Ravin's Lair

Hugs!
Stacey Malerne

Ravin's Lair

by

Stacey Palermo

JADA

Ravin's Lair

Cover Photography by Stacey Palermo
Cover Design by AngeliQue Shatzel
Author Photograph by AngeliQue Shatzel
Interior Design by Robert Garcia .www.gpsdesign.net

Published in 2005 by JADA Press
Jacksonville, Florida
www.JadaPress.com

ISBN: 0-9764-1153-9

Printed in the United States of America

For my daddy
Who taught me that anything was possible
If you reached for the stars and took it.
May the wind fill your sails and take you
To the places of your dreams.
I love you.

My mom, your never-ending support, and love.
My brother, my best friend.
I love you both.

My editor, J.L. Goldsworthy at The Printed Page,
Thanks for all your hard work.
Jada Press, thanks for everything.

For my husband,
Thank you for your patience.
For my children,
Thank you for your encouragement.
I love you all dearly.
Never stop believing in yourself
And never stop reaching for the stars.

AngeliQue,
For teaching, listening, and learning
With me.

My Shadow,
For always being by my side when I needed
You the most.

A special thanks to my models,
Carrie and Carl, thank you so much.

"Whoever says that there is no magic has never gazed towards the stars."

Ravin stood under the darkened sky. Her head hung low as she ignored the light rain that fell against her body. She gently laid the white rose on her fiancé's casket as she said goodbye. What should have been the beginning was now the end.

One

Six Months Later

"Ravin honey, Brett's here." Her mother held open the bedroom door.

"Thanks, Mom," she moaned miserably, burying herself under her blankets.

"Ravin! Get up!" Brett said brushing past Ravin's mother and bouncing into the room.

Ravin rolled over groaning. "Why?"

"You promised to take those pictures for me, remember?"

Ravin rolled her eyes under the covers. Why couldn't they accept the fact she was not ready to face her life?

"Now get up we have work to do," Brett demanded.

"No." She pulled the blankets closer to her body.

"Stop feeling sorry for yourself! I can't take it anymore," Brett stammered, wanting desperately to pull her friend from this rut. It hurt seeing her in so much pain.

"I don't recall making you a promise." She closed her eyes, wishing she would just go away.

"Well, you did. I cancelled that overpriced hack you told me to, and now there isn't enough time to get anyone else."

Ravin sat up, gazing dismally at her best friend.

"Last week, you promised to help create my portfolio," she advised, "a portfolio, I might add, that I need by next week!"

She lay back down ashamed. "I remember now."

"So . . ."

"So I wasn't thinking straight," she uttered, knowing she couldn't go back on her word no matter what.

"So too bad! You promised, now get up!" Brett dragged the blankets off the bed and tossed them on the floor.

"Brett—"

"No. You listen to me," she demanded, "You've been in this room for almost six months now. It's time to leave. I won't take no for an answer. You gave me your word and you're going through with it."

Ravin locked eyes with Brett. She was amazed at Brett's behavior; it was very out of character for her. "Fine, you win." She threw her legs over the side of her bed and contemplated how she could pull this off. She'd always had an interest in photography, enough to have taken courses during high school. "Give me a minute."

Brett nodded and bounced out of her room. Ravin's mother closed the door, offering her a warm smile.

Ravin lay back down, resting her arm over her eyes. Her mind went back to the events of her fiancé's death. Her mother had suffered the same horrible fate, losing her husband in a similar manner, and yet she wasn't hiding in her room.

A short while later, Ravin led Brett to the abandoned warehouse a few blocks from her house. Her bodyguard Pauly followed behind, unsettled by the location.

Ravin felt a surge of exhilaration from the familiar feel of her camera fitted into the palm of her hand. Forgetting the world around her, she escaped behind the eyepiece and let her intuition tell her what to do. Posing Brett aroused a new feeling, something she hadn't experienced in school. Graduating early never gave her the chance to finish the last class—fashion photography.

"Rave, I don't like this place," Pauly protested quietly from behind her, rocking on his heels.

"Relax, Pauly," Ravin stated calmly. Pauly was always on guard, and although it was necessary, it could be awful annoying.

Ravin Capello was a quiet person by nature, the exact opposite of her best friend Brett Santana. Brett's bubbling personality craved the attention Ravin gave her in the spotlight. Ravin was dangerously beautiful and amazingly intelligent, which confused people when she opted to hide her black opal eyes behind the locks of jet-black hair that covered her face.

Brett Santana shared a special friendship with Ravin. They had been inseparable since the tender age of two. Brett had always dreamed of being in the limelight, and modeling was her way of accomplishing that goal.

Ravin watched her friend come to life through the eye of her camera. She was a natural.

Roxi Tavern was a very important agent. She noticed Brett at the deli she worked. After watching her mildly saunter around, flirting with customers, Roxi knew Brett had what it took. She was slender and graceful, and her sapphire blue eyes reflected off her honey blond hair. The only thing left was to find out if she photographed well. Roxi knew she had to take this treasure before anyone else did.

Ravin smiled to herself as she shot the last few frames. She knew that these pictures would make or break her friends' dreams. She lowered the camera, and Brett noted a small spark glisten in her deep black eyes.

"What?" Ravin questioned, wishing she hadn't felt so free and in control again. She couldn't allow Brett to think that she was right, that being behind the camera could bring her back to the world.

"We're done," she stated coldly as she tucked the last roll of film into the case.

Brett leapt off the windowsill. "Excellent! Wanna go for lunch while these get developed?"

Ravin's fear rushed back and she felt caught in the headlights. "No."

"Why not?"

"Don't push me, Brett."

Brett let out a sigh, thinking about her spending more time in seclusion. She knew she saw the spark and she prayed it was enough for Ravin to come back. "Fine," she muttered quietly "I'll stop by when these are finished." She knew she couldn't push anymore, but she would never give up on her best friend.

Pauly stood back and watched. He could see Brett's disappointment. He had seen the same spark and hoped this would help Ravin end her months of self torture. He followed Ravin as they split up and reflected back seven years before the time her father had hired him to protect her. They had become close over the years. After her father's death and the death of her fiancé, Pauly had become her only true confidant. He understood her in ways no one else ever would. He was the only person that shared in the secrets of her past.

Two

Marco Deangelo read the headlines as he and his fellow bandmates waited for their manager. *Mafia style murder reported in broad daylight. Witnesses state that passer by saw the man gunned down before they were thrown into another car. No leads yet as to who the two young women were that witnessed the shooting, or which families were involved.*

He couldn't believe the violence that consumed people today. It brought back many memories he had tried so hard to forget. The only thing that kept him from his past was his future. Being one of five band members of an up-and-coming group, he put all his energy into his dreams.

Ben Grey owned JAM Records and managed some of the groups under his label. He had a knack for finding talent and a fathering disposition that kept them happy. His favorite new find was a group called Jaded. Five exceptionally talented and devastatingly gorgeous guys made up the group. Brody was the youngest to join the group, almost fifteen years old and seven years younger than Nico, who was the oldest. When Ben saw the connection between the five of them, he signed them immediately. Several months after finding the right music and wardrobe, he sent them to play at the local high schools to see if his vision would come to life. Immediately, they made history. They had taken the town by storm, and quickly became a household name. Before they knew it, they were the hottest group around.

Marco settled into his new lifestyle, looking back at the beginning. His dark brown hair was now cut in a fashion that he would not have chosen, another grand idea from their public relations person. Their inability to change their appearance without her consent infuriated them all, but Marco knew that this was all part of fame. Fame dictated what, who, and why they did what they did. He knew it would take time to adjust.

Three

"Yes, can I help you?" the woman asked, leaning over the dark wooden desk as Brett approached.

"I have an appointment with Roxi Tavern."

"And your name?"

"Brett Santana."

"One moment please." She flipped open her appointment book. "Yes, Miss Santana. Please follow me." She stood and proceeded to Roxi's office. She quietly knocked on the door before opening it.

"Miss Tavern, Miss Santana here to see you."

"Thank you, Michelle. Please come in and sit down, Brett." Roxi walked over to her couch. Brett followed full of nerves. This was her first attempt at a modeling job and she was more nervous than she thought she would be.

"Were you able to put together a portfolio?" She smiled sitting across from Brett.

"Yes, I was."

"Great. I hope it didn't set you back too much. I've seen girls spend thousands of dollars on a portfolio with no real hope of making it."

"No, it didn't cost much at all." Smiling, she handed Roxi the portfolio that she and Ravin had put together. "I don't know if it's as professional as it should be . . . I've never done anything like this."

"Didn't the photographer supply one for you?" she stated casually as she opened the first page, Brett's face silhouetted against a dirt-covered window. Her breath stopped.

"No, I'm afraid I didn't go to a professional photographer," she confided hoping it wouldn't hurt her chances.

Roxi glanced up at her in shock. "Well then, who did these?" She flipped through page after page of perfect shots, each one unique.

"My best friend."

"Your friend?" She asked, impressed with her audacity to come for an interview with a non-professional portfolio.

"Yes." Brett gazed at the floor almost wishing she hadn't listened to Ravin. She knew in this business, they frowned upon going against the grain.

"Well, I am definately hiring you so cheer up . . ." She smiled. "But I wonder if I can get your best friend in here too."

"You're kidding! You're hiring me this quickly?" She sat motionless. Shock fought its way through and won.

"Yes, dear, this quickly. I knew you'd make it the moment I saw you. All I needed was to see if you photographed well, which you do. As for your friend, I'd like to try to work with her too . . . if you think you can arrange it."

"Really? You don't even know what she looks like."

"Not for modeling, for her photography skills."

"She's not going to believe this," she sighed in amazement.

"Has she been studying long?"

"No. Well . . ." She sank back on the couch sensing the tension leave. "She did take some courses in high school, but I don't know how far she got."

"Is that so? She has no formal training. Does she shoot a lot?"

"No, this was a first for her."

"Well then, she's a natural. If you can arrange it, I would like to meet her. I love finding fresh new people to work with. Ask her. See if she would be interested."

"I will." Brett smiled at her good fortune.

"Let me show you around." Brett followed Roxi out the door and down the hall. "Well, I've just moved into this building, so some things are still under construction. This will be the main studio where we'll be doing most of the photo shoots. The reception area is over there. I'm sorry there isn't anyone here for you to meet."

"That's okay. This place is great."

"Good, this will be your home away from home. I do have to warn you though. I share this building with my partner, Ben Grey. He owns JAM Records, so you will probably run into a lot of musicians. We'll have a meeting at the end of the week regarding how we are all going to interact with each other."

"I understand, but won't it be cool to meet some of them?"

"Yes, that's why I want this meeting. I want to make certain that when *my* girls are talking with *his* boys, you don't come across as crazy fans. Instead, I want my models to behave like they are equals, if not better."

"I think I understand."

"Good. I'll let you go and tell your family. Hopefully you can get your friend in here to meet with me about a job." She handed her a three-ring binder. "The first page of this notebook has your schedule on it. I expect you to have read this by tomorrow and be here on time. Don't worry about make-up or clothes. We'll take care of everything."

"Thank you so much, Ms. Tavern." Smiling, she hugged the notebook close to her chest.

"Please call me Roxi."

Brett ran to Ravin's, excited to share the good news. She knew her father wouldn't be home from work yet and her mother passed away when she was younger. Ravin's family had taken her in as one of their own, and she knew Mrs. Capello would be as proud as if she were her own mother.

"Ravin!" she yelled running into the kitchen. "I got it!"

"Oh, that's wonderful, Brett!" Mrs. Capello embraced her. "That's just fantastic."

"Great!" Ravin replied, trying to appear happy for her friend.

"It is, and you know what Roxi told me?" She looked around and smiled back at Pauly. "She wants to meet you. She wants to give you a job as a photographer, although I'm sure when she sees you, she'll try to get you to model, but she wants to hire you."

"Oh, Ravin, how wonderful! I told you those pictures were exceptional!" her mother boasted.

"That's great, but I don't know."

"Why not?"

"Because I don't know anything about fashion photography."

She suddenly felt panic rise through her.

"But you can learn!" Brett threw her arms in the air.

"No." Ravin stood up and escaped out into the garden. Brett's face dropped as she watched her best friend walk away from an incredible opportunity. She glanced over at Pauly and Mrs. Capello in shock. Pauly shook his head and went out after Ravin.

"She's got the talent," Mrs. Capello told Brett. "I know she has the talent. If we could just get her to come back to us, the way she was before." She shook her head.

"I know. Hopefully Pauly can help."

Pauly sat down on the bench next to Ravin and took her hand. Together, they gazed out at the array of flowers spread out before them.

"So?" he asked after a long silence.

"So what?"

"Pretty good opportunity, don't you think?"

"No."

"No?"

"I don't know anything about that kind of stuff."

"Sure you do, you know what matters."

"And what would that be?"

"How to make the model look good. You've always had a knack for that kind of stuff."

"No, I haven't."

"Sure you have. I remember when you were little, you used to set up all your dolls in different outfits and pose them."

She thought back to her innocent days and hid a smile. "God, you remember that?"

"Sure."

"Pauly." She turned to him and sighed, "I'm not ready for anything this big. I just lost my father and my fiancé."

"Okay, losing your father will always hurt, and Dominic has been gone for six months now. It's time to take off the black and get back into life. You're only eighteen. You have your whole life in front of you. Take the chance now while you still can. This opportunity won't come around again. This is the once in a lifetime."

They talked for over an hour and everything she had stored up inside came pouring out. It was the first time she had ever talked about Dominic's death and how she felt it was her fault he lost his life. Pauly told her the facts about his murder and assured her that it had nothing to do with her.

She felt better after their talk, better than she had in a long time. When Brett returned later that night, Ravin admitted that this was her chance to shine. Photography was a passion of hers. She told her to set up a meeting with Roxi.

Four

Five Years Later

Ravin stepped out into the hallway from the darkroom at JAM Records. She slid on a pair of black sunglasses and leaned against the wall, waiting for her eyes to adjust to the light. After five years in the darkroom, this took longer to achieve. A group of musicians talking to Benny pulled her attention over, one stood out among the rest. His dark hair and smoldering eyes captivated her. No man had managed to capture her attention since Dominic, but something about this one caused a stir from deep inside that she had never felt before. She dropped her black leather duffel bag to the floor and waited for Brett, trying to reverse the images rushing through her mind.

Marco slid his hands from the wall behind his head when he saw her out of the corner of his eye. She was leaning against the wall wearing a pair of tight jeans ripped at the knees and a fitted black muscle shirt. In one hand, she held a black leather jacket that she let hang to the floor, in the other, the strap to her black duffel bag. He examined the way her back arched, revealing her bare stomach as she leaned her head back. His eyes followed her long wavy black hair as it descended down past her soft face and across her exposed shoulders.

"Marco!" Nico slapped his arm.

"What?" He quickly looked back at Nico embarrassed. Nico took notice of Marco's diversion and let out a low whistle.

"We still need a photographer, JAM needs the cover pronto," Vinny chimed in.

"Sorry, what?" He turned unable to shake her from his mind.

"Marco, could we please pay attention? We still need a photographer."

"What would you like me to do? I'm not the one who ran off to marry some bimbo," Marco snapped.

"Well, we'd like your opinion," Vinny prompted.

"What do you think, Ben?" Marco looked over at Benny for reassurance.

"I'm not sure, give me a minute." Ben tapped his finger on his memo book.

Roxi sauntered down the hall with her nose in her appointment book, almost running head on into Cole.

"Hi, boys!" She looked up in time. "Why the long faces?"

"Hi, Roxi, our photographer bolted on us. We need the cover, like yesterday!"

"Benny? What happened to Andrew?"

"Ran off with Chastity to get married or something," Vinny uttered with a defeated look.

"That sucks. What about that new photographer you hired?"

"He's not good enough yet, at least not for these guys." Benny laughed as he shifted his feet. "What about you? Can we use yours? I'll pay top dollar."

"Let me check my book." She flipped open her appointment book and then glanced down the hall, catching Ravin out of the corner of her eye. "Okay, Thursday morning. Say around seven?"

"That would be great, Roxi. I owe you big!"

"Oh, you will, Ben, you will." She laughed as she strolled away. "I'll break the news and then you're on your own."

"Where?" he called out to her.

"I'll let you know," she called back over her shoulder.

Marco leaned against the wall, oblivious to the conversation. He wasn't sure why this girl intrigued him so much. He could see that she was beautiful—that was obvious. Her fitted clothes outlined her petite frame perfectly. But he knew there was more to it than that, something he could sense, something deeper.

"What was that all about?" Nico asked concerned.

"Nothing for you to worry about. Okay so we're set for a photographer. I'll send over the ideas and a copy of the CD, and hope for the best." Ben gazed over at his prize band.

"So?" Vinny questioned, his anticipation reaching a high.

"Is he any good?" Cole questioned.

"Well, *she* is very good, one of the best." Ben proclaimed.

"So, why haven't we used her before?"

"Well, she um . . ." Ben paused, "She hates shooting for musicians."

"She does? Why's that?" Cole urged.

"She could never deal with their egos, at least that's the rumor floating around," Ben whispered.

"That doesn't sound very fair," Cole stated.

"But you don't have egos, right? At least you won't when you're doing the shoot with her," Ben hinted.

"Right, no egos. What exactly does that mean?" Brody asked sarcastically.

"Don't act like the world owes you anything, and don't treat her like hired help," Ben demanded.

"Got it." Nico shook his head.

"A chick photographer, huh?" Cole dropped his shoulders in worry.

"Don't worry, Cole. She's probably more professional than any guy we've ever worked with." Ben began pacing. He felt a little apprehensive about hiring her, but what choice did he have now?

Marco's gaze slipped away from Ravin, still wondering what drew him to her. His eyes wandered back to his group knowing that was where his attention needed to be. Reluctantly, he turned his back and asked, "Okay, when and where?"

"Thursday, seven a.m."

"What did Roxi mean when she said that she'll break the news and you're on your own?" Nico asked as they walked back into the meeting room.

"Ravin's a pain in my ass. Don't worry about it," Ben stated, patting Nico on the shoulder.

"Pain in the ass?" Nico's head swam with dread.

"Don't worry. She'll do a great job. She's one of the most talented photographers out there. We just don't agree on everything. Not a problem." Ben tried to ease their minds, or was it his own? He wasn't sure.

"Should we bother sending her our ideas?" Marco finally returned to the conversation.

"Yes, of course. Can't say she'll use them, but at least we can try. I'll have a messenger send them over to her." Ben glanced over at the somber faces of his prize band. "Hey! It'll be fine, relax." Ben told them to go back to the hotel and get some rest.

All Nico heard was 'hard to get along with', and he was already dreading the shoot. But under the circumstances, they had no other choice, except maybe to postpone the album release, which was out of the question. They went back to the hotel, each with something on their minds.

Nico worried about the photo shoot.

Cole and Brody worried about what prank awaited them back at the hotel.

Vinny just wanted to get back to writing his music.

Marco couldn't stop thinking about the girl he saw in the hallway. She didn't fit. She was mysterious, in a way, different.

Five

Ravin and Brett walked down the street toward Ravin's warehouse. Pauly hung back for a moment, his eyes ever watchful in the darkness.

"So, did you see Jaded there tonight?" Brett asked, smothering her excitement.

"No, Brett, I didn't notice," Ravin lied.

"Oh yeah, like I'm gonna believe that. Marco Deangelo was standing in the hallway staring at you!"

"Get a life, Brett!" she joked.

"I've got a life, Rave. It's you who lacks one. I go out on dates and hang out at the clubs with real people. And what does Ravin do every night? I'll tell you—she spends it in her darkroom at home, alone!"

"Well, let me tell you something—if I didn't spend all my spare time in the darkroom developing *your* pictures, you wouldn't be on every magazine cover would you?" Ravin teased.

"True. Okay, I give. Well, just in case you *were* interested, Marco Deangelo *was* staring at you. You do know who they are, don't you?"

"I don't think so. You know I don't follow the groups, not like you and Mia anyway."

"Well then, let me fill you in." Brett laughed as they rounded the corner to Ravin's place. Just as Ravin slid the key in, Brett told her everything she knew about the group.

"So what, Brett? You know I'm not interested. Not after what happened with Dominic."

"Dominic! When did you start thinking about him again?"

"I think about him all the time."

"Well, it's time to stop. Right, Pauly?" she asked over her shoulder.

Pauly smiled, knowing better than to get into this conversation. The subject of Dominic was too painful for Ravin and Pauly still felt guilty about it.

"When I'm ready. Anyway, even if I did find a boyfriend, when would I possibly have time for him?"

"You'll make time. I do!"

"Oh yeah, and the last one was just great," she huffed. "He loved all the time you gave him, all the time in the world to sleep around."

"Don't start, Rave. At least I'm trying."

"Well, don't start with me then. I'm trying to make a career."

"Rave, give me a break! You're the most sought after photographer around. I know how much Roxi pays you. And I know you get a cut from every shoot you do."

"Oh, really? And how do you know all this?"

"Roxi slipped one day when I was renegotiating my contract."

"Yes, I do well, but I'm going for something different. It's hard to explain."

"Well, when you figure it out, let me know."

"That reminds me." She tossed her keys on the table. "I've got to call Roxi. She asked me for a favor Thursday."

"Okay, I'm jumping in your shower."

Ravin slipped into her small office connecting the living room. She placed her black bag in the corner and sat down at the large granite desk. As she dialed Roxi's home number, she leafed through some proofs that lay on the desk. There was no answer so she tried the office.

"Hello?"

"Hi, Rox, thought you'd be home by now. It's past eight."

"Just hanging out talking to Benny. What's up?"

"You mentioned you wanted a favor, but you didn't tell me what you needed."

"Oh yeah! Actually, it's a favor for Benny."

"What?" she sighed, no longer wanting the details.

"Yes, his band Jaded needs a photo shoot done. Hold on I'm putting you on speaker. Okay Benny, tell her what you need."

"Hi, Ravin. Jaded is about to release their fourth album and they need the cover shot before next week."

"What happened to your photographer?"

"He split to Rio to get married or something."

"That's too bad. But don't you have a back-up?"

"Yes, but he isn't nearly good enough for this. That's why I'm asking you. I know you can get it right and you'll do an incredible job."

"Well, thank you, but—"

"But listen, I know we don't agree on much and I know you hate musicians. Lord knows you've told me enough times, but just this once, please?"

"Ben, listen to me. I deal with egotistical models all day and I can tell you that they aren't half as bad as musicians are. I don't like shooting them and you know it."

"But what if I promised that they would behave, act like normal people and not cop any attitudes? Would you consider, *please*?" he begged and crossed his fingers under the desk.

"Okay, let's just say that you ask them to do this. Who's to say that they will?"

"I'll bet my life on it."

"Not good enough." She stood up and started pacing around her office. She felt an unusual flittering run through her stomach as she thought about Marco in front of *her* camera.

"Ravin, I will triple the pay! Please?" he pleaded.

"Fine, but just this time. And they have to follow my rules," she demanded.

"Not a problem! Not at all, what do you want from them?" he rung his hands together.

"First off, check their egos at the door, no security, PR people, girlfriends, mothers . . ." She paused, thinking about Marco for a brief moment. "And they can't cop an attitude with me or they'll hear it. Ask Rox, she knows." She could hear Roxi laughing in the background and knew they were both thinking about the last time Ravin blew up at a model.

"No problem. We'll see you around seven then. I sent over a list of their ideas and a copy of their CD. Read them over, listen to the music, and get inspired."

"Anything else?" she asked sarcastically, wishing she had never made the call.

"Nope, that's all. Roxi?"

"Not from me. I'll talk to you tomorrow, Rave."

"Okay, bye."

Ravin hung up the phone and leaned back in her chair. Musicians, she thought to herself—great. They had bigger egos than models. She was just about to get up when Pauly walked in the door and handed her a small package.

"Thanks, Pauly, I was expecting this."

"Who's it from?"

"Benny."

They exchange looks and he waited until she opened it. Ever since her father's death Ravin had received threats from the rival family on and off. Pauly kept his guard up at all times. Out of habit, she showed him the contents and he walked away.

She sat back in her chair, flipping through several pages of notes Benny had sent along with the CD. All of the boys had written down their ideas, all very similar concepts. She pulled out her CD player and popped in the disc. Putting up her feet and closing her eyes, she let the music tell her what to do. It was one thing that had an instant effect on her. She could hear Marco's deep raspy voice echoing through her earphones, song after song. Brett would never give up if she knew that Ravin secretly followed the group. Allowing herself to relax, she dreamt about Marco's strong arms, the way his muscular stomach tightened when he danced on stage. Lost in her fantasy, she almost didn't hear the phone ring.

"What's up?" Ravin answered, looking at her caller ID.

"I knew Thursday stuck in my head for some reason. That's when they're painting the studio." Roxi sighed.

"That's right, now what?"

"Think we can do it at your studio?"

"I guess," She sighed in defeat.

"You're a dream, Ravin."

"Why are you doing all of this, Rox?"

"I own Ben. I owe him a break."

"Why?"

"Long story, let's save it for the plane ride."

"Okay, this time."

"Thanks, babe. I'll bring them over around seven."

"I'll be ready," she groaned inwardly.

Ravin walked around picking up after Brett. She had moved into her warehouse three years ago and renovated most of it. She added an upstairs apartment, where Brett stayed when they repainted her apartment. She also added twelve bedrooms across the other side for guests, not that she ever had any, and one right next to hers for Pauly. Downstairs, she built several studios, some with permanent props and some she left empty. She added a gym and a music room for Brett and Mia, complete with a black grand piano.

Six

Thursday morning came quickly for Brett. She woke up early to get ready and picked out the perfect outfit. She made coffee and smiled when Mia came in with the same enthusiasm. Ravin sat hunched over her proofs from the previous day.

"Coffee?" Brett cautiously entered her office.

"Thanks." She stretched her arms above her head.

"How long have you been up?"

"I don't know, didn't look. What are you doing up so early?" Like she even had to ask.

"Just wanted to give myself enough time to get ready. What should I wear anyway? I've never had the pleasure of working in the background with you."

"Working in the background? God, you make it sound like I don't do anything."

"You know I didn't mean it that way. I'm just so used to having clothes picked out for me and everything. I've never worked with you without being in front of the camera."

"I know! I'm just pulling your chain Brett. I can't believe you're nervous."

"I am not!" she protested, trying to hide the fact she was.

"Yeah right! If you weren't nervous, you wouldn't be up at five o'clock in the morning." She chuckled.

"You know me too well, Ravin Capello. Okay, okay I'll find something to wear on my own." She sulked out of the room.

"Wear something comfortable!" Ravin called out after her, laughing.

"Ravin." Mia poked her head in the door. "It's six o'clock. Want us to wait for you?"

"No, go ahead. I'll be down in a few." She sat back in her chair, looking at the clock. She wasn't happy with Roxi for doing this to her. She knew she didn't like to shoot musicians. She hoped they followed her directions not to bring their "people" with them. Ben promised that he had explained how she needed total quiet. With a heavy sigh, she walked into her bathroom and jumped into her waterfall shower. She thought about the ideas the boys had sent over and couldn't shake the feeling that something didn't fit. Over and over, she went through each song, thinking about how Marco looked and the way he sang. She tried to clear her mind, to shake Marco's image from her head. She needed a clear head to come up with something spectacular. As if on cue it hit her. She jumped out of the shower excited and got dressed.

Seven

Marco awoke early, unusual for him, but he couldn't shake the image of the captivating girl he had seen the day before. Something stirred deep inside him. He stood in the doorway of the balcony, looking out over the city, thinking about her until Vinny interrupted followed by the waiter.

"When is Roxi coming to get us?" Vinny asked, pouring them both a cup.

"Roxi? I thought Ben was picking us up." Marco looked at him puzzled.

"Nope. Roxi is taking us. And get this, this photographer won't let us bring any security or assistants. Nobody! Can you believe the audacity of this girl?" Vinny threw his hands in the air.

"When did all this come about?"

"Yesterday, haven't you been listening at all?"

"No, I guess not. We can't bring anyone?"

"No."

"I wonder why. Doesn't sound too safe."

"Roxi assured us that nothing will go wrong."

"How does Nico feel about this?"

"What'd you think? He's a wreck."

"I bet."

"Anyway, you better get ready. She'll be here in a half hour."

The boys nervously waited for Roxi to show up, and when she did, their security guards escorted them out to her car. On the way Roxi, explained how Ravin worked, what to expect from her, and what she expected of them.

"Remember, she doesn't usually shoot for musicians. She's doing me a huge favor. She's doing you a *huge* favor, so don't blow it."

They agreed to be on their best behavior and did a double take of the warehouse as she pulled up to the door.

"This is it?" Cole asked, trying to conceal his laughter.

Roxi stopped at the door and turned to them. "This is her studio. I know it looks like crap on the outside. I've tried to get her to spruce it up, but that's the way she is. Believe it or not, it's quite amazing inside."

She opened the outside door and led them into a small entrance-way. As she keyed in the password on the console, Nico swung around when he heard the outside door lock shut. He relaxed knowing she at least had some good security.

Roxi led them into the spacious studio. "Welcome to Ravin's Lair, boys." Laughing, she took their coats and set them on one of the many black leather couches set in different social arrangements. "I must go now, so you behave."

"You're leaving us?" Nico questioned.

"You're in good hands, trust me." She patted Nico on the arm, turned, and left.

Marco looked around the warehouse decorated with four black leather couches. Each one rested on a large leopard print rug, all offering a different angle to view the expansive warehouse. Half walls separated areas into specific rooms and enormous chandeliers hung from various parts of the ceiling. Whoever decorated this place had a unique style and great taste.

"Hi." Brett bounced in.

"Hi, it's Brett . . . right?" Vinny asked, hoping he wasn't wrong.

"I'm glad you remember." A smile rose from within as her eyes connected with his.

"How could anyone forget?" he laughed nervously.

"Well, good morning and welcome. Please sit, make yourselves comfortable." They sat down looking around. "Ravin should be down any minute."

Marco sat down on the couch and felt butterflies run through his stomach. He wasn't listening to the conversation; he was too busy thinking about the girl who had stolen his thoughts.

"Ravin?" Nico asked surprised. "*Thee Ravin Capello?*"

"Yes! You know her?" Brett always felt proud when people called her *Thee Ravin Capello.*

"I only know her reputation. I can't believe she's doing our shoot!"

"This . . . is good?" Cole asked slowly.

"Good? My God, Ravin Capello is like the best photographer around! She's . . ." He paused. "She's like a legend in fashion photography! She did that one shot I've got on my wall back home, the one swimsuit picture with like ten models in bikinis standing on the airplane." His voice was full of excitement.

"I remember that shot. I thought for sure I was gonna fall off the damn plane." Brett laughed, remembering it well.

"You were there?" Vinny asked.

"Yep, second from the right."

"I'll have to take a look at it when I get back home."

"Maybe if there's time, I'll show you her wall of fame. I think that shot is up there."

"Wall of fame?"

"Yeah, she just started putting up unusual shots on the wall one day. That's how it started, I guess."

"Hi!" Mia squeaked as she popped in from nowhere.

"God, Mia! Stop doing that!" Brett jumped out of her skin.

"Sorry, Brett." She chuckled. "You know you're starting to get jumpy like Ravin! You two need to relax! Anyway, good morning, boys. Ravin will be down in a minute. Can I offer you coffee or juice? Which I see Brett hasn't shown you yet." She threw her a look. "There are also bagels and muffins. Help yourselves." She giggled. "And I need to get your styles. They sent over a whole slew of clothes and I don't know who wears what."

"Great." Nico helped himself to a glass of juice.

"Thanks, Mia. I was about to show them to the table." Brett glared at her. Mia winked back and smiled.

Brett entertained everyone while Mia jotted down notes. Marco sat impatiently after finding out Ravin was the girl in the hallway at JAM. His stomach twisted uncontrollably.

Ravin strolled onto the set with her dark black hair up in a clip, a few wisps hanging down around the sides of her face, hiding her dark eyes. She wore her favorite low-rise jeans and a black cropped shirt that almost reached down to her navel. Marco saw her from across the room, watching her carefully as she gave her assistant directions. That same feeling stirred from a place he never even knew existed.

As Ravin went through her regular routine of checking out her equipment, she felt someone moving up behind her.

"Morning." Vinny approached her.

"Hey," Ravin replied shyly.

"You must be Ravin?" Vinny asked surprised.

"Yes, Ravin Capello." She looked up as she took his hand.

"Wow, I'm honored. I've seen your work. You're pretty incredible."

"Thank you. Ben didn't tell you I was doing the shoot?"

"No, he didn't."

"Well, we should probably get started." Eager to get this over with, she looked back down at her camera.

"Sure thing." Vinny walked back over to his friends. Thinking Ravin was behind him, he turned to introduce her.

"I thought she was behind me, but I guess she's ready." He said confused.

"So, where is she?"

"Setting up."

"She didn't like our ideas, did she?"

"She had something better in mind." Randy walked up behind them. "Hi, I'm Randy." He extended his hand, "I'm one of her assistants."

"Nice to meet you, Randy." Nico shook his hand. "So, what's she got planned for us?"

"You'll see." He smirked, "She wouldn't tell you, would she?"

"We haven't even met her yet," Cole laughed.

Randy chuckled. "Well, she tends to work like that. Half the time her models come expecting to do certain shoots and end up doing a totally different cover."

"And she gets away with this?" Brody laughed.

"Have you seen her work?" He raised an eyebrow.

"Not really, nothing specific. She's doing us a favor; our photographer couldn't do the shoot. We're kinda left in her hands, hoping she can pull off a halfway decent album cover for us."

"Halfway decent is something you won't get from Ravin," he said with a straight face.

"Excuse me?" Cole panicked. He saw a smile grow across Randy's face.

"No, she gets it perfect the first time. Don't worry about it, guys. Even though she doesn't usually do this type of work, I've seen her pull off some pretty incredible shit."

"Honestly?"

"Honestly," Randy reassured them.

Brett walked over and asked the boys to follow her to wardrobe. Mia was waiting with clothes laid out for everyone.

"Okay, give me a few minutes to remember names. Cole?"

He stepped forward.

After a few moments of handing out clothes, the girls left the room to allow them some privacy. They each walked out in a different style, but matching color. Marco liked his best of all; a black leather jacket and bandana around his head definitely suited his personality.

"Good choices. Whose idea?" Vinny asked, shaking his head in acceptance.

"Ravins. She thought these would fit better with her vision." Mia winked. "I'll let her know you're ready." She disappeared in a flash.

"Ravin, they're ready," Mia whispered.

"Send 'em in." She finished hanging the tarp with Randy.

Mia left to gather up the boys. When they returned, they were all looking around surprised. She had set up a city park bench complete with a street lamp. Overhead, she laid out a tarp to darken the set and give the appearance of a dark foggy night.

"This is cool," Nico said looking around.

"Thanks." She jumped off a stack of boxes.

"So, you didn't like our other ideas?" Cole questioned.

"Well, they were good but . . ." She paused looking directly at Marco. "They fit better with your last album. This one doesn't make me think of steel and chrome. It makes me feel . . . dark city streets." She shook her head. "It's hard to explain. It's just something I feel."

"Well, whatever it is you feel, go with it," Nico said impressed.

"Thanks," she uttered shyly. "Okay, you there." She pointed at Cole. After a few minutes of positioning everyone, she took a step back to examine the set. Without warning, she began snapping pictures, stopping occasionally to change a pose, fix a shirt, or adjust a prop. Stepping back again, visions began to swamp her head. She went back over and messed up Vinny's hair a little, untucked Cole's shirt, and finished up with Marco. She brushed a strand of hair out of his face and stepped back again. Again, she stepped forward and pulled open his shirt more to expose his chest. He watched her expression as she admired his tattoo. She felt the electricity run through her fingers as she touched him. Marco closed his eyes; the rush of instant excitement surprised him. He quickly eyed Vinny to bring him back to reality before he lost control. Vinny smiled, knowing the feeling all to well. She adjusted his shirt again, and still not happy she handed her camera over to Randy. His body tensed up when she lightly brushed her fingers across his neck as she straightened his collar. Randy handed her camera back and she began shooting while she tried to control her breathing. She didn't break stride, handing Randy the used camera and receiving a fresh one. The boys were impressed with her speed and attention to detail. She unloaded twenty rolls of film within a few hours. Content with what she had, she sent them off to lunch.

"That's it?" Brody laughed.

"For now," she replied coldly. She handed Randy the last roll and asked him to put everything in the developer.

"So, what's next?" Nico asked pulling off the leather coat.

"Ben asked me to do a cover with the group and then some singles for the inserts, whatever the hell an insert is."

"You don't know much about music, do you?"

"No, but I'm sure you'll want to teach me," she remarked sarcastically.

"The inserts are singles where we write thank you notes to our fans and families."

"That's very sweet." Her big black eyes looked up at him.

"Sweet? I've never heard it put that way. But hey, we're just grateful for all of this, especially at the last minute."

"No problem." She laughed, edging her way to her darkroom. She felt a little uneasy with them being so nice. She had expected them to be like other groups, but they weren't. They were very friendly. It made it harder for her to dislike them, harder for her to forget about the way her hands had quivered when she touched Marco.

"Are you having anything for lunch?" Marco said with a smile, wondering why he felt flushed.

"No, thank you. You eat." She smiled. "Marco . . . right?"

"Yes, Marco Deangelo. Thank you, Ravin. This has gone quick so far, completely different than what we're use to."

"That's why I told you not to bring other people."

"Why is that?"

"Too many people around to distract you. I need your full attention without interruptions."

"You've got my attention." He cocked an eyebrow.

"Good, go eat. I'll be done with these soon." She smiled again and walked away wishing she could figure out what he was doing to her.

"See you later." He shook his head. No one had left him with a loss for words before. There was just something about her, something in her eyes, her smile. He couldn't put words to the way he felt. Marco glanced down at his hands and didn't know why they were sweating. He closed his eyes briefly and slipped his hands into his pockets as he walked over to the lounge.

Ravin slipped into the darkroom with Randy. "How's it going?" she asked sliding onto her stool.

"Good, just about done. You okay?" he asked as he flipped on the red light.

"I'm fine, why?"

"Nothing." He smiled as he turned around. He had noticed the connection between her and Marco.

"I think I want to set up the pipes and pulleys."

"Sounds good."

"Yeah."

"Want me to print these first?"

"No, I'll print 'em. You go have lunch."

"Okay, then I'll start setting up."

"Okay."

Randy left her scanning the negatives into her new computer. Still new to digital, she gave in and found this way of looking at the proofs indispensable. She still preferred the old format for printing, but this gave her a good enough print to see what she had. She hit the print button, walked out of the darkroom, and sat on the couch next to the door.

As she leaned back and closed her eyes, she thought about the way her body responded to Marco's touch. Her hands shook with curiosity and fear. Her heart pounded heavily in her chest as the image of Marco's gaze seared through her mind. She needed to clear her head. She needed to re-connect with her perspective. She took a deep breath and concentrated. She had at least five more hours before she could breathe without Marco's presence occupying her time. Her thoughts quickly flashed to her past, as much as she tried to push it away.

The black Lincoln driving by, the window slowly opening . . .

She jolted herself from the painful memory. She couldn't allow herself to fall into her thoughts again. She had work to do and she needed to stay focused. Five years ago, when Roxi hired her, she had vowed not to let her past haunt her. Every ounce of energy she had went into her photography. Within a year, she had become the top photographer around. She kept her loyalties to Roxi and even to a man she thought she loved . . . until now.

Eight

Ravin carried the proofs back to the lounge. Happy with the results she handed them to Nico and sauntered over to the buffet table.

"Hey, Rave." Brett spoke as Ravin poured herself a cup of coffee and leaned against the table. She always loved to watch people's expressions when they weren't looking. The room was silent as she studied their faces, especially Marco's. Her eyes drifted over his dark hair, down his soft boyish face. His eyes were a deep chocolate brown, but very soft. She could see so much emotion in his eyes. Her gaze continued to wander down his strong jaw line, admiring his goatee. He was wearing a black mesh shirt, and she could make out the muscles in his arms and the strength of his chest. She wondered how it would feel to have his arms wrapped around her, holding her tight.

"What's up, Rave?" Brett whispered in her ear, causing her to jump back into reality.

"What?"

"You in there?"

"Huh?" She smiled.

Brett smiled back, seeing a small amount of normalcy seep back into her best friend.

Ravin glanced back at the group of guys huddled over the proofs when Nico looked up at her.

"I don't know what to say."

Anything, she thought as she twisted her coffee cup in her palm. Instead, she just smiled.

"These are unbelievable!"

She walked over and sat next to Marco on the couch. They went through each photo, setting aside the ones they didn't like. She explained what she saw for the single shots and asked for their opinions.

Sitting so close to her made Marco's stomach flip. He looked over at her, watching the curve in her neck. She smiled at him as she tucked a few strands of hair behind her ear. Why did this one girl make him feel this way? What was is about her? His eyes wandered over her soft face and he studied they way her mouth turned into a smile so delicately. She sensed him looking at her and turned to him. Marco caught his breath, looking back into her black opal eyes, fascinated by the way the colors changed from moment to moment.

"My ideas sound okay with you?"

Marco sat speechless.

"Honey, with your talent," Cole paused. "You tell *us* what to do."

Everyone agreed that Ravin had full control. She was pleased.

"Rave, wanna help me out?" Randy walked over.

"Sure." She turned to the boys. "See you in ten." She turned back to catch one more glimpse of Marco as she walked away.

"Did you see that, Mia?" Brett whispered still leaning against the buffet table in awe.

"You know I did."

"I've never seen her like that. She was like—" There were no words to describe it.

"Like a normal girl attracted to a guy?" Mia whispered.

"Quite possibly. Mr. Marco may just be the guy to pull her back into the real world."

"Think?" She exchanged looks with Brett.

They both shook their heads in agreement. Mia happily bounced off to set up the wardrobe, knowing the rest of the day would go smoothly, and if nothing else, at least a little more interesting.

Nine

Brett sat back talking to the boys while they waited for Ravin to finish setting up. They all went through the pros and cons about each other's careers. After debating, they all agreed that leading a normal life would be great sometimes. Being able to walk down the street or eat out at a restaurant without people stalking them would be something new to all of them.

Marco sat back. Normal would be great, he thought normal wasn't so bad. A loud crash wrenched him from his thoughts.

"Ravin!" Brett ran up ahead of everyone. "What happened? Are you all right?" She watched Ravin get up off the floor and dust herself off.

"Fine." She rushed over to the other side of the huge pipe that was now lying on Randy.

"Randy man, what the hell happened?" she asked laughing.

"Beats the shit out of me!" he sputtered, still trapped under the pipe.

"You hurt?" she asked, pulling up one side of the pipe so he could slide out.

"No, you?"

"No."

Marco watched her raise the pipe off Randy. Her strength took him by surprise.

"What the hell happened?" Nico asked running up.

Randy stared up at the ceiling, trying to figure out why it gave out. Ravin walked away, shaking her hands by her side. Marco followed her around the corner as everyone helped Randy with the pipe. She stood with her hands down on the table looking at the floor.

"You okay?" He reached out, touching the small of her back. He could feel her body trembling.

"I'm fine." She felt his hand glide across her back as she turned, leaving it to rest lightly on her waist.

"You're shaking," he spoke quietly.

"You're touching me." She gave him a look of disapproval as she walked away.

He followed her back to the set and watched her climb into the rafters to clamp down the pipe again.

"Okay, let's get this done," she said, convinced it wasn't going to move again. She looked back at Marco, feeling a little bad, dismissing him the way she had, but how could she allow herself to care for another man?

She moved toward him. "Thanks for being concerned," she stated shyly.

"Just wouldn't want anything to happen to you."

"I appreciate it, thanks." She bit her top lip.

"Okay, let's finish up." He smiled. He knew he got to her, he knew there was a connection.

"Okay, who's first?" she asked, picking up her camera.

Mia changed the boys and sent them in to Ravin one at a time. She saved Marco for last, secretly hoping it would spark something more.

Brett felt torn between watching Ravin shoot Marco and going back to the lounge to talk to Vinny. Mia winked at her, telling her to go. She would report anything interesting. Brett skipped off to see if she could spend more time with Vinny and maybe even get a date.

Marco walked out onto the set with the same clothes as before. This time though, she changed his shirt to a silver button down and asked him to put the bandana back on.

"Is it straight?"

"Yep." She looked up briefly. "Stand in the middle over there and duck." She went over to the wall and dropped down a pulley tied with a piece of thick rope at both ends. He didn't duck and jumped back when it fell in front of him.

"I told you to duck!" she said with a laugh. "Stand with your arms up, like you're leaning on a door frame." She lowered the pulley a little more and stood back to examine it.

"What do you want me to do?"

Oh . . . she thought to herself, absolutely anything.

"Arms up, pull your body forward a little."

He did so.

"A little more." She peered through her camera. "Comfortable?"

"No problems."

"Good, don't move." She stood up again and grabbed a roll of tape from her bag.

"And what may I ask do you plan on doing with that!" he asked playfully.

She raised her eyebrows and smiled. Confusion flooded his mind. She stood in front of him and reached behind his back. She thought of what she would like to do as she pulled his shirt back, revealing more of his chest and stomach. As she taped his shirt back, she could smell the musky scent he wore and it sent a chill up her spine.

Marco stood as still as he could. He felt her hot breath on his neck. He tasted her perfume as his heart pounded uncontrollably in his chest. He had no idea what it was about her, but it drove him crazy. He knew that if she didn't back away soon, he wouldn't be able to stop himself from kissing her.

She felt it too. She locked eyes with him as a feeling of intensity shot through her. She closed her eyes after turning back to her camera, remembering the way he smelled, the heat, the way her heart danced in her chest.

"Okay," she said as she regained her composure. "Your shirt was hanging too low." She shot the rest in silence.

When she finished, she walked Marco back to the lounge and apologized for all the delays. She offered them the chance to stay and wait for the second set of proofs.

"You're gonna leave us?" Cole asked.

"Well, someone's gotta print these." She smiled.

"So . . . you aren't gonna stick around?" Marco questioned hopeful.

"Sorry," she said lightly.

Marco felt discouraged; he wanted to sit with her and get to know her better. He watched her saunter off to her darkroom, wishing he could follow.

* * *

After an hour of badgering, Brett gave in and told Marco where her darkroom was. Brett knew Ravin would give her hell, but who was she to stop Marco from trying. She couldn't help thinking that he might be the one guy that could break the celibacy Ravin had cloaked herself in for the last five years since Dominic's death.

Marco found the darkroom easy enough. He paced outside the door for ten minutes before knocking on the door.

"Come in."

"How?" he questioned, feeling silly.

"It's a revolving door. Be prepared. It's very dark in here. When you get through, stop. I'll come over and walk you around."

He pushed through the door, confronted by total blackness. "Ouch!" he muttered, stubbing his toe.

"Sorry, I told you it was dark in here. I can't turn on the red light yet." He jumped as he felt her take his hand and guide him to the stool near her work area.

"So, tell me, Ravin, what is it that you do in here all alone in the dark?" he asked playfully.

"Wouldn't you like to know," she teased.

"Ooh, tell me," he answered back, seeing a different side of her emerge in the darkness. She took him through the process gradually. He watched her bring a negative to life on a blank piece of paper. He had never known exactly how this worked or how time consuming it was. They spent three hours in the darkroom, talking and printing the group's pictures. She hadn't felt at ease with a man in a long time. The only other person who had ever talked to her in her darkroom was Pauly; this was the first time that somebody was interested in what she did more than how she looked.

"So, what did Ben tell you about me?"

"Ben?" He paused, not sure if he should say anything.

"Yeah Ben, did he tell you that I was a pain in the ass too?"

"Um . . ."

"I'll take that as a yes."

"You know about that?"

"Sure, Ben and I have never seen eye to eye." She laughed. "Actually, he hates me."

"Why?"

"Well, it bothers him that he can't impress me with his list of celeb friends and all that crap. He told Roxi that I just don't belong in this business if I don't hob-knob with the important people."

"Really? Does anyone impress you?"

"I guess, but nobody surprises me. When did he tell you all this?"

"That day at JAM when you were standing in the hallway acting all cool with your shades on."

"Tuesday?"

"Yeah."

"Well, I wasn't trying to be cool."

"No?"

"You'll understand when we're finished."

They sat in silence for a few minutes, unsure of what to do or say. She wanted to kiss him, but she was too scared.

"I was wondering if you'd like to go out or something. I mean, if you're interested."

"I um . . . I'm not sure what to say."

"Listen, I'm sorry. I didn't mean to make you uncomfortable. Forget I even said anything." He pushed back his embarrassment.

"No, I think I would like that."

"You think?"

"Well, it's been a long time since I've been involved with anyone."

"How long?"

"Five years."

"You haven't dated in five years?" he asked surprised.

"Yes." She seemed to feel embarrassed for the first time.

"Why? I mean, look at you. You are beautiful and extremely nice." He shook his head. Nice?

"I . . ." She sat speechless. She'd had men try to pick her up many times before, but she never felt an interest . . . until now.

Marco felt his way down the table. The red light didn't give him enough confidence not to. He took her arms and tried to look into her eyes, seeing nothing but the blackness in them. Ravin trembled with anticipation. What would she do if he kissed her? Her mind raced with thoughts, and her heart pounded with a mixture of fear and need. He slowly leaned into her and touched his lips to hers.

"I'm sorry," he stammered, taken aback by the intensity of the kiss.

"It's okay." She leaned against the table, catching her breath.

"No, that was out of line, even for me."

"It's okay. You just . . ."

"Surprised you?" he laughed.

"Yes, I have to admit it's a first."

"Sorry, I've never done that before. You just caught me off guard."

"*I* did?"

"You know what I mean."

"No, not really. I've never felt this way before. This is all new to me."

"Well then, let me show you." He reached out, taking her chin with his finger and pressed his lips to hers again. She melted into his arms, feeling the passion take over her body and reaching down to her soul. Marco slid his hands down her sides, wrapping them around her waist as he pulled her into him. Ravin lost herself for a moment, reveling in this new feeling. Slowly, he broke away, not releasing her from his embrace. If he only knew what he was doing to her. He leaned his head to hers in silence.

"We should go. The pictures are done." She muttered.

"Yeah, they're probably wondering where we are." He wished time would stand still.

"Yeah." She stepped away.

"Hey." He brushed his finger across her cheek. "I want to spend some time with you. I want to get to know you."

"I'd like that." Her heart pounded and her head swam with a mixture of feelings. Fear and want struggled to take control and she didn't know which one would win.

"Possibly where there's light?" he snickered.

"Let me grab my proofs." She reached over and slid them into her bag. "You didn't happen to bring your sunglasses in, did you?" she asked, sliding hers onto the front of her shirt.

"Why would I?"

"You'll see." She slipped her glasses on and led him out to the couch.

"Now I know why you asked, I can't see a damn thing!"

"Sit. Your eyes will adjust in a few minutes."

"How long does it take?"

"You? Probably only a minute."

"And you?"

"At least another hour."

"An hour! Why so long?"

"When you spend as much time in the dark room as I do, you kinda become nocturnal."

"So . . . you do better in the dark, huh?" he asked playfully.

"Something like that," she laughed shyly.

"Okay, I can see now, sort of. You wanna go show these off?"

"Sure." She stopped and turned to him. "Listen, I don't know if I'm ready . . ." She paused not wanting to hurt his feelings.

"To let anyone know . . . don't worry about it. I understand. I don't even think I'd be willing to let the guys know that I jumped the gun—so to say. When you're comfortable, you let me know."

"Thanks. You're a lot different than most guys I meet."

"I hope that's good?"

"It is." She smiled lightly as she looked up at him.

"Good, I would hate to think my mom didn't raise me right."

"She did a fine job."

"Thanks. So are you going to tell me why?"

"Why what?"

"Why you don't date and why you aren't comfortable with anyone knowing. Brett is your best friend, isn't she?"

"Yes, she is, and as for the dating thing, that's a story for later." She avoided the question and began to walk back to the lounge.

"Why?"

"Assuming I'm not a conquest?"

"No, I don't play games like that."

"You don't, huh?"

"You don't trust men, do you?"

"No." She looked down at the ground. He gently pushed her in front of him and followed her back to the lounge.

"That's okay, I'll earn it," he whispered as they walked up to the lounge. He could feel her smile from behind. He would earn it if it took a lifetime.

Brett watched them walk up and she knew immediately that

something was different. She smiled casually at Ravin and looked over at Marco. His eyes sparkled as he sat with his group. Brett knew something had happened, and she hoped Ravin would confess that evening.

"Got the proofs done." She handed them to Nico.

"Great!" Nico started looking through them. "Ben called, he wants these by tomorrow if possible. He set up a meeting and he wants you there too, Ravin."

"Great," she mumbled under her breath. She went over and poured another cup of coffee.

"I'm hungry," Brody pouted.

"You're always hungry!" Nico laughed.

"What'dya say? Want to go out and get something to eat, Brett?" Vinny secretly crossed his fingers behind his back.

"Sounds good. Ravin, wanna join us?" Brett tempted.

"Not really. I've gotta finish up some more work. You guys are welcome to order in if you'd like."

"Marco, are you staying or coming out with us?" Brett asked looking at Ravin.

"I'd rather stay if it's okay with Ravin."

"Fine with me as long as you don't mind watching me work."

"Not at all. I'll stay and order something."

"Suit yourself. Hey, don't forget to call Tony. Let him know you're staying."

"I will." He sat back on the couch and picked up the proofs she had just finished printing. Somehow looking at pictures of himself didn't seem so conceited. She had captured something that no other photographer had been able to find before.

Brett pulled Ravin aside. "This okay with you?"

"Sure, Pauly's here."

"I meant that Marco's staying here with you. I don't want to push you, but . . ."

"Yes, Brett, its okay with me."

"Be good." She smiled.

"I will. *You* be careful."

After seeing everyone out, she sat down on the couch and watched Marco examine the pictures.

"Are you hungry?" she asked, pulling her legs up to her chest.

"Yes, wanna order something? My treat."

"Sure, what do you want?"

"I've got a taste for Chinese." He nodded.

"Sounds good, what do you like?" she pulled out her cell phone and placed their order.

"You should call Tony, whoever he is." She looked up at him.

"He's my security guard."

"Oh, then definately call him," she warned.

He pulled out his cell and told Tony where he was and the address just in case. "So, you live here?" he asked, hanging up his phone.

"Where did you think I lived?"

"I don't know, not here. I thought this was your studio."

"It's both."

"Do you pull your bed out of the wall or something?" he joked, looking around theatrically.

"Ha! No, I built an apartment upstairs," she said over her shoulder as she got up to answer the door.

Marco followed her over paying the delivery guy and grabbing the food.

"Upstairs, huh? I should have known." He nodded as he placed the food on the table.

"Known what?" she questioned opening the bags. She smiled apprehensively.

"That you would live somewhere like this."

"Why do you say that?"

"Well, you're an artist, it just fits."

"I see, what would you like to drink?"

"Whatever."

"Water, wine . . ."

"Wine's fine."

"I'll be right back." She disappeared upstairs with Pauly's dinner and returned with a bottle of wine and glasses.

"So, this is just a lounge area? It's pretty cool in here."

"Thanks." She felt a little embarrassed. He couldn't help staring at her. She looked so beautiful with her dark hair falling across her face. And her eyes, they were so dark and mysterious, but at the same time so loving and sensual. But it was her smile, however, that kept his attention. Something in her smile looked angelic and mischievous at the same time. Her smile drew him in and kept him captivated.

"What?" she asked modestly.

Her words broke his trance, "What?"

"You're staring at me."

"Sorry, I can't help myself. Something in your smile that . . . I don't know. I can't explain it."

"Oh." She glanced down at the table and fiddled with her wine-glass.

"It's not a pick-up line," he assured. "Never needed them."

"Really? Tell me Marco, how is it that you get the girls?" she teased.

"I don't, they just follow me. I have no choice but to talk to them."

"I see, and how many girls do you average in a week?"

"None. I had a girlfriend a while back, but that's been over for a while. I haven't seen anyone since. It's pretty tough to date when you're traveling around the world all the time."

"True."

"So, tell me, why is it that you haven't dated anyone in five years," he asked matching her sarcasm.

"Long story." She looked down at her hands. Dominic was her first lover—and last. She was too embarrassed to admit that she was wrong, or even that she had fallen for him. Dating was a painful game, one she wasn't prepared to play. At least not yet.

They sat and talked the rest of the night. She walked him around and showed him her "Wall of Fame", telling him some of the stories behind the pictures, but mostly she listened all night. She was good at avoiding discussions about herself and turning the table back to him.

"Hey!" Brett bounced in hours later.

"Hi, hon, how was dinner?"

"Good and yours?"

Ravin smiled at her.

"Marco, Nico is outside. He said if you want a ride to get off your ass and get out there." She laughed, falling onto the couch.

"Thanks." He looked over at Ravin, "I had a good time. I hope I can see you again."

"Me too." She walked him to the door. "I'll see you tomorrow at the meeting."

"Oh yeah, until then." He lightly kissed her cheek and wished her a goodnight.

Brett bounced behind her all the way upstairs, digging for information. Ravin revealed nothing.

Ravin fell into bed thinking about Marco. She thought about how good he made her feel, and it terrified her to think of being with someone else. She knew Dominic loved her, even though he wasn't a good man. Dominic made her feel wanted, a feeling no other boy had ever given her. Growing up was difficult with everyone knowing she was off limits. With two older brothers and Pauly around her all the time, she was amazed that she even got Dominic. She accepted his faults, even the mortal sins. She knew about his other women and his kids. No one was aware that she knew, and she never knew why she loved him. But he loved her, enough to marry her after making her pregnant. After his murder she didn't know what to think. She has always wondered if his death had something to do with her.

Marco was different. He didn't know about her past. He was interested in who she was now. Or was he? All these questions raced through her head as she lay in her bed. Why was he so interested? She never gave him a reason; she never gave anyone a reason. She was good at closing people out. Letting them in was too complicated. In the back of her mind, she knew the war wasn't over. People made appeals all the time and the one man she feared had a big family.

She closed her eyes, hoping this night would be different. Maybe tonight she would sleep.

Bang! Bang! Bang! Nooo! Dominic! The black Lincoln drove up as the barrel of a gun slipped out the half-opened window.

She was up again at three, the same time every night. This night was different though. Thoughts of Dominic and Marco tore through her mind. She tried to pick through her proofs, but she kept pulling out ones of Marco. "Why now?" she whispered to his picture. "Why now?" She gave up and headed down to her gym, knowing that the only way to release her anger was to hit her kickboxing bag. Pauly watched from the shadows, wondering what was running through her head. He knew she would struggle with the idea of dating another man, and there wasn't a thing he could do to help. This was hers, all hers to deal with. He could only offer his thoughts if she asked. He hoped she would, and then he would tell her what he thought.

Ten

Marco awoke earlier than usual. Thoughts of Ravin's mesmerizing smile were still fresh in his mind. Mindlessly, he walked into the bathroom and stepped under the cold water. He could remember exactly how she looked, how she smelled, and how she attentively listened to his stories.

"Hey, Marco!" Vinny yelled, following room service in.

"I'll be out in a minute," he answered, wrapping a towel around his waist.

Vinny graciously tipped the waiter and closed the door behind him. "So . . . how was your dinner last night?" Vinny smiled and helped himself to a cup.

"Fine, and yours?"

"Very good. I think Brett and I hit it off pretty good."

"That's great. She's nice, pretty too." Marco couldn't even compare her to Ravin. Vinny and Marco had very different taste in women.

"So, tell me, what's she like?" Vinny asked curious to see if Marco figured this one out.

"She's different."

"How different?"

"In a good way different. She's smart, has a good sense of humor. She's . . ." He paced around the room. "It's hard to explain. There's just something about her that draws me in, and once I'm there, there's no escape."

"That's pretty deep, Marco. My question is this: What did you two do last night?" He smirked.

"Nothing, talked mostly. She showed me around the warehouse and stuff."

"Sounds boring."

"Why? Was your night that much more interesting?"

"To be honest, it was. We went out clubbing after dinner. She has a lot of energy!"

"Meaning?" Marco raised his eyebrows comically.

"Ha, funny." Vinny forced a laugh as Cole walked in. "Hey, Cole, what's up?"

"Got a half-hour. Better get ready." He poured himself a cup too.

"For what?"

"For the meeting. Apparently, Ravin called and moved it up. She said it interfered with her entire day. Ya know, like she's the only one with appointments."

"Don't say that. That's not how she is. Remember, she did this as a favor. We broke into her schedule. Of course, it'll screw up her whole day by adding a long meeting."

"Man, he's already defending her!" Cole snickered.

Marco glared at him and slammed the bathroom door behind him.

"Hit a nerve, did we?" Cole looked at Vinny dazed.

Eleven

"So . . ." Brett lay on Ravin's bed, waiting for details.

"So, what? I told you everything last night. What more is there to say?"

"You told me nothing! I want you to say that you're interested in him and that you would like to attempt to be normal."

"Why Brett? What's in it for you?"

"Well, the fact that he spends every waking moment with Vinny doesn't hurt."

"Oh, I see, you like Vinny, huh?"

"Of course! He is so hot! And he can dance."

"Well, now that's important, isn't it?" Ravin snapped as she raced around the room.

"What crawled up your ass and died?"

"Excuse me?" She swung around to look at Brett.

"You heard me! What crawled up your ass and died? For the first time in five years, you spend time with a guy that *isn't* Pauly and all of a sudden you cop an attitude with me."

"I'm sorry, I'm tired. I didn't sleep at all last night."

"You never sleep, so how can it be worse?"

Ravin shrugged, digging through her closet.

"How much sleep did you get?"

"About an hour."

"Are you still having those nightmares?"

"Yes."

"Ravin, that's not healthy. You should see someone about that."

"I did. He gave me sleeping pills and told me it was all in my head."

"I'm sorry, I didn't know. Anyway, where are you going so early?" she asked, watching Ravin pull on jeans.

"I've got to go to the meeting with Ben and the guys. Apparently, they need me to help pick out the cover. God knows why."

"Ooh, can I come?"

"Not to the meeting, but if you want to hang out at Thrill, get dressed."

"Ya know, Ravin," she announced, walking out of the room. "It won't go away."

"What?"

"Marco, he's under your skin now. That won't go away." She smiled and walked out.

Ravin's head filled with a landslide of emotions. A small part of her was excited to see Marco again, but another part was full of warning and fear.

"What'dya think, Pauly?" Brett whispered to him as they entered the building.

"About what?"

"Marco."

"No comment at this point."

"Don't you think it's good that she's starting to see other people?"

"If it suits her."

"You are absolutely no help, Pauly, you know that?"

"That's not what I'm here for." He glared at her.

"When you two are done talking about my personal life, I'd like to tell you that I don't know how long this will take."

"I'll be here." Pauly sat on the front couch with his book.

"Can I walk to the conference room with you?" Brett pleaded.

"If you must," she sighed, picking up her black duffel bag and portfolio.

"I must, I must," Brett urged.

"Fine, but don't distract me. I need to get through this. Okay?"

"Okay." She glanced back at Pauly then whispered to Ravin, "It won't go away."

Ravin glared at her as she walked the rest of the way in silence. She tried to push her thoughts of Marco out of her mind and focus on her work. He'd been in her head since the shoot. Having him stay for dinner was huge for Ravin. Part of her desperately wanted to get out of her body and be free. The other part was terrified of the thought of falling in love with someone else.

Brett walked quietly beside Ravin, hoping she could at least get a chance to say hello to Vinny. She knew they had hit it off well, and even better, they understood each other. They shared similar life-styles and the same values.

Ravin took a deep breath and held the doorknob, trying to focus her thoughts. When she opened the door, Brett peeked in and waved to Vinny. He smiled and waved back. Marco, who was slouched in his chair, immediately sat up as she strolled in, sitting at the opposite end of the table, and proceeded to ignore him while sifting through her bag.

"Good morning, Ravin." Ben smiled shifting his papers.

"Morning, Ben . . . boys." She looked directly into Marco's eyes, wanting nothing more than to walk over and wrap her arms around him.

He tried to read her face; she acted completely different from the night before.

Ben sensed some tension and started the meeting. Ravin pulled out the enlargements of choices they had made the day before. Ben studied them carefully, asking everyone around the room to offer their opinion. Even Ravin gave her choice. After another hour of dis-cussing photos, inserts, and setting up another photo shoot for the promotional posters, they ended the meeting.

Ben sat back in his chair, happy with the work Ravin had done, but slightly confused by her coldness.

Vinny split as fast as he could to find Brett.

Nico, Brody, and Cole went to go find some fun of their own.

Marco cautiously followed Ravin out of the conference room and down the hall. She stopped in front of a room long enough for Marco to see where she had gone. He followed her in.

"Hi." She stood waiting by the door.

"Thank God! I thought you were pissed at me or something."

"No, why would you think that?"

"Well, you didn't say two words to me in there."

"Work is separate from everything. I take my work very seri-ously."

"You take life too seriously." He leaned against the doorframe, crossed his arms over his chest, and smiled.

"What's that suppose to mean?"

"Nothing bad, you're just a lot more closed off than I imagined."

"You don't live my life."

"What's that suppose to mean?" he mimicked.

"Nothing."

"Do you have to work all day?"

"Yeah."

"That stinks."

"Sorry."

"Can I at least walk you to wherever you need to be?"

"Sure." She smiled sweetly and stopped him again, holding her hand in front of his chest. "Please don't take this the wrong way, but . . ."

"Uh oh."

"This place thrives on rumors and I'm a *very* private person."

"I get it."

"Marco, it's not that I want to pretend there isn't anything between us. I just . . . I just don't know how long it'll take me before I understand all that I feel."

"So, you do feel something?"

"Yes, I do. Did you think I didn't or something?"

"I wasn't sure. You're not very open, ya know."

"I know."

"Listen, it's our secret, but only for now. I don't know how long I can take not telling the world about you."

"Well, you'll have to wait. At least for now."

"I understand. Really, I do. I know how hard it is to have any kind of privacy."

"Thanks." She led him back to the lounge and asked him to wait while she talked to Roxi and Michelle. She watched him as she compared schedules and smiled every time he looked up at her. Eventually, he sat down with Cole and tried not to pout.

"So . . . she got under you skin?"

Marco looked over at Cole and smiled at his question. "I guess she did. I didn't expect her to have such an impact on me so fast."

"I've never seen this happen to you before."

"It never has. What is it about her, Cole? She's like . . ." He shook his head hoping it would clear his thoughts.

"Like she's got you under her spell?"

"Something like that. I mean she's very nice, little quiet for my taste, but nice."

"If you say so. She doesn't talk much, does she?"

"Well, no . . . I did most of the talking, but . . . I just can't put my finger on it."

"So, go for it."

"Ya think?"

"I do."

"I want to, but we're leaving for L.A. tomorrow."

"So, ask her to dinner or something for tonight. Tell her you're leaving tomorrow. Tell her you want to get to know her better and that you'll be back next week. The worst thing that'll happen is she'll say no." Cole shrugged.

"Sure, she'll say no and we'll be with her next week and I'll feel like a total ass."

"So what? It wouldn't be the first time!" Cole stood up and walked away laughing before Marco could take a swing at him.

"Excuse me, Ravin?" Marco interrupted.

"Hold on, Roxi." She walked over to the side with him. "Sorry, I'm so busy."

"That's okay. I was wondering . . .," he asked looking up at her smile, "if you would like to go to dinner or something tonight?"

"Tonight?" She looked disappointed.

"We're leaving for L.A. in the morning. We have to shoot our first video. But we'll be back next week, so I was hoping if you weren't too busy, we could do something tonight before I have to go."

"Well, I've got a location shoot at three. That's probably gonna take me through dinner. I can develop tomorrow, but I can't get out of the shoot."

"Really, where?"

"New Haven."

"Why there?"

"They have a great lighthouse."

"Cool."

"Maybe you can meet me up there. You know, pick up some

dinner on the way." She shocked herself by asking, hoping it was the right thing to do.

"Are you sure?"

"Yeah," she blushed. "Maybe you can ask Vinny to come too. Brett's in the shoot. We could all hang out after. It'll give you someone to talk too until we're done."

"Are you sure? I don't want to interfere with your work and stuff."

"No, I want you to." She felt a sudden rush of nerves.

"Okay, it'll be me and Vinny, but we'll have to bring at least one bodyguard. I hope that won't be too much."

"I'm use to it. Pauly goes everywhere with me."

"One of these days, will you please tell me why he's always with you?"

"Same reason as you."

"Ravin . . ."

She just smiled at him and he wasn't sure if he was ready to know the answer.

"Listen, I've got to get ready to go soon. I'll have Roxi give you directions and see you there around five, five thirty?"

"What do you want me to bring?"

"Something warm, it gets cold out there at night."

"Okay, and food? What kind of food would you like?"

"Surprise me." She smiled and started walking into the back. She turned back and smiled at him as she turned the corner.

Marco walked back to Cole with a smile on his face.

Twelve

Marco, Vinny, and Tony walked along the beach watching Ravin shoot a handful of models.

"Pretty nice life, don't ya think?" Tony commented, looking at all the models. "Who's who?" he asked.

"Brett's the model in the black two-piece." Marco pointed, "And Ravin's the one with the camera." He stated proudly.

"Ravin's the photographer? That's right, Vinny's got the model." He shook his head. "Not bad guys, not bad at all."

"Thanks," Vinny boasted.

"Hey, there's Pauly." Marco pointed over under the trees. "I think I'm gonna go talk to him."

"Who's Pauly?" Tony asked Vinny, watching Marco approach Pauly.

"From what I get, he is Ravin's bodyguard. I have no idea why she needs one, but hey! What do I know?"

"Ravin has a bodyguard, huh?" He suddenly wondered what Marco was getting himself into.

"Hey, Pauly right?" Marco said walking up.

"Yeah, Marco."

"Well, it's nice to meet ya." He shook hands with him.

"Sit," Pauly offered.

"Thanks. I guess I need to get to know you a little. Ravin hasn't said much about you."

"Naw, she never does."

"Can I ask why?"

"Why what?" Pauly asked, enjoying the sight of Marco as he squirmed.

"Why does she need you? What's up?"

"She'll tell you when the time's right."

"Brett told me you've been with her for like fifteen years."

"About that."

"Okay, so you won't tell me. Can we talk about her?"

"What would you like to know?"

"Anything."

Marco and Pauly talked for a long time while they both watched Ravin work. Marco admired the way Pauly looked after her and he felt at ease with him. Pauly got to know Marco pretty well and liked him right away. He could tell Marco was a stand-up guy and not after anything but her company.

"Is there a town nearby?" Marco asked looking around.

"About two blocks over. Why? What do'ya need?"

"I told Ravin I would pick up some dinner. I would like to get some wine too."

"Sure."

"You want anything?"

"Whatever."

"What does she like?"

"I'll give you clue to Ravin." Pauly playfully smiled.

"What's that?"

"She's simple, very easy to please. She *doesn't* like big impressive things."

"I'll keep it simple. Like what . . . sandwiches?"

"Yes, she's more of a sandwich girl than a fancy seafood dinner girl. Get my drift?"

"Yeah thanks, that helps to understand her."

"Good."

Marco got up, told Vinny and Tony where he was going, and promised to bring back enough for them all.

"Hey Marco!" Vinny called out. "Bring Tony."

"Yeah, I'm coming with you." Tony got up.

"Pauly will take care of me, right Pauly?" Vinny laughed. Pauly just nodded never taking his eyes off Ravin.

"See you later." Marco walked down to Ravin and told her he was going to get some food. She promised she would be finished in an hour or so.

Marco went out and bought all the things he needed for their picnic. He also picked up enough for Vinny and Brett. He then headed back, stored the things he'd bought, and sat on the beach watching Ravin work the models. She was quite impressive, the way she used her camera. It was almost as if she were dancing with it.

After an hour, she finished and packed up her cameras. She sent them back with Randy, along with the film and extra people she used for the lighting.

"We're done," she said walking up.

"Good, are you hungry?"

"Not really." She pulled his arm up and looked at his watch. "It's only five-thirty."

"So, is everyone leaving?" he asked, looking at Roxi as she packed the models into the van.

"Yeah, except Pauly."

"Of course. I've got a picnic planned if that's okay. Thought it would be nicer out here than in a loud restaurant."

"That sounds good. Vinny and Brett too?"

"Well, they have their own. Vinny wanted to spend some time alone with her."

"Really? I'm glad. She's kinda gotta a thing for him."

"She does? Good, I was hoping he wasn't chasing his tail. He does that sometimes, reading affections wrong."

"Yes, she's a good person. She would never lead him on."

"I know, just . . ." He smiled.

"Being protective," she said understanding.

"Yeah. So, want to sit?"

"Sure.

Marco spread out the blanket and pulled the cooler over. He reached in and took out the bottle of wine and glasses. "Glass of wine?"

"Sure."

"I don't want you to think that I'm trying to get you drunk or anything though. I bought water too."

"I don't get drunk, Marco."

"No?"

"No." She took the wine and settled back on the blanket. She was more nervous than she thought she would be. What were they supposed to talk about all night? Were there any rules about dating? She looked over at Brett talking and laughing. Her body language was so relaxed and animated. Ravin felt uncomfortable. She looked over at Pauly talking to Tony, wishing she could ask him what she was supposed to do.

"So, tell me something," Marco finally said, watching her looking around restlessly.

"Like what?"

"Like why you look like a nervous wreck?" he chuckled.

"Sorry. I just don't know what to talk about."

"You can start by telling me why you don't like dating."

"It's a long story, Marco."

"I don't have anywhere to be." He looked at her serious.

"I'm not ready to tell you that."

"Why?"

"Listen, I had one boyfriend. I got hurt. I'm not the kind of person who would go out and have that happen again. Okay?" she snapped.

"Okay. Would you rather spend the rest of your life without loving anyone than risk getting hurt?"

"Yes. I'm very happy with my life."

"That's just crazy, Ravin. You have so much to give. Don't waste it."

She sighed and looked out at the water. Trouble was brewing, and she didn't want to chase him away. But how was she going to explain her life? How could she tell him that the Mafia had killed her first boyfriend and that they were eventually going to hunt her down and kill her too? This wasn't a normal lifestyle. This was her life and she feared it more than anything. The last thing she wanted to do was risk the life of someone else, someone as special as Marco. Part of her just wanted to curl up in his arms and feel loved and protected, and the other part of her screamed in fear. She shivered at the thought.

"Cold?"

"A little."

"Here." He reached into a bag and pulled out a new sweater he had just bought. "Put this on."

"Oh no, I couldn't. I've got a coat in the car."

"Take it. I just bought it. I don't need it."

"Are you sure?"

"Would I offer if I wasn't?"

"Thanks." She sat up, pulling it over her head. She reached up and pulled out the clip from her hair. Marco watched as she shook her hair loose, allowing it to fall down past her shoulders and across her face. Who was this breathtaking woman sitting here with him, and why did he even deserve such a chance?

"Okay, so you aren't use to dating, but I need to ask you if there's any chance of you and me?"

"I want to Marco, part of me wants to so badly." She paused, trying to think of a way to explain her feelings.

"Listen, I can take this real slow if that's what you need. I have no problem with that."

"You don't?" She felt suspicious by his sincerity.

"No, I don't."

"Slow is good. Slow would help me feel more comfortable."

"Good. Slow it is, but I have to tell you that I can't get you out of my head. I may want to talk to you a lot. Is that okay?"

"Yes."

"And I want to kiss you right now." He reached over and touched her cheek gently.

"You do?"

"Yes, I do, so you need to tell me to stop when you're uncomfortable and I'll stop. I don't know how slow you want to go. You need to tell me."

"Okay." She leaned over and kissed him. He gently took her face in his hands and pulled her away. He looked deep into her eyes and saw the apprehension below the surface.

"Do you trust me?" he whispered.

She looked at him without answering.

"Do you trust anyone?"

"No," she added shyly.

"I can assure you that I will not hurt you, physically or emotionally. I'm not like that. I never will be like *him*." He drifted to the memory of his father.

"Him?" she asked confused.

"My father."

"I don't understand."

"He abused us. He was a drunk."

"I'm sorry."

"Don't be. Because of him I'm a better person. I will never hurt another person as long as I live."

"I think I can trust you eventually."

"Good." He leaned over and touched his lips to hers. Running his hands down her shoulders, he felt her body quiver. His heart raced and his blood went hot.

Ravin's head spun with anticipation and fear. She didn't understand how she felt. Her body ached with every touch.

The evening soared by, and Marco couldn't get the answers he sought so badly. So many puzzles entwined her, like her distrust and her timidness toward men, but most of all, her need for Pauly.

"So, what time is your flight tomorrow?" she asked, pulling her arms around herself to keep warm.

"I think it's around ten. I'm not sure."

"You aren't sure? How can you not know when you're leaving?"

"Ravin, I just do what they tell me to do." He laughed.

"You do, huh? Do you always do what they tell you to do?" She cocked her head to one side.

"Only when it has something to do with the band." He chuckled. "Come here, you look like you're freezing." He held his arms out to her.

"I am." She crawled over and sat back against his chest. She felt his heart pounding strongly.

"What do you have to do tomorrow?"

"Couple shoots and *a lot* of darkroom time."

"Sounds boring."

"Not really, I like being by myself."

"Why? Don't you like other people?"

"Yeah mostly, but I seem to have lost a lot of patience with people. I guess when you work with so many models who expect you to tell them what to do, you wonder if there's anyone out there who can think for themselves."

"They aren't all that bad, are they? I mean, Brett seems pretty intelligent."

"It has nothing to do with intelligence, but I do expect a small amount of thought to go through their heads when they're up there posing. I shouldn't have to tell them how to do their job."

"I guess. I can't be that objective though. I'm one of those people who expects someone to tell me how to stand and smile."

"That's different."

"Why?"

"Do you expect them to tell you how to sing?"

"No."

"Is your main job singing or modeling?"

"Singing, and I get your point."

"Precisely, their job is to model . . . and they should know how."

Ravin was comforted watching Brett and Vinny arriving to join them. She felt the pressure lift of her shoulders, and she knew she wouldn't have to hold the conversation alone anymore.

Marco fell into bed that night thinking of a way to get closer to Ravin. It seemed impossible with his schedule, but Brett had promised that she would come around. He fell asleep trying to decide which kind of flowers would suit her best.

Ravin fell asleep that night hopeful that maybe they would stop soon. Maybe . . . if she was lucky Marco could make the dreams go away.

Noooo! Dominic! Bang! Bang! Bang! Nooo! Dominic! The Black Lincoln—gun barrel—gunshots echoing. Flashes of that day ripped through her head.

Thirteen

"Hey." Marco quietly leaned on the doorframe watching Ravin finish her morning shoot.

"Hey. Aren't you suppose to be on a plane?" she asked barely looking up from her camera.

"Soon. Just wanted to stop by and say good-bye, for now at least."

"I never did like good-byes," smiling, she looked up. " When are you coming back?"

"So, you are interested?" he teased, lifting an eyebrow.

"Well yeah, I am." She looked down at the floor. She could feel her heart quicken as he looked into her eyes.

"Good, then I'll be back." He smiled "Want anything from sunny California?"

"No." She smiled back at him.

"Good, get back to work. I'll see you Thursday." He winked with a sly smile.

"Okay."

"Okay." He leaned over and kissed her gently on the lips. Ravin closed her eyes, unsure of this new feeling, but certain she wanted him to come back.

Ravin secretly watched him leave with Vinny and Cole. She watched the way he walked with confidence, the way he turned back and looked for her one last time. His dark eyes scanning the reception area for her. Her heart quickened as she thought about the way he had touched her face before kissing her, the way his lips felt touching hers. She wasn't sure what these feelings were or where they came from. He made her feel dizzy with anticipation. She wondered briefly if this was how love truly felt. Somehow it made her feel safe, and more important, she felt wanted.

Marco sat on the plane and closed his eyes, Ravin's beautiful face monopolized all of his attention. He thought about how her eyes sparkled in the light and how she looked when she shook her hair loose the night before on the beach. It was a vision that would never leave him.

Fourteen

"Ravin!" Lainey screamed from down the hall.

Ravin poked her head out of the studio. "What?" she asked abruptly.

"You got more flowers." She smiled as she carried them to her.

"Thanks." She admired the latest delivery. For the last six days, Marco had sent her a bouquet of flowers. After two days of roses, she was happy to see that he had changed over to daisies. Brett admitted to telling Vinny that she liked daisies the best.

"So?" Lainey asked jumping in place.

"What?"

"Who's sending you flowers?"

"None of your business." She walked away pulling out the card that read: *Dear Ravin, Looking forward to seeing your beautiful face. Seems like too long since I've seen your smile. Marco.*

"Ravin, why won't you tell us who they're from? Do you have a secret boyfriend you aren't telling us about?" she asked sharply.

"Lainey, my life is mine, not yours." She turned and walked down the hallway.

"Hey." Brett walked up behind her, causing her to jump.

"Hey."

"Why are you so jumpy?"

"Sorry, I didn't hear you coming. Hey, are we doing that shoot today or what?"

"I don't know yet. Roxi said she'd let us know. What are your plans tomorrow?"

"Nothing, why?" Ravin looked at her quizzically.

"Marco's coming back."

"Yeah?"

"You didn't make any plans with him?"

"Was I suppose to?"

"Well yeah! He's only been sending you flowers everyday. I can't believe you didn't make any plans yet."

"Did you?"

"Yes, Vinny and I are going out to dinner and maybe my place. Depending on how dinner goes." She winked mischievously.

"Oh." She looked at the floor ashamed.

"Have you even talked to him?"

"No."

"Why not!"

"Couldn't think of anything to say."

"You *are* kidding me, right?"

"Brett." She swung around and looked at her best friend, wishing she knew what to do.

"Okay, let me take care of it for you." She walked away dialing her cell phone. Ravin sighed and wished she knew what she was supposed to do, how she was supposed to act. She watched Brett sitting on the couch, laughing and smiling on the phone. Ravin felt a twinge of jealousy toward Brett. She was so at ease with men. Ravin didn't know why she wasn't. Or did she?

"Hey." Pauly put his hand on her shoulder.

"Hey."

"Roxi wanted me to ask you if it was okay to give Marco your cell number. Apparently, he's been trying to get a hold of you."

"What do you think, Pauly?"

"Well, I don't know him that well."

"What does your gut say?"

"I say get to know him. He seems like a good guy. He's taking the time to get to know you."

"I have no idea why I'm so scared."

"Ravin, you are a beautiful woman, and to waste that by never sharing your life with another man would be a crime. I know it's been a long time and I know Dominic hurt you, but you can't let him pave the road for every other guy. Not all guys are like that."

"I know all men aren't like that. I just never wanted to take the chance."

"Well, you have to."

"But—"

"No. Don't start analyzing this. He seems like a great guy. Give him the benefit of the doubt. I ran his record; it's as clean as mine, so if that's what you're thinking . . ."

"That doesn't say much!" she remarked with a laugh.

"You know what I mean."

"I know, Pauly, I know. I just don't know what to do? How do I act? What am I suppose to say?"

"Ravin, do what feels right. Do whatever makes you feel comfortable, but most important, make sure you tell him why. You don't have to tell him the whole story, but at least tell him that Dominic hurt you and that you need to take it slow. If you tell him why, he'll respect you and he'll take it slow. Unless my instinct is wrong, then he'll dump you and treat you like shit." He laughed.

"Funny, is that what you would do? Respect a girl if she told you that?"

"Yes, I would. If I was honestly interested in a girl and she needed the time to adjust after a bad breakup, then, yeah, I would."

"Well, it wasn't a bad breakup, was it?" She looked at him, her eyes moist with the pain of the memory.

"Well, no, but just be honest with him. That's what's important."

"I told him to go slow."

"Good."

"Pauly, he's sent me flowers everyday. Is that slow?"

"Sure, he's just interested in you. He wants to show you, that's all."

"Okay."

"Ravin! Phone call!" Michelle called sharply from across the room.

Ravin nodded and turned back to Pauly. "Thanks." She stood up on her toes and kissed his cheek. They exchanged smiles and she went to the desk to pick up her phone call.

"Hello?" she asked as she watched Brett laughing on the phone with Vinny.

"Hey, you are *not* an easy person to get a hold of." Marco laughed.

"Hi, how's L.A.?"

"Good, lonely but good." He was so happy that she recognized his voice. "We'll be in tomorrow, and I was wondering if you wanted to do something."

"Yes, I would, but first we need to talk."

"Uh oh, that doesn't sound good. About what?"

"We can talk tomorrow."

"You're gonna make me wait until tomorrow?"

"For what?"

"Usually when a girl says *we need to talk* its not very good news."

"Well, it depends on how you take it I guess."

"So, tell me."

"Tomorrow."

"Now."

"It's just about taking it slow. I am interested, but I just need time to adjust, explain some things. Is that okay?"

"Whew! Yeah, that would be fine. But we talked about going slow. Am I rushing you? I need you to tell me if I am."

"Well . . ."

"Flowers too much?"

"A little. They're beautiful and I love them, but it scared me a little."

"Scared you?"

"I'm just trying to be honest. Yes, the six bouquets of flowers freaked me out a little. One would have been fine."

"I'm sorry. I just couldn't stop thinking about you. I thought you were mad or something. You didn't call."

"I couldn't think of anything to say, and before you say anything, Brett already yelled at me."

"She did, huh?"

"Yeah, see . . ." She looked around at some of the models watching her. "We'll talk more tomorrow, okay?"

"Okay. What's your day look like tomorrow?"

"What time do you get in?" she asked, reaching for her schedule.

"Eleven."

"Let's see, three shoots at eight, ten, and two, and of course darkroom time."

"Great, so I'll wander down after our meeting with Benny. You'll be at the studio, right? Or are you shooting at the warehouse."

"Studio."

"Good, 'til then?"

"Okay." She blushed, relieved that he couldn't see her.

"See you tomorrow." He hung up quietly and Ravin leaned against the desk.

Brett wandered over when she was done. "So? What'cha doing tomorrow?" she taunted.

"Ha ha, Brett. I'll see him after his meeting. Then I have a two o'clock shoot, so I have no idea after that."

"Good. Now that's what I wanted to hear. You wanna go get some dinner later?"

"I would, but I think I'm gonna get some take out and get caught up in the darkroom. Then I won't have so much to do tomorrow."

"Good idea. Want some company?"

"Sure."

Fifteen

"They're here," Brett whispered to Ravin.

"Okay." She laughed.

"When are you going to be done?"

"I thought they had a meeting?"

"Benny's sick, so they cancelled. Marco's looking for you."

"Send him back. I'm gonna be at least another half hour." She shot daggers at Carlos. "Unless my model cooperates, then I can be done sooner and he can go back to bed!" she yelled bitterly.

"Okay."

Marco walked up quietly and leaned in the doorframe. Watching Ravin was never boring, he loved the way she moved behind the camera, like a tiger stalking its prey. He noticed Carlos looking at him and smiled, trying to be friendly, but he didn't acknowledge Marco. Models, he thought to himself, what an interesting breed. Randy whisked her cameras away when Ravin finished. Carlos walked over and put his arm around her. Marco watched Ravin shrug him off, but Carlos tried again.

"Carlos, back off!" she threatened, putting her film in her bag.

Marco couldn't hear what he said to her, but he was ready to walk in at a moment's notice. He saw Pauly sitting in the corner watching too. Ravin brushed him off again, but this time he grabbed her arm and spun her around. Pauly sat up and Marco waited to see what he'd do first. Before he knew what happened, she had grabbed Carlos by the arm and threw him to the floor in one quick motion. Marco watched him go down and Ravin scream at him. He looked over at Pauly, who went back to reading his book with a slight smirk on his face.

"I guess I don't have to worry about you, do I?" Marco said with a smile as he leaned in the doorway.

73

"Hi." She walked over. He looked over her shoulder and watched Carlos dust off his ego.

"Sorry, Rave." He scampered away.

"Remind me not to get on your bad side," Marco stated.

"He does that all the time. You think he would have learned by now," she huffed.

"Want me to talk to him?"

"No, Pauly tried once. Carlos is just stupid. He thinks he's irresistible or something. You should be use to that though, all those girls throwing themselves at you."

"Yeah, but I don't throw them on to the floor! And no, you don't get use to it, at least I don't."

"Good."

"So, are you done? Can we go somewhere and talk?"

"Yeah, I just need another minute and we can go." She picked up her bag and he followed her out to the reception area. She handed Michelle some papers and checked the book.

"I'll be back for the two o'clock."

"Don't bother, Lainey's sick."

"Cool."

"Keep your cell on though in case Roxi wants to talk to you about it."

"Okay." She walked Marco out back to the garage.

"Isn't Pauly coming?" he questioned.

"Not with us, but he'll be around."

"As in?" he asked confused.

"You won't see him, but he'll see us."

"So, he's not the same kind of bodyguard as Tony, is he?"

"No." She unlocked her Durango. Marco looked at the SUV and back at her. "What?" she asked mildly.

"Not the kind of car I expected you to drive."

"What did you expect to see me in?"

"Something smaller. So what is Pauly's job?" he pressed trying to get back on the subject.

"To protect me." She started the engine.

"From who?"

"Whoever would want to hurt me," she stated uneasy.

"Why doesn't he walk with you?"

"Because he can see more behind me, I don't know! He's giving me space, so we can talk."

"Where are we going?"

"To the river."

"The river? You aren't gonna like fit me with cement shoes are you?" he joked.

"No, we don't do that anymore," she spat sarcastically.

Marco looked at her confused. "C'mon, spill it."

"I will. I'll tell you everything I can today, but first I need food."

"Can we take it with us?"

"Sure, the deli sound good to you?"

"Fine with me." He sat back concerned. He wondered what she was going to tell him. She drove him out to her favorite spot overlooking the East River. She parked the truck and dug out their sandwiches.

"So what's this horrible thing you have to tell me before we can go forward?"

"Well, it's not that horrible, at least I hope not."

"Ravin, you can tell me anything. I want you to trust me."

"Well, that's a good place to start. Trust is very hard for me."

"Why?" He shifted in his seat and gazed into her dark eyes.

"I was engaged five years ago."

"Engaged ... to be married?" He was not expecting to feel jealous.

"Yes." She took a deep breath. "I was engaged to Dominic Scalise, and he wasn't very good to me. He always had girls on the side and even another wife with kids. But I chose to overlook that because he was the first guy to ever pay any attention to me—"

"I find that hard to believe."

"Well, you didn't grow up with Pauly and two older brothers, did you?" She tried to laugh. "Anyway, he died, about a month after my father."

He reached out and touched her hand, gently stroking the top with his finger. "I'm sorry. I didn't know you lost your father too."

"Yes, so I'm sorry if I'm a little closed off."

"Ravin, don't worry about that. I can deal with that as long I know that you want to try to move on with me. I like you and I want to get to know you better, but before I do, I need to know if it's something you want too."

"I do, I'm just scared. I don't know why I loved Dominic so much. He did hurt me and I don't ever want to feel that kind of betrayal again. That's why I never bothered dating. I find it to be too painful, at least for me."

"I understand, and let me assure you that I can only handle one woman at a time." He smirked to lighten the mood that slipped away.

"Thank you." She smiled, feeling better for having told him. For the first time in a long time, she looked forward to being with another man.

Sixteen

"What time is it?"

"Wow, it's almost five thirty." Marco looked at his watch.

"Think we should call somebody before they worry?"

"Yeah, probably. Nico must be out of his mind."

"Is he always this protective? I mean, can't you like go out and do things alone."

"Yeah, but I don't have Tony with me and we *are* in New York. While we're on tour or in the process, he tends to keep close tabs on us."

"Doesn't that bother you?"

"Not really. We made a pact when we started off that we would always take care of each other. The band wouldn't be the same if one of us weren't there."

"True. Well call him and tell them all to meet us at my warehouse. We can order in dinner."

"You sure?"

"Yeah, I'd cook something but I never have any food there. I pretty much spend all my time at the studio."

"You can cook, huh?"

"Yes, I can cook." She grinned.

"How long until we'll be there?"

"Like ten minutes."

Marco called Nico and they all met at Ravin's. They ordered in Chinese. Brett was happy to see her best friend acting like a real person and putting aside some of her fears. She knew it was going to be a great summer.

Pauly even stayed and got to know the entire band. He felt an instant connection with Marco and Nico, and he felt at ease with them around.

"So, Pauly, tell me something I need to know about Ravin," Marco said after she went upstairs.

"Like what?"

"Like, is she this hard to get to know or is she playing games?"

"I thought she took you to the river to talk."

"Yeah, she told me a story about how her ex-boyfriend hurt her. Everyone has a story like that, even me."

"What else did she tell you about him?"

"Not much, that's why I'm asking you. Trying to get any information out of her is like pulling teeth."

"Dominic was her first boyfriend, her first love and her first lover. He lied, cheated, and stole from her. And then they shot him to death in front of her. She's been this quiet ever since. She wasn't always like this. She was more like Brett. It hit Ravin hard, *really* hard, so she has every right to be weary of men in my opinion. Just keep talking to her. Eventually you'll break down her walls and she'll let you in, although I'm not sure you will want to once you do." He let out a small laugh.

"He was shot and killed in front of her?" he stammered in disbelief; she only told him a small part of the story.

"Yes, she and Brett were walking down to meet him at the jewelry store to pick out their wedding bands and he was shot and killed in front of them. I only wish I could have gotten there sooner." He said, drifting off into a memory he would rather have forgotten.

"You have got to be kidding?"

"Why the hell would I kid about something like that!"

"Sorry, I just." He shook his head, "I didn't even think."

"Don't worry about it. Just don't tell Ravin I told you. She really is excellent once you get to know her, and a lot of fun when she relaxes."

"Does she ever?"

"What?"

"Relax?"

"Not that I've seen in a while."

"Well, we'll have to work on that now, won't we?" He gave Pauly a devilish grin.

*   *   *

Marco spent the week with Ravin, mostly he spent it in the dark-room with her working, but more important he took the time she needed. The more time they spent together, the more she opened up. Something began to spark between them, something she knew was very powerful. Every time he came near, her heart ached with an inner longing, and when he touched her, it was almost unbearable. The feelings he aroused in her made her feel like her skin was on fire. She had never felt such powerful emotions before and part of it scared her. But every time she felt anxious, she reached over and took his hand. It had a calming effect on her until he would reach over and caress her face. Then it would start all over again.

Seventeen

"Marco man, get up!"

"What! I'm up!" He bolted up from his warm bed.

"We got to get going; we've got to be at Ravin's in a half an hour." Vinny slammed the door shut. Marco rolled over, annoyed at Vinny for interrupting his dream. Slowly, he got out of bed and shuffled sleepily to the bathroom.

Cole was sitting at the table drinking coffee when he walked out in a towel.

"Why is it, man, that *every* time I get coffee sent up, you guys are always drinking it?" he said with a laugh, pulling out a pair of baggy jeans from his suitcase.

"I don't know, I guess yours tastes better." He laughed.

"Funny, Cole. Have you seen my favorite yellow shirt?" he asked, looking around the room.

"Yeah, I think Brody took it."

"Man! I wanted to wear that today."

"Sorry, I didn't realize it was so important! Wear something else."

"I don't have anything else clean."

"Go dig through my stuff."

Marco shook his finger at him and walked into Cole's room. He flipped open his suitcase and found a suitable replacement.

"We're leaving in two minutes," Nico advised him as he walked by.

"Fine, let me grab my bag."

"Ravin, what do you want to set up?" Randy asked as he walked into her apartment. Ravin walked out of her bedroom, her eyes glazed over from the lack of sleep.

"What?"

"God, you look tired."

"I am. What did you ask me?"

"I asked what you wanted me to set up."

"Benny just wanted them in front of colored backdrops."

"That's it? I thought these were for posters and stuff."

"They are."

"And this is as creative as you're going to get? Colored back-drops!"

"Randy man, I don't think I've gotten more than four hours of sleep in three days. My heads a little blurry today. Okay?"

"You know what you need?"

"I'm afraid to ask." She rubbed her eyes.

"One of my special morning after drinks."

"Your what?" she asked, pulling her hair back into a ponytail.

"Morning after drinks, I make them up when I get a hangover."

"I don't have a hangover. I'm just tired."

"Well, they work well for being tired too. Trust me, don't you?"

"Sure, whatever." She sat on the couch and put her face in her hands. Randy returned five minutes later with a tomato juice concoction and forced her to drink it. They went downstairs and began setting up. Brett arrived with Mia in tow, her arms filled with bagels and muffins. Brett immediately pulled out the large coffeepot and Mia went to set up wardrobe. Ben asked if she could shoot them at her warehouse again, offering her more money and informing her that the boys were more comfortable there. She agreed. Since she'd much rather have them at her place anyway. She had their full attention and got to spend more time with Marco without prying eyes around the studio.

"Good morning." Brett smiled as she opened the door to let them in.

"Good morning, Brett," Cole mimicked her walking in.

"Why do you take such good care of us?" Nico asked, pouring some juice.

"What can I say? We love you guys."

"Where's Ravin?" Marco asked, looking around.

"I saw her around somewhere."

"I'm gonna go find her." Marco walked around looking for

Ravin. He quietly walked up to her sitting against the wall and sat down in front of her.

"Hey," he whispered, trying to look into her face. She slowly looked up, blinking her eyes.

"Hi."

"What'cha doing?"

"Nothing." She hesitated as she stood up.

Marco reached over and grabbed her arm before she lost her footing. "Are you okay?"

"Yeah, I'm fine." She stretched her arms above her head. "Just didn't sleep too well last night."

"No? Why not?"

"Just couldn't."

He reached for her hands, "Can I get you anything?" he asked, looking at her exhausted eyes.

"Coffee would be a great start." She smiled.

He leaned in closer. "Mind if I kiss you?"

She just smiled and allowed him to take her to the safe place where his eyes always led her. She felt the electricity run through her, the mix of emotions that coursed through her every time he touched her. His kiss was soft this morning, but it possessed the same intensity as before.

He leaned his forehead against hers and whispered, "Can I buy you a cup of coffee?"

Ravin smiled and took his hand, and together they walked out to the lounge. Brett beamed as they walked in. They all sat down and talked about what Ravin had in mind for the day's shoot. She knew she didn't want colored backdrops, so she sat back and told them to spit out ideas. She listened to them as they came up with different ideas, feeding off the stuff she shot earlier. She felt Randy's morning after drink kick in. This incredible surge of energy rushed through her and her leg started bouncing.

"Uh oh," Brett radiated.

"What?" Cole looked around. Brett pointed to Ravin's leg and they looked back at her confused.

"What?" Cole asked.

"You guys are in for it now." Brett laughed. Ravin exchanged glances with her and the girls winked at each other. "Yeah," Brett whispered nodding her head.

"Could either one of you explain what you are smiling about?" Nico asked, confused.

"I think we might be leaving the warehouse. You should call back your troops."

"Leaving? Why would we be leaving?" Nico became concerned.

"Ravin's got that look in her eye again. I know that look."

Ravin sat with a smug smile on her face, nodding as they looked over at her. She quickly got up, went to get Randy, and told Mia the change in plans. Nico immediately got on the phone and called back their security guards.

"So, where are you taking them?" Brett whispered as Ravin packed her cameras.

"Not far."

"Not far? Where?"

"The empty lot down the street."

"Really?"

"Yeah."

"I'll get your coat."

"Thanks." She smiled, loving every second when something hit her this intense. Maybe that was why she felt so drawn to Marco. He gave her the same intense feeling.

"What do you need Ravin?" Randy called out, running past her.

"Don't know yet. I haven't been there in a while."

"Call me when you get there and I'll be over in a minute."

"Make sure the guys change before they leave here."

"Got it."

"Oh, Randy!" She spun on her heel.

"Yeah?"

"Thanks for the drink." She smiled.

"It was only tomato juice and hot sauce . . . and a little secret ingredient." He winked.

"I know, but I needed it."

"Well, go before it wears off!" He laughed and threw her bag to her.

Ravin ran down the street with Pauly. She surveyed the empty lot and pulled out her light meter, checking the amount of light she would need. She called Randy and asked him to bring her two portables as she started setting up the old wood and barrels.

"What's going on? Does she do this often?" Marco asked Brett as they walked briskly down the street.

"She use to. It's been a long time since she's been inspired like this."

"So, this is somewhat normal for her then? I shouldn't be concerned that she's lost her mind?"

"No, Marco, she hasn't lost her mind." She laughed. "If anything she's found it again. This is the Ravin I know, the one who goes off on a whim and makes you do bizarre things. But I'll tell you this, her best work is when she's in this kind of mood."

"Really? What should we expect?"

"Expect to do things that you would never dream of doing. That's about all I can say. I have no idea what she has up in her head. I just know it's gonna be good."

"I guess we'll have to trust you guys." He spotted Ravin and headed over to her.

"Marco!" Brett grabbed his sleeve pulling him back.

"What?"

"Don't, not when she's working, e*specially* when she's in one of her moods."

"Why?"

"Trust me, don't be the boyfriend. Be the client."

"Okay."

Pauly leaned against the brick wall watching the security guards scouting the area. *Amateurs,* he thought to himself mocking. *If they only had a clue.*

"Okay, here's the deal." She took a deep breath and proceeded to meticulously position them. "Just go with me, whatever I shout out—do. Got it?" She shot the group in the empty lot with a rejuvenated feeling. Randy ran around in the background, holding up the reflector to block out some of the light.

She emptied her camera and grabbed a new one. "Okay, change positions."

"Can we have a minute; let the blood to go back to the bottom of my legs." Vinny laughed stretching.

"Sorry, yeah, take a second." She rushed over to pull out some more wood for them to sit on. Pauly got up and helped this time. He hated watching Randy struggle when Ravin was in her swing. She positioned them carefully, diligently fixing their hair and clothes. She saved Marco for last and took extra time adjusting his shirt, allowing her fingers to run across his chest. It sent an extra charge through her, a feeling she wished she could bottle up and use whenever she needed.

Marco shuttered every time she touched him. Her fingers delicately brushing across his chest with such intensity, startled him. She stepped back before he could react and began snapping pictures. Two hours later, she packed her last roll of film and handed her bag to Randy.

"Okay, we're done."

"Great, that was kinda fun." Nico jumped down off the wood.

"Ravin, I'll bring this all back and start these right away," Randy said packing the lights.

"Please." She smiled.

"Rave!"

"Yeah?" She turned to Brett.

"Roxi called. Lainey's sick again. You get the day off."

"Cool. What's she sick with today?"

"Who cares? Can I steal Vinny now?"

"Yeah sure. They can all stay if they want."

"Good."

"That was different." Marco cautiously walked up behind her.

"Sorry, sometimes it gets out of control."

"I loved it. You're nuts!"

"Gee thanks."

They watched the others head down the street.

"Ravin, I can't help myself anymore."

"What do you mean?"

"The way you were touching me over there. I'm sorry, but you are driving me crazy."

"So . . ." She was confused.

"So, I'm telling you this because my emotions have taken over and I'm afraid of how they're going react to you."

"Marco."

He stopped her by leaning over and kissing her. Every emotion stirring in him came to the surface. All the energy she gave him from her touch came pouring out. Ravin's head spun. She gave in and allowed herself to feel what he did to her. Pushing her up against the wall of the building, he ran his hands up her back and dug his fingers into her hair. Ravin gently touched his chest, allowing herself to become free. Her touch became stronger and more aggressive as she slid her hands up his chest and around his neck. She could feel her knees weaken as Marco pressed his body against hers. She reached up and grabbed his fingers in hers and he pushed them up against the wall above her head. Her breath quickened, and her heart beat faster and faster until he stepped back. He suspended her arms above her head and looked deep into her dark eyes.

"Sorry," he whispered.

"Don't be." She looked up at him.

He cracked a smile. "I don't want to rush you. I told you though, I can't stop myself when I'm around you. I know you probably aren't ready for this."

"If I wasn't before, I am now." She pulled him to her, kissing him with all the passion she felt.

Pauly leaned against the wall with a hopeful smile on his face. This made him happy as he turned away and surveyed the area.

Eighteen

"What's it going to be today?" he leaned on the doorframe of the studio.

"Hi." She spun around.

"Hungry? It's almost two-thirty."

"I don't know if I'll have time today. Sorry." She sauntered over holding her camera.

"That's okay. What'cha got left to do?"

"This shoot, developing, and a meeting at four."

"Will you at least call me when you're done?"

"I can do that. I shouldn't be any later than five."

"That's fine. I'll go out shopping or something."

"Okay. Are you guys all coming over for dinner tonight?"

"Is that an invite for everyone?"

"Yes."

"Sounds good. What time?"

"Around six? I'll pick up something on the way home."

"Okay, here." He dug into his pocket and pulled out fifty dollars. "I can't let you pay for everyone."

"Don't worry about it." She pushed his hand away.

"Ravin."

"Listen, when you're out can you pick up some more wine and bottled water?"

"Yeah sure, but . . ." He started to say as she backed away.

"But nothing." She smiled and went back to work. Marco stood in the doorway still holding out the fifty.

Ravin looked back one last time and winked at Marco. He waved goodbye and winked back at her.

"Pauly!" she called out, unloading another roll from Lainey's shoot.

"Yeah?" he called back from the hallway.

"Can you call Momma's and get some take out?"

"Sounds good. What'dya want?"

"Enough for everyone, whatever. You know I'm not picky."

"For what time?"

"I told Marco to have them there at six."

"I'll take care of it."

"Thanks, Pauly! I'll be in the darkroom."

Pauly pulled out his cell phone and called her mom's restaurant. He talked to her brother Nicky after placing his order.

"What's up, Pauly?" Nicky asked, sensing Pauly wanted to tell him something.

"Nothing really, Ravin's got a boyfriend now."

"Oh really? When did this happen? I thought she gave up on men."

"Well . . . this one slipped in."

"What's he like, Pauly? Is he good enough?"

"Yes, he is. His name is Marco, and before you say anything else, yes, I did all the usual. He's clean."

"Good. When do I get to meet him?"

"When Ravin's ready I'm sure she'll bring him around. She's struggling with this whole thing, though."

"Why?"

"I'm not sure. I don't think she's ever gotten over Dominic. I think she's scared."

"Of what? Why the hell is she torturing herself? What the hell is there to be scared of?"

"Honestly, I don't know, but she's trying and we all need to support her."

"I get it, so this guy's okay? Is he good to her? What kind of job does he have?"

"He's very good to her. She explained a little of her past with Dominic and told him to take it slow. He is, as for what he does? Well, you may not like it."

"Why?" Nicky demanded.

"He's a musician. He's in the group Jaded."

"Never heard of them. A musician, huh? Well at least he ain't no model." He snorted.

"Yeah, she'll tell you all about him later. I don't want to give away too much."

"Got it. Keep an eye on her Pauly."

"I will."

"All right, see you in a while."

Pauly and Ravin swung by and picked up the food on the way home. She told them she was running late and promised to call Nick the next day and tell him everything about her new boyfriend. Her mother looked into her daughter's face and knew it was more than that.

"Sorry we're late!" she yelled, walking in with arms full of food.

"Man, how much did you get?" Cole asked, taking some of bags from her.

"Apparently, Pauly couldn't decide what he wanted." She laughed over her shoulder at him.

"Lead the way." Marco said, taking the rest of her bags toward the lounge.

"Let's eat upstairs." She smiled.

"You sure?" he asked.

"Yeah."

Sensing the confusion, Brett asked, "Marco, is this your first time upstairs?"

"Yes."

"Ravin, you've never had him upstairs?"

"No," she said, embarrassed.

"Wow!" Brett said shocked. "You'll love it. It's pretty cool up there."

"Listen." She swung around. "I don't know how clean it is in here. I don't spend a lot of time here."

"Don't worry about it." Marco smiled.

She opened the door and let everyone in. Marco handed Brody the bags and he, Brett and Cole brought the food into the dining room. Ravin set her black bag down, turned to Marco, and smiled.

He took her face in his hands and kissed her lightly on the forehead. "Give me a tour?"

She smiled and took his hand. It wasn't a long tour, but a huge

step for her. She showed him the two bedrooms and her office, and
then they went back to the living room.

"It's not much, but its home." She squeezed his hand.

"It's perfect. Let's eat."

"So, what else do you have jammed in this warehouse of yours?"
Nico asked over dinner.

"Well, you've seen most of the downstairs and across the hall
over there." She pointed out the one window. "I have like twelve bedrooms."

"You're kidding? Twelve bedrooms! What the hell do you need
with all those bedrooms?"

"Honestly, I have no idea why I built them." She always wondered herself.

"Well, you have to do something with all this space. Why did
you decide on a warehouse anyway?" Marco asked curiously.

"It fit my needs. I looked at houses, but they were too small. I've
always wanted a studio and darkroom in my house. When I couldn't
find anything, my brother suggested a warehouse. I saw this and fell
in love, so I bought it."

"I think it's pretty cool. I mean, you can do just about anything
here and never have to leave your house."

"Pretty much, that's why I wanted it. Eventually, I want to move
the studio in here permanently."

"Why haven't you?"

"No time."

They talked all night; Pauly enjoyed having other people around,
something he didn't realize how much he had missed.

Nineteen

Marco lay in bed, visions of Ravin wandering through his thoughts. He looked over at the clock. It was almost seven-thirty. He wondered if she was still sleeping and imagined her lying in her bed with her black hair fanned out across the pillow. He pictured her dark olive skin peeking out from under the sheets. The knock on the door dragged him out of his daydream. He walked over and let in room service, followed closely by Cole and Vinny.

"Why are you up so early?" they asked.

"Dunno." He said. "Why are you here so early?"

"Talked to Ben. He just got off the phone with Brett. She offered Ravin's place for the meeting. Guess Ben couldn't get a hold of her. Anyway, Brett said that Ravin had a meeting room in her place. It would be quieter and safer. Word is out. Look out your window," Cole complained short of breath.

Marco got up and glanced out the window. There were at least two hundred girls standing outside the hotel, screaming their names. He loved what he did . . . except this part.

"Anyway," Cole said, pacing the room, "I guess we're supposed to go to Ravin's. I don't see why it would be any safer."

"Nobody would suspect us to be there. Ben's right. Does Ravin even know?"

"I don't think so, but you better pack. We're leaving now." Vinny turned on his heels and walked out. Cole sat down and watched Marco throw things into his suitcase.

"You really like her, don't you?"

"Yes, I do. I don't know what it is about her. I can't put my finger on it. It's weird. I've never felt like this before."

"You're in love, Marco. It's so obvious."

"Shut up! I've only known her a month."

"That's all it takes sometimes, especially when you find your soul mate." He smirked.

"Soul mate? Get real."

"Think about it. Let's go."

"What about my coffee?"

"I'll make you some at Ravin's." He laughed.

Marco zipped up his bag, wondering how they were going to get out this time. He had to admit their security guards were getting inventive.

Nico opened Marco's door. "Let's go." He stated straight-faced and serious.

They walked up to the roof and climbed into the helicopter.

"What's all this for?" Marco asked, buckling his seatbelt.

"Bomb threat." Nico said gravely. This had happened once before in Germany. They took it very seriously.

"Shit! Where are we going?"

"Ravin's. I just talked to her. She assured us that nobody could find us there. She's also getting some extra people there for us."

They flew in silence; take the good with the bad. They always followed that. After five minutes, they landed on top of a building next to Ravins. Three unknown men stood up top waiting. Cautiously, they got out, security guards on full alert.

"Who's Tony?" Leonardo asked as he stepped forward. "Rave sent me. I'm Leonardo. Let's get these guys inside." He shook hands with Tony. "Follow me." He ducked his head as the helicopter took off.

They followed Leonardo down the staircase. Ravin and Brett were waiting at the bottom. Ravin ran over and took Marco's hand.

"You okay?"

"I am now." He smiled. Pauly led them through a maze of tunnels coming out in Ravins warehouse.

"This is just cool!" Brody squealed. "It's so cloak and dagger. I just love it!"

Marco looked at Ravin differently. He wasn't aware of this part of her life. She never talked about her past.

"Pauly, could you show these guys their rooms please?"

"Follow me, guys."

She grabbed Marco's sleeve and pulled him aside. "I hope you aren't mad at me?"

"Why would I be?"

"Benny called this morning and told me about the bomb threat. *I* told him to do this."

"Who are all these people?"

"Mostly family."

"You aren't um . . ." He didn't want to say it.

"No, my dad had a lot of friends before he died."

"Sorry."

"I'll understand if you can't handle this." She motioned to the half dozen soldiers.

"Why wouldn't I?"

"Well, you know."

Marco wrapped his arms around her waist and pulled her against his chest.

"Not even these guys could keep me away," he whispered in her ear.

Pauly looked over his shoulder and smiled. Leonardo flashed a look at Pauly, making sure Marco wasn't out of bounds. Pauly nodded his approval.

"Okay, show me my room. Are your clothes taking up all the closet space?" he laughed grabbing her hand.

"Very funny, follow me."

She led him over to the rest of the guys as they huddled outside their rooms trying to figure what was going on. Ravin told them she would get some food and to let her know if they needed anything specific.

"You aren't going out alone," Leonardo stated.

"No, Pauly always come with me," she assured him.

"Yeah, we'll pitch in some money too," Nico added, pulling out some cash.

"Fine. This place is pretty huge, so you should be able to get some privacy. You can't see anything from the outside, so no one will be able to see you in here. There's a piano downstairs and you can go outside. I had them open up the middle of the warehouse to put in a yard."

"Cool."

Vinny looked at her excited "You've got a piano?"

"Yeah, an old Grand. I can't tell you if it's in tune, though. You'd have to ask Brett. She plays, not me."

"You wouldn't happen to have any weights?" Nico thought he'd shoot for the moon.

"Yeah, I have a stocked gym downstairs to the right, but it's mine from three to six." She stressed.

"You work out that late? How? You're always at the studio."

"Um . . . actually at three in the morning."

"You get up that early to work out? Are you nuts?" Nico blinked with surprise.

"She's usually up then anyway," Brett cut in, walking up with a handful of sheets. "Here's the deal: She never sleeps. Ever!"

"Why don't you sleep?" Marco asked, concerned.

Ravin shrugged.

"Who's up for exploring?" Brody asked. "Hey, anywhere off limits?"

"Pauly's room. It's next to my apartment."

"Got it, let's go." Cole followed him.

Vinny asked Brett to check out the piano with him. Nico went with Tony and discussed what was happening. Ravin stood looking at the floor.

Marco took her hand. "Let's go. Show me around, my little nocturnal, non-sleeping princess."

"Please don't ever call me princess!"

"Sorry, but I bet I can get you to sleep." He winked devilishly at her.

Twenty

A few hours and a few hundred dollars later, Ravin, Brett, and Pauly returned with more food than she had ever purchased. Benny had moved the meeting to four o'clock and the girls started cooking.

After the meeting, they served dinner and happily crowed around the dining room table.

"This is great. I have to admit, it has been a long time since we had a real home cooked meal," Cole said, helping himself.

"Thanks." Brett blushed.

"I didn't know you could cook so well. Wanna marry me now?" Vinny half joked.

"Sure! But I didn't do much. Ravin did most of it."

"So you can cook too?" Brody asked.

Marco leaned over the table, watching her.

"I'm Italian and Greek, what else can I say?"

"A lot! You can cook and take fantastic pictures. Is there anything else I should know?"

"In time." She smiled.

Marco gazed into her mysterious dark eyes and wondered how much more she was hiding.

"I talked to Ben. The concert is still on," Nico said over the table.

"Great! I'd hate to let the fans down, especially the ones who will benefit from the proceeds," Vinny said excited.

"Concert?" Brett looked up at him.

"Yeah, next Thursday. Wanna come?"

"I'd love too!"

Marco glanced over at Ravin, who was sipping her wine and silently watching everyone. She turned her head and beamed fondly at him.

"What?"

"Coming?"

"To what?"

"Our concert. You, Brett, and Mia, front row, of course. It's a lot of fun," he teased.

"Now why would I want to come to a loud concert filled with screaming teenagers?" She couldn't stop herself.

Marco's face went blank until he saw a smile unroll onto her face.

"I'm kidding!" She laughed.

"Yeah, come on, Rave. It'll be fun. We always have a blast," Brody pleaded.

"When?"

"Next Thursday, starts at seven."

"Of course, we'll come."

"Great! We'll get everything set up for you. Limo, tickets, backstage passes. Everything!" Vinny boasted.

"I think we can handle getting there," Mia said shyly.

"Not for this, you will all be treated like royalty."

"That's not necessary," Brett said quietly.

"Brett, don't argue with him. If he wants to get us a limo, he can," Mia said hoping to get the celebrity treatment for once.

"Okay, okay! I just don't want you to think I need all this royalty treatment."

"I don't." He winked.

They all spent the night in Ravin's apartment, watching movies and telling stories. Ravin spent most of her time just watching the people that had filled her home. Every now and then, she and Pauly exchanged glances, neither sure how everything had changed so abruptly. All she knew was that having them all around her was contagious and she didn't want them to leave. She leaned back against Marco's chest and knew that she never wanted him to go. She was falling in love with him and wasn't sure what to do. She took Pauly's advice and just let it happen, hoping nothing bad would ever happen to him.

Twenty-One

"Dinner alone tonight?" He slid up behind Ravin.

"Sounds good to me."

"I sent the guys out, let us have some time alone."

"They agreed, huh?"

"Sure, why wouldn't they?"

"Just kidding. What do you want?"

"You," he regarded provocatively. "Let me take care of you for a change."

"It's not necessary."

"Don't argue with me," he said playfully. "You've cooked for us for the last two weeks. It's my turn. Let me cook for you."

"You can cook?"

"Sort of, nowhere near as good as you, but I can make the basics."

"Okay, I guess. You won't . . . like . . . burn down my kitchen or anything, will you?" She laughed.

"No. What do you want?"

"Surprise me." She leaned in and kissed him. Over the last few weeks, she had fallen in love with him. She hadn't told him, of course, but she felt it.

"Well, what do you want?" he teased her, backing away.

"I told you, surprise me." She paused. "I've got to get to the studio. Some of us still have to work, ya know!"

"What time are you coming back?"

"I hope by four. I've got a shoot at ten and then some serious darkroom time."

"Don't stay away too long."

"I'll hurry." She kissed him lightly and left.

Marco went shopping, buying all he needed for the evening

meal. He spent the day planning everything to be just right. He decided that this was the night that he'd win her heart; he didn't know that he already had.

Ravin looked at the clock in her darkroom and rushed through the last prints. It was almost four-thirty and she hated to be late.

"Sorry I'm late!" She rushed into the living room.

"You aren't." He called out from the kitchen.

"Smells good! Do I have time for a shower?"

"Plenty."

"Good, I'll be back in a few." She ran into her room, tossing off her clothes. After a quick shower, she hurried into her closet and picked out a pair of tight black pants, cut very low at the waist, and a white button-down shirt. She went back into the bathroom and applied a small amount of mascara and some gloss across her lips. She threw her hair up in a clip and went into the kitchen to help.

"I'm done," she said, as she walked in.

"Damn that was quick."

"I'm fast. Pisses Brett off." She laughed.

"I bet! Of course, you don't need to do anything. You're perfect the way God made you."

She smiled at him a little embarrassed. She still had to get use to compliments.

He seated her at the table that was adorned with candles and wine, and served her the only meal he knew how to make.

"Sorry, this is about all I can handle." Slightly embarrassed, he suddenly wished he had taken home economics in high school. "I hope you like fettuccini."

"Peanut butter would have been fine." She smiled and tasted his cooking.

"How is it?"

"Fabulous! I think this is better than mine. What's your secret?"

"I won't tell!"

She laughed and threw her napkin at him. During dinner, they talked about her shoot and the upcoming concert. He cleared the plates, refusing to let her help, and brought her more wine as they sat on the couch.

"I've got strawberries and whip cream for dessert. I couldn't think of anything else."

"Sounds good. I love strawberries."

She sat back while he went to get them and wondered if other men were like this too. Was Vinny doing something nice like this for Brett? She shook the thought out of her head when he set the tray down on the table.

"You know what I like more than strawberries?" she asked, dipping her finger in the whipped cream.

"What's that?"

"You." She smiled as he grabbed her finger and licked off the whipped cream.

He took her wineglass and set it on the table. Knocking it into the bowl, he spilled some wine on the wood.

"I'll get a towel," she said, heading into the kitchen.

He followed her and pushed her up against the refrigerator. The kiss was hard and intense. He held her wrists above her head as she dug her nails into the back of his hands. His body pressed against her as he moved down her neck. She arched her back unable to control her feelings.

"I'm sorry," he said, letting go and taking a step back.

She grabbed the front of his pants and pulled him back to her. With her other hand, she took the back of his neck and pulled him against her body. Her kiss was provocative as she slid her hands down his chest. Slowly, she began untucking his shirt. He responded and unbuttoned the bottom button of her blouse. Then he stopped again.

"Are you sure?" he asked breathlessly.

"I can't wait anymore."

She grabbed his shirt and dragged him into the living room, pushing him onto the couch. She leaned over and touched her mouth to his as he pulled her onto his lap. Her hands trembled as she pulled off his shirt, touching his hot skin. Marco's fingers shook as he unbuttoned the rest of her blouse. His lips touched every part of her skin as he slid it off her shoulders. Ravin threw her head back. His lips felt like fire on her skin. She closed her eyes as he ran his hand up her neck, pulling out her hair clip. Her hair fell across her bare shoulders as she tried to breathe. Her head swam with passion as he lifted her off the couch and laid her on the floor in front of the fire. He touched every part of her, slowly and attentively. Ravin dissolved under his touch.

They made love on the floor in front of the fireplace. He ran his fingers up and down her leg. His touch was so gentle and so exciting at the same time. She rolled over onto her stomach as he explored every part of her. Her head was spinning. The emotions he brought out of her were so powerful; *this is how it's supposed to be*, she thought. She closed her eyes and said goodbye to Dominic.

She rolled back over when she realized he had stopped touching her. He propped up on his elbow, watching her. She looked deep into his eyes as hers misted over.

"What?" she asked.

"Nothing." He smiled.

"Why are you staring at me?"

"How could I not? You're so beautiful."

"Yeah, you're just saying that to get me in the sack." She laughed quietly.

"No." He reached out and touched her face.

She closed her eyes and a single tear rolled down her cheek. He gently wiped it away.

"What's wrong?"

"Nothing."

"Nothing?"

"No."

"Why this?" He held up his finger.

"I'm scared."

"Of what?"

"You getting hurt, like they did to Dominic."

"I won't."

"Just scared."

"Is that why you don't sleep?"

"Yes."

"You can now." He brushed a strand of hair from her face.

She looked into his eyes and said quietly, "I think I've fallen in love with you."

"I know I've fallen in love with you." He leaned over and kissed her. He wrapped his arms around her and held her close to him.

It was the first time in five years that she felt safe. It was the first time he felt sure about anything.

"Come on." He took her hand and pulled her up. "This floor's getting uncomfortable." He led her into the bedroom. She stopped and lit the fireplace and they settled into her bed.

"Do you have a fireplace in every room?"

"Just about."

He pulled her against him. This time he made love to her intimately.

She fell asleep in his arms.

Bang! Bang! Dominic! Nooo!

She bolted up, covered in sweat. It happened every night at the same time. She looked over at the clock and then down at Marco. Three a.m. and he was peacefully sleeping in her bed. She had fallen in love with him fast and it scared the hell out of her.

Just as she was about to get out of bed she heard him mumble. "Get back over here." He said reaching for her.

She smiled and crawled back under his arms. He held her close and didn't let go. She eventually fell back to sleep, but it only lasted an hour. The nightmare returned, and this time she got out of bed and went down to her gym. It was the one thing that could take her mind off her dreams.

Marco rolled over reaching for her. He rubbed his eyes and looked around. It was a little after six and he had an idea where she was. He grabbed his pants and wandered down to her gym. Standing in the doorway, he watched her work out with her kickboxing bag. She wore a tight black muscle shirt and cut-off shorts. She looked sensational with her hair pulled back in a ponytail. He couldn't believe the amount of power she released as she punched and kicked the bag. He leaned on the doorframe and watched.

She gazed over and saw Marco leaning in the doorway. He looked incredible with his messy hair, bare chest, and rumpled jeans with the button undone and bare feet. She wished she had her camera.

"Hey." She walked over to him. "I hope I didn't wake you." She kissed him lightly.

"No. Your absence did."

"Sorry."

"It's okay. Come here."

"Yuck, I'm all sweaty."

He reached over and grabbed her waist. "That's the way I like you!" he teased, pushing her back into the gym. He leaned up against the pillar and pulled her against his chest. He slid his hands across her back as he eagerly kissed her.

She slid her hands up his chest and pushed him away. "I need a shower," she said holding him off.

"Let's go," he said with a devilish grin. He chased her up the stairs into the bedroom. They fell onto the bed laughing.

"Gotta work today?" he asked, rolling her over onto her stomach.

"Yeah. Oh, that feels good," she said as he massaged her tired muscles.

"Who are you shooting today?"

"Hmmm, huh?" she purred. He had strong hands and he knew how to use them.

"I asked who you were shooting today?" He leaned into her neck, brushing his lips across her shoulder.

"Not shooting, developing your cover today."

"Want some company?"

"I'm only gonna be downstairs." She rolled over, running her fingers under the waistband of his jeans. She slowly traced to outline of his firm stomach muscles.

"Then I can make you late." He bent down, touching his lips to her neck.

She wiggled out of her shorts, and his hands immediately moved down pulling at the edges of her panties. Ravin pushed down his jeans in between breaths. He crawled onto the bed, pulling her up with him as he caressed her thighs. He pushed her muscle shirt over her head, running circles around her breasts with his tongue. Ravin lay back and closed her eyes. She wondered if and when she was ever going to fall back down to earth. She hoped she never would.

Marco made love to her with intense passion. Their bodies moved together as one, as if they had been together forever. She had fallen hard for him, and she swore that she would never let him get away.

Twenty-Two

"Hello?" Marco answered his cell phone.

"Hey, Marco, it's Benny."

"What's up?"

"We need to get together to discuss the video. You guys coming in today?"

"I guess so. What time?"

"Around eleven?"

"We'll be there." He hung up and took a deep breath as he headed downstairs.

"What's up, man?" Nico looked up from his papers as Marco walked in.

"Benny wants us in at eleven."

"Today?"

"Yeah."

"For what?"

"Next video." He looked around thoughtfully.

"I see we've made it to the next level?" He eyed Marco's mood; he also noticed that he was still only wearing his pants.

"Yeah." He smiled.

"Any good?" Nico snickered.

"You have no idea." He closed his eyes blissfully.

"I can imagine. Get dressed. I'll tell the others."

"Thanks."

Marco walked down to Ravin's darkroom, not caring that he still hadn't gotten dressed. He quietly knocked on the door.

"Come on in, Marco."

"How'dya know it was me?"

"Cause I know you can't get enough!" She laughed.

"I think you've got me all wrong." He snickered. "We have to go to a meeting at eleven. We have to start pre-production for the next video."

"Okay, but before you go anywhere, I want some snapshots of you looking like that."

"Rave! It's like pitch black in here. How can you possibly know what I'm wearing?"

"Do you know that's the first time you called me Rave?"

"You aren't answering the question."

"I told you, I can see better in the dark."

"Okay fine, but one of these days I'm gonna find a use for that night vision of yours."

He felt her take his hand, and before she could lead him out the door, he took her by the shoulders. He pressed his forehead to hers and whispered, "I wouldn't mind one of you too."

They walked out of the darkroom and over to her black leather couch. She carried her two cameras and a smug look on her face.

"Trust me?" she asked in a naughty voice.

"You know I do," he replied, pulling her down onto the couch with him. She pushed him back, trying to get up. Her camera clicked rapidly. She had him lounge around and not look directly at her. After following him around the warehouse for a few minutes, she let him off the hook and told him to get dressed for his meeting.

"What about it?"

"What?" she asked, confused.

"A picture of you?"

"I don't think I have any."

"Take some."

"I'll think about it." She leaned her head on his chest. He wrapped his arms around her and held her. "You're driving me crazy! Now go away!" she giggled.

"Well, I know when I'm not wanted!" he said playfully. He pretended to push her off his chest, but she wouldn't let him go. She rested her head back on his shoulder. Marco whispered, "I love you," in her ear. She felt her heart jump.

"I love you too," she said softly. He wrapped his arms around her tighter as a tear ran down her cheek. He silently wiped it away.

"Go get dressed. You have to get to your meeting and I have to get these pictures finished. I promised Benny I would have them done by six."

"I'll let him know they are on the way." He kissed her gently.

"Thanks. How long do you think you'll be?"

"Not sure, why?"

"If I finish up early enough I might go shopping."

"Oh yeah? For what?"

"Film. I want to see if they have anything new. I have a jeans add coming up. Maybe something will click."

"Okay, want to go out for dinner tonight?"

"I'd like that." She kissed him on the nose and sent him to get dressed.

"Want me to stop before I leave?"

"If you want."

"See you in a few." He let go of her finger, went upstairs to shower, and get dressed.

Ravin went back into her darkroom and developed the pictures she had just taken of him, thinking about what he had said about having a picture of herself. She had never taken a picture of herself before.

Ravin asked him to call her cell if he got back before she did. He promised he would as he said goodbye.

After they moved in, they found out that the bomb scare was just that, a scare. Ravin sent everyone else home and Pauly got to know their bodyguards better as they made a little group in the back. They all took turns making rounds at night just in case.

Twenty-Three

Brett showed up a half-hour after Ravin called ready to shop. They strolled down the street, stopping off at Ravin's favorite stores. Pauly followed in his car, keeping a close eye on her.

"You know something I don't?" Brett asked, watching her buy several new tanks and shorts.

"Why would you say that?" She smiled.

"Best friend intuition? You're buying all these new summer outfits and it's not quite warm enough yet. Are you going somewhere?"

"Honestly, we are." She looked over at her.

"We?" She pushed her around so she could see her face.

"Well, you are the top model, aren't you?"

"Another location! I was just getting close to Vinny. Rave, by the time we get back, he'll be off to L.A. for his next video."

"Don't worry about that."

"So what? Where is Roxi sending us now?"

"L.A."

"You're kidding! For what?"

"Aztec Jeans."

"Why L.A.? Can't we do the shoot here?"

"Jerry wants it shot in the desert."

"The desert? I have to stand in the desert in jeans!" She stifled a scream.

"You make it sound so bad, Brett. It's not like we spent four days shooting the swimsuit issue in thirty degree weather, or don't you remember that?"

"Oh, like I could every forget that! I thought I was gonna die from pneumonia."

"So, a few hours in the desert shouldn't be too bad. Anyway, the research is finished, the location is set, and I'm doing the shoot. It won't take long. It's a jeans ad, for crying out loud."

"Marco know yet?"

"No, Roxi just called me a few hours ago."

"Great, she plan on telling me anytime soon?"

"I told her I'd tell you."

"When?" She stood with her hip out, something she only did when she was mad.

"Next week." She turned and paid for the clothes.

"Why are you buying all this new stuff? You hate shopping, and you don't usually care what you have on."

"Yeah well, the guys might just happen to have a few videos to do out there, and maybe they'll need more shots for calendars and stuff. The desert's a pretty cool backdrop, don't you think?" Her sly undertone snickered.

Brett looked over at her best friend and recognized the look in her eyes. She had plans and they included Marco and the boys. "Videos? Calendars? I think I've got it. How the hell did you pull that off?"

"To be honest, Roxi did. She was talking to Benny when Jerry called. They thought it would be great."

"Do the guys know yet?"

"Benny's telling them today."

"So, who else is going?"

"As in models?" she said, leaving the bags with Pauly as she set off for a cup of coffee.

"Yeah, who am I doing the shoot with?"

"I think Roxi said that Lainey would be there with Carlos."

"Ugh, I have to shoot with him?"

"Fraid so, but hey, Vinny will be there. Maybe he can, ya know, beat him up or something."

They both broke out laughing as they walked down the street. Neither one of them noticed the black Lincoln coasting down the street. Pauly, however did and his guard went up as he dialed Nick's number.

"Okay, we did the shopping thing and lunch. Now what?"

"Camera store."

"For what?"

"Film."

*   *   *

Ravin called Marco from the camera store and asked if he could let the delivery guy in.

"How long?" he answered.

"He may beat me there, he may not."

"Okay hon, do I need to pay him?"

"No, it's all paid for. Maybe slip him a twenty and I'll pay you back."

"I'll take care of it."

She hung up her cell, thinking how great it was to have him in her life. On the other hand, she was still terrified that something might happen to him.

Pauly hung back, watching the Lincoln. He kept one eye on the car and the other on Ravin. His right hand slid down the side of his waist and rested on the butt of his gun. He was fully prepared to use it—just in case.

Ravin saw the car out of the corner of her eye. She quickened her step as it drove by. She looked back at Pauly, eyes distressed. His face was blank and she knew it wasn't good.

Marco answered the door, knowing it was Dave delivering the film. He held the door open to let him in.

"Hi, I've got a delivery for Ravin."

"Yeah, bring it in." Marco held the door.

Dave brought in four boxes and left them in the hallway. Marco handed him a fifty.

"Thanks, man!"

Marco looked around at the boxes curiously. He couldn't believe this was all film. He walked around them slowly, sizing them up when Cole walked by.

"What the hell you doing?" he asked, causing Marco to jump.

"Ravin got a delivery from her camera store. I can't believe this is all film."

"She bought film? In four huge boxes? How much film can she go through?"

They both broke out laughing, still circling the boxes. They didn't hear the girls walk in; they looked at each other and smiled. Brett shrugged, not sure what they were doing.

"Are you . . . like . . . marking your territory or something?" Brett asked.

The boys both jumped embarrassed at being caught.

"Ha! Just trying to figure out what's in here."

"Well, open them," Ravin said as she put down her packages from her shopping trip.

They all sat down and ripped open a box. She directed them to unload all the film and pile it up near her darkroom. Marco held up a new camera and asked her where she wanted it. She took it from him and tore open the box. He got up and sat behind her wrapping his arms around her waist.

"New camera, huh?"

"Yeah." She smiled.

"Like you really need another one, don't you?" he teased.

"It's a digital. I don't have a digital."

"Is that so? Are we finally going to follow the times?"

"Well, not entirely, at least not until I see how good it is."

"I see." He gently kissed her neck. "Are we still going out?"

"Yes. What time?"

"I haven't made any plans yet. Tell me where you want to go; I should make reservations or something."

"No, I'm taking you somewhere special to me." She looked over at Brett. Brett smiled and nodded.

"Oh, really? Where?"

"You'll see."

They put away her film and started upstairs to get ready. Marco took her bags and followed her up. He chased her into the bedroom and pinned her down on the bed.

"Oh, if we didn't have dinner plans, the things I would do to you," he said insidiously.

"Ha ha! I'm hungry."

"Where are you taking me anyway?"

"Surprise," she said, going into her closet.

She turned and watched Marco dig through his suitcase and wondered if she should spring this on him. After last night, she told him he could stay in her room with her if he was comfortable with that. They were leaving next week and something told her deep inside that her mom should meet him. She knew this was the one person she could spend the rest of her life with.

She pulled out her black leather pants and a white sheer sweater.

She went into the bathroom to touch up her makeup. When she came back out, Marco had put on a pair of black loose-fit jeans and a bronze button-down. She stopped in the doorway, watching him standing there with his shirt open, putting on his gold chain. It reminded her of their first shoot together, the way he stood there with his shirt open, showing off an incredible body. She smiled at this perfectly wonderful guy standing in her room.

"What?" he asked, without looking up.

"Nothing."

"Why are you smiling like that? What are you up to?"

"Just happy."

"I make you happy?" he asked relieved, moving toward her.

"You make me happy." She smiled suggestively.

He wrapped his arms around her waist and touched his lips to hers.

"You make me happy, *very* happy," he said.

She rested her head on his chest. He moved his hand up and held her head close to his heart.

"You're good for nothing, boy!" rang in his head. Why didn't she leave him? He knew why. He would find them if she ever left. Instead, she toughed it out, hoping someday her nightmare would end, and she and Marco could move on. His father was an abusive drunk. He hardly ever hit them, but the words hurt more. His father died drunk behind the wheel of the car. Unfortunately, he took an innocent family with him. Marco and his mother didn't grieve for his father. Instead, they grieved for the family he killed. He vowed never to be like his father. He would love unconditionally and purely. Ravin made this easy for him.

Pauly pulled the car up to the curb outside. Tony got out first, followed by Marco and Ravin. Marco looked up and saw the big red sign that read Capello's.

"Capello's?" he asked, looking at her.

She looked at Pauly, who moved back, taking Tony with him.

"Sorry, I didn't mean to spring this on you so soon."

"Family?"

"Yeah." She looked down at the pavement.

Marco took her hands and looked into her face. "I'm looking forward to it. Is your mom here?"

"Mom and two brothers." She smiled.

"Two? Oh man, I'm dead." He laughed.

Pauly walked up and patted his back. "You'll do fine, man. If I like ya, they'll like ya."

Pauly entered first, looking around. Ravin and Marco followed hand in hand, and Tony came in last looking around. *Straight from the Godfather movie* he thought to himself.

"Pauly!" a high-pitched voiced shrieked from across the room. His sister came running through the restaurant throwing her arms around her big brother. She turned and hugged Ravin, and her mouth dropped when she introduced Marco.

Ravin walked over to her brother Joey and hugged him tightly.

"Been a while, Sis. Who's the beefcake?"

"Marco Deangelo."

"Good girl. Mom know?"

"That's why I'm here. Go get her."

"Bossy, aren't we?"

"Listen, he's important to me, I want to do this right."

Joey nodded and went back to get their mother and older brother Nick. Nick came out first, shook hands with Pauly, and kissed his sister.

"Nick, this is Marco. Marco, this is my oldest brother, Nick."

They shook hands, her brother carefully checking him over.

"And this is my other brother Joey."

Another handshake.

"And my mom."

"Mrs. Capello, nice to meet you," Marco said nervously.

Nick walked over to Pauly and Tony. "Who's this?" he nudged Pauly.

"Tony."

He extended his hand; Nick shook it, giving Pauly a confused look.

"Tony is Marcos' bodyguard." He smirked.

"What the hell does he need one for?"

"You are kidding me, Nick? You don't know who that is?" Pauly's sister asked, utterly shocked.

"No," he replied, looking back over at Marco. "Never seen him before."

"Oh my God! That's Marco Deangelo!" she shrieked.

Nick stood there dumbfounded. "From the group Jaded?" still nothing from Nick. "My God Nicky! They are like huge! Do you like totally live in a hole or what? They are like the hottest group in the world, and I'm talking the *whole* world. They are so excellent! And he's even more gorgeous in person; I can't believe he's here!"

Pauly grabbed his little sister by the arm and glared at her, "Not a word little girl!"

She sulked off, pouting. She wanted desperately to tell her friends that he was there, but she knew not to overstep her brother.

Ravin, Marco, and her mom sat down in the back booth. Ravin kissed everyone on the way back, saying hello. Mrs. Capello ordered them diner and wine, and talked with her daughter and her new boyfriend. Ravin's mom liked Marco instantly and Joey did too. Nick was going to have to trust Pauly and relax. He trusted Pauly completely; after all, he had been protecting his kid sister for years.

Pauly watched out of the corner of his eye. The black Lincoln drove by for the third time. Either they were stupid or dispensable. He knew Tony would be useless in this kind of situation. After all, he was more like a bouncer. His only job was to keep the girls from jumping the stage and tearing off their clothes. He wasn't prepared to deal with what Pauly needed that night. If anything went down, he was glad it would be there. He looked around into the eyes of his friends and family. They knew the look and went on full alert. But how to tell Ravin? He knew she had seen the car. He wasn't sure if she had seen it the other day. He wondered if Marco spoke Italian. There was only one way to find out.

"Ravin, *dobbiamo andare presto.*" Pauly said.

She looked up at him in disbelief. Why did they need to go soon and why was he speaking Italian? Something was wrong; she could see it in his eyes. She knew the Lincoln was near and she noticed how quiet it had gotten. She knew that everyone was ready to fight and she needed to go—now. Although she was surrounded by people that would give their lives for her, she would be much safer at home.

"What did he say?" Marco asked, looking around. The air seemed thicker, more serious. "What's going on?"

"Nothing." She forced a smile.

"It's late, honey, you two should go. This is not a nice neighborhood when it gets late."

"Sure, Momma?"

"Sure, baby. Are you working tomorrow?"

"Yeah, I've got a morning shoot."

"Call me. Marco, it has been a treat meeting you. I'm glad you came." She stood up, kissed her daughter, and then turned, hugged, and kissed Marco. They said goodbye to everyone and headed for the door where Tony stood waiting.

"Where's Pauly?" Marco asked.

"Getting the car," Tony answered. He looked over and Nick escorted them out to the car. Pauly rushed off speeding down the road to get home.

Marco shook his head in confusion. "Would you please tell me what the hell is going on?" he demanded.

Ravin was looking out the back window and turned to him, "Nothing, don't worry."

"I wasn't until now. Why the hell is Pauly driving so fast? And why are you two looking out the windows? What's going on? Tony? You better tell me something." An edge of impatience crept into his voice.

Ravin glared at him making sure he kept his mouth shut. "Nothing, man. Just though I saw some unfriendly teenagers walking the streets looking for trouble is all."

Marco leaned back in his seat, unhappy with the answer he gave him. Pauly immediately got on the phone once they got back to Ravin's. He was screaming at someone in Italian and Marco wished he understood what he was saying.

Ravin changed into a pair of doctor scrubs and a tank top. She poured two glasses of wine and sat down next to Marco on the couch. He looked into her deep black opal eyes, the colors weren't changing like they usually did. Right now, they were black, deep jet black, and full of fear and anger.

"Please tell me," he pleaded.

"When I'm ready," she said without looking at him.

"Are you or we . . ." he stammered, "in danger?"

"No," she said sharply as she slid her hands under his shirt and caressed his stomach. He laid his head back and closed his eyes. Her touch was so soft and relaxing. He turned to look at her again, her face, usually soft and inviting, was empty and full of thought. He knew she understood what Pauly was saying on the phone. She even shouted out a few things herself. He couldn't shake the feeling that she was involved with the Mafia. He couldn't think like that. He couldn't accept the idea that the love of his life was involved in something so horrible and wrong.

"I didn't know you spoke Italian."

"There's lots you don't know about me."

"Like what?" he asked, trying for any kind of information.

"Like I can speak Italian, Greek, Spanish, and Latin." She forced a smile.

"You're kidding!"

"No."

"Wow, four languages, that's pretty impressive."

"No, it's not."

"Sure, it is. Four is a lot."

"Yeah well, my father spoke Italian, my mother spoke Greek and Latin, and I took Spanish in school."

"Teach me?"

"All of them?" She looked at him quizzically.

"No, but maybe a few choice phrases." He smiled devilishly.

"I can teach you a choice phrase in sign language!" She laughed as he grabbed her hand to stop her.

"You're funny!" He pushed her onto her back and pinned her down.

"Kiss me." She touched his cheek with her finger. She wanted to remember him this way, just in case.

"Never on command!" He pushed himself up.

She reached over, took his face in her hands, and kissed him intimately. Marco couldn't help himself; he took her in his arms and let his feelings for her come back up to the surface.

"Tell me," he pressed again as she snuggled against his chest.

"Hey, did Benny talk to you guys today?" she asked, changing the subject.

"Yeah, pretty cool, huh?"

"I think so. You can show me around." She smiled as she ran her finger up his thigh.

"You've never been to L.A.?"

"Nope, everywhere else, but not L.A."

"You're kidding?"

"Nope."

"Well then, I'll just have to give you my tour." He smiled.

"I look forward to it."

He reached up and ran his fingers through her hair, thinking about what had happened that night. They went to bed and fell asleep in each other's arms. Marco fell asleep wondering if it all was just a coincidence. Ravin fell asleep, scared that it was happening all over again.

Twenty-Four

"The limo will be here at six to pick you up. I told the crew what to do for you. Tony's in charge of you, so keep tight with him okay?" Marco asked, running around the room like a crazed maniac.

"I'm bringing Pauly. And a few of his friends."

"Yes, of course. I told Tony."

"You better get out of here. You're driving me nuts." She laughed.

"Why am I driving you nuts?"

"All this pacing around, you honestly look nervous."

"I do?"

"You do."

"I guess I do, but the second I'm on stage, it all goes away."

"Well, go away. I'll see you there." She kissed him quickly and walked him to the waiting group by the door.

"Ravin! The limo's here." Mia called up to her.

"I'll be right there," she called out from her bedroom. She looked in the mirror one last time wondering why she was doing this. She put on her black belt and tied the front of her shirt.

The limo ride to the concert was exciting for Mia. She was usually the one riding with Ravin in her Durango. Ravin looked around in shock when they pulled up to the stadium. There were thousands of screaming girls, praying to get a glimpse of them.

The limo stopped in front and Tony opened the door for them. Three other security guards helped the girls into the back where the boys waited.

Ravin walked back with them. She couldn't believe the chaos.

There were people running everywhere backstage screaming into headsets. Pauly's eyes scanned every inch. He couldn't keep up with everyone. He and Ravin exchanged looks, both glad she wasn't in show business.

"Hi!" Marco bounced up behind her, scaring the hell out of her and putting Pauly on edge even more.

"Hey!" She said quietly, still looking around cautiously. The way she was raised, scenes like this were just avoided. Too many people only meant too much room for error.

"This way." He took her hand.

She followed behind him with Pauly on her heels. Marco wore a black leather vest and black baggy pants. When he took her into the back room, she noticed they all wore similar clothes. Brett ran over to Vinny full of excitement. Mia found Nico pacing around the tables. Ravin's eyes scanned everything. She had an uneasy feeling in the pit of her stomach.

After fifteen minutes, someone escorted them to their seats. Ravin looked around as the band came out on stage and thousands of girls started screaming at the top of their lungs. Pauly wished he had brought some earplugs. For Ravin, part of her was proud to see Marco up on stage doing his thing. It was interesting to see his work in action, but at the same time, she had an unnerving feeling that she couldn't shake.

During the second act, the band sang a love song. Marco looked right into her eyes as he sang. She felt like a schoolgirl, this weird giddy feeling coming over her. She almost let her guard down, feeling happy and having fun, but just as the concert started winding down, it began. People were noticing Brett and asking for her autograph, some even asking if she could get them a job. Ravin could feel her become more and more uncomfortable and she sensed trouble. The crowd was getting rowdy and there was no way out. Girls were rushing the stage, screaming and throwing things up to the boys. Ravin looked over at Pauly, and her eyes told him to get her the hell out of here. He grabbed Tony by the shirt and told him they needed to go immediately.

"Follow me." Tony grabbed Ravin's arm. Brett and Mia were grabbed as they were escorted through the crazed fans and down through the tunnel under the stage.

Ravin's head began to spin. This reminded her of the times that her father would vacate the family during the rough times.

"If you want to leave now, I'll tell them to meet you at the warehouse."

"Which would be better?" Brett asked.

"Have them meet you there. I don't think you want to be here when they get off stage. It gets a little crazy sometimes."

"This happens all the time?" Ravin looked at him astonished.

"Every concert," Tony said proudly.

"This is nuts," she said, listening to the screaming.

"Get in; they'll be there in a half-hour." Tony opened the door for them.

They drove off quickly and quietly with Leonardo at the wheel. Pauly insisted on hiring his own driver, knowing he could get them out safely in case something went down. Pauly sat up front, thinking a little differently about Tony now that he saw what he did. He was still more of a bouncer, but it took a different kind of person to deal with this. He knew Tony couldn't handle his kind of work. And he certainly couldn't handle Tony's job. He would probably end up shooting everyone. Pauly didn't like busy crowds; he was a quiet person who liked controlled situations. That was why he never left Ravin. They were a perfect match.

When the boys arrived at the warehouse, they were exhausted, exhilarated, and concerned. They noticed the crowd getting a little crazier than usual, and Marco watched Tony escort them out early.

"Ravin, hon, are you all right?" he asked, reaching for her hand.

"Fine, why?"

"You looked a little jumpy out there."

"Too many people, makes me uneasy."

"I'm sorry. If I would have known you didn't like crowds, I would have put you in the box. Why didn't you tell me?"

"I don't know. I guess I was trying to be normal." She forced a laugh.

"What's that supposed to mean?"

"I don't like crowds. That's all." She smiled and touched her cheek to his chest. What he didn't know was that the black Lincoln had been following her for the last few weeks. It only meant one thing. After Pauly did a little checking, he found out that it wasn't over.

Twenty-Five

Bang! Bang! Bang! Noooo!

Ravin sat up in bed covered in sweat. She glanced over at Marco sleeping quietly and slipped out of bed. She threw on her sweats and went down to her gym.

Pauly came in when he heard her, "Can't sleep?"

"No, what's happening?"

"Go back to bed, Rave. It's done."

They stared at each other for a few moments. Pauly didn't say anything else before he walked out. Ravin stood in the middle of her gym, gazing out the door. She wasn't sure if they had killed the men in the Lincoln or not, and if they had, was she the person who asked them to? Had she turned into everything she despised about her heritage? More importantly, were either of her brothers involved? She knew what went on during the wars, because her father had told her things. He told her names, dates, and even where to find the proof if she ever needed it. She never knew why he had told her all of this, but she had a feeling that he needed someone to know and her brothers would be bigger targets than she would. But her father was wrong; they had murdered him because of what he'd done. She knew the men in the Lincoln were after her because of what she knew. Because of her, Carlos Penelli was sitting in prison for the crimes he had committed.

She sank to the floor and leaned up against her boxing bag. Putting her face in her hands, she took a deep breath and tried to clear her mind. She was still in danger, and as a result, she was putting Marco directly in the line of fire. Worse yet, she was putting the whole group in danger. But how could she let Marco go now? She

119

was so in love with him that it overwhelmed her. She had never experienced such feelings before, the way time seemed to stand still just before he kissed her. She knew she only had two choices. She could go back to the life she had made for herself alone, back to the way it use to be when she was safe and the only person in danger. The other choice was to tell Marco exactly what was going on and hope he understood. Even if he did, how could she be sure he would be safe? How could she be sure they wouldn't drop her trail and go after him to prove a point?

Pauly stood in the shadows, painfully watching her. He knew what she was thinking. He knew she had to make a decision and it had to be all hers. He was prepared to protect them all if that's what she decided. The conversation he had with Nick was about just that. Nick was prepared to give him the help he needed if she continued to see Marco. Pauly already had people lined up and doing the research to find out everything they could. It wouldn't be long before he had all the information he needed to go forward, if that was what Ravin wanted.

Ravin never got her workout in. Instead, she paced and sat and thought. Pauly stood in the shadows the whole time, wondering what she would decide.

Eventually, she went upstairs and crawled back into bed. She noticed it was five a.m. and Marco had to be up by six. He started shooting his new video that day. She tried not to disturb him, but when she climbed into bed, he rolled over and slid his arm around her.

"Get your workout in?" he mumbled.

"No," she whispered staring at the ceiling.

"No?" He propped up on his elbow. "Why not? What were you doing down there so long?"

"Thinking. Go back to sleep. You've got to be up in an hour."

"What were you thinking about?"

"Nothing." She ran her hand across his chest. It felt different from before, as if deep down she knew it might be the last time. Marco could see her face in the moonlight filtering through the window. He could see she was different. He knew she had something heavy going on in her mind and he wished she would tell him so he could help her.

She fell into a fitful sleep, waking up every fifteen minutes. Eventually, she gave up and watched Marco get ready for his video shoot.

"Are you coming to see me for lunch? Maybe hang out and watch a while?"

"Lunch I can do. Hang out and watch? Well, that might not be helpful to you." She laughed, sticking her leg out from under the sheets.

"You need to stop doing that!" he said, trying to get ready.

"Sorry."

"No, you aren't. I've been bugging you for weeks. My turn, huh?"

"Maybe!"

"See you later?"

"Yeah."

He sat on the edge of the bed. He cocked his head to the side and gazed into her eyes, touching her face effortlessly. "Will you tell me what's going on up there?" He ran one finger up through her hair.

"When I'm ready." She looked away.

"When you're ready, I'm here. No matter how bad it is, Ravin, I'm here. I always will be." He left discouraged, knowing something was eating at her and she wasn't willing to share.

Ravin pulled on her scrubs and a long sleeve shirt, and then headed down to the darkroom. She finished developing the pictures of Marco and laid them out on the table.

"Come in."

"Hey, Rave." Pauly came in handing her coffee.

"What's up?"

"You okay?"

"Yeah."

"Just checking. Ya know." He felt her pain and it was killing him.

"I know."

"What'cha got?"

"Pictures of Marco. What'dya think?"

Pauly walked over looking down the table. "Good, but I wouldn't expect anything less."

"He's gorgeous, isn't he?"

"I wouldn't know. I like this one." He picked up the shot of Marco, his back facing her as he stood in a lit doorway.

"Me too." She looked down at it. She couldn't believe how hard this was.

"You really do love him, don't you?"

"Yes, I do. But . . ."

"But what?"

"But it won't last."

"Why do you say that?"

"I can't put him in danger. I can't put the whole band in danger like this. Marco's too important to more people than just me. I have to let him go as soon as I get back from L.A."

"Ravin, what are you talking about?" Pauly was shocked to hear this from her.

"Pauly, I've got hit men following me around trying to kill me! What if they miss and hit him? What if they grew brains and thought it would hurt more if they killed him? It's already happened once. He's too important to his fans. I can't be responsible for that."

"Ravin, you have officially lost it." He turned and faced her. "First of all, if they really were hit men, you'd already be dead. Second, I wouldn't let that happen. I didn't know Dominic was getting the hit until five minutes before it happened, and it had nothing to do with you. He was skimming money off his pick-ups and meeting with the boss's girlfriend. Sorry, he wasn't faithful to you. I didn't know that either."

"Yes, you did. So did I."

"And third, if you left Marco, you would be the most miserable pain in the ass, and I couldn't deal with that. These men we're dealing with are wannabes. They have no idea what they're doing. They're basically trying to scare you."

"And how do you know Carlos Penelli isn't sending them."

"Because I know. And so do Nick and Leonardo. We've already taken care of it, Ravin. Leonardo went to visit them yesterday."

"He did?"

"Yes."

"And you don't think it'll happen again? You don't think I'm in any danger? What about what my father told me, all that information? They know I know, and they killed him because he told me."

"Yes, they did, and they watched you for two years. Eventually, they gave up, knowing you weren't going to tell anyone."

"So, they think I've forgotten?"

"No, they check up on you, I'm sure. But as long as you keep your mouth shut, they'll leave you alone."

"Pauly, there's always gonna be someone with a hot temper out there, someone who won't do it the old way."

"I know. Why do you think I've never left your side? Nick has more under control than you think. He's exactly like your father, only smarter."

Ravin leaned against the table, digesting all this information. She hadn't known Nick was so involved, and she didn't know that Dominic was stealing money or messing with the boss's mistress. That would explain a lot, except why she had to witness the brutal attack.

"I should go and thank Leonardo."

"Probably."

"I've gotta meet Marco for lunch today."

"Don't wait too long."

"Think it's over? Do you think they won't try to hurt me? Or are they just waiting for the right moment?"

"Hard to tell, but I think you should put your guard up a little. You've let it fall since Marco came into your life."

"Yeah. Life imprisonment inside my own head."

"Let me know when you're ready."

"You're taking me?"

"For now, Nick's orders." She nodded her head.

Oh Marco, she thought, *what am I going to do?* She wandered upstairs to get dressed.

"Hello?" she answered, stepping out of the shower.

"Hey, babe, it's Brett."

"Hi, hon, what's up?"

"Gonna pick me up?"

"Vinny tell you what time?"

"Yeah, he just called. They're breaking for lunch around one."

"Okay, I'll pick you up."

"What are you doing 'til then?"

"Some business to take care of. I'll try to get there as early as I can."

"Need any company?"

"No. Thanks though."

"Are you okay?"

"Not really?"

"I know something's wrong. I can hear it in your voice."

"It's nothing. I'll see you later."

She hung up and slipped on her black leather pants. She thought of Marco as she tied up the front of them and put on burgundy sweater. She kept her hair down, letting the wild curls circle her face. She wasn't in a good mood. She felt depressed, angry and abandoned all at the same time. Now she had to thank Leonardo and Nick. She grabbed her black bag and headed to the door with Pauly.

They spent almost two hours in the old neighborhood. She thanked Leonardo and his boys, and then spent some time with her brothers. She assured him that she was fine, but Nick knew better. He knew she was struggling with something, and he had a good idea what it was. She told him how long she planned to stay in L.A.

"You sure you should still go?"

"Nicky, I've been traveling around for years now. I'm not gonna let them run my life. I never have and I never will. Pauly's coming anyway."

"You have let this run your life; you've been alone until now."

"That had nothing to do with them." She glared at him.

"Fine, as long as Pauly's going."

"I've gotta go."

"Hey!"

"What!" She could feel the anger rising.

"I like him." Nick looked at her.

"Who?"

"Marco, I like him. I think he's perfect for you."

Ravin smiled at her brother. His acceptance meant so much to her. Under different circumstances, she would feel happy, maybe someday.

Ravin picked Brett up at twelve-thirty.

"Sorry I'm late," she said as she got into the truck.

"I knew you'd be here sooner or later. Let's go. I can't wait to see Vinny."

"You really like him, don't you?"

"Yes, I do, as much as you like Marco?"

Ravin was silent. She never thought about this. If she did leave Marco, Brett and Vinny would still be together. How would she handle seeing Marco and not be able to touch him or feel his hands running through her hair?

When they reached the set, they went up to the door.

"Sorry, ladies, this is a closed set," the man guarding the door said.

"They're expecting us," Brett said matter-of-factly.

"And you are?" he asked with attitude.

"Kidding right?" Brett matched.

"No, you are?"

"Ravin Capello and Brett Santana," Ravin said with no patience for playing games.

"Terribly sorry," he said, shaking his head, "I didn't realize, please go right in."

Brett said a few choice words under her breath and Ravin withdrew further into her head. When they walked in, the boys were singing and dancing for the camera. Benny waved them over as soon as he saw them.

"Hi, Ben," Brett greeted.

"Hey, girls, glad you could make it."

"So are we. I'm so glad you were able to get this one shot here, Ben. This is really cool," Brett said excited.

Ravin sat in the chair nearby, watching. Marco saw her and smiled. She watched him dancing in perfect sync with the other guys. He was just too perfect for her. She didn't deserve him. She could see the muscles in his stomach working hard as his shirt flew around while he danced. She had to tell him, there was no way around it. He needed to know that if he was going to continue to see her that his life would be in danger. She got up and walked over to the empty section of the warehouse. She didn't want anyone to see how upset she was. She could see little details in the ceiling from the lights filtering over from the set. She found a pillar and leaned up against it, sinking deeper in thought.

Pauly watched her from the entrance of the warehouse. He knew he couldn't help her, but if Marco came to him, he would explain everything, whether Ravin wanted him to or not.

After half an hour, the boys broke for lunch. Vinny was the first off the floor, running to greet Brett.

"Where's Rave?" Marco asked, walking up out of breath.

"Over there." She pointed. "Sulking or something."

"What? Why is she sulking?"

"I don't know what's wrong with her. She won't tell me anything anymore. She's in her own little world."

"Her own little world, huh?" Marco mumbled, feeling a tinge of concern.

"Yeah," Brett said smugly as she curled her finger around Vinny's. "She's got a lot on her plate; she's been working a lot."

"Working, huh? You think that's it? Or does it have to do with me?"

Brett shrugged her shoulders. "Well, Ravin's definitely moody today. I'm just warning you, and I have no idea why, so don't ask." She smiled and pulled her attention back to Vinny.

Marco quietly walked over and found Ravin leaning up against one of the pillars. He stopped before reaching her and watched her. Her head was leaning back against the column and her eyes closed. He tiptoed up to her and gently kissed her chin.

"You shithead!" she screamed, swinging at him.

He grabbed her wrists and pushed them back up against the pillar in defense. "Sorry." He chuckled, not letting go of her arms. He could tell she was still struggling, but she wasn't trying very hard. He stepped closer and touched his lips to hers, feeling her body give in. Slowly, he let go and slid his hands down her arms, kissing her passionately. Her hands instinctively wrapped around his neck, scraping it with her nails. He stepped back, knowing what that did to him and looked at her.

"Don't start something you can't finish," he said, out of breath again.

"Sorry." She sighed.

"What's wrong?"

"Nothing."

"Bull." He could hear it in her voice. "What's wrong?"

She let go of him and stepped away."Nothing! God, why does everyone keep asking me that?" She walked back to the lunch table. He followed her, grabbing her hand and swinging her around.

"Don't ever do that again," she said, suppressing her anger.

"Sorry, but Rave, something's wrong. Did I do something to piss you off?"

"No, it has nothing to do with you okay?"

"Okay. Are we okay?"

"Yeah, fine," she snapped.

"Are you hungry?" he asked, knowing not to push her.

"No." She knew she shouldn't take this out on him or Brett. It wasn't their fight and they shouldn't have to suffer because of her. "No, thank you. I'm not that hungry. But you eat. You need your energy." She smiled, trying hard to change her mood.

"You sure?" He began to say until he looked at her face. "If you want to talk about anything, bounce your frustrations off me, you just let me know." He smiled and kissed her cheek.

She smiled at how truly wonderful he was.

After lunch, the boys went back to the set to finish the video. Ravin and Brett went back to the magazine.

"I've got to talk to Roxi," Ravin said.

"Oh yeah? What are to two conjuring up now?"

"She wants to talk about the L.A. shoot."

"Well, if you want some company, let me know."

"Sure, it affects you too."

Ravin walked into Roxi's office with Brett in tow.

"Hey, Roxi, what's going on?"

"Hey, Rave, Brett. Glad you're here. I just got off the phone with Jerry."

"How is Jerry?"

"He's good. He rented that location for you. You've got it for three days."

"Three days? Not like putting a time limit on perfection!"

"That's the best he could do. Anyway, you'll be able to pull it off. I've got the best for you to work with."

"You got to choose the models?"

"Yep."

"Great! Who?"

"Well, Brett, of course, Carlos, Lainey, and Steel Roberts."

"Fantastic! I love working with Lainey, and Steel ain't too bad either," Brett said excited.

"Good, it should go well then. When do we leave?"

"Well, a little earlier than we thought. You guys need to be there Thursday morning to start."

"Thursday? But today's Tuesday. That doesn't give us a whole lot of time to get ready." Brett pouted.

"Can you swing that, Ravin? Packing all your equipment?" Roxi questioned, ignoring Brett's mild tantrum.

"Do I have a choice?"

"Well, not really. Don't forget you still have to shoot Anyssa tomorrow and Carlos."

"Yeah." She sighed.

"Can you do all that? I need to know, I don't want to postpone her shoot again. She's still so new and I don't want her running off to another agency."

"No, I can do it. I'll just use my spare camera tomorrow and pack up my good one tonight. What time?"

"Plane leaves tomorrow night at ten. I will pick you up at nine."

Ravin and Brett left the meeting with Brett complaining the whole time. Ravin tried to keep her head together and block her out. It wasn't fair to blow up at her now. Brett went back to her apartment and started packing for L.A.

Ravin wanted to walk around the park for a while, but Pauly didn't think it would be a great idea. He offered to drive her around and she settled with that. She needed to be moving to think, and although driving was not the same as walking, it was the next best thing. After a few hours, they headed back to her place to start packing. If she got it all done quickly, she would have some time left to spend with Marco.

"Hey, babe," he said quietly as he entered the darkroom. The lights were all on and it was the first time he saw how big it really was. "Wow, this place looks so different when you can see."

"Yeah," she said quietly as she put her camera into a travel bag.

"Still grumpy?"

"I'm not grumpy!" she said a little on edge.

"Yes, you are, but I guess everyone's entitled to a bad day."

"Thanks." She looked over at him as he sat on the edge of the table. "Sorry, I don't mean to take it out on you."

"That's okay, as long I know I didn't do anything wrong."

"No, you didn't do anything wrong." She smiled and leaned against the table.

"Good. Why are you packing?"

"We're leaving tomorrow night."

"Leaving? Where?"

"L.A."

"I thought we weren't going until next week?"

"It's been changed."

"Are you still shooting us in the desert?"

"Yes, Saturday. Friday after TRL Benny has you flying out. Then Saturday, I'll do the shoot in the desert. I only get the location for three days."

"Bummer. So, this is our last night together."

"Well, for a few days."

"It's gonna be torture."

"Funny." She started packing again.

Marco walked over and touched her arm. She turned around and let him hold her. She felt so safe wrapped in his arms. How could she ever let him go?

He put his chin on her head and sighed. Holding her calmed him in a way nothing else did. He wondered for a moment if he should leave the group. Touring was going to be so hard without her and thinking about it was agony.

They spent their last night packing and talking about his video. She avoided every question she could and tried to act normally. He saw through her and felt a helplessness wash over him. If only she would tell him, he would be able to help her. He held her all night long as she tried to sleep. Every time she did, she woke up on the verge of tears. Her nightmares were worse and her mind was racing. Most of the night, she held Marco's arm and stared at the light dancing behind the window.

Twenty-Six

Ravin got out of bed at four; she thought about working out but decided against it. Instead, she went down to the piano room and worked out her fingers on the keys. She wasn't that good, but she could play a few songs. She didn't hear Marco follow her out. Marco noticed Pauly standing in the shadows. Both of them watched and listened to Ravin.

"What's going on Pauly?" Marco asked, concerned.

"Did she tell you anything?"

"No."

"She's got a lot on her mind right now, I can't say what."

"But—"

"But the advice you're looking for is just to give her some space. She really needs a little space."

"From me?"

"Not just you, everything. She tends to bottle things up, and I can tell you it's about to blow."

"What can I do to help her?"

"Don't smother her or she'll lose it."

"Thanks." He turned to look at him. "But you can't tell me what it's about?"

"Not really, at least not yet."

"Does it have anything to do with me?"

"Marco, she has fallen in love with you very fast. She told me, and honestly, I think it scared the hell out of her. She's never experienced a simple boyfriend; she went from Dominic right to you. I think she's just very confused and a little overwhelmed right now."

"Things did move fast, didn't they? I mean, we met and the next thing we know, we fell in love with each other. Then we had that

130

bomb scare and she insisted that we move in here." When Marco thought about it, it was fast.

"Yeah."

They stood there and watched her for a few more minutes. Pauly finally went back upstairs. Marco slowly walked into the room and sat next to her.

"Hey," he said quietly.

"Hey, I didn't wake you up, did I?"

"No." He started playing a song on the piano.

"That's nice." She laid her head on his shoulder.

"Doesn't have any words yet."

"No? Why not?"

"Can't put any to it yet."

"Oh. It's still nice."

"Ravin, I think I know what's wrong. I was talking to Pauly and he explained a few things."

"He what?" She sat up quickly, thinking Pauly had given Marco the whole story.

"I agree things did happen very fast between us. I mean, it wasn't that long ago that we didn't even know each other." He looked over at her as he continued playing the tune that stuck in his head. "I fell in love with you faster than I imagined possible. I didn't believe in that whole love at first sight thing until I met you. It scares me a little too, and then moving in here."

"Marco—"

He put his finger to her lips. "Let me finish. You've had a secluded lifestyle, and within a month, you met me, fell in love, and had me and four other guys move in here. That's a lot for anyone, especially someone like you. I know you're scared. I am a little too. It's okay, as long as we're honest with each other."

He looked down into her eyes. They were soft and loving again, but still filled with fear and sorrow. She put her head back on his shoulder.

"I don't want to smother you. That's the last thing I want to do. You need to tell me to back off a little when you feel that way. I can't help myself around you sometimes. I don't know why, but I just have to be around you. You make me happy, even if I'm just watching you work."

"Marco, I do love you, and I am scared."

"That's good. I'd worry if you weren't."

"There's more to it than just that."

"I'm sure there is, but we don't have to talk about it now." He put his hand on her leg.

"Play for me," she said quietly and closed her eyes.

Marco played for over an hour. He wasn't sure if she fell asleep or not, but he had never seen her *this* quiet. Ravin kept her eyes closed and let the music run through her soul. The music always told her what to do.

Twenty-Seven

"How long do you think you'll be at the studio?" Marco called into the bathroom.

"I don't know. Depends how long the shoot takes."

"Who ya doing today?"

"A new girl, Anyssa, and Carlos."

"Oh, him."

"Yeah, him," she said as if his name left a bad taste in her mouth.

"Maybe I'll stop in for lunch." He thought for a minute. "Or not?"

"I'd like that. I have no idea when though."

"I'll stop by. If you don't have time, that's okay."

"Thanks."

"For what?"

"The space."

"Just tell me when you need it and you'll get it. I just want to make you happy."

"You do." She kissed him gently. "I have to go. I'll see you for lunch."

Ravin pulled into her parking spot and got out of her truck. She heard a loud smash and spun around. Twenty feet behind, an elderly woman sat in the middle of the sidewalk with a shopping cart full of cans sprawled out in front of her. Ravin turned to go into the studio with her heart racing, but before she could get inside, a homeless man grabbed her arm and asked for money. Pauly quickly pushed the man away and took her arm.

"Why the hell didn't you wait for me?" he barked furious.

"Sorry."

"Ravin, you need to pull it together and fast. You can't just take off like that."

"I said I was sorry! *Okay?*" She was more agitated then he knew.

"Fine, but don't get so pissy."

"Don't tell me what to do, Pauly. I have enough people telling me what to do."

He glared at her and she stormed into the back of the studio.

"What's wrong with her?" Roxi asked after watching the scene.

"She's real pissy today, Roxi, tread carefully." He walked away, miserable.

"Great," Roxi groaned.

"Ravin, are you back here?"

"Yeah, Rox. What's up?" She stepped out from behind the backdrop.

"You okay? Pauly said you were in a mood."

"Whatever."

"Listen, I could care less what mood you're in. You have to shoot a new kid this morning; I can't afford to lose her. Do you think you can show her what kind of family agency this is?"

"Roxi," she replied, her demeanor changing, "I'm sorry, yes I will be fine. I will not let this one go."

"Thank you."

"Sure." She smiled. As soon as Roxi left, she flipped up her middle finger and went back to fixing the backdrop.

Forty-five minutes later, Roxi showed up with Anyssa on her arm.

"Ravin, this is Anyssa. Anyssa this is Ravin, our head photographer," Roxi said sweetly, almost making Ravin heave.

"Nice to meet you, Anyssa."

"Same," she said with all the confidence and cockiness of a seventeen-year-old.

"Do you know how or what you are supposed to do?"

"Yes, Roxi explained everything to me."

"Good. I usually don't say anything while I'm shooting unless, of course, I need to. If you know your body and the poses, you won't need to listen to me. Although if I do give you a direction, I expect you to follow it."

"Understood."

"Let's get started." Ravin set her up in front of the backdrop and told her what she was looking for. Anyssa was a natural, which was a relief to Ravin, but she also had a lot to learn. Ravin's biggest problem with her was the attitude.

After three hours, Anyssa got into the groove. Ravin was as nice as she could be, but still on the edge.

"Ya know what I could use?" Ravin turned to Randy.

"What?"

"My digital."

"You're gonna shoot with your digital?"

"Yes, I am," she said sharply.

"Okay." Randy backed off. He turned to get it and saw Pauly just shake his head. That only meant Ravin wasn't happy today.

"Here ya go."

"Thank you, Randy." She turned and started shooting with her new camera. Being able to see Anyssa immediately relaxed her a little. She only spent another half-hour with her and finally let her go. Randy took her cameras and rushed off to get the film developed before she could bite his head off.

"Ravin, you better chill out," Pauly said out of the side of his mouth.

"Sorry. I can't seem to get it under control."

"Do you have time for a break?"

"No, I've got to shoot Carlos in twenty minutes. Why?"

"Thought I'd run you over to the gun range and let you blow off a few rounds to get it out of your system."

"I don't have the time, nor do I want to shoot a gun."

"Rave, you have to deal with Carlos. Trust me. By the end of that session, you'll want to."

"Thanks Pauly, but I'll pass. Marco said he might stop in for lunch. Can you make sure he finds me please?" she said as sweetly as she could.

"He is?"

"Yes, we had a talk this morning. Apparently, after you did," she added with a frown, "about smothering me and how scary it is to have this all happening so fast."

"You talked?"

"Yes."

"And?"

"And everything is okay."

"Good. I don't want you to lose him."

"Neither do I, Pauly."

"Good, come here and give your big bro a hug."

"Big bro, huh?" She walked over and wrapped her arms around Pauly. She loved him like a brother.

"Okay Ravin, I'm ready!" Carlos sauntered down the hall.

"Look out world," she said sarcastically. She slid back into the studio, dreading the thought of shooting him. So far, her morning sucked and now Carlos was just making it worse. It was as if he fed off her moods and enjoyed playing her last nerve.

Marco walked into the agency and spotted Pauly down the hall.

"Hey," he said walking up to him.

"Hey, Marco. Good morning?"

"Yeah, I think I get it. How's she doing?"

"You don't want to know. She has had a real crappy day. Just warning ya."

"Great, where is she?"

"Studio three."

"Thanks."

Pauly nodded as Marco walked down to the studio. He leaned in the doorway, watching Ravin attempt to control Carlos. After a few minutes, he was sure Carlos was purposely trying to aggravate her.

"Carlos, could you please do your job!" she shouted after posing him for the third time.

"I am. I just like it when you touch me."

"Go to hell!" She stormed back to her camera.

Marco looked over at Randy who honestly looked scared.

"Can we please try again?"

Marco watched Ravin for another twenty minutes, knowing she was losing patience. Then it finally hit and she lost her temper.

"Carlos you fucking bastard! I don't have time for this. Do your damn job!" she screamed.

Everyone down the hall heard her and looked over. Pauly ran to the doorway to see what was going on. Marco held him back, wanting her to blow off the steam she needed.

"Why don't you do *your* fucking job, you little bitch! You're supposed to make me look good."

"Nothing could make you look good! Now do your fucking job!" she shouted again.

Carlos took his time and screwed it up again.

"I don't have time for this! I'm done!" she screamed and threw her camera against the wall shattering it into small pieces. She stormed out of the studio, shoving Pauly and Marco out of her way.

Carlos looked stunned, not expecting her to get angry. He always played with her and she never lost control.

Marco turned to go after her, but Pauly grabbed his arm. He held tight as Marco tried to break free.

"Pauly!" he yelled, struggling.

"Marco, this would be the worst time. Trust me, she needs to leave."

"What if she gets hurt?" he asked, worrying she'd get in a car wreck or something.

"It's bullet-proof. They can't get to her if she's in her truck," he said, not realizing who he was talking to. He quickly shook his head and pulled out his cell.

"Yeah, she bolted. Follow her," Pauly said into the phone.

Roxi ran up after hearing the screaming.

"What the hell was that?" she asked out of breath.

"Ravin threw her camera against the wall!" Carlos said, trying to play the injured bird.

"Shut up, Carlos! What the hell did you do to her? I told you to behave today. I warned you. If she doesn't come back, it'll be your fault! It will also be the end of your career!" She turned on her heels and looked to Pauly for answers.

"Well?" She threw up her arms.

"What?"

"Where the hell is she?"

"I don't know." Pauly threw up his arms.

"Shit!" Roxi paced, unsure if she was frightened for Ravin or mad because of what she had done.

"She'll be back," Pauly assured her.

She turned back into the studio and looked at the shattered camera sprawled across the floor. She looked up at Randy. "Did she get anything?"

"I think so; I'll put them in now and see."

"If not," she said, shaking her head, "I'll have to use something old."

Ravin recklessly drove her Durango into traffic. She didn't know where she was going and she didn't care. All she cared about was getting away. She had to get away from everyone and go somewhere quiet. After a while, she found herself at the beach. She got out of her truck and walked down to the shore.

Roxi helped clean up the broken equipment and thought about all the changes she had seen in Ravin recently. She knew Marco meant a lot to her and she knew about her past. After Pauly explained about the black Lincoln, Roxi got nervous. She dreaded this day and knew it would eventually come. She just wished it hadn't come so soon, but she already had another photographer in mind.

Marco looked around feeling helpless, Pauly was on the phone again and he walked over.

"Pauly, we've got to go and find her," Marco insisted.

"I already know where she is. You should just go back to the warehouse."

"But—"

"Look, I know you want to help her, but you can't. There's nothing you can do."

"Fine, can I ask you something though?"

"What?" Pauly said, losing his patience.

"What did you mean when you said her truck was bullet-proof and that as long as she was in it, they couldn't hurt her?"

"Nothing."

"Pauly, tell me," Marco demanded.

"It's nothing, really."

"Why would she be driving around in a bullet-proof truck if it was nothing?"

"Marco, back off." He stormed away.

Marco felt restless as he headed back to the warehouse. Something was going on that they weren't telling him and it stung. He was used to protection and he knew what it involved. Who was she and what was all this cloak and dagger shit? He sat down on the couch in the lounge and thought about every aspect of his life with her. The pieces started fitting together after a couple hours. She had plenty of friends that looked more like thugs and she was Italian. Her boyfriend was murdered and so was her father. Those were facts, but what didn't fit was why she was involved. Although it explained Pauly better, it didn't explain why she needed him. Could she possibly be involved with the Mafia? No! He shook it from his head. Not her. The one person he truly loved could not be involved in something so violent and wrong. Marco began pacing the warehouse. He continued to pace until she walked in the door four hours later.

"Hi," she said embarrassed walking up to him.

"Are you okay?" he grabbed her arms and looked into her face.

"Yeah, better now. Listen—"

"Whatever, I'm just glad you're okay."

"As I was going to say . . . I'm really sorry. I'm sorry for pushing you, yelling at you, and losing my temper."

"That's okay. It happens." He looked at her desperately wanting to ask her. She was leaving in a few hours and didn't want to spend it arguing. "Did you finish packing?"

"Yeah, this morning."

"Good, do you need me to hold you?"

"I think that would be perfect."

"Come here."

He took her over to the couch and sat down with her. Ravin curled up on his lap and laid her head on his chest. She always felt safe there, but for how long?

"I'm not trying to make you mad, but I need you to tell me what's going on. This is more than you're letting on. Pauly let something slip after you left. He said that as long as you stayed in your truck, you were safe. Something about it being bullet-proof. Now I know what that means, and I know you are in some kind of danger. I need to know why and from who. I want to spend my life with you, but I can't if you aren't honest with me."

Ravin didn't answer. She knew that she had to tell him, but this just wasn't the time. All she wanted was to feel him surrounding her. He reached up and stroked her hair.

Pauly stormed in, talking fast on his cell phone in Italian. He looked over saw Ravin on Marco's lap and pointed at her. "I'm pissed at you," he bellowed.

She stuck up her middle finger and didn't move from Marco's lap. Marco let out a small chuckle and felt good about winning over Pauly.

"Ravin, Roxi just called. She'll be here in an hour," Pauly said into the room.

"Thanks." She pushed herself off Marco. "Thank you."

"For what?"

"Holding me."

"Anytime."

He gently brushed his lips across her forehead. She looked up and kissed him gently on the mouth. She knew she could never let him go and she was going to do whatever it took.

"Let's go get your bags." He took her hand.

They went upstairs to gather her things. He put her bags by the door and walked into the bedroom as she was putting the last few things in her carry-on.

"Nick will be over to show you how to lock up," she said as he walked in. "And he'll be watching the place while we're all gone. He always does, so don't be surprised if he just pops in."

"That's fine."

"Don't worry about him, he likes you," she said reading his mind.

"Good, maybe we'll get a chance to get to know each other."

"Maybe."

"And I'll see you Friday night."

"Yes."

"Good, come here." He pulled her over into his arms. He kissed her tenderly, not wanting to let go. She looked up into his warm brown eyes and fell in love all over again.

She gave him one last kiss before saying goodbye. Marco watched her leave with Roxi and wished her a good flight. After she was gone, he felt empty as he wandered into the piano room.

Twenty-Eight

After settling in their seats in first class, Ravin laid her head against the window. Flying was not her favorite thing to do, but she learned how to get through it. After take off, the flight attendants began to serve drinks, but Ravin declined.

"What's the matter?" Brett asked.

"Nothing."

"Then why the hell are you throwing cameras around? I heard what happened today. Tell me what's going on, Ravin."

"Just a lot happening in a short time." She closed her eyes.

"True, but that's not all. I know you, Ravin, and I know it's got nothing to do with Marco. You're on edge, Pauly's on edge. What is it?"

Ravin just looked at her. Brett knew they were following her again. She looked down at her hands. When she left the old neighborhood, she left all that behind.

"They're back?"

"Yes."

"Who?"

"Brett, I don't want to talk about it. I need to concentrate on this shoot." She looked at Brett's expression. "I'm not keeping anything from you. I'm just tired and confused, and I need to get through this photo shoot."

"Okay, if you need me . . . " She began to say.

Ravin smiled and put her head back on the window.

She soon fell into a fitful sleep; visions of the desert broke through her thoughts of Marco. She could see the ghost town and Marco standing in the middle of the deserted road. Little by little, the images came before her. Her shoot with the boys now etched in her mind, she knew what to do. All she had to think about was what to do with the man she loved and how to deal with her past.

Marco lay in bed thinking how lonely he felt without Ravin. He would be with her in two days and he hoped she would be the way she was before. This new personality scared him, the temper, and mostly the silence. He didn't like not knowing what was going on in her head and in her life. If she would only tell him, he would feel better about it, unless it was bad, unless she was going to leave him. He would not be able to handle that. He thought about leaving the group again, not that he wanted to. But if it kept him closer to Ravin, he would sacrifice his career for his happiness. He knew he would never find another person like her. They were so alike in many ways. They were both creative and passionate. Mostly, it was the way she made him feel. The way his skin felt like it was on fire when she touched him. He thought about the way she stroked his chest and ran circles around his stomach. He drifted off to sleep, imagining her next to him.

Twenty-Nine

Ravin and Brett landed at the Los Angeles airport at three o'clock in the morning. After several delays and layovers, they were both glad to be there. They piled into the waiting car, exhausted and feeling the effects of the change in temperature.

"How long until we're at the hotel?" Roxi asked the driver.

"About fifteen minutes."

"What's the game plan?" Ravin asked.

"I'm not sure. I have to see if the others are in yet. We have the set for three days so we can start whenever."

"Brett, how much sleep do you need?" Ravin asked.

"Couple hours at least."

"I want to start as soon as possible."

"Okay, I'll make sure everything's ready to go for you."

"Thanks, Rox. Oh, I'm real sorry about yesterday."

"That's okay. You scared me a little. I've never seen you lose it like that."

"Sorry."

"Just don't pull that again. It took me two hours to calm Carlos down."

"Calm him down? He started it."

"Well, he claims he was an innocent bystander, although I know better. Don't worry about it, Rave. Maybe this will straighten him out. Go and get some sleep. I'll call you when the girls are ready."

"I'll be wandering around, getting things together."

"Keep your cell on."

Ravin went up to her suite and flipped open her suitcase. She pulled out a pair of shorts and a tank top. After a quick shower, she grabbed Pauly and headed down to the courtyard. She sat down at the edge of the hot tub and dipped her feet in. Ideas came fast and she jotted them down the best that she could. By the time she was finished Pauly came over with two cups of coffee.

"Thought you could use some. You didn't look like you got any sleep on the plane."

"Thanks. Pauly?" she asked as he walked over to the lounge chair.

"What?" he yawned.

"What are your thoughts?"

"About what Rave?" He was tired, *real* tired, and he didn't want to fight with her anymore.

"Marco."

"Rave, I'm too tired to fight with you."

"I don't want to fight; I want your honest opinion of Marco. I don't want to talk about anything but him."

"You want my opinion?"

"Yes."

"I think he's a great guy. I think he's good for you, and as soon as you get into the swing of it all, you two will be great together."

"Really? How long will it take?"

"What?"

"Getting into the swing?"

"I have no idea."

"Yeah, so it calms down?"

"The relationship? Yeah it eventually calms down and life goes back to normal." He winked at her and stretched out on the chaise lounge.

Ravin wondered if it was too early to call Mia in New York. She looked at her phone and saw it was four thirty. After a minute, she figured it wasn't too early and dialed her number.

"Hello?" she answered sleepily.

"Hey, Mia, it's Rave."

"Hey, I thought you were going to L.A.?"

"I'm here."

Mia looked at her clock, seven thirty. "What time is it?"

"Four-thirty."

"What can I do for you?"

"I need you to call me with a list of sizes on the boys, you know, shoes, jeans, shirts, even hat sizes if possible."

"Hat sizes?"

"Yeah, cowboy hats."

"That sounds interesting. Where are they?"

"They're at the warehouse. They have to finish the video today, and then tomorrow they're doing TRL. After that, they're flying out here."

"When do you need this?"

"ASAP. I had another vision."

"I see. That would explain the early phone call."

"Sorry, I hope I didn't wake you up."

"No, that's okay."

"Hey, how was your location?"

"Great."

"Excellent. Tell me everything when you get here."

"When I get there?"

"Yeah, I need you here."

"What for?"

"To model. I've already booked your seat. You'll fly in with the guys."

"You're kidding? Can I sit next to Nico?"

"You can sit on his lap for all I care!" She laughed.

"Okay, I'll get these sizes and call you back."

"Great, thanks. I have no idea when they're leaving, but Benny will know where they are."

Ravin sat back, pleased with her thoughts. She curled up next to Pauly and they both watched the sunrise.

"Yeah?" Ravin answered her phone.

"We're all set," Roxi said on the other end.

"Girls?"

"On the plane."

"Equipment?"

"Just waiting on you."

"Darkroom?"

"The hotel rented some darkroom time for you at Paramount Studios at your convenience."

"That's pretty impressive, Rox. How'd you pull that one off?"

"Well, I did mention that you were not only shooting for Jerry, but the guys too. I guess that helped."

"Cool. Give me five minutes and I'll be out front." She shook Pauly awake as she dialed Marco. She hoped she wasn't interrupting him.

"Hello?" he answered quickly.

"Hi, Babe."

"Ravin! I'm glad you called."

"Are you shooting?"

"No, they're doing Brody right now."

"Good, how's it going?"

"Good. Why didn't you call this morning? I was hoping to talk to you earlier. I was worried."

"You were?"

"Yeah, until Mia came over and started measuring us."

"She did?"

"Yes, she wouldn't tell us for what, but she said you had some kind of vision and we were required to give in to her measuring tape."

"I only needed your sizes; she didn't have to go that far."

"Yeah well, she did. You should have seen Cole's face when she walked in and he was standing there in his boxers." Marco laughed.

"Really?"

"Yeah. She told us you called her this morning, so I figured you got there okay. I would have liked a call."

"Sorry. Still getting use to that whole checking in thing."

"I'm not asking you to check in, but when you fly halfway across the country, I would like to know if you got there safely."

"Point taken. Listen, I'm running late, so hold on." She put down her phone while she changed her shirt. "Just changing my clothes. We're on our way out to the desert."

"Wish I was there helping you out of your clothes," he said in a devilish voice.

"Funny."

"Will you call me tonight?"

"Yes, but I have no idea when I'll be back."

"Call me anyway. I'll leave my cell on your empty pillow."

"Thanks for the guilt trip. Now I miss you."

"You do?"

"Yes and I love you. I've gotta fly."

"I love you too. I'll talk to you tonight."

Ravin smiled as she ran down through the foyer. She jumped into the car and they took off to the airport.

They flew out in a small plane, which Ravin decided was worse than a big one. Once they landed, she scouted the area as the crew set up shop. She really wanted to get this done in one day. It was only nine a.m. and the heat was just bearable. She couldn't imagine what it was going to be like by noon. After finding her spot, she set everyone up and began shooting. Fortunately, her models were very eager to get back into their air-conditioned hotels and cooperated fully.

After a quick lunch, she asked everyone for another hour. She could have been done earlier, but Randy had to stay back.

"How do'ya think it went?" Brett asked Ravin as they walked back to the plane. It had only taken them another hour or so to finish and she was grateful. The heat was heavy and thick, even under the tent.

"Pretty good."

"You aren't happy with it are you?"

"Why do you ask?"

"You didn't give it a hundred percent. What do you have up your sleeve?"

"Nothing! Why?"

"Because, Ravin, I know you too well. This wasn't the real shoot, was it?"

"Shh." Ravin put her finger to her lips. "We'll talk back at the hotel."

"Buy me dinner?"

"Room service coming up!"

"That's all I'm worth to you?" Brett mocked.

"Very funny. I was gonna wait for Marco."

"I know, I'm kidding. He told me all the places he was taking you."

"He did, huh?"

"Yes, he did. I hope you brought a nice dress."

"No, I don't think I even own a dress."

"Well, we'll have to fix that, won't we?"

"Why?"

"Because he wants to take you out for a nice dinner."

"Can he do that?"

"L.A. is a very different place. They treat celebrities like normal people out here. It's not like New York, where he wouldn't be able to walk down the street without people noticing him. Out here? They're all famous, so nobody cares."

"Cool."

"Yeah, so we'll shop. Rodeo Drive, maybe Sunday."

"Sure."

Both girls went back to their adjoining rooms and took showers. They ordered room service and collapsed on the couch.

"So, what's the secret?" Brett asked, finishing her fries.

"What?"

"Why aren't you using any of the shots from today?"

"How do you know I'm not?"

"I know you. What's your plan?"

"Maybe I'll use them, but I thought it would be even better if the boys were in it. I already talked to Ben and he said it was okay as long as Jerry gave them something. I talked to Jerry and he was thrilled. He just wasn't sure if he could afford them. That's were I left it. I'm working on some charity from Benny and hope Jerry will be able to do something for them. As far as I know, they are now working on a publicity exchange."

"That is fricken awesome!" she shouted, excited. She then paused and looked over at Ravin. "What about me?"

"You're still in the shoot. I thought I'd have you, Mia, and Lainey."

"Ravin, you are a genius."

Thirty

"Hey," Ravin said softly over the phone.

"Hey, baby. How'd it go today?"

"Okay, you?"

"All done. Took us a little longer than usual though. The director was an idiot."

"Oh yeah? Why's that?"

"He couldn't decide what he wanted. Anyway, your shoot went okay?"

"Yeah, I guess. I wasn't real happy with the models."

"No? I thought Brett was there."

"She was fine. They were all fine. They just didn't have what I was looking for."

"So, I don't need to skip TRL and kick anyone's butt!"

"No." She laughed, knowing he was talking about Carlos. "That won't be necessary." For the first time in a few days, she felt relaxed.

"Do you have to re-do it?"

"Probably."

"Sorry, wish I was there."

"Why? You can't change the fact that they didn't have what I was looking for."

"No, but I could be there giving you a back rub or relaxing in the hot tub or something."

"I've already been in the hot tub. I'll take the back rub."

"You have! With who? When?" he said, taunting.

"Relax. Three this morning with, well, wouldn't you like to know," she teased.

"Pauly?"

"Yeah, sort of."

"Sort of?"

"He was crashed on the lounge chair next to me."

"That doesn't count."

"Guess not."

"I miss you," he said quietly listening to the thunder.

"Me too." She walked out onto the balcony. She could smell the ocean and hear the waves crashing onto the shore.

"Are you on the ocean?"

"Yeah, it smells good out here."

"I love the ocean. It's thundering here."

"I'll trade ya."

"Really? I thought you would love the ocean."

"Why?"

"Sparks creativity."

"Does it now?"

"Yes, it does."

"No, you do," she said yearning for his touch.

"I do what?"

"Spark my creativity, among other things." She giggled.

"I spark your creativity?"

"Yes."

"Wow, I'm honored."

"Take it easy, Marco."

"No, seriously. I've never had anyone give me such a compliment."

"Bull."

"Serious."

"Then I take it back. I can't have you thinking I'm a nice girl. That's just not right." She laughed.

"Funny. You aren't a nice girl. You're an incredibly smart, and unbelievably sexy woman."

"Stop."

"Why?"

"Because."

"Rave?" he asked after a long silence.

"I miss you."

"There's more—what?"

"I need you. I need to hold you."

"What's wrong?"

"Nothing, everything . . ." She sighed and looked out at the ocean. "It's just that a lot has happened to me in a short amount of time."

"Things did happen between us fast, but I wouldn't change anything."

"I know, neither would I. It's just a big change for me. I never thought I would depend on anyone else, and now I find myself needing you, relying on your touch to soothe me." She silently wiped the tear rolling down her cheek. "I just . . ."

"Ravin, God, I love you. I've been so scared that you were backing away from me. I thought you were leaving me. I know it's a lot and it's fast, but I can't control how I feel about you. I just wish I was there to hold you."

"I know. Me too."

"Listen, get some sleep. You sound really tired, and if I keep talking to you, I'm very likely to fly out there tonight. You're driving me nuts."

"I am?"

"You do every second of the day."

"Ha! I love you. I'll see you soon."

"Okay, I love you too."

She hung up the phone and looked out at the black ocean. She listened to the waves hitting the shore and felt the breeze brush across her face. *What now?* She thought. She knew she wouldn't be able to sleep and she didn't want to bother Brett this late. The only other thing to do was to walk. She pulled on her jeans and a long-sleeve shirt and headed out the door.

"Where ya going?" Pauly asked, closing his door.

"I thought I'd go down to the bar or something. Wander around."

"Why didn't you let me know?"

"Sorry. Just . . . thinking."

"It's okay; I'm used to you not telling me when you're going somewhere." He laughed as they went downstairs.

They found a quiet spot at the end of the bar and ordered two glasses of wine. Pauly noticed two men out of the corner of his eye. They weren't dressed right for L.A., their first mistake. Ravin noticed them too. She looked over at Pauly.

"This isn't over, is it?"

"'Fraid not."

"Think it's for me?"

"Can't be sure. They seem pretty interested though."

"We know anyone around here?"

"Not sure. In Vegas, we do. I'm gonna make some calls." He pulled out his cell phone.

Ravin positioned herself behind Pauly, giving her a perfect view. She memorized every detail of their appearances.

"All set. Johnny's coming up from Vegas with a few friends."

"Johnny who?"

"Johnny Giovanni. I don't know if you remember him or not. He moved out of the neighborhood when you were about eight."

"I remember." She looked down at the ground. Her past ran through her head. She tried so hard to separate herself from the lifestyle her father had led. She hated every bit of it.

"Wanna go back to your room?"

"No."

"You'd rather be a sitting duck?"

"No, I'd rather not let them run my life, Pauly. This was my father's lifestyle, not mine. I'm not playing this game."

"It wasn't your father's either. He just got caught up in it. You *do* know that, don't you? You know he was never a part of all this?"

"He wasn't? Then why were there always threats and . . ." She threw her hands in the air. "And all this shit around?"

"Like I said, he just got caught in the middle. Your father was a very proud person, the kind that didn't turn his back on friendship and loyalty. When he opened his restaurant, they tried to use him. He wouldn't let them run it, but he said he wouldn't stop them from meeting there. It was the only way to keep the peace. Otherwise he would have been pulled in."

"Why is it you seem to know more about my father than I do?"

"He talked to me a lot, told me things he couldn't talk to your brothers about and things he shielded you from, or at least tried. Ravin, he never wanted you to see this part of his heritage. That was why he left Italy. He wanted a better life for you, your mother, and your brothers. He wanted the American dream. It didn't start off that way, and in the end, it didn't end up that way. No matter what he did, they pulled him back. He could only hold them off to a point."

"So, he truly wasn't involved with the Mafia?"

"No, and neither are your brothers."

"How?" She always wondered how Pauly knew what she was going to say before she had a chance to say it.

"No, your father did everything he could to stay out. He never used them for favors, money, or clout. Everything he had, he worked for on his own. The only thing he did was feed them and give them a safe place to eat, somewhere to call theirs."

"So basically, he was the club owner and they paid him well."

"Yeah, but he never took the extra money they offered. He said that would give them reasons to ask for favors."

"What did he do?"

"Told them the way it was."

"He stood up to them?"

"Yes."

"Then that's what I'm gonna do."

"You are, huh?"

"Pauly, my very best friend is here. The one man in my life that means more to me than you is coming tomorrow and I really don't intend to risk their lives. I won't lose Marco the way I lost Dominic. I won't." She shook her head. "They can't have him."

Pauly smiled. He knew she was more like her father. They sat back and waited for Johnny. Her only concern was for Brett and Marco. She didn't care what happened to her. She pushed back her fear and let her anger take control.

After a while, she went back upstairs to try to sleep, knowing very well the dreams would be there and wishing Marco was there to hold her when she woke up from them.

Bang! Bang! Bang! Noooo! Not Marco, please!

Ravin woke up covered in sweat. She sat in bed and cried for the first time in five years.

Thirty-One

Mia jogged up to the boys as they walked through the airport.

"How was TRL?" she asked rushing them onto the plane.

"Good, as usual," Nico said proudly.

"We should be in L.A. around nine."

"Great."

Marco sat back in his seat, wondering what Ravin was doing, and what she was wearing. She had called him earlier, telling him to meet her at the hotel. He asked what was wrong, hearing something different in her voice. She assured him it was nothing. She had spent the day shopping with Brett and was just tired. He wasn't buying it; restlessly, he waited to get there.

Ravin paced around her suite waiting for Marco to arrive. Pauly had moved Brett across the hall and set up house with Johnny and his men next door. Ravin didn't know who they were and they said that was best. She walked into Pauly's room and glanced over as he sat at the table with Johnny.

"What's going on?" she asked.

"Nothing, just making some plans."

"Is there any way this can get done without any violence?"

"I'll try." Johnny snickered.

"Seriously."

"Rave, we're gonna do everything we can to get this done without anyone getting hurt, including them," Pauly reassured her. He knew she hated the violence. In fact he did too.

"Anything I can do?"

"No. When's Marco getting in?"

"Another hour."

"Good."

"Why?"

"Cause he can keep you out of my hair," Johnny said, laughing.

"Funny." She turned sharply and walked out.

"Let me know when he gets here, okay?" Pauly said, looking over his shoulder.

"I will."

She walked out, not knowing what she was going to do for another hour. What she really needed was her boxing bag.

"So, what's up with little Ravin? Man she has grown into quite the woman!" Johnny said, watching her leave the room.

"Yeah, she turned out pretty good," Pauly said embarrassed. She was like his sister and it felt strange to have a friend make comments about her.

"So . . . who's this Marco guy? He any good for her?"

"Yeah, he's a good guy, treats her right. He's in the band Jaded, and apparently they're pretty big."

"I've heard of them, took one of my girlfriends to their concert last year. They're pretty good, if you like that stuff."

"Yeah, had to go to one myself. They aren't bad, not my style though."

"So, not only do we have to watch Ravin, but we have to make sure none of these guys gets hit too?"

"Pretty much."

"Nothing like a little chaos to bring a smile to my face, man."

"Can we handle all seven?"

"Seven?"

"Yeah, Rave, Brett, and the guys."

"Oh yeah, seven," he said counting in his head. "Not a problem."

Pauly sat back in his chair wondering why he was doing this. He hadn't been involved in a shakedown in over five years. He had never been involved in the shooting part. He was the eyes and ears. Pauly had a sharp mind and a way with people. They trusted him instantly and this was how he gathered information.

"Pauly, come here a minute."

"Yes, Mr. Capello," Pauly said cautiously, approaching his boss.

"This is for you," he said as he handed him a small gun. Pauly looked at him puzzled.

"I don't know what to say."

"Say thank you, Pauly."

"Thank you, Mr. Capello, although I'm not sure I understand."

"Pauly, you know this neighborhood is getting worse everyday and I want you to continue to work for me. You do a great job watching out for my little princess and all the other odd jobs. I would feel better knowing that you're carrying a piece to protect yourself and my little girl. Do you know how to use it?"

"No, sir, I have never shot a gun before."

"Well then, let's go."

Mr. Capello took Pauly by the arm and drove him over to the shooting range. Teaching him was as fun as it had been teaching his own two sons.

Pauly spent all of his spare time at the shooting range learning everything he could about guns. The owner of the range told him he was a natural, but he wasn't sure if that was a good thing or not. At least, it would please Mr. Capello.

Marco got off the plane to the waiting car. He sat in the back impatiently, shaking his leg.

"Will you cut that out!" Cole asked.

"What?"

"Shaking your leg like that. You've only been away from her for two days, man! I can't imagine what you're gonna be like when we go on tour."

"Sorry." He stopped, or tried. He couldn't help being nervous. He knew something was wrong with Ravin and he needed to see her. He needed to see her eyes; her eyes would tell him everything.

As soon as they reached the hotel, Marco ran to the desk and picked up his key. As he walked off the elevator onto the floor, he noticed them right away. One at each end of the hall and two sitting in front of the two doors. They all sat up as Marco emerged from the elevator. He looked at his room number and slowly walked up to the room. The man sitting next to the door looked up to him.

"Are you supposed to be here?"

"Yes," Marco said, confused.

"Who are you?"

"Marco, why? Who are you?"

"Go ahead." He waved him in.

"Gee, thanks." Marco slipped the key into the door, still staring at the guard. He quietly opened the door and stepped in. Ravin was standing in the door leading out to the balcony. She turned around as he silently closed the door.

"Hey." She smiled.

"Hey." He looked at her; he could see the concern in her face as she walked up to him. He dropped his luggage and met her halfway.

"I'm so glad you're here." She wrapped her arms around him. His concern left him as soon as he felt her arms around her neck.

"I missed you," he said, kissing her passionately.

"I missed you too." She rested her head on his chest.

Pauly poked his head in the door after Marco arrived. He saw Ravin wrapped in his arms.

"Have a good night, Rave, Marco."

Marco shook his head as Pauly closed the door.

"Come here," she said, taking him over to the balcony. They sat outside listening to the ocean.

"Will you now please tell me what's going on?" he asked.

"I told you. Nothing."

"Well, if nothing is wrong, why are there so many of Pauly's friends outside?"

"How do you know whose here?"

"Well, there's one at each end of the hall, one outside your door, and one outside Brett's."

"Okay, already, we aren't sure, but Pauly and I spotted someone downstairs yesterday, someone from the old neighborhood."

"I don't understand."

"I have done everything possible to leave my past . . . in the past. My father was friends with a lot of shady people." She looked at him, hoping he would understand. "He knew a lot of things about them, bad things. When he told me—he was murdered. They killed him because he told me. Dominic was murdered because he worked for the Mafia, as a runner. I didn't know this when I was with him, of course. Thanks to my father and Pauly, I led a pretty sheltered life, but apparently he was stealing money from his pick-ups or some-thing and sleeping with his boss's mistress. That's why they killed Dominic. My father was killed because of me, because he told me secrets that put a man away in prison for life." She took a deep breath and glanced to see his blank expression. "I never expected anyone to bother me at this point. If I knew they would come back, I would have never let you into my life. But you're here now and the only thing that matters to me is that you are safe. These people you see around are friends from the old neighborhood. They aren't hit men or Mafia, just friends who have legitimate jobs, but they have a lot of respect for my family."

"So, you aren't in the Mafia?"

"Is that what you thought?"

"Sort of."

"Marco—"

"Ravin, I don't even know where to start. Can you assure me that you and your family are not involved in the Mafia in any way?"

"Me? Yes, I can assure you that I am not in the Mafia. I can assure you that my brothers are not. When my father came over from Italy with his friends, he opened the restaurant. He wanted the American dream, they all did. Unfortunately, the jobs that his friends took didn't give them that dream, so they did what they knew. But my dad didn't. He made his dream work. When these friends started coming to the restaurant to talk and eat, he couldn't tell them to go. He showed his respect by allowing them into his place and feeding them. They tried to give him more money, but he wouldn't take it. Instead of money, he asked that they didn't pull him in and that they would watch out for him and his family. So, that's what they did. They enjoyed his food, paid him well, and looked after us. The peo-ple you see here, Johnny and everyone, they're all the sons of my father's friends."

"And Pauly?"

"Pauly lost his father when he was young; he died in a plane crash. His mom asked my dad to look after him and give him some work to do to keep him off the streets. When I was growing up, the neighborhood started changing. The gangs were trying to take over, so my dad asked Pauly to watch over me. Right before my father died, he asked Pauly to protect me no matter what. Pauly promised my dying father that he would and that the only thing that could stop him was death. That's why Pauly's still with me, that and because it isn't over yet." She sighed looking into Marco's blank expression. "Marco, Pauly has stayed with me because he promised my father he would. He grew up me with, like a brother, and he has watched out for me since I was nine years old. In my family, respect is extremely important. That has nothing to do with being in the Mafia"

Marco looked over at Ravin with mixed emotions. He didn't know whether to hold her or walk out on her. He feared she was involved with the Mafia, but from what she told him she really wasn't. Even so, violence was violence no matter what name it took. He got up and started pacing the room, trying to sort out this new information. Ravin knew this was big, maybe too much for him to deal with. She prepared for him to leave her, even though she knew that she would fight for him. She didn't say anything, but instead watched him pace around the room.

"So—there are men here that are trying to kill you?"

"I don't know what their intentions are, but that's the assumption."

"So, you guys are gonna hunt them down and kill them first?"

"No, Marco, we aren't killing anyone."

"So why are all these guys here?"

"Protection. Mostly for you, the guys, and Brett."

"Protect us?" he asked, shocked to hear her say that.

"Yes." She looked up at him with teary eyes.

"What about you? Whose gonna protect you? Aren't you the target?"

"Yes, I am."

"Why?"

"Because of their secrets, they don't want them told."

"Did you plan on telling someone this? Is this why they're after you?"

"No."

"Then why the interest now?"

"I don't know? That's what Pauly intends to find out."

"I see. Is this the last of it? Once these people are . . . dealt with . . . will there be any more?"

"Not unless Carlos Penelli breaks out of prison."

"Who the hell is Carlos Penelli?"

"The one man I put away for life." She looked down at the floor. "The only man I am truly afraid of."

"So, you did tell, to some point."

"I put him away, but not with any of my father's information. Unfortunately, nobody thinks that."

"Before I can think about this anymore I have one more question. Tell me the honest truth." He sat on the edge of the coffee table and looked into her eyes. Right now they were black, as black as can be, and they weren't dancing with any colors. They were cold, black, and scared. "Have you ever killed anyone or shot anyone?"

"No! God, Marco, how could you ask that?" She stood up abruptly.

"Has Pauly?"

"No! Neither has Pauly. We don't go around shooting people, Marco. I hate violence; I hate the thought of it all. I can't change my past and I can't change the way my father lived his life. I have changed mine and so has my family. Like I told you, we aren't *in* the Mafia!" She stomped over to the other side of the room.

"Have you ever shot a gun?"

"Yes, my brother taught me years ago, but I have never used one outside the shooting range and I don't own one."

"Does Pauly?"

"Yes, he and about seventy-five percent of the population in New York."

"I need to take a walk," Marco said. "I'll be back in a while."

He stood up and walked out of the room. Ravin stood there feeling empty. For the first time in her life, Pauly was not the only one she confided in. Even Brett didn't know most of it. She wanted to run after him and erase everything she had just said, but she understood how he felt. She knew the overwhelming feeling that was running through him. She got up and walked back into Pauly's room.

"What's up?" he asked, surprised to see her.

"I . . . um . . ." She pulled him away from Johnny. "I just told Marco everything. He went for a walk."

"Johnny, can you tail Marco?"

"Yeah." He got up and left.

"You told him everything . . . as in?"

"Everything."

"Wow." He sat on the bed. "I didn't think you'd tell him everything."

"Well, I thought it was important. I thought he should know every aspect of my life, even the past."

"How'd he take it?"

"He was very quiet, asked a few questions, and left."

"I see. What do you want me to do?"

"I want this to end without killing anyone. I don't want Marco to think that we do what they do."

"I can't promise anything."

"But you can promise me that you will not kill anyone unless you absolutely must."

"You know I couldn't kill anyone. How could you think that?"

"I don't. I just need you to reassure me so I can reassure Marco."

"Okay. What now?"

"I don't know. I guess I just have to wait for him to come back, if he ever does."

"Let me know if you need anything."

"I will. Just make sure he's protected."

"I will."

She turned around and strolled back into her room. She lit the fire and poured a glass of wine.

Marco walked down to the courtyard unaware that Johnny was tailing him. He sat down on a lounge chair overlooking the ocean and thought about everything Ravin had told him. He needed someone to talk to, someone who understood his feelings about violence. He pulled out his cell phone and called Cole. Of all his bandmates and best friends, Cole was the most level-headed with him.

"Yeah?" Cole yawned.

"Sorry to wake you, man, but I need to talk."

"Where are you? Why aren't you with Ravin?"

"I need to talk."

"Okay, where are you?"

"Courtyard."

"I'll be right down."

Within minutes, Cole was downstairs sitting next to Marco. "What's up?" he asked.

Marco sat with his elbows on his knees. "Ravin just told me something, and I don't think I can handle this."

"What did she say?" Cole asked, looking at his friend. His pain was visible on his face.

"Well, you know those guys sitting guard outside her and Brett's doors?"

Cole shook his head looking at him. He had a feeling that what was coming next wasn't going to be good.

"Well, apparently . . ." Marco took a deep breath. "Apparently someone from the Mafia is after her."

"What?" Cole shouted, never expecting to hear such a thing.

"Yeah, my reaction too."

"Why?" He shook his head, "I mean, why would they be after her? Marco, man, what the hell is going on?" Cole asked, suddenly afraid for his best friend.

"She watched her father murdered, and her fiancé murdered too. I guess by the same guy, I'm not sure, but anyway, she told me that her father told her *things* before he died. She assured me that her father was never involved in the Mafia and I believe her, but she did put this Carlos guy in jail for killing her father." He took a deep breath.

"Marco, that doesn't explain why they're here," he pointed out.

"Yes, it does. She said they've been following her around for years, checking to make sure she wasn't telling anyone the information her father had given her. She isn't sure why they are trying to do this now. She hasn't said anything to anyone." He shrugged. "She doesn't know exactly why they're here. That's why Pauly called up a few friends to protect us."

"Us? Why would they be here for us? Why not for her?"

"That's what I asked. She was more concerned about our safety than her own."

"What? Does she have a death wish or something?"

"No," he spat. "She just . . . she just said that she was worried about us getting hurt."

"So . . . what's the problem?"

"What do you mean, what's the problem?" he asked, shocked by the question.

"Seriously, Marco, where is your problem with this? I am not asking in a mocking voice here. Are you afraid of something happening to us or her? What scares you so much about this that you felt the need to call me down here in the middle of the night."

"Cole, she's tied in with the Mafia!" Marco sat up, shocked that Cole couldn't see the pain he felt.

"Marco, do you really think she's involved with the Mafia?"

Marco looked at him, his mind reeling with unanswered questions.

"Reach deep down and tell me what your gut says. Do you honestly think that Ravin is in any way involved in this other than as a victim of circumstances."

"I don't know, Cole. That's why I called you. You've always been the voice of reason with me. What should I do?"

"What options are you talking about?"

"Should I leave her?" He dreaded even saying it aloud.

"That's a little abrupt, isn't it?"

"Is it?"

"Do you believe that she isn't involved?"

Marco gazed up at the stars, searching for the right answer. "Yes." He looked back down at Cole. "I think I do. I mean, if she says she isn't, but, I don't know the whole story either. I don't know why they would even be around her. Her father came straight from Italy. His business worked and his friends did what they knew. That's what she told me anyway, so he let them stay and eat at his restaurant. They looked out for him and his family. She told me that was his request, not to pull him in, just look out for his family."

"So, he told her secrets and some Carlos guy killed him in front of her?"

"I don't think she was meant to be there, but yeah, that's what she said. She turned him in and he's now serving a life sentence."

"Does she think he's behind this?"

"She isn't sure. That's what Pauly is supposed to find out."

"So, why don't you hold your decision off until you know why she's being followed? I mean, if they came to kill her, or whatever, don't you think that you would like to help stop that? You do love her, don't you?"

"Of course I do!" Marco yelled, looking over his shoulder at Cole. "Of course I love her," he muttered to himself.

"Well, I think you need to find out the rest of the story before you go off half-cocked and break up with the best thing that has ever happened to you. Ravin loves you, otherwise she wouldn't have told you all of this. Follow your heart, man. Listen to your instincts." Cole slapped Marco's knee, left him to think over the situation, and headed back up to bed.

Eventually, Marco headed back upstairs, still unsure what he was going to do.

He slid his key in the door as quietly as he could. Slowly, he opened the door; Ravin was sitting on the couch with her legs curled under her. She had a blanket covering half her body and her head was lying on her arm. He wasn't sure if she was asleep or not, nor was he sure if he was ready to talk to her. He tiptoed over to her. When he saw she was asleep, he gently lifted her off the couch and carried her to bed. After he covered her, he sat on the edge of the bed watching her. Struggling with his feelings about her past, he watched her for the rest of the night.

Three hours later, he watched from across the room as she woke up suddenly in a cold sweat. She sat up in bed and looked around. She didn't see him sitting on the chair in the corner as she got up and went out onto the balcony. He sat and listened to her cry, feeling helpless and scared. He had finally found the woman he could spend the rest of his life with and he couldn't bring himself to make a decision.

Thirty-Two

Ravin was the first person on the plane. She watched Marco board alone with the rest following behind. He slowly walked over and sat next to her.

"You okay?" he asked quietly.

"Yeah sure, why wouldn't I be?" she said coldly.

"You were crying last night."

"How would you know?"

"I watched you."

"You never came back last night."

"Yes, I did. Who do you think put you in bed?"

"That was you?"

"Yeah. Who did you think it was?"

"Pauly."

"Of course." He looked out the window. "Did you have another nightmare?"

"Of course."

"Are you ever going to tell me what they're about?"

"You really wanna know?"

"Yes. Maybe I can help."

"I doubt it, but okay."

She sat back and told him every detail of her dreams, how every night she watched Dominic get shot, how she heard the sounds of the gun shots and saw him fall to the ground covered in blood. She also told him that the last few nights it was him falling covered in blood.

Marco looked at her in utter astonishment. He never realized how bad Ravin's nightmares were. He reached out and took her hand.

"I'm sorry, I didn't know. Can I do anything?"

"No." She closed her eyes and squeezed his hand as the plane took off.

"Don't like flying?"

She shook her head. "I don't want you anywhere near this Marco. You know that, don't you?"

"Nothing's gonna happen to me, trust me."

They flew to the desert in silence. Ravin didn't know what to say and neither did Marco. She had made up her mind not to let him go and now he was the one leaving her. How could everything have gone so wrong? She tried to make small talk with Mia and the other guys.

Brett watched her carefully, trying to think of a way to fix this.

When they reached the ghost town and unpacked the plane, Ravin went to walk around. She asked the boys to get into wardrobe and, then pulled out her camera. She wished she hadn't smashed her new digital. It could have come in handy. She found a quiet spot and perched herself on the fence post, watching the wind playing games with the light. This was going to be a tough shoot and a long day. Marco stood in the doorway of the tent watching her. Part of him wanted desperately to run over and hold her. The other part was so scared of her past.

They each came out wearing a pair of Aztec jeans, a white muscle shirt, and cowboy boots carrying their cowboy hats. Ravin felt inspired. They looked great. She led them out into town and positioned them in front of the old building. She clicked away, wishing she had her music.

"Think you've got enough?" Nick asked, pulling out a sandwich.

"I'd like some sunset shots. You guys are holding up great," she said, sipping from her water bottle.

"Thanks, we're having a good time."

"You work well together, better than most of my models." She forced a smile.

"It's five o'clock now and you want sunset shots. So, like a couple more hours?"

"I guess. I'm gonna re-group for a bit, so take a long dinner." She forced another smiled and walked away.

"Marco man, what the hell's going on between you two? She's not happy and neither are you." Nico turned to him after Ravin left.

"Nothing," he said quietly.

"Anything you want to talk about?"

"Not really." He slumped off to the other side of the tent. Sitting alone, he sipped his water and watched Ravin walking around town.

"You sure you wanna be out in the open when it gets dark?" Pauly asked, walking up to her. She turned quickly.

"Why do you ask?"

"Not sure," he said, looking around. "One of Johnny's guys saw a car about a quarter mile down the road.

"Shit. Do you think they came here?"

"Probably. They're looking for them right now."

"Do you think they can find them first?"

"Probably. If I know Johnny, he most likely has and is taking care of things as we speak. He knows how you feel . . ." Pauly looked at her reassuring. "But I thought you should know just in case."

"Thanks, Pauly."

"Are you two okay?"

"No, we aren't." She looked down at her hands.

"Want me to talk to him?"

"No . . ." She sighed. "He has to make the decision, not me."

"Let me know if you want anything." He patted her shoulder. "We've called in a car; it should be here in a while." He smiled and walked away.

Ravin walked back to the tent and asked them to follow her out to the dirt mound. She started to take the singles when a loud rumble of thunder rolled in. She looked out at the sky and watched the clouds roll in; the rain came fast and felt good. Pauly ran over with an umbrella and protected her camera.

"Marco!" she yelled to him under the tree. He looked over at her. "Mind getting wet?"

Her smile was magic.

"Where?" he asked.

"On the mound. Start with the shirt and hat on then take them off."

He obliged and Ravin ran through three rolls of film. Eventually, the rest of the guys came out, each one adding to the picture. Mia hesitated, not sure about rain and white muscle shirts, but when Brett ran out jumping into Vinny's arms, she gave in. Ravin smiled and let out a small chuckle as she watched five very wet guys and two very wet models run through the rain.

Ravin stood under the umbrella watching Marco. The rain was hitting his tanned body as he held him arms in the air and closed his eyes. She took as many pictures as she could, giving up when she ran out of film.

"Come on, Rave! It isn't fair that you stay dry!" Brett shouted.

Ravin smiled and handed her camera to Pauly. He walked back to the tent and packed it away. Her assistants packed up the plane.

"We have to go now, before this storm gets worse," one of them said.

"Ravin, should I tell them to go?" Pauly asked, "We have a car."

"Sure," she said and sat under the tree watching them play in the rain.

"Marco man, whatever the problems you two are having, you've got to drop it. Go and talk to her," Cole said, noticing her sit under the tree alone.

Marco knew he was right; he strolled over to Ravin and held out his hands. "Come here," he said, pulling her up to her feet. "Get wet with me."

Just as she walked into the rain with him, they heard a gunshot. Ravin swung around from the force and Marco threw her to the ground. She forced him off as she looked around. Vinny and one of Johnny's men covered Brett. Nico, Cole, and Brody were safe. Pauly came running over and dove down next to Ravin and Marco.

"Where did that come from?" he asked out of breath.

"Over there." She pointed.

"What the hell was that?" Marco screamed at her. He looked in her face and saw panic.

Pauly grabbed them both and pulled them over to the tree. "Keep down and stay quiet." He whistled over to Johnny.

Johnny whistled back, indicating everyone was fine.

"I can't see shit out here. It got dark real quick, Ravin did you see anything?"

"I can see everything, Pauly." She looked up at him.

"What? What can you see? How many, where?"

"The shot came from over there." She pointed and Pauly turned around. "But I can hear him over here." She pointed in the opposite direction.

"There must be two! Can you see either of them?"

"Not unless they move," she said, holding her arm. She could feel the blood seeping into her shirtsleeve and her arm throbbing. She didn't dare say anything.

Marco sat against the tree, his heart pounding so hard that he thought it would explode out of his chest. He held onto Ravin's trembling hand.

"Pauly, don't you have a gun?" he whispered to him.

"Yes."

"Well, why aren't you shooting back!" Marco screamed, concerned for Ravins life and the lives of all his friends.

"What?" Pauly asked confused.

"Shoot back," he demanded.

"Marco, I'm not a violent person. I don't think I could do that." He was just as shocked to hear himself say that as Ravin was. Marco broke free and crawled over to Johnny.

"Listen, I hate violence," he whispered to him, "but I hate dying more. Do something! We have to get the hell out of here!"

"Marco! Get back here!" Ravin demanded. She sat up against the tree holding her arm.

"Ravin, did you get shot?" Pauly pulled her arm over to him.

"Yeah, it's just a scratch though. I'm fine."

"We have to get out of here. We're sitting ducks. There are too many of us."

"Do you have a plan?"

"I think so. Stay here and stay down." He crawled over to Johnny.

Ravin sat against the tree still holding her arm, all alone. This was the way she wanted it though. If she went down, she wanted to be alone. As long as Pauly could get the rest out safely, she would stay here and sacrifice herself.

Marco looked over at Ravin alone against the tree; he could make out most of her face and knew she had her eyes closed. What he couldn't figure out was why she was holding her arm like that. Slowly, he crawled back to her.

"Hey, are you okay?"

"Fine, why?"

"What happened to your arm?"

"Nothing, I'm fine."

He pulled her hand away and saw the blood soaking through her sleeve. "Ravin! My God, you're bleeding! Did you get shot?" he shouted.

"Yes," she said quietly.

"We need to get out of here. Can you see them? Can you tell one of the guys where they are so they can shoot them?"

"Why would you want that? You hate this!" She waved her hands in the air.

"Ravin, I want to get you out of here. You need to get to the hospital."

"No. Everything will be fine."

He took her shoulders and pulled her against his chest. He pulled the muscle shirt out of his waistband and tied it around her arm. Pauly came back with Johnny and two other men. The others were inching their way back to the car. Ravin could hear Brett explaining what was going on and felt relieved that she didn't have to explain it all over again.

"Marco get back to the car. Ravin and I are going to stay here."

"I'm not going anywhere."

"Marco, get out of here!" Pauly demanded.

"No."

"Fine, Ravin?"

She pointed out where she had seen them and Johnny's men went after them. After a few minutes, they heard the signal and Pauly grabbed Marco and Ravin and ran for the car. Marco was relieved not to hear any gunshots. As soon as they got to the car, everyone shouted at Ravin, asking questions.

"Shut up!" Marco shouted. "Let's just get the hell out of here."

He held Ravins hand the whole way back. She leaned her head against his shoulder and quietly fell into a daze. The car was silent; all Ravin could hear was Pauly explaining to the guys what was happening. They all sat stunned and uneasy in their seats. No one but Cole knew this about her and they were all sworn to secrecy.

"Pauly," Marco murmured quietly, "Ravin's hurt."

"Yeah, I know."

"She's too quiet."

Pauly leaned over and touched Ravin's face. It was cold and wet.

"Rave." He shook her gently. "Rave!"

Her eyes fluttered open. "What?"

"Just making sure you're still with us." She smiled at him and closed her eyes again.

Once they got back to the hotel, Pauly bandaged her shoulder. He promised Marco that it wasn't bad and she would be fine. He left him alone with her while he went into the other room. They heard screaming in Italian. Ravin understood every word he said to her brother Nick.

"Want me to run you a bath?"

"Sure," she said very quietly.

"Anything else?" She just looked at him. "Are you hungry?"

"A little."

He called up room service and had them deliver sandwiches. After they ate, he started her bath and went back into the room to pull out some clean clothes for them to wear. He cleaned up and poured some wine.

"Want some company?" he asked, holding two glasses of wine.

"Sure."

He handed her the wine, slipped out of his clothes, and slid in behind her. She pulled his arms around her and leaned back against his chest.

"Have your feelings for me changed?" she asked.

"Yeah, I think they have."

"I'm sorry. I didn't think I could hold onto you after all this."

"Well, I can tell you that I still love you more than anything, more than I've ever loved anyone in my life. When you're not around, my heart feels empty, but when you're by my side, the love is so full. When you told me last night what was happening, I was angry. I was hurt and mad, mad at you for making me feel like I couldn't be with you. I've still got a lot going through my head, and after today . . ." He sighed. "I'm not sure what to think. Ravin I love you, but I hate what's happening to you, and I'm mad because there isn't anything I can do about it. But I'll get through this, just as you will. When you asked for space, I gave it to you, and now I'm asking the same."

"I know."

They sat quietly for a while unable to jump over the uncomfortable hurdle that stood between them and happiness.

"Let's get out. This water's getting cold," he said, pulling her up carefully.

He wrapped her in a towel and led her into the bedroom. They got dressed and sat down on the couch. Ravin leaned her head on his shoulder and closed her eyes. She drifted off into a restless sleep.

"Everything okay man?" Pauly tiptoed into the room.

"I think she'll be okay."

"And you?"

"We'll see. Hey, Pauly, thanks . . . for everything."

"No need, I put my life before hers. You never have to say thank you."

"I feel I do. You're a good friend, to her and me."

"Thanks. See you in the morning." He winked.

"Yeah."

Pauly walked away and turned back to watch Marco hold her. He knew how much they loved each other, and he hoped they could get through this.

After a while, Marco carried Ravin to bed and climbed in next to her. He didn't wrap his arms around her like he usually did. Instead, he sat up on his elbow and watched her. Ravin slept almost through the night.

Thirty-Three

"Morning," Marco said as Ravin opened her eyes.

She looked up and saw him watching her. "Morning," she said rubbing her eyes.

"Sleep okay?"

"Almost."

"You didn't wake up like you used to."

"No, but I was up half the night."

"But you didn't wake up in a cold sweat, did you?"

"No, but before we go on with this can I get some coffee?"

"Sure, sorry. I had some sent up already." He got off the bed, poured her a cup, and brought it over to her in bed.

"Why are you being so nice? I thought you hated me."

"I never hated you!"

"Sorry. I have a headache and I don't want to fight."

"Good. Get dressed."

"Why?"

"Because I want to take you out for breakfast."

"Marco, I don't feel in the mood to go out."

"It's not far." He pulled her out of bed, forgetting about her arm.

"Ow!" She let go of his hand.

"Oh my God! I'm so sorry! I forgot! Are you okay?"

"Yeah, I'll be fine," she said, holding her arm. She watched a new stream of blood trickle into the bandage.

"Oh, Rave, I'm so sorry! I made it bleed again. Let me get Pauly. He'll know what to do."

"No, let him sleep. It'll be fine." She unwrapped the bandage and walked into the bathroom to put on a new one.

Marco waited for her to come out of the bathroom. He heard the

shower turn on and waited half an hour for her to come back out. She
walked out wrapped in a towel.

"Sorry, I was already in there . . ."

"It's okay. Washing away the past?"

"Yeah, something like that."

"Good, throw on something and come to breakfast." He held out
his hand.

She slipped on her scrubs and a T-shirt. "Where to?" She took
his hand and he led her out on the balcony. She sat down at the table
he had set up and looked out at the ocean; the sun was rising and
turning everything a vibrant golden red. Marco poured her another
cup of coffee and sat down with her. He opened the silver cover and
set it aside. Inside were a half dozen bagels and cream cheese and a
long black velvet box. She looked at the box and back at him.

"What's that?"

"I got this for you in New York." He picked it up and handed it
to her.

Slowly, she opened it revealing a beautiful diamond tennis
bracelet. "Marco, this is gorgeous. I can't accept this. It's too
much."

"No, it isn't." He took it out of the box and fastened it onto her
wrist. "I saw it in the store and thought of you." He watched her eyes
sparkle as she admired the bracelet.

She leaned over and kissed him. "Thank you. I feel bad; I didn't
get anything for you."

"You've already given me more than I deserve." He sat back and
glanced out at the sunrise. "It's almost as beautiful as you."

"Thank you."

"Ravin, I know I drove a wedge between us. I'm sorry. I've had
time to think about this and I know that I don't want to lose you over
it."

"I know, Marco, I know. It's just . . ." She looked back out at the
water. "If you can't handle my past, we shouldn't be together. I can't
promise you that it won't come back again."

"I know."

"Listen," she said facing him, "I made the decision to fight for
you. But I can't if I'm not sure that's what you want. So until you're
sure . . . then maybe we should slow down."

"Ravin I don't want to slow down and I don't want to lose you over this."

"But you aren't sure you can deal with this, so until you are—"

"I can deal with this; I just don't know exactly what's going on. I know you told me, but it's just gonna take some time to sink in." He looked out at the water. "I don't know what to expect. How can we be sure that you'll be safe? That's all I care about, your safety."

"And all I care about is yours. I don't care what happens to me, but I can't be responsible for you or any of your bandmates getting hurt."

"Ravin, that's ridiculous. How can you not care about yourself?"

"It's not that I don't care. I've just accepted that someday I might. I'm not afraid of death, only the death of those I love."

"You're crazy."

"Say whatever you want, that's the way I feel. I can't help it. I just know that I'm not going to run anymore."

"Is that what you've been doing?"

"Well, not running. More like hiding. I've never been in the limelight because I was afraid. Roxi said I could make it so big if I modeled, but I was scared to put myself out there."

"You would be a good model, a great one. You're so gorgeous, you would be on every cover."

"That's why I choose to stay behind the camera."

They sat quiet for a few moments. Marco sat and thought about what she had said about death. He watched the sun as it brightened her face. She was so beautiful and so calm. Her face had changed since the previous night. Then it was full of fear and anger. It was now calm and full of thought.

"So, what's on the agenda for today?" he asked quietly.

"I need to develop."

"Can't you do that tomorrow?"

"I guess. I just thought it would be nice to get it out of the way. Anyway, I'm dying to see how those rain shots turned out."

"How long would it take?"

"Couple hours."

"A couple hours? You? Yeah, right." He laughed.

"Sure, if I only print out the proofs and don't get involved with any enlargements."

"Forget it. You can't help yourself."

"Probably not. What did you have in mind?"

"I don't know, just thought we could do something."

"Like what?" She smiled.

"Whatever we wanted." He smiled back.

"Okay, I'll print tomorrow."

They spent the day with their friends on the beach. Ravin tried to relax, but she remained quiet most of the day. Pauly assured her that everything was back to normal and that Johnny had taken care of everything. She snuck away for an hour and called to thank him.

Thirty-Four

"Marco," Ravin said, shaking his shoulder.

"What?" he grumbled, rolling back over.

"Get up!"

"Why?"

"You have a meeting in an hour."

"Shit!" he muttered and rolled over, rubbing his eyes.

"Why are you so tired?"

"I don't know. It must have been those margaritas."

"You did toss back a few." She laughed.

"Yeah, I guess I did. What time are you going to Paramount?"

"In about ten minutes."

"Gonna be gone all day?"

"Probably."

"Call me every few hours. Let me know how you're doing please."

"Sure. When's your last meeting?"

"One o'clock. It shouldn't take too long."

"Call me when you're finished." She kissed him goodbye and left for the studio.

Ravin got into the waiting limo and began shuffling through her bag. She wasn't sure what to expect when she got to Paramount. She knew this was a favor, and favors usually didn't pan out the way she wanted them to.

When she arrived, she was surprised to receive the celebrity treatment. Ravin wasn't aware that her reputation had spread this far. Alex and Mark introduced themselves and walked her back to the darkroom.

"Hi," she said extending her hand.

"I'm honored to meet you, Miss Capello," Alex said, shaking her hand eagerly.

"Well, nice to meet you."

"We're here to help. Work the machines, whatever."

"Thanks, that'd be great."

"Good, how many rolls do you have?"

"Oh, I don't know. Maybe a hundred?"

"Shit! I guess you don't fool around."

Ravin wasn't sure what to think of Alex. Mark was very quiet and stayed in the back, warming up the machines.

"You really dumped a hundred rolls of film on two shoots?"

"Yes. I guess."

"Wow, so maybe the rumors are true, huh, Mark?"

"What rumors?" She asked, curious.

"That you don't dick around, among other things," he said loading the film into the processor.

"No, I don't dick around, and what other rumors are flying around here?"

"Ah . . . nothing."

"Tell me. Trust me it won't bother me."

"Well, rumor has it that you're hard to work with. You won't accept anyone else's ideas."

"True. I am hard to work with. Let me ask you something. Have you ever seen those people singing karaoke?"

"Sure."

"What do you think about that?"

"Some people shouldn't sing." He laughed.

"Exactly, some people shouldn't do things they don't know how to do, so they shouldn't judge those of us who do." She sarcastically raised an eyebrow.

"Point taken."

"How long will these take?"

"Usually about twenty minutes a double roll."

"Okay, I'll be right back. I've got to make a phone call."

"I'll be here."

Ravin left the room, wondering why she was always stuck with the talkers. She held her phone in her hand, wondering who she could call when it rang.

"Hello?"

"Hey. Where are you?" Pauly asked.

"At Paramount. What's up?"

"I'll be there in a few minutes."

"Pauly! What's going on?" she shouted as he hung up the phone. She paced the hallway nervously, and then quickly dialed Marco's cell.

"Yeah?"

"Thank God! Are you okay?"

"Ravin?" he asked surprised. "What's wrong?"

"I don't know. Pauly just called me."

"What did he say?"

"Nothing! He asked me where I was and then he told me he'd be here in a few minutes and hung up!"

"Ravin, settle down. You're safe there if anything's wrong. Do you want me to come over?"

"No, stay there. I just needed to make sure you were all right."

"Everything's fine here, but I'm worried about you."

"I'm sorry; I should have waited for Pauly before I called you. I must be interrupting your meeting. I just got scared. I can't lose you."

"Honey you aren't gonna lose me. I'll be there as soon as I can."

"No, stay there. At least I know where you are. I'll call you when I hear from him."

"Okay and not a minute later. I love you."

"Love you too." She hung up the phone and continued pacing the hallway.

"The first few are done," Alex said hanging out the door.

"Great, I'll be right there. I'm waiting on someone out here."

"Who? I'll wait, tell her or him where you are."

"Thanks, his name is Pauly." She described him and went in to print the proofs.

"Damn it! I hate coming in here when it's dark!"

"Pauly!" She swung around. "What the hell is going on!"

"Nothing." He let out a small laugh.

"What the shit was that call for! You scared the hell out of me!" she yelled at him through the darkness.

"Sorry." He laughed. "I didn't mean to scare you. Thought you'd be over this jumpiness by now."

"Yeah, right."

"Talked to Nicky, told him everything. He's pissed that you haven't called him."

"Yeah, when?"

"Yeah well, he's pissed. Anyway, he's glad you're okay. He wants to fly out here."

"Why?"

"He thought that since everything's over and done with, he'd like to spend some time with Marco. Get to know him before you get in too deep."

"You came down to tell me this?"

"And to give you this."

"Outside." She took his hand and led him out the door. She took the black box from him and opened it. Inside was a pair of beautiful black opal earrings.

"Who are these from? They're gorgeous."

"From me," he said shyly.

"You? Pauly! Thank you. But why? You've never done anything like this."

Pauly reached over and held her arms, looking directly into her eyes. "Ravin, you are the most beautiful, smartest, and bravest woman I know. You are also the most stubborn, pig-headed, and biggest pain in my ass. I never thought I would need you to protect me. Without your sight, we might not have been able to get away the other night. The black opals represent the darkness in your eyes that you see through everyday, whether it be in your troubles or the night. I've never given you anything before because I never wanted you to feel like I wanted you other than a friend. Now that you have Marco, I feel like I can give you these without you thinking something weird."

"Pauly, I don't know what to say." She hugged him and wiped a tear from her cheek.

"Thank you will be fine."

"Thank you. I love you Pauly, you know that. You know I couldn't have gotten through this without you."

"I know. Now get back to work. Marco told me he wants to go out to some club tonight, so I've been told to get your ass in gear."

"Me?"

"Yeah, you. You tend to lose track of time in there."

"No, I don't."

"Yes, you do. Oh and by the way, if you want some help taking those shots of yourself, just ask!"

"How?" she wondered aloud.

"Give me a break, Ravin! I know *everything* you do."

"Everything?" she said with a sarcastic smile.

"Yes, everything." He winked.

"I may take you up on that."

"I'll see you later. Don't be late!"

"I won't."

"I'll be out front waiting."

She walked back into the darkroom smiling. She pulled out her phone and dialed Marco.

"Yeah?" he answered, worried.

"Are you ever gonna say hello first?" She snickered.

"Rave! Are you okay?"

"Yes."

"What was that all about?"

"Pauly just wanted to talk to me and give me a pair of earrings."

"What? He gave you a pair of earrings?"

"Yeah, I'll tell you about it later. Go back to your meeting."

"Done."

"Already?"

"Yeah, director bailed on us."

"You're kidding?"

"No, we'll talk later though. I want you to hurry up and finish. I want to check out a club or two with you."

Thirty-Five

"Yeah?" Marco answered the phone in his usual manner.

"Hi, Marky!" A familiar squeaky voice chirped on the other end.

"Tammy?" he asked, shocked to hear her voice.

"Yes! How are you?"

"What do you want?" he asked, dreading the answer.

"We need to talk, Marky. I know you're in town. I saw you guys leave the hotel."

"About what?"

"Can you meet me?"

"Not really, I'm kinda busy."

"I only need a few minutes. I'm downstairs in the lobby. Meet me please?"

"Fine, I'll be down in a minute." He hung up the phone, wondering what she wanted. She hadn't called him since they'd broken up eight months ago. Why now? He walked down to the lobby with a bad feeling in the pit of his stomach.

"What do you want, Tammy?" he asked, walking up behind her. His mouth dropped when she turned around.

"Hi, daddy!" she patted her enlarged belly.

"What the hell are you talking about?" he said, pulling her aside.

"What do you mean?" she pouted.

"Why did you call me Daddy?"

"Well, obviously because I'm pregnant with your child, silly."

"That isn't mine!" he yelled, pointing at her stomach.

"How dare you! Of course, it's yours. Who else's would it be?"

"You tell me! Maybe that guy you were screwing around with when we broke up."

"Marky, don't say that. That isn't nice."

"First of all, don't call me Marky! Second, I don't care if it's nice. It's the truth and you know it!"

"Don't yell at me! This is yours."

Marco paced around, knowing this was the worst thing that could happen at the worst time. He sat Tammy down and tried to talk to her. She was convinced the baby was his and wouldn't listen to him.

Ravin and Pauly stood in the doorway, watching the scene with Tammy and Marco. Ravin immediately shut down her feelings and walked away. Pauly grabbed her arm and told her to deal with it. In Marco's profession, she was going to see a lot of this. She controlled her anger and walked up to him quietly.

"Hey, Marco." She forced a calm tone in her voice.

"Ravin! Hi . . . um . . . this is Tammy," he said, standing up quickly.

Ravin smiled and extended her hand. "Hi, Tammy. Nice to meet you." She looked down at her stomach. Her fears built up higher.

"Hi! Are you a friend of Marky's? He's so great, isn't he? I just love him to death. We're gonna have a baby."

"Really? How wonderful for the two of you." She glared at him.

"Of course, this is a huge surprise to him." She giggled, "He's been so busy recording. I didn't want to distract him."

"Of course." She smiled and turned to Marco. "I guess it must be a pretty big surprise. And after all this time, who would've guessed?" She smiled seductively and patted the side of his face before she walked away.

"Who was that?" Tammy asked with attitude, crossing her arms over her chest.

"No concern of yours." Marco paced around for a minute before deciding to go after Ravin. Tammy tried to stop him and he pushed her aside oppressing as much anger as he could.

"Marky! Where are you going!"

"I'll deal with you later." Storming off, he went to look for Ravin. He ran upstairs almost slamming into Vinny.

"Vinny! Have you seen Ravin?"

"No, what's going on?"

"I'll explain later. I've got to find her. Is Brett in her room?"

"Yeah." Vinny looked confused.

Marco rushed to her room almost breaking the door in. "Brett!"

"Hey, Marco, nice wife."

"Shit! She isn't my wife. She's my ex-girlfriend. We broke up over eight months ago."

"Well, I guess she forgot to tell you something then, huh?"

"No, she wasn't pregnant then. I don't know whose baby that is, but I can assure you it isn't mine."

"Think so?"

"I know Tammy. She got knocked up and thought she could pin it on me."

"Why?"

"Money." He looked around nervously.

"So, why are you telling me?"

"Because I want you to know the truth. I need to find Ravin. I need to explain what's happening before all hell breaks loose."

"Too late for that. She's pissed, beyond pissed. It took her five years to open up to another guy and see what happens? I can't fix this Marco, and I don't know if you can either."

"I can."

"How? You have a very pregnant ex with a pretty convincing story. It won't be easy."

"Brett, do you trust me?"

"Yes."

"Good." He told her what he needed her to do. They had rented a beach house for the summer and he asked her to try to get Ravin there. He would clear this up soon, and if Ravin wasn't going to talk to him until then, at least he knew where she would be. He ran downstairs to look for her and found Pauly. Pauly pointed to the beach and offered to talk to Tammy. Pauly believed him. The facts were pretty cut and dry.

Marco walked down the beach, watching Ravin pace through the surf. He wondered what she was thinking as he quietly walked up behind her. He touched the small of her back, but she turned and stepped back.

"Go away, Marco," she said coldly.

"No, not until you let me talk."

"About what? You're going to be a father, which is great. I'm happy for you."

"Ravin, I don't know where to start." He took her hands in his and led her up the shore. He sat her down on the sand and looked into her face. "Tammy and I broke up over eight months ago. She wasn't pregnant then. We broke up because she was cheating on me."

She gave him a hardened gaze.

"I don't know who that baby's father is." He sighed, looking into her face. It was blank and dark.

"Why is she saying it's yours."

"Why do you think? She always cared more about my money than me. The guys she likes are low-life's. They don't have anything to give her."

"And you do?" She put her head down drawing circles in the sand.

"You believe me, don't you?" His eyes pleaded.

"I don't know, Marco. I need some time." She got up and walked away.

Marco didn't try to stop her. He knew it would only make things worse.

After a while, he headed back to look for Tammy. He found her sitting with Pauly and walked over.

"Hey, Pauly." he said distressed.

"Hey, Marco. I was just having a talk with your friend here. Hope you don't mind." Pauly winked at him. Marco knew his intentions.

"No, I guess not." He sat down and waited for Pauly to lead him.

He tried to listen, but his mind kept going back to Ravin. He thought about what she was going through and how hard this was going to be on top of everything else.

"I'm going for a walk." He stood up.

"Bring your cell in case I need you," Pauly said.

Marco shook his head and wondered what he would do to Tammy.

Picking up her bags, Ravin knew leaving was her best option. But where? Where could she go to forget about him, somewhere he couldn't find her? She grabbed a taxi and headed off to the airport. When she got there, she bought a ticket to Italy and called the hotel to leave a message for Pauly. She also called Nick to postpone his trip and promised to explain once she got to Italy.

She felt like a coward sitting in the terminal. It wasn't normal to run away so fast, but she never knew what normal was, especially in a relationship. She knew Pauly would understand her message; she knew he would stay back and make sure Marco took care of his problem. Hopefully, she would be able to accept him back, but only if the baby wasn't his as he promised. Pauly would find out, Pauly would take care of it. What if he couldn't? What if the baby was Marco's? Her head swam with questions and made her feel sick. She closed her eyes and thought of somewhere that made her feel safe. The only place she could think of was in Marco's arms.

"Now boarding Flight 1184," she heard over the loud speaker.

Ravin got up and boarded the plane. She sat back in first class and tried to shut down her mind.

Thirty-Six

Marco walked back up to their room and noticed that all of Ravin's things were gone.

"Brett!" he called into the adjacent room.

"What!" she yelled back as she threw her clothes back on. Vinny still lay in bed with a smug expression on his face.

"Where'd Ravin go?"

"I don't know, why?" she asked, walking into his room.

"Where is she? Her stuff's gone. Didn't you tell her about the beach house?"

"Yes, I did. She probably took off."

"Where? Why?"

"Where? I don't know. I didn't even know she'd left. She didn't tell me anything. And why? Well, you figure that out."

"Is Pauly still here?"

"I don't know." She turned on her heels and went back into her room.

Marco ran downstairs and found Pauly at the bar reading a letter.

"Pauly! Where's Ravin?" He ran up out of breath.

Pauly handed him the message and studied his face as he read it.

Pauly, I went home. Don't tell Marco where I am, I need time to sort this out. I hope it works out in my favor, but if it doesn't, what can I do? You know I'll be fine. Don't come after me. I talked to Nick and he's fine with it. Take care of Marco and Brett for me. I'll contact you soon.
Ravin

"Where is she?" Marco asked.

"Don't know." He smiled.

"Yes, you do! Tell me, Pauly. I need to straighten this out with her."

"First, you need to straighten things out with Tammy."

"Nothing I can do until the baby's born. She said she would give me a paternity test then."

"When is she due?"

"Five weeks."

"Well, my friend, you have five weeks until you can clean up this mess. Then Ravin will listen to you. Until then, I would leave her alone. She's a lot more stubborn than you think." Pauly patted him on the back.

"I can't take her back!"

"I'm not telling you to take her back. Just be nice until you can get the test done."

"Fine!" He stormed off.

Thirty-Seven

Ravin gazed at the grapevines that went on for miles as she sat out on the terrace. She was glad she had come to Italy. The break was good for her. Pauly had come to visit, bringing letters from Marco that now sat in front of her unopened. She tried to convince herself that she didn't care, but deep down, she would never get over him. He had touched her heart in a way like no one else.

"Ravin, are you ever going to join the real world?" her great aunt Josephine asked.

"Eventually, Mimi, eventually."

"Not good enough. You are young, very young, and you need to let go of this old soul of yours. Go and be free. Take this boy back. Tell him you love him."

"I can't do that, Mimi, not after what happened." She shook her head and gazed back out at the vineyard.

"Ravin dear, look at me." She turned Ravin's face to hers, "Forgive the boy. It was something that happened before you met him. He is your soul mate. You belong together. This is why Dominic was taken from you. You were meant to be with Marco."

"How can I be sure?"

"Do you trust me?"

"Of course, I do, Mimi."

"Good, come with me." Mimi was Ravin's favorite aunt. She led her upstairs to a room filled with old boxes and trunks. She pulled out a box and blew off the dust.

"In here are letters that your uncle had written me from the war. Read them. You'll understand."

Mimi left the room and Ravin pulled out the letters. She read each one and was shocked to find out that her uncle had fathered a

189

child while he was at war. Her own life followed Mimi's perfectly.

Ravin wiped the tears from her face as she put the letters away. She walked back out onto the terrace where Mimi waited.

"Well?" she asked.

"What happened? Where's the child? What did you do?"

"Unfortunately, the mother and child did not survive the attacks on their town, but I did forgive your uncle and we went on to live very happily."

"How?"

"Go back to L.A. and look into Marco's eyes. That's were you'll find the answers."

"Mimi, I don't think I'm as strong as you."

"Ravin! You are so stubborn! Swallow that pride of yours and go. That was his past. It always comes back to haunt you when you are happy. When you are with Marco, before you found about this, did you ever think about Dominic?"

"Yes."

"Did you feel guilty?"

"Yes."

"That is your past haunting you. You and your dreams, you let them plague you. Are you still having those nightmares?"

"How do you know about my nightmares?"

"Pauly, he also showed me the letters. Have you read them?"

"No."

"Good. I will make you some coffee and you will sit down and read them. That's an order."

Mimi disappeared into the kitchen and returned with a carafe of coffee. She held out the letters and Ravin reluctantly took them, carefully opening the first one.

Dear Ravin,

Where are you? Pauly won't tell me anything. All he says is that you are okay. I don't believe him. I'm not okay. You know how much I love you. Doesn't that count for anything? I know I've screwed everything up, by not understanding your past and now with Tammy. I know the baby isn't mine, and I'll wait to prove it. I just wish you were waiting by my side, helping me through this. I can't do any-

thing except think about you. The way you look at me, the way your hair brushes across my chest, it all makes me crazy. I can't stop thinking about the first time I saw you at JAM, the way your tight jeans hugged every curve, that black muscle shirt that clung to your body, the way your hair hung down across your face.

I remember our first photo shoot with you, the way I felt when you leaned over me to fix my shirt. God, Ravin! You set my skin on fire! Can't you see we're perfect together?

Ravin, I miss touching your face, I miss running my fingers through your hair. I lay in bed wishing I could hold you, touch you. I miss making love to you, the way you smell, and the way your back arches when I brush my lips across your neck. Ravin, I love you. I miss you, I need you. I know deep in my heart that you feel the same. Come back to me, please.
All my love forever,
Marco.

Ravin sat back and wiped the tear from her cheek. She remembered how Marco used to wipe them away. She missed him more than she thought possible. She reached for the last letter.

Dear Ravin,
I don't want to live this life without you. I don't want to say goodbye. I want to spend the rest of my life with you. I don't know how it happened so fast, falling in love with you. It took me by surprise. My love for you is so intense. Sometimes, when I lay in bed thinking about you, my heart aches. I can hear your voice, smell your perfume . . . I'm going crazy not knowing where you are or if you're okay. Please, I want 'til death do us part' to be with you, and only you.
Love,
Marco

Pauly stood in the doorway as a smile ran across his face. He knew Tammy went into labor the night before and he would be hearing something anytime now. He looked over at Mimi.

"Fly the boy in, Pauly; I'll take care of the rest." She smiled.

Thirty-Eight

Marco looked through the glass at the hospital, watching Tammy's newborn baby boy. The DNA test was finished and now he just had to wait for the results.

"Yeah?" he said, answering his cell.

"Hey, it's Pauly."

"Thank God! Where are you? Where's Ravin? Is she okay?" he asked quickly.

"Relax! Everything's fine. Where are you?"

"Hospital."

"How'd it go?"

"Fine. They are both fine. The doctor said she went early, but the baby is fine."

"And the test?"

"Done, just waiting for the results."

A nurse walked up behind him and handed him a sheet of paper.

"Still there, Marco?" Pauly asked sensing the silence.

"Yeah, the results are here."

"Well?"

"Well, from what I can make out of this, there is a ninety-nine percent chance that I am *not* the baby's father." He breathed a sigh of relief.

"Excellent! Go to the airport. I have a ticket waiting for you."

"You do? To where?"

"Just go. Plane leaves in two hours."

"I'll be on it." He hung up and went to wish Tammy well.

Leaving the hospital, he called Nico. He knew they were all anxious for the results too. He also told him he had to fly out.

"Where?" Nico asked.

"Pauly didn't say. Listen, I know this is going to throw off the schedule. I'm sorry, but if I let her go . . ."

"No, don't worry about it. You've been pretty useless anyway. Marco if you let her go, you'll be even more useless. We were going to spend the next week working with the director on the video. We can do it without you."

"If you need me—"

"Go! We'll call if we need you."

"Thanks, Nico. You have no idea how much this means to me."

"I know, and I bet it'll make a great song too."

He hung up as they reached the hotel and ran upstairs to grab his bags. Brett smiled at him in the hallway and Vinny wished him luck. He was at the airport with half an hour to spare and stopped at the newsstand to buy some pens and paper. He followed the ticket he picked up and realized he was on his way to Italy. *So that's were she's been hiding,* he thought to himself. He settled back in first class and began writing. He didn't stop until the plane landed.

Pauly stood at the gate waiting.

"Hey!" Marco said excited.

"Hey, flight okay?"

"Yeah sure." He looked around. "Where's Ravin?"

"Doesn't even know you're here yet."

"She doesn't?" He had been hoping that she'd be there waiting for him.

"Nope, let's go." He picked up one of Marco's suitcases and led him out to the car. Mimi sat in the back, waiting.

"Marco, this is Aunt Josephine, better known as Mimi. This, Mimi, is Marco."

Marco sat in back of the car, looking at her and wondering why Ravin wasn't with them. Mimi sat and looked at Marco; he was everything she hoped he'd be. So far.

"Well, it's very nice to meet you, Marco. Take off the glasses. I need to see your eyes." Marco obliged, smiling at this older version of Ravin.

"It's nice to meet you, although I wish I knew more about you. Ravin doesn't talk about her family much."

"Really? Doesn't surprise me. That girl doesn't talk much. Never used to be that way though."

"No? What happened?" he asked curious. Maybe he could finally find out some things that Ravin would never talk about.

"A conversation for later, my dear. You have exceptionally nice eyes, my boy. I see now what Ravin likes most about you."

"My eyes, huh?" He felt very comfortable around her, an instant connection.

Pauly drove back the whole way smiling.

"Yes, dear, you have very honest and loving eyes, a very rare tribute I see in men these days. And I've seen many suitors coming for all of my many nieces. Now, Ravin does not know that I have brought you here. She is very upset about the setback in your courtship, but, my boy all will be well soon."

"How can you be sure? She *is* very stubborn. She won't accept my letters, phone calls . . . not that I've even known where she was. I'm worried about her, especially after the whole desert thing."

"What happened in the desert Pauly?" she asked, looking up at him.

"Nothing, Mimi."

"Don't give me that!"

"Just finishing up some past grievances."

"With who?"

"We'll talk later, Mimi."

"You better!" she demanded. She turned to Marco again, turning her voice soft and sweet. "Marco, I'm taking you back to my vineyard. In the back of the property is an old stable house. It's set up for you and Ravin. I will drop you off and settle you in. Then Pauly will take Ravin out and leave her with you. You two will tend to your wounds. Whether you get back together is beyond my control, but if I know my favorite niece, all will be well."

"Think so?"

"I do. See her uncle also fathered another child, during the war. I know that you are not the father to this new child, yet she does not. But because I know human life, I know that this will not affect the way you two feel about each other. Loving people is easy, but to be in love, truly in love the way the two of you are, that's not something you can do on your own. That's special, and once you find it, you can't make it go away. No matter how hard *she* tries. So I've arranged this meeting to bring you back to her."

"Mimi, you are probably the only person who has understood how I feel about her." He looked at her with a new respect. "I can't get her out of my head."

"Don't try. Soul mates never leave, not even in death."

"Can you have more than one?"

"Not living, but they can be reincarnated."

"How can I ever thank you?"

"Treat her well." She kissed his cheek as they pulled up to the stable house.

Marco got out, looking at the breathtaking view. Pauly pulled his suitcases out of the trunk and walked inside with him.

"The fridge is stocked, fresh beds, towels, the usual."

"Thanks."

"How long you want before I bring her out?"

"I don't know, I wouldn't mind a shower."

"Well, you can take a bath, but not a shower. Sorry." He chuckled. "Just be lucky you have running water!"

"Funny."

"I'll have her here by five. Gives you two hours to clean up."

"Thanks."

"No problem." Pauly turned to leave.

"Hey!" Marco called out.

"What?"

"I don't know how to thank you, man. This means the world to me."

"Yeah, I know, just getting her out of her pissy mood will be thanks enough." He left the house laughing.

Marco wandered around briefly, checking the layout of the small house. Each window had a spectacular view of the vineyards and mountains in the distance. He grabbed his suitcase and found the bedroom. He pulled out some clean clothes and stashed the rest in the corner.

The hot bath felt good. It washed away all the bad things that had happened in L.A. He carefully dressed and splashed on Ravin's favorite cologne. He had never worn Polo before, but when he found out that the smell alone drove her crazy, he went out and bought some. It was a little muskier than he normally wore, but he had grown to like it.

When he was happy with his appearance, he walked into the living room. He quickly lit a fire in the fireplace, knowing how much she loved watching the fire. His watch said he still had fifteen minutes before she arrived. He pulled a bottle of wine from the fridge, found some glasses, and poured himself one. He thought about how good it would be to see Ravin again, how empty he felt without her.

Thirty-Nine

"Ravin, are you ready yet?" Pauly called to her.

"Yeah, where are we going anyway?"

"Surprise."

"Pauly, I'm not in the mood for surprises."

"Why not?"

"Because I'm not."

"Did you call Marco yet?"

"I tried. Nico said he's gone."

"Where?"

"He didn't know. Probably off with . . ." She tightened her hands into a fist and mumbled something under her breath.

"No, I know he's not."

"How do you know?"

"I spoke to Nico this morning. Tammy had the baby this morning. It's not his. The test came back negative."

"It's not his?" she gasped, finally allowing herself to feel guilty.

"No, so let's go already."

"Where? Why won't you tell me?"

"Just shut up and let's go. We've gotta stop somewhere first."

"Why are we going out here?" she asked, looking out the window.

"Mimi needs something from the closet. She said you know where some red box was? I have no idea what she's talking about, but she said you would know."

"Yeah, I know she used to keep her favorite jewelry in it. What does she want that for?"

"How am I supposed to know? She told me to have you get it before we go out."

198

"Fine, I'll be right out."

She got out of the car and walked to the door. She could smell the fire and noticed someone was there. She turned to get Pauly to go in with her, but he was already driving away.

"That bastard!" she said under her breath. She touched the doorknob and felt butterflies run through her. Quietly, she opened the door. She could smell his cologne immediately. Her stomach started doing flips and her knees instantly went weak. Pausing in the doorway, she watched Marco walk out from the kitchen. Her heart jumped and she grabbed the doorframe to hold herself up. She couldn't believe how unreal it felt to see him, his dark eyes looking at her with as much passion as she felt.

"Hi," he whispered. He began walking over to her, but stopped before reaching her. Looking at her face brought an overwhelming feeling over him. His love for her hit him hard, over and over again. His hands began trembling and tears filled his eyes.

"What are you doing here?" she asked softly.

"Mimi."

She should have known she was up to something. She walked over to him and touched his hands gently.

"You okay?" he asked, feeling her hands tremble.

"I am now." She looked up at him. He gently wiped the tear rolling down her cheek.

"I am sorry," he whispered.

"I know, I understand. I should be the one to say I'm sorry. I ran out on you like a little kid. I'm embarrassed that I did that. I should have stayed with you, worked it out."

"It's okay. Just don't ever run away again please. I was so worried about you. I haven't slept in weeks."

"Me neither." She gently slid under his arms and laid her head on his chest. Marco wrapped his arms around her. He could feel her heart beating fast next to his.

"Hungry?" he asked, not removing her from his embrace.

"Let me guess, Mimi supplied food too?"

"Oh yeah, there's enough for a few weeks in there."

"I'd rather just hold you."

"Good, me too. I started a fire. Sit with me." He led her over to the couch and sat her down. Kneeling on the floor in front of her, he held her face in his hands. He looked deep into her eyes as a tear ran down his cheek. "Ravin, I love you more than anything in this world. You mean more to me than everything. I . . ." He paused, reaching into his pocket. "I had plans in L.A., but I think this is even better." He pulled the ring out of the box and held it to her finger. "Ravin, will you marry me?"

She looked at him in shock. She was not expecting this; even before Tammy appeared, such a thing never crossed her mind. She closed her eyes and let her emotions answer.

"Yes, I will," she whispered.

The feelings overwhelmed her. Marco slid the ring onto her finger and pulled her into him. It was the first time he had held her in three weeks and he never planned to let go. Leaning down, he took her chin in his hand and looked into her black opal eyes.

"I'm going to take care of you forever."

"I love you, Marco. I always have. I'm sorry for taking off."

"That doesn't matter anymore. I'm here with you now and I plan on staying. No matter what, I love you. We'll take this day by day if that's what you need. Just don't ever leave me again."

"I won't." She leaned in and kissed him. She dissolved with his touch and melted into his arms.

They fell onto the couch, hands roaming over each other's bodies. Ravin pulled his shirt out and began unbuttoning it. He pulled her shirt over her head and kissed every piece of exposed skin, working his way down her stomach.

"This is new?" he whispered and touched her new piercing on her navel.

"Like it?"

"Love it," he said, kissing around it carefully.

She slid his shirt off, running her hands up his chest. Her hands shook from a mixture of emotions. Entwined in one another's arms, Ravin's head spun as she grew feverish with desire. Marco picked her up and carried her into the bedroom, laying her carefully down on the edge of the bed. He slowly unbuttoned her jeans, running his hands underneath the waistband. Ravin gasped with every touch and she slid them off. Marco slid her up onto the bed more, rolling her over onto her stomach. He kissed every part of her body as if it were the last time he would ever touch her. He noticed another new addition to her. She had added a new tattoo. He stopped to examine it carefully.

"What does it mean?" he whispered.

Ravin smiled and rolled over looking into his eyes. "Like?"

"Like? All these changes, what's up?" he asked, making small circles around her nipples with his finger.

"Don't know," she moaned.

"Don't know? Something must have triggered this. I never thought you'd get a tattoo or a belly button ring."

"Marco?" she groaned.

"What?"

"Shut up and make love to me," she demanded, grabbing the back of his head and pulling him down to her. He crushed her with a kiss and she reveled in the strength, the feel of his body, the smell of his skin. They spent the entire night in bed together, touching and exploring like they did the first time.

After a few hours, Ravin went into the kitchen and returned with a bowl of pasta and a loaf of bread. They picnicked in between their lovemaking.

Ravin fell asleep on his chest, feeling consumed with happiness and contentment. She slept through the entire night without a single nightmare.

Marco held her in his arms and watched her sleep. He felt complete with his soon-to-be wife in his arms. For a short time, he felt bad leaving Tammy at the hospital alone with a new baby and no means of support. Maybe he could talk to Ravin about giving her some money to take care of the baby. He didn't love her, but he wasn't heartless.

Pauly and Mimi quietly drove down the lane toward the stable house. They saw the glow of the candles in the bedroom and knew their mission had been successful. Each had a fulfilled feeling in their hearts as they drove back to the main house.

Forty

Ravin awoke around six and gazed over at Marco stretched across the bed on his stomach. She lightly touched his back, watching the muscles quiver under her touch. Lying next to him, she traced the muscles up his spine, through his hair, and back down again.

"I don't have anymore energy left," he muttered half asleep.

She laughed quietly. "I was just touching you."

"I know you, girl. You're too much for me to handle." He rolled over.

Her fingers moved across his jaw line and down his neck. "I wasn't asking for anything." She continued running her fingers across his chest and down his stomach.

"You weren't, huh?" he asked in a disappointed manner.

"No, I don't think I could move from this spot anyway."

"Did I wear you out?" he regarded provocatively.

"Oh yeah, but I loved every second." She laughed.

"You did, huh? Well, I guess I'm gonna have to think of a way to get you out of bed and take you to breakfast."

"Think you can?"

"Oh, I know I can!" he said, tickling her.

She jumped up and wrapped a sheet around her naked body.

"Come here," he said pulling her down onto his chest. He kissed her deeply and pushed her onto her back kissing down her neck.

"I thought you didn't have enough energy left?" She smiled suggestively.

"I just got my second wind." His lips moved down her neck to her breasts, kissing each one attentively.

* * *

202

"You didn't bring any clothes, did you?" he called to her in the bath.

"Why would I have? I thought Pauly was taking me out to dinner."

"Of course. It's weird you know?"

"What's weird?"

"Yesterday, I was at the hospital in L.A. waiting for the DNA tests, and then next thing I know, I'm on a plane here."

"So *how* did all this happen anyway?" she asked, walking into the bedroom wrapped in a towel.

"What?"

"Everything? How did the test turn out? How did you get here? How did you know where I was?"

"Wow, a lot of questions. The test turned out in my favor. I'm not the father. Pauly called me while I was at the hospital. I was on the phone with him when I got the results. He told me to pack my stuff and get to the airport. He had a ticket waiting. I didn't know where I was going until I got on the flight. He and Mimi picked me up from the airport around three and brought me here."

"You met Mimi then?"

"Yeah, I love that woman! She's very inquisitive and super sweet."

"So, I take it she likes you."

"I think so; she told me that you and I are soul mates, like her husband and she are. She told me about the other baby he fathered too."

"She told you that?"

"Yeah."

"I can't believe she told you that!"

"Maybe she thought it pertained to our lives somehow."

"I never though about it that way. That's why she had me read all those letters. God, I feel like an idiot." She looked down at her hands.

"Why would you feel like that?"

"Because I didn't catch on to what she was doing! I spilled my guts to her, told her everything about us, about what's been going on in my life and the changes in the last few months."

"You didn't see it because you were so caught up in it. The baby scare, the desert. Ravin, you've been through a Mafia war, an upside-down relationship, and the pressure from work. All in a couple months. I don't know anyone else who could handle that."

"It wasn't a Mafia war, Marco."

"It looked like that to me. They tried to kill you. By the way, how's your arm?"

"It's fine. Just don't let Mimi hear about it. She'll have the whole family out there."

"Come here." He sat her on his lap. "Now that I've got you, I want to know something."

"What?" She slid her fingers through his hair.

"Stop teasing me. I want to know if you really want to marry me."

"Are you insecure about this or something?"

"A little. I've never asked anyone before."

"Yes, I want to marry you, but only if you promise me something."

"Anything, name it."

"Promise me that you won't have any other girls popping up pregnant and that you'll try to understand my fears."

"No other girls, I promise. Well, I can't promise that they won't try to accuse me or claim anything. It's part of the lifestyle. As for your fears, I can't protect you from them if I don't know what they are."

"Deal." She pushed him back on the bed and kissed him passionately. They both sat up when they heard the knock on the door.

"You aren't dressed. I'll get it." He turned back and stopped in the doorway. "You don't have any other relatives lurking around, do you?"

"Yes, tons. It's probably Mimi or Pauly though."

Marco laughed and answered the door. Pauly stood outside with an overnight bag and a smile.

"Hey, Pauly, come on in."

"No thanks. Clothes for Ravin." He handed him the bag. "I can report back that everything is as it should be?"

"Yes, even better."

"Good, Mimi will be happy. It'll be nice for her to think that she won this round, if you catch my drift?"

"Yeah, I get it."

"Good. Dinner tonight at the house at five. No exceptions."

"I'll let her know."

"Oh, Marco?" he said turning back.

"Yeah?"

"Dress decently." He smiled and got back into the car and drove away.

"Who was it? Pauly?"

"Yeah, he dropped off a bag for you. And he told me to tell you that dinner is at five, no exceptions, and for me to dress decently."

"Oh no, you know what that means?"

"I'm afraid to ask, what?"

"Well, you asked if I had any other relatives lurking around. Guess what?"

"They'll be here tonight?"

"Yep."

"Uh oh, I'm in trouble."

"You'll be fine."

"Listen, if you don't want to tell anyone about our engagement I'll understand."

"I think this is a perfect time to tell them."

"Yeah?" He smiled.

"Yeah, did you bring anything nice?"

"I doubt it." He looked through his suitcase while Ravin pulled out fresh clothes from hers.

"Not much," he said dryly.

"I guess I'll have to take you shopping then." She smiled at him.

"Oh really?" he said, surprised. "I thought you hated shopping."

"I still do, but I would like to get something special for tonight."

"Maybe something to show off that sexy tattoo and belly ring!" he said, raising his eyebrows up and down.

"Sexy tattoo?"

"Well, yeah. What is it anyway?" He sat on the bed pulling her over and lifting her shirt to look at it.

"Egyptian."

"Interesting."

"You don't like it, do you?"

"Yes, I do! It's just a surprise. I didn't think you would ever get one."

"Well, I loved yours, so why wouldn't I?"

"I don't know, and why did you pierce your navel?"

"I have no idea honestly. I can take it out if you want me to."

"No, leave it. I think it's sexy."

"Get dressed. I'll take you to breakfast and then we'll go to a few shops I know."

"Do you want to stop and see Mimi first?"

"No, we'll surprise her later."

They got dressed and walked outside. Marco looked around at the miles of grapevine and turned to her. "How are we going to get anywhere? Pauly drove down here. I can barely see the house."

"Follow me." She grabbed his hand and led him around the back of the stable house to the barn. She swung open the doors. Inside sat a black Ferrari.

"*Whose* is this?" he tried to hide his excitement. Ravin smiled and opened the drivers' door. Marco slid in next to her. "Well?"

"It's mine," she said proudly.

"Yours! You have a Ferrari?"

"Yes, is that a problem?" She smirked. She knew how much he loved fast sports cars. She could imagine how he felt about this car.

"No, not at all! I just never even imagined you would have a car like this."

"Why? You don't think girls like fast cars." She turned on the engine and Marco held his breath as he listened to the engine purr.

"It's just—you have an SUV at home. I though that was more your style."

"I like my truck, but I *love* this car."

"So, why is it here and not in New York?"

"Could you imagine what would happen to this car in New York? Anyway, Roxi would think she was paying me too much if she knew I had this."

"True."

She sped out of the barn, flying through the gears. She looked over at Marco's face. His expression was priceless. It was the same expression her brothers had when they learned she could drive a five-speed. Flying down the dirt road, she honked the horn as she sped past the house. Mimi and Pauly were on the terrace smiling.

"Holy shit!" Marco screamed as she took the turns at seventy miles and hour.

"Is this too fast for you?"

"As long as you can handle it, go, girl!"

She took him through the winding hills as fast as she could handle. Marco laughed the whole way.

"I can't believe you!" he said to her as they got out at a local diner. "I've never seen this side of you."

"I only let go like this here at home."

"Speaking of home," he said as he held open the door for her, "where are we anyway?"

"What do you mean? We're in Italy."

"Well, I know that! What part?"

"Pauly really didn't tell you anything, did he?"

"No, not really. He put me on a plane and picked me up at the airport. I just had enough time to wash up and start a fire. Then you showed up."

"Were you listening on the plane at all?"

"Honestly no, I was writing."

"Oh really? Writing what?" she asked, looking over the menu.

"Songs," he said as the waitress asked for their order.

"Songs? About what?"

"You." He looked around. Everyone was staring at him.

"Me, huh? I'd like to read them, if that's okay with you."

"One condition."

"You and your conditions." She laughed. "What?"

"Tell me why all these people are staring at us."

"They're probably wondering who you are."

"I take it they know you?"

"Of course, I grew up here."

"So, are you going to tell me where 'here' is?"

"Is it bothering you that they're staring at you?"

"Yes, it does," he stated nervously.

"Why? And we're in Ravenna."

"Ravenna?"

"Yes, that's were Daddy got my name from. Why is it bothering you that they're staring at you? You should be use to it by now." She snickered.

"You never get use to it, Ravin, and I know they aren't staring at me for the usual reason. They are here to protect you, and *I'm* the enemy this time."

"No you aren't. I can't believe they scare you."

"They do!"

"You think they're gonna blow your head off, don't you?" She teased.

"Well, the last bunch didn't have a problem shooting at me."

"Different set of circumstances. Anyway, they weren't aiming at you."

"Still."

"Still, Marco, it's not like that all the time. To be honest, that's the first time anyone's tried to hurt me." She whispered across the table. "They use to just follow me and send me threatening letters, but even that hasn't happened in three years."

"You never told me that."

"Why? Would it make a difference?"

"Yes, it does. When you told me about what was happening, I was upset. I thought this happened to you on a regular basis, I had no idea. I meet this fabulous woman and find out that the Mafia is after her. What am I suppose to think?"

"Shh. Don't let anyone hear you . . . please," she begged.

"You didn't tell me it hasn't happened in a long time. You didn't tell me that this wasn't normal. I thought it was."

"I'm sorry, I didn't even think about that. It didn't occur to me that you didn't know." She sighed and looked out the window. "I feel like I've known you forever. I'm comfortable talking to you."

"Okay, but now that I know this new information." He took her hand. "It makes me love you even more." He smiled and squeezed her hand.

He still felt a little uneasy, but she kept reassuring him.

"Shopping?" she asked, reaching the car.

"Show me the way." He held open the driver's door.

She handed him the keys and walked around to the passenger side. "You drive."

"Are you sure?"

"You can drive a stick, right?"

"Of course."

"Well then, let's go." Marco hopped into the car with a huge smile. Ravin smiled at the men standing on the sidewalk watching.

"Tell me where to go." He pulled out.

Marco drove her around, stopping off at the few stores that were in town. They picked up a few outfits each before deciding it was time to go back and get ready.

Mimi greeted Ravin's mother and her two brothers.

"So, Mimi, what's this all about?" Nick asked concerned.

"Nick, my boy, can't I just have a party for Ravin? Do I need a reason?"

"It'd be nice."

"You, my boy, are too negative. I flew Marco in yesterday, and then Pauly dropped Ravin off at the stable house. When we drove out there last night, the candles were lit."

"What's that suppose to mean?"

"Don't you ever pay attention, Nick?"

"I guess not, Mom."

"Ravin left Marco in L.A."

"Why?"

"Apparently, his ex-girlfriend showed up pregnant or something."

"He knocked up some broad and now he expects to get together with my little sister?" Nick said furiously.

"Nicky dear, the test came back negative. Marco wasn't the father of this child. He tried to tell Ravin, but she ran home to forget about him. She couldn't handle the pressure of losing him."

"So, were having a party for her because he wasn't the father to this girl's baby?"

"They never get it do they?" Mimi said to Ravin's mother. She smiled and shook her head.

They set about getting the house ready and cooking the feast. At about four-thirty, all of Ravin's aunts, uncles, cousins, and family friends began arriving.

"Are you ready?" Marco asked Ravin nervously.

"Just about," she called out from the bathroom.

She had dressed Marco in a pair of black dress slacks and a

black silk button down. He looked incredible, especially in black. For herself, she chose tight black low-rise pants and a black sheer sweater.

"Let's go," he said impatiently.

"I'm coming!" She walked out of the bathroom, putting in her silver hoop earrings.

"Not yet!" He laughed and threw his arm around her waist.

She kissed his nose and pushed him out the door. They got into the Ferrari and drove up to the house. Before getting out of the car, she twisted the three-carat diamond ring on her finger and turned to him.

"Listen, my family's kinda strange."

"How strange?"

"You'll see. Just be nice, but mostly be you. I want Mimi to see the man I fell in love with."

"I can't believe I'm nervous!"

"Look at me." She pulled him to her. She gazed into his eyes and felt strong, stirring emotion rise through her.

When she opened the door, she noticed Joey first. She ran over and threw her arms around him. "What are you doing here?" she asked as she spotted her mother and oldest brother. Tears threatened her eyes as she hugged her mom hello. Mimi stood in the doorway pleased.

"Attention, everyone," Mimi called out. "This is Marco." She put her hands on his shoulders.

Marco felt all eyes fall on him. Ravin walked up and stood next to him, slipping her arm around his waist. She looked at her mother when she stated proudly, "This is Marco, my fiancé."

A silence fell over the room; her mother walked up to Ravin and Marco and kissed them both. As the rest of the family congratulated them, Mimi stood in the doorway smiling. She couldn't believe how lucky she was to be here for this.

Embraced into the family, Marco enjoyed this new feeling. After dinner, the men went out on the terrace to enjoy drinks and cigars while the women finished in the kitchen and admired Ravin's new engagement ring.

"So, Ravin dear, any thoughts on what kind of wedding you want?"

"No, I haven't, Aunt Isabella. He only asked me last night."

"Leave her be, Isabella. Let it sink in before we all start making plans," her mother said, warding off the family.

"I'm going to see if the guys have eaten Marco alive yet," Ravin said, making her escape. She went out to the terrace and saw Marco talking to her uncles.

He watched her out of the corner of his eye. The way she interacted with her family was so different. She was so relaxed and at ease, and he was amazed at the difference. He held out his hand as she walked up to him. She wrapped her fingers in his and led him off to the side.

"How ya doing?" She smiled.

"Fine, you?"

"Good. Are they treating you okay?"

"Yeah. I'm having a great time. A little overwhelming, but I really like your family."

"You don't have a big family, do you?"

"Nope. Just my mom and her parents. I think I have two cousins and an aunt somewhere, but I haven't seen them since I was real young."

"So, this is pretty intense then, huh?"

"Yeah, a little."

"This isn't even half of them. This is only part of the family from town."

"You're kidding?"

"Nope."

"When can we escape?"

"What'dya have in mind?"

"Just want to be alone for a few minutes."

"Follow me." She took his hand and led him down the steps to the yard. They walked over to the hammock and sat down. He pulled her onto his chest and wrapped his arms around her.

"So, what's up?" she asked.

"Just need to be with you. They keep asking what kind of wedding we want. I didn't have any kind of answer for them. I guess it's something we need to discuss, huh?"

"No."

"Why not?"

"Because."

"Ravin, no secrets."

"Dominic and I made plans. Big plans, cake, flowers . . . the works. The day we went out to pick out our rings, he got killed."

"Pauly told me that had nothing to do with you. He said he was skimming off the top or something."

"When did Pauly tell you this?" She looked at him surprised.

"In L.A."

"Really? What else did he tell you?"

"That's about it. So, because of Dominic you're nervous about planning our wedding?"

"Sort of. Marco, you just asked me last night. It hasn't sunk in yet."

"Its definitely hit me. I was planning on doing this back in L.A. When Brett told you that you needed a nice dress, it was for this reason. I had the fancy restaurant all set up and everything."

"Really?" she asked saddened.

"Really."

"I feel bad now."

"Don't. I still got a chance to ask you, didn't I?" His arms wound around her, pulling her to his chest and holding her close.

"Yes, you did. And honestly, I think I liked this proposal better than a fancy restaurant."

"Figures."

"Why do you say that?"

"Don't take this the wrong way, but you're simple."

"I'm simple?"

"Yes, *you* are simple. You like the simple things in life, walks on the beach and candlelit dinners for two with hot dogs and a lounge chair. Flashy things don't impress you."

"Truth, loyalty, and honesty do though."

"Of course, with the exception of the Ferrari."

"That doesn't count though."

"Why not?"

"Because it's a car."

"So?"

"So, it's a car. It doesn't count."

"Why?" he teased.

"The only thing that impresses me about the car is the way it handles, not how much it costs or who makes it. It's the performance that impresses me."

"Oh . . . so performance impresses you, does it?" he said playfully.

"Oh yes, your performance, stamina, and endurance impress me." She laughed.

"Yes well . . ." He leaned back, "Everything about you impresses me."

"You're kidding?"

"No, I'm not."

"Why do I impress you?"

"Your strength."

"My strength?"

"Yes, you are the strongest, most level-headed person I know. You don't care what people think about you and you have incredible confidence in yourself. It shows in everything you do."

"Is that so?"

"Yes. Ravin, I don't know how to express what I feel. I'm not sure there are even words to explain the feelings I have. All I know is that when you left, my heart dropped through the floor. When I didn't know where you were, I worried so much I couldn't even eat. Nico just about beat the hell out of me trying to keep me concentrating enough on the video. I guess you could say when you left, you took my heart with you, because it sure wasn't with me."

"I'm sorry."

"Stop saying that. We're here together, where we belong. I told you I wasn't gonna let you go easily. I love you too much. I know we belong with each other."

"I'm glad you're here. I've been lost without you too. I should probably apologize to Pauly for driving him crazy."

"You drove him nuts, huh?"

"Yes, he tried everything. He took me to Milan to do a few shoots. He took me to the island spa. He tried everything, nothing worked, not even the food."

"I can tell. You look like you lost a few pounds."

"I have not!"

"Sure, you have. I can tell. I know every part of your body and the tattoo wasn't the only change. I wasn't the only one who noticed either. Nick asked me if you were sick, although I think he was secretly wondering if I had gotten you pregnant or something."

"You're kidding." She looked at him.

"No."

"What did you say?"

"Nothing. I didn't know what to say."

"Great."

"Rave, he's pissed at you. You didn't call him when you came here. You didn't stop in New York. He's been going nuts."

"He knew where I was."

"Yeah but—" He looked out at the grapevines and back at her. "He's your brother and he feels like a father to you. He was worried and he didn't know how to fix it."

"Fix what?"

"Your pain. He couldn't fix your pain and neither could I. You have no idea how frustrating and hard it is to feel so helpless like that."

"I called him."

"Well, you better talk to him. Let him know what's going on."

"I will, tomorrow. Tonight is about us."

"Should we go back to the party?"

"Probably."

"You don't want to go?"

"Not really. I'd rather grab some more wine and walk back to the stable house with you."

"Walk?"

"It's a beautiful night. The vineyard's peaceful. I've spent a lot of time walking through thinking about you."

"You did?"

"You were on my mind every second of every day, Marco. You should know that."

"I do, but you aren't the most open about your feelings."

"I know, I'll work on that."

"As long as I know you love me, that's good enough."

"I'll love you until death do us part."

Marco stood up and pulled Ravin off the hammock. They headed back to the party, hand in hand. Ravin could feel the ring twisting on her finger and it felt good. Most of all, it felt right.

"You two are still here?" Uncle Tony asked as they walked up.

"It's my party, Uncle Tony." She laughed.

"Go. Get the hell out of here. Enjoy being young. Go frolic in the grapevines, I've taken your Aunt Isabella there enough times!" he roared.

Ravin and Marco burst out laughing and went inside to talk to her mother.

"Hi, Mamma." She walked up behind her.

"You two are still here?"

"Why does everyone keep asking that?"

"Just thought you'd be off by yourselves somewhere."

"Well, I guess we'll go then. Just wanted to get some more wine."

"Ravin honey, I packed all your things and had Pauly put them in your car. Stay at the stable house as long as you like."

"Thank you, Mimi. Thank you for everything, for putting up with me, but mostly for bringing Marco back to me."

"I just followed your heart for you. Sometimes you young kids need a kick in the ass! I won't expect you at breakfast, but you are welcome." She kissed Ravin and Marco and shuffled them out the door.

"Momma! How long are you staying?" she called out.

"A few days. We'll talk tomorrow."

Marco held open the door for Ravin as she slid into the seat of her car. They drove back to the stable with Ravin promising him a walk through the grapevines. They made love under the moon that night. It was the most magical thing that had ever happened to either one of them.

Forty-One

Marco brought their coffee into the bedroom and looked at Ravin sitting on the bed with her cell phone in her hand.

"I haven't turned this on in three weeks. It's time I came back to the real world, huh?" she looked up at him.

"I think your first call should be to Brett. She's pretty worried about you."

"Have you talked to her?"

"Yeah. She spent a lot of time trying to persuade me that you were fine and you'd be back soon. She's a pretty great person, doesn't deserve being left out."

"I get the point, although she should know me well enough."

"She does. She said she knew where you were, but she wouldn't tell me."

"Mind if I call her?"

"No, I wouldn't, but I think she would. She might still be sleeping. It's earlier there."

"True, I get so confused with these time zones."

He lay on the bed next to her and rested his hand on the small of her back.

"Hello?" Brett answered quietly.

"Hate me?"

"Ravin! My God! Are you okay?"

"Of course, I am."

"Were the hell are you?"

"Italy."

"Thought so. Where's Marco? Have you heard from him at all?"

"He's here next to me."

"Thank God!" she stated and then yelled out to Vinny, "Ravin's on the phone. She's with Marco."

"How's everything?"

"Fine. We haven't worked much since you left. So, what's going on? Tell me everything, Ravin. I'm so pissed that you haven't called me at all."

"I'm sorry. I needed to be alone. Get myself together."

"So, how did Marco find you?"

"Mimi and Pauly brought him here. I didn't know anything about it."

"So, you were forced to see him? I hoped you worked things out?"

"Yes, as a matter of fact we did." She winked at Marco.

"Vinny wants me to tell you to tell Marco that he's gonna have to be back by Sunday. They're shooting the video Monday morning at seven."

"We'll be there."

"You coming too?"

"Yes, I'm coming back. Just gonna stay today and we might leave tonight."

"Well, let me know. I can arrange whatever you need."

"Thanks, Brett. Oh, by the way, how's Roxi? Is she pissed?"

"Oh yeah, you didn't call her either."

"Sorry."

"Don't be. I'd do the same thing. Anyway, she's been able to use some leftover shots from past sessions, so she's been able to keep up the magazine. But she really needs you to come back."

"I'll call her later."

"Rave, you've gotta hurry back. I've got so much to tell you."

"Stuff you can't say now?"

"Exactly."

"I'll see you tomorrow, hon. Listen, tell the guys so they don't worry about Marco."

"I will. Hey, did everything turn out okay with you two?"

"Even better than I imagined."

"Excellent! He told you the baby wasn't his?"

"Yes, he did."

"Good, I'll let you go. Let me know what time your flight is tomorrow."

"I will. Love you, hon."

"Love you too. Bye."

Ravin was relieved Brett wasn't too angry with her. Of course, now she had to call Roxi and that would be a different conversation altogether.

"Everything fine?" Marco asked.

"Yeah, she's gonna tell the boys that we'll be back tomorrow."

"Tomorrow, huh?"

"Yes, is that okay?"

"Well, I suppose so. I'd much rather hang out here with you forever."

"So would I, but I have to get back to work. So do you. You have a video shoot Monday morning at seven."

"Okay, as long as you're coming with me."

"I'll come to L.A. with you, but I'm not sure how long I'll be staying. Roxi needs me for the magazine."

"I know, but you have to at least give me the weekend in L.A."

"I promise."

"Good. What should we do today?"

"I want to spend some time with my mom and brothers."

"Of course, but I have two questions I want to ask you."

"Shoot."

"First, we will at some point need to talk about our wedding. I know you're uncomfortable with it, so I'll let you lead the way. But, Ravin, I don't want you to avoid this. I'll need an idea so I can arrange our tour around it, okay?"

"Okay."

"Second, is there any reason why Pauly didn't need to come with us into town?"

"I'm home, no surprises here." She looked down, playing with her fingers.

"What do you mean?"

"Ya know, Marco, the whole world isn't out to get me." She pushed herself off the bed.

"I know. You never really sat down and explained the whole story to me."

"I know and that's something I have to do before I marry you. I need you to know my entire past, as I need to know yours. But I'll need a little time to put it all into words and find a time that we won't be interrupted."

"I'll make the time." He walked over to her and wrapped his arm around her waist. "I'll make the time." He whispered as he kissed her.

Forty-Two

Ravin hated leaving her family behind, but duty called. She sat back on the plane and rested her head on Marco's shoulder. Roxi had faxed the itinerary she had set up for L.A., and although she was mad at her, she was happier that she was coming back. She pulled out her black book and started writing notes for each day.

"Roxi keeping you busy?" Marco asked, looking over at a very full week.

"You have no idea." She shook her head.

"Well, I guess she wants to either make you catch up or torture you."

"More like torture. Do you realize I'm shooting every day this week?"

"Everyday, huh? Anytime to schedule me in?"

"Let me check." She laughed. "Depends how much time you want and what part of the day!"

"I'll take what I can get. I'll probably have the same insane schedule you do. Nico said we have a lot to do. Apparently, I set us back a few weeks."

"I'm sorry, Marco."

"Don't be. It was worth it."

"Hey, look at this!"

"What?"

"I already have you scheduled in." She pointed to Wednesday afternoon.

"Oh yeah?"

"Looks like you have another photo shoot to do."

"You're shooting it?"

"Yep!"

"Good. I love working with you."

"So do I." She smiled and kissed him gently.

Marco kissed her back and pulled out his black book. "Love me?"

"You know I do." She smiled.

"Good. Now leave me alone; you aren't the only one who got faxes today." He playfully pushed her away.

They sat side-by-side jotting notes in their books as the ground below slipped away. Between talking and working, the flight went by quickly. They arrived in L.A. around two o'clock and walked out of the gate hand in hand. Brett and Vinny ran over when they saw them.

"Ravin!" Brett shouted as she ran up to her and gave her a huge hug.

"Hey, Brett, how are things?" she choked out as Brett hugged her.

"Look at you! You look so good!" Brett beamed, holding her at arms length.

"I don't look any different than before. You look different, you cut your hair."

"Yeah, like it?"

"I do, looks good on you. Hey, Vinny." She leaned over and kissed his cheek; he hugged her and kissed her back.

"Hey, Marco. How was the flight?"

"Boring. All she wanted to do was work."

"Very funny, Marco. You were the one with your face stuffed in that book," she said playfully.

"Rave, there's something different about you. I can't put my finger on it." Brett looked sideways at her.

Ravin and Marco looked at each other and smiled. She told him Brett would know she just had to wait until she figured it out. They jumped into the limo and sped off for the beach house.

"Ravin, what is that on your finger?" Brett asked, pulling her hand closer. "Oh my God! Is this what I think it is?" She looked up at Ravin as a huge smile spread across her face.

"Something you want to tell us, Marco?" Vinny asked.

"I asked Ravin to marry me," he said with a proud smile.

"Well, I guess congratulations are in order!"

"Thanks, man."

"The first to go. Wow!"

"I can't believe this! Ravin, when? How? I need details!" Brett shouted, still staring at the ring.

"We'll get into it later," she said covering her mouth in a yawn.

"Along with how the hell you two got back together."

"I'll tell you the whole story. First, I want a shower and some food."

"Me too, I'm starving," Marco said, stretching out in the back seat. He closed his eyes and let his mind drift away. He was looking forward to going back to the beach house with Ravin. He couldn't wait to walk down the beach with her and make love to her on the sand.

"Where's Pauly?" Brett asked.

"Vacation."

"Comfortable with that?"

"Why wouldn't I be? Marco's here. He'll watch over me, right?" Ravin nudged him.

"Huh?"

"Are you in there?"

"Sorry, what did you say?"

"Brett asked where Pauly was. I told her I sent him on vacation and that you would watch over me."

"Damn right I will." He squeezed her hand.

"I guess that's settled. Where do you want to eat tonight?"

"It doesn't matter to me," Ravin said, looking over at Marco for his opinion.

"I'm game for anything. Somewhere close by though. I've had enough traveling for a few days."

"Sounds good to me," Ravin said, yawning again.

"We could all walk down to that little dive down the beach." Brett suggested.

"Yeah, great cheeseburgers there," Vinny said. He looked over at Marco and Ravin they were both fast asleep. He and Brett exchanged glances and shrugged.

"Hey, Rave, Marco wake up! We're here." Brett slapped her leg. Ravin blinked and sat up. She looked out the window at the beach house.

"I thought we were going back to the hotel."

"No, we checked out the day you left. We've all been staying here."

"Cool." Ravin gently touched Marco's face. He was still asleep. "Hey, wake up."

Marco sat up and looked over at the beach house. A smile spread across his face.

"I suppose you stole the good room?" He looked over at Vinny.

"No, we left it for you."

"You're kidding?"

"Yeah, you called dibs on it. You get it."

"Awesome! Wait until you see this bedroom. It's so great."

"I'm looking forward to it," she said getting out of the limo.

"Hey! Anyone here!" Vinny called out as he opened the door.

"Hey Vin, Brett," Cole said, walking by. He almost didn't notice Marco and Ravin come in behind them. "Marco! Ravin! I can't believe you're here. Are you okay?"

"Yeah fine." She smiled and hugged him.

"Nico! Marco and Ravin are here!" he yelled out back.

Nico and Brody came running in, pulling Ravin into a bear hug.

"What's going on? Are we back together?" Nico asked.

"Yes, we are." Ravin smiled.

After a refreshing shower, Ravin sat at the edge of the bed watching Marco finish dressing. She slid on a pair of tight black running pants and a half shirt. She walked over, slid on her three-carat engagement ring, and applied a small amount of eyeliner. She grabbed her clip and was about to put her hair up.

"No, wear it down," he said taking the clip from her hand.

"Why? Do you like it down?"

"Yes."

"It's messy!"

"No, it isn't. It's sexy."

"But the wind's gonna blow it all over the place." She looked over at his face. His big brown eyes begged as child would for candy. She shook her hair loose, and Marco smiled, winning a small battle. He grabbed the back of her neck, kissing her eagerly.

"Let's go, Rave! I'm hungry," Brett yelled in.

"We're coming," she yelled back. She grabbed Marco's hand and walked out into the living room.

As they sat at the table, Ravin looked around at probably the best friends she'd ever had. Happiness swept over her and a smile spread across her face.

"What are you smiling about?" Brody asked, looking over at her.

"You guys."

"What about us?" Cole asked.

She looked over at Marco; he set his hand on her leg and smiled. "Okay, here goes."

She took a deep breath and held up her hand to show off her new ring. Nico almost dropped his cheeseburger and looked back and forth from Ravin to Marco.

"Are you kidding me?" he bellowed.

"Nope," Marco replied with a proud smile on his face.

"Is that what I think it is?" Cole asked, shocked.

"Yes."

"Holy crap! I can't believe this!" Nico ran over and pulled Ravin into an enormous hug. "This is great! Congratulations!" He shook Marco's hand.

The rest of the night went by quickly. They caught up on every-thing from the video to tour dates. Ravin felt guilty every time Marco apologized for all the delays. The rest of the guys all assured them that she was more important and Marco's happiness was the key to success for the next tour. They talked about her career and their visit to Italy. Marco told them about the Ferrari she had hidden away— and how well she drove it.

"God, she took you for a ride in that car?" Brett sighed.

"Yeah, why?"

"I'm surprised you're still here. She's tried to kill me in that car I don't know how many times!" she laughed.

"I wasn't trying to kill you!"

"You certainly drove like you were."

Ravin dismissed her with a wave of her hand.

"She drives like a maniac," Brett added.

"No, I don't, at least not with anyone else with me."

"You drive faster?" Marco looked at her in shock.

"Yeah, I've pegged it a few times."

"Who the hell taught you to drive like that?" Cole questioned.

"Pauly, for defensive purposes, or at least that's what he said."

For Ravin, the night ended perfectly. She felt safe and loved around her friends. She just wished Pauly had been there to enjoy it.

Thirty-One

Ravin sat on the beach with her black notebook, watching the sunrise. Marco was right; the ocean did something for her creativity that she just couldn't stop. She would have preferred to have him with her, but she didn't want to wake him. She set her mind free and wrote down ideas for the photo shoots Roxi had set up for her in L.A. She didn't hear Marco walk up behind her.

"Damnit, Marco! Don't do that!" she shrieked as he sat behind her and wrapped his arms around her.

"Sorry, I thought you heard me coming."

"No, I didn't."

"What'cha doing out here all alone? Pretty girl like you shouldn't watch the sunrise by herself."

"I didn't want to wake you. I've been up for a while."

"I know. I saw you leave around four. Are you having nightmares again?"

"No, well sort of. Nothing to stop me from sleeping. I'm just not use to so much sleep now. I guess it'll take a while to get back to normal."

"Never thought about that. What'cha writing?"

"You know," she said as she turned and looked at him, "you were right about the ocean."

"Oh yeah? About what?"

"Creativity. I can't stop it."

"Told ya. Amazing isn't it?"

"Amazing yes, and powerful too. I was lying in bed and all I heard were the waves crashing on the shore. It's very . . ." she paused for the right word.

"It's the rhythm of the waves that do it to you."

She smiled, knowing there was another meaning in there some-where. He read her mind and playfully smacked her shoulder.

"Dirty mind."

"I didn't say anything." She smiled seductively.

"What time do you have to go today?"

"By ten. You?"

"Nine o'clock meeting, then I guess we go right into the second video."

"Will you be gone all day?"

"Probably, and probably most of the night. I've got a lot of catching up to do—and don't say you're sorry."

"I'll try to swing by for lunch or dinner or something, unless they don't let you eat."

"We eat." He chuckled. "I'd have to call you with a time though."

"That's fine."

"Want anything to eat?"

"No, but a cup of coffee would be great right about now."

"Okay, I'll get it. You work."

"Thanks, babe." She watched him walk back up to the house and jotted down a few more notes.

"Ravin, where do you want this set up?" Randy asked, popping his head in the door.

"Randy! What are you doing here?"

"Surprise! Roxi flew me out. Thought you might need some experience to help you catch up."

"You have *no* idea. This is awesome."

"Good, let's get to work." He walked over and gave her a hug.

She filled him in on what they were shooting and he went right to work, falling perfectly in step with her.

Alex and Mark looked at this new guy and wondered what he was doing. *They* were hired to help Ravin, after days of begging and a little bribing.

"She must know him or something."

"Ya think, Mark? I think he's worked with her before."

"Does this mean we're out?"

"Not if I can help it." Alex set down the lights Ravin had requested and walked over to her.

"Okay Ravin, what do you need me to do?"

"Hi, Alex . . . yeah . . . can you get me the box of film in the back and my black bag please?"

"Yeah sure," he said confused. "Want me to help with the lighting?"

"No thanks. I think I've got it under control." She smiled and walked away.

"What's that all about?" Randy asked, walking over to her.

"That was Alex. From what I here, he did a lot to get to work with me, and I think I bruised his ego sending him for my bag and film."

"Aww, poor thing. Yet another youth scarred for life by the famous Ravin Capello."

"Very funny, Randy!"

"Yeah, yeah. You setting up this?" he asked, picking up another prop.

She shook her head and finished setting up the models. Alex returned with her film and black bag.

"Okay, here we go. Randy?" She looked over at him. He picked up the first camera he had lined up on the table and handed it to her. He then reached over and flipped on her stereo. Music blared from the speakers and that was the last thing she said.

Alex and Mark watched in amazement. Randy knew every move she made before she made it. He had the cameras loaded in record time and stood waiting for her to hand off the used one. They worked remarkably well together, and in a pinch, it showed.

With Randy here, she knew the day would be shorter. Once she finished the first shoot, they walked back to the darkroom together without looking back.

Forty-Four

Marco and the boys worked their asses off to finish the video. After ten hours, the director called it quits. They asked if it was possible to finish that night.

"Aren't you guys tired?"

"Well yeah, but if we only have a few more scenes to do, we'd rather finish it up tonight. We've got two other videos to do this week," Nico told the director.

"Not to mention a concert, publicity, and three photo shoots," Brody added for the effect.

"Fine with me, as long as you guys are willing."

After three more hours, they finished their second video. They were all exhausted, but it felt good to get one more thing behind them. Marco's disappearance to Italy set them back a few weeks.

"Did you talk to Ravin today?" Cole asked, waiting for their turn on the set.

"I talked to her after lunch."

"How's she doing?"

"Good. Roxi flew Randy in to help her out. She's happy about that. I guess the guys they hired to help her weren't very good."

"Oh no? I wonder why." He chuckled sarcastically.

"Probably because she's a pain in the ass to work with!"

"I can't believe you just said that!"

"Why? She is! Even she knows it."

"I didn't have a hard time with her."

"Yeah, but you were on the other end of the camera. She's pretty abrupt with her demands. It took a few years before Randy was able to work with her. They have been together for almost five years now, and he knows everything about her."

"Where is all this coming from, man?"

"Pauly and I were talking in Italy. He was telling me how she got started and stuff."

"I see. Anything interesting?"

"The usual, except that she's been gifted from the start and that she's always been very guarded—even more than she is now."

"Wow. Well, I'm glad she's opened up." Cole snickered, wondering how she could have been even more guarded than she was now.

"Me too. What time is it? I can't find my watch."

"It's almost ten-thirty," Cole said, looking down at his watch. He let out a small yawn and wished they could finish up.

"That's a wrap!" the director called out.

"Cool," Marco whispered.

Cole smiled grateful as his wish came true. After packing up they all headed back to the beach house to relax.

Nico walked into the living room first and saw Brett and Mia spread out across the floor in front of a large poster board. "What exactly are you two doing?" he asked, laughing.

"Well, let's see. They're eight of us, all with crazy schedules for a week or so. We decided to make out a schedule so everyone knows where they are suppose to be and at what time," Mia replied with a smile.

"What a great idea!" Nico said, looking down at the schedules.

"Thanks." Mia smiled.

"Yes, Mia is the official organizer." Brett looked up.

"That's great. We could use one of those." Nico smiled.

Mia smiled, looking up at Nico. His face went soft as he smiled back at her.

Brett's eyes scanned from one to the other watching their expressions.

"Where's Ravin?" Marco asked, walking back out of his bedroom.

"She isn't back yet," Brett stated as Vinny pulled her up off the floor.

"Where the hell is she?" Panic bubbled from deep down in Marco's gut.

"I guess she's still working," Brett stated calmly.

"She couldn't possibly be shooting this late!" Marco looked around for her, thinking.

"She's probably developing, Marco."

Marco pulled out his cell phone and quickly dialed her number. He walked out onto the back deck, waiting for her to answer. After letting it ring a dozen times, he hung up and paced around the deck. Pauly was still away and he had a funny feeling deep inside. He wasn't sure what it was, but he knew he didn't like not knowing if Ravin was all right.

"Brett! Do you know where she was developing from?" Marco asked quickly as he rushed into the room.

"No, I don't know. Mia?" Brett questioned.

"She isn't picking up her cell. She always picks up her cell!" Marco spat.

"Yeah, but not when she's in the darkroom, Marco. You know she can't have it on when she's in there," Brett replied dismissively.

"I know." He looked down at his phone again and decided to try again.

"Sorry, Marco," Ravin said into the phone.

"Thank God, are you okay?"

"I'm fine. I'm on my way home now. I heard the phone. I just didn't get there in time."

"What were you doing?"

"Are you sounding jealous?"

"No. Sorry I just got scared for a minute. Pauly's not with you and I don't know—"

"Don't worry, Marco."

"Okay, I'll try not to worry so much," He said, thinking there was no way that would happen.

"I'll be home in fifteen minutes or so." She clicked off her phone and sped down the highway to the beach house.

Forty-Five

"Ravin! Let's go!" Brett yelled from the front door.

"I'm coming! Relax, Brett. We'll be there."

"I know, I just haven't seen Vinny in three days. I miss him."

"I know I miss Marco too. We'll be there before you know it," she said shaking her head and locking the front door.

The boys were away on location, and this was the first day off the girls had to go and see them. The beach house had become their home on the West Coast, although Ravin missed New York more than she thought she would. She had become the hottest photographer on both coasts. When word got out that she was out west and taking jobs, calls came in daily. Everything from Hollywood stars and their families to ad campaigns and model portfolios desperately wanting her service. She was busier than she ever had been in her career. Randy stayed on, splitting his time between both coasts, but he wasn't enough; she hired three more assistants and had Mia on the set with her daily. Mia kept Ravin organized. Even the poster board at the house had become invaluable. Everyone relied on it to know where to be and when. Ravin's brother Nick came out for two weeks and went back and forth to her shoots with her. This made Marco relax and tend to his own work. He came back full speed and finished the music to the songs he had written on the plane. Ravin got a personal concert and smiled proudly. The rest of the band was impressed and almost grateful to Ravin for leaving him; after all, they were only a few songs short for their next album.

Ravin pulled her rented Durango onto the set and looked around. Everyone seemed to be sitting around, and she didn't think that was how it was suppose to be.

"What's going on?" she asked, walking up.

"Director hasn't shown up yet." Marco pushed himself out of his chair to hug her. He rested his head on her shoulder and snuggled into her neck.

"Where is he?"

"Jack's trying him again."

"I'm sorry," she said, waving to Jack. She and Jack had met a week ago during another shoot for a female rock group he was managing. She must have made quite an impression on him, because he had requested more sessions from Roxi.

"I'm just glad you're here."

"Me too. If there's anything I can do, let me know." And with that, she playfully smacked his arms as he raised his eyebrows up.

"Later, my boy! Later!" She laughed.

"Hey, Marco. Hi Ravin. Nice to see you again." Jack walked up, tucking his cell phone into his pocket.

"What's the story, Jack?"

"Still can't reach him. I talked to his neighbor and he said he hadn't seen him either."

"So, what the hell are we suppose to do?"

"I'll have to think about that. Give me a few to figure something out."

"You better do something."

Jack Gallivan sat on the edge of the sound stage, talking with the head of production.

"Jack, I don't know what to tell you. We haven't heard anything yet."

"Think we should start without him? I mean, we only have today to use the sound stage."

"I'd say yes, but I don't have anyone available to send out to you, unless you think you can do it yourself."

"Me? I've never done a video alone."

"I know."

"Ravin Capello is here."

"Ravin Capello? The photographer?"

"Yes."

"Why's she there?"

"She's tight with Marco."

"Really? Well, if you want to ask her to help, go for it, as long as everyone's good with that. Talk to the band, talk to the crew. Give it a shot. If anything you'd end up with rolls of useless film. That'll cost a lot of money if nothing turns out."

"I know. That's what I'm worried about."

"On the other hand, if she can get most of it, you'll be all right."

"True. I'll ask her."

"If she says no, just follow the story board and do what you can."

"Thanks."

Jack paced the ground, trying to figure out what to do. Asking Ravin would be risky. Or would it? She knew about lighting, and camera angles, and she definately knew the band. The more he thought about it, the better it sounded. If it didn't turn out, he could always blame her.

"Ravin, could I talk to you a minute?" Jack called out.

Ravin looked at Jack and shook her head. She looked at Marco and shrugged her shoulders.

"I'll be back."

"Sure." Marco smiled as she walked away.

"What's up, Jack?"

"What would you say if I asked you to help me direct the video?"

""I'd say you're nuts." She laughed.

"Honestly, what would you say?"

"Are you serious?"

"Very."

"What about the director?"

"I called the production company. They haven't heard anything either. They asked me to give it a shot."

"So, why are you asking me?"

"Well, I don't know this group at all and I haven't done many videos. I know you're close to them, and I know that you are an incredible photographer. You know about lighting and angles. That's where I'll need your help."

"You are kidding?"

"No, I'm afraid not. If we don't use this stage today, we lose out. It's booked for the next two weeks."

Ravin leaned against the stage and thought for a moment. She knew she could handle it, but she wasn't sure how everyone around her would deal with it.

"Well, I guess if they're gonna lose all sorts of money."

"You are a lifesaver."

"What do I do?"

"Well, first let me introduce you to the crew, and then we'll go back and look over the storyboard. I'll show you what they had in mind."

"Where's Ravin?" Brett asked, walking over to Marco.

Vinny sat next to him and pulled Brett onto his lap.

"I don't know. She went over to talk to Jack and I haven't seen her since." He looked around the set for her.

"What's going on, man? Are we just gonna sit here all day?"

"I have no idea, but we better do something soon." Marco shifted in his chair. He couldn't handle sitting around doing nothing when there was so much to do. He looked over at Vinny when he waved over to Ravin, walking up with Jack at her heels.

"Okay, here's what's happening." She motioned to Nico, Brody, and Cole to join them. "Jack still can't get a hold of the director, so with the blessings of the production company . . ." She paused, looking at everyone. "Jack and I are going to do it."

She watched all their mouths drop in amazement.

After a few seconds, Nico chimed in. "I think that's a great idea! Who knows us better? You're a fantastic photographer. Directing can't be that different."

"Well, it is, but you're right. I do know you well and I know lighting. So with Jack and the crew's help, I think we can pull it off."

"Let's get to work!" Marco stood up, grabbed Ravin by the arm, and steered her off to the side. "Sure you want to do this?"

"Why? If anything it'll be fun."

"Do you trust Jack?"

"I'm not sure, but I get the impression you don't."

"He's just so . . ." He glanced over at Jack, his body language mimicking that of a snake. "Inexperienced."

"Yeah, I know, but he showed me the cameras and I've talked to some of the crew. They're willing to give me their all. All I have to do is make sure it turns out the way it's supposed to."

"Oh, not too much pressure, Rave!"

"You know I work better under pressure! Anyway, you'll lose out if we don't try. If we do, one of two things will happen: We get no usable footage and waste the stage, or we get some usable footage and don't waste the stage."

"Good point, so now what?"

"Get your ass into wardrobe!" She laughed.

"Ooh, she's already acting like a director! Love you." He gave her a quick kiss on the cheek.

Ravin sat in the director's chair next to the camera screen and told Jack to get it into gear. The lighting crew talked to her throughout the day, asking her to speak up if the lighting wasn't right. She sat back, watched her boys singing and dancing on cue, and viewed it as it all came to life on the screen.

After a full day of shooting, Ravin was happy with how it turned out. She was told that the film would be ready the following morning if she wanted to view it.

"Ravin, it's been a pleasure working with you," Jack said, walking up behind her.

"Thanks, Jack. It was fun."

"You did a great job. You're a natural."

"Well, I wouldn't go that far."

"My boss will. Are you gonna be around tomorrow?"

"Most likely. Marco can always get a hold of me if need be."

"Excellent, see you tomorrow."

Ravin joined Marco and the boys around the buffet table.

"Where else would I find you, Brody?" She laughed. "How do you think it went?"

"I thought it went great. You sure looked comfortable sitting there." Cole laughed.

"Yeah well, I didn't feel comfortable. I think Jack's up to something."

"Why do you say that?" Cole cocked his head looking at her.

"Instinct. He just seemed to drop it on me too easily. Don't you think?"

"I think you should trust your instincts. I thought it was a little weird to just throw you into the director's chair, but, hey what do I know?" Cole laughed.

"I agree. Follow your instincts, Rave." Brett shook her head as she pulled a root beer out of the cooler.

Ravin sat on Marco's lap and tried to push back the bad feeling that hung heavy around her. She felt that Jack was up to something as soon as they began shooting when he stepped back and let her take over. She felt exhilarated directing, but at the same time, she felt stifled not being able to control the whole video. Jack sat in the background, fielding phone calls and doing pretty much nothing. That was the first tip that she was in for some friction. She wasn't sure from which side.

After they wrapped up, Ravin and the rest of the guys went back to the hotel. Ravin was up most of the night studying the storyboard and making one of her own.

Forty-Six

"Jack!" Mason yelled from the editing room.

Mason Reid was the head producer on this project and one of the heads of the studio. Jack walked in with his tail between his legs ready to blame Ravin for whatever was coming at him.

"Yes, Mason?"

"Jack, did you have anything to do with this video?"

"I'm not sure what you mean." He sat nervously on the couch.

"Did you shoot any of this video? It's a real simple question, Jack."

"No, sir, Ravin did all the work. I tried to stop her, but . . ." He paused.

"She's good."

"Good?" Jack asked, surprised.

"Yes, Jack, very good. I want her to finish up the video." Mason stood up, a motion for Jack to leave and that the conversation was over.

"But, Mason, she's never done anything like this before. She has no idea how to shoot a video."

"I tend to disagree. At least she knows what the hell she's looking at. And you, my friend, are going to stand behind her and give her anything she needs. *Is this understood*? I hear any problems coming from you and you will not work in Hollywood again."

Jack stood up and nodded. He knew not to mess around with Mason Reid. He could get kicked out of the business with one phone call from him.

Mason picked up the phone and dialed the hotel number that Marco and the guys were staying.

"Hello?" Marco answered the phone.

"Marco? This is Mason Reid." Marco sat up in bed quickly.

"Mason, how are ya? What's going on? Did you find our director?"

"Yes, I did, but it isn't Tom. He's in the hospital. He wrecked his car the other night."

"That's too bad; I hope he didn't get hurt to bad."

"He'll be fine, two broken legs and a mild concussion."

"Wow! I can't believe it. So, you found another director?"

"Kinda. I was wondering if you knew how to get in touch with Ravin Capello?"

"Want me to put her on?"

"She's there?"

"Yeah." He smiled.

"Boy, you didn't waste any time!" He laughed, obviously unaware of their relationship.

"Mason Reid for you," Marco said, holding out the phone to Ravin as she came out of the bathroom.

She looked at him confused. "Who is Mason Reid?"

"Head producer." He smiled.

She took the phone and sat on the edge of the bed wrapped in a towel. "Hello?" she asked slapping Marco's hand away from the towel.

"Ravin, Mason Reid here."

"Hi," she stammered unsure why he was calling her.

"I went over yesterday's film and I'm impressed."

"You are?"

"Yes, I am. See, I know you did all of this. I have my spies. I like the way you look at things."

"You do?"

"I do. I was wondering if you would like to finish it?"

"You would?"

Marco looked at her, his eyes begging for information.

"Yes, I would." He laughed.

"Sure. What do I do?"

"Come to my office and we'll discuss everything."

"What time?"

"As soon as you can. I don't want the band to lose any more money or time on this project. I'll send a car for you. Oh, and if you have any ideas you want to put into this, please bring them."

"Mason wants me to shoot the video," Ravin told Marco after she got off the phone.

"You're kidding me? Rave, that would be so great!"

"Marco, I don't know the first thing about shooting a video."

"Come here." He pulled her over and wrapped his arms around her waist. "I know you can do this. I don't know much about it either, but if Mason thinks you can do it . . . well, you can."

"Marco—"

"No, Ravin, listen. How easy is it for you to do a photo shoot without Randy?"

"Well, not easy . . . but I can still do it."

"I know, but with Randy there, how easy is it?"

"I don't see what you're getting at."

"What I'm getting at is this. With the right people behind you, you can do anything."

"I'm not finding the same confidence you seem to see."

"Well, that's why I'm here. Do you want me to go with you?"

"Yes."

"Give me a minute and I'll throw on some clothes."

"Thanks." She restlessly walked over to the closet and pulled out her favorite black leather pants and a gauzy white top.

"Ready?" he asked, buttoning his shirt.

"Yeah, oh wait!"

"What?"

"He asked me to bring any ideas I had for the video with me."

"You have ideas?" he asked shocked.

"Yeah, I couldn't sleep last night."

"So, that's what you were doing."

"Yeah." She looked at her hands, embarrassed.

She picked up her black bag and they walked out. Marco slipped his finger through hers.

"Are you having nightmares again?"

"Once in a while, but they aren't bad."

"No?"

"Not anymore." She smiled at him. "Not since you came along."

Downstairs, they got into the waiting limo outside and drove off. Ravin wrapped her hand around Marco's and they rode quietly to Mason Reid's office.

"You look nervous." Marco squeezed her hand.

"I think I am." She tried to force a smile.

"Wow, this is a first."

"Yeah."

"I didn't think you got nervous."

"Well, there's a first time for everything. Hey, did you let anyone know we were going?"

"Oh my God! I forgot!"

"You better call." She looked at him sternly.

"Yeah, I'll give Vinny a call."

"No, call Nico or Cole. Let Brett take care of Vin." She smiled devilishly.

Marco smirked and dialed Nico's number. "Nico, who's there with you?"

"Nobody." He paused. "So you two are going where?"

"Mason's office."

"Okay, let me know what's happening."

"Yeah. Hey, Nico!"

"What?" he scowled.

"Who's there?" Marco asked laughing.

"Nobody! Goodbye, Marco." He hung up the phone, rolled back over, and put his arm back around Mia. She closed her eyes and they fell back to sleep.

"Someone there with Nico?"

"He said no, but I know I heard someone next to him."

"Wishful thinking, Marco."

"Not this time," he said, knowing his best friend had a new comfort.

"Marco! Great, I'm glad to see you," Mason greeted them and patted Marco on the back.

"Hey, Mason, this is Ravin."

"Well, it's very nice to put a face to the name. Your reputation precedes you."

"Thank you."

"Come, sit down. You two want coffee? Maybe some muffins or bagels?"

"Coffee," Ravin said, sitting at the large oak table. She looked around the conference room. The walls were covered with music posters and gold and platinum albums.

"Sounds good." Marco sat next to her.

"Sandra, could you bring in some coffee and refreshments for our guests please?"

"Right away, Mr. Reid."

Mason sat down across the table from them and folded his hands together. Within minutes, Sandra had returned with coffee and a tray of breakfast deserts.

"So, Ravin, I was watching your footage this morning, and I was very pleased. As you know, the director we had hired is in the hospital and won't be able to continue this project, so I would like to give you a shot to finish it up for us."

"What about Jack?" she asked.

"What about Jack? Well, he's not ready to do this. He proved that to me yesterday. See, he didn't know I had my people there watching him after he said he'd do it. I wasn't happy with his lack of enthusiasm. You, on the other hand, impressed me."

"All I did was watch the screen and tell the guys what to do. The camera guys did all the work."

"True, but that's only because they knew what the story board was and started before you stepped in. The thing is that I like the way you look at things. You have a very keen eye for detail and you seem to understand how to make things work in your favor."

"Not all the time."

"I disagree. I want to try you out. We've already lost time and money."

"Exactly, you have already lost time and money, so why have me do it? I have no idea what I'm doing, and you can't be sure that I'll be able to pull it off. Why can't you just put another director on the job?"

"Do you know how much that will cost?" Marco broke in.

She looked at Marco and back to Mason as he shook his head. She started to feel ganged up on until she thought about it. They would lose the whole video without someone to finish it, and it would cost a lot more money to hire a new director, not to mention the setback in schedules.

"Fine, teach me." She gave in.

"First, tell me what kind of ideas you came up with." Mason snickered.

"How do you know if I did?"

"I know you're kind, Ravin. You are an artist; you are also

involved in the group. Surely, you have an idea how you would like to see their video turn out."

"True." She smiled at Marco.

She began to present her ideas. The changes were small but dramatic and unbelievably good. Mason was impressed, so much that he had his best crew sent down to the set to teach Ravin. He knew that for the first few videos she would need the best crew until she got the hang of it.

Leaving Mason's office, Ravin's head spun with ideas and fear. She worried how it would turn out, if at all, and how the rest of the guys would react. They were already on their way to the set, and Ravin had to tell them she was the one and she had made changes.

Marco sat back in the limo and watched this wonderful woman by his side. His feelings for her intensified every moment he knew her, and her abilities surprised him every day.

"Hey, Marco, Ravin!" Cole yelled as they pulled up.

"Hey, Cole," Marco answered as he watched them whisk Ravin away.

"What's going on?" Cole asked in the confusion.

"Catch this one." He laughed. "They want Ravin to direct the video."

"You're kidding? Is that where you went this morning?"

"Yeah, straight to Mason's office."

"They want her to finish the video?" Cole gaped at Marco.

"Yep, and she's making some changes too."

"Does Nico know yet?"

"No, we just got here."

"This is so cool. We've got to find him." Cole pushed Marco and they went off to find Nico.

Ravin spent the first hour talking to the crew. She learned where everything was and who was in charge of what. They warned her about Jack and what he was up to, assuring her they only answered to Mason. She told them she understood and had a feeling he would try to pull something. They explained how the chain of command worked in Hollywood and what she needed to do to get the video shot in time.

She spent the next hour with Jenna, the band's choreographer. They hit it off immediately. Jenna loved the ideas Ravin had for the rest of the video. She showed her a few moves that would fit well with the changes and pulled in Vinny and Brody as they were walking by.

"Do this, guys," she told them, showing them the moves she came up with. The boys followed along, matching her step for step. Ravin was impressed.

"What do you think?"

"I like it, easy to do." Vinny shrugged.

"Comfortable?"

"Always with you, Jenna!" Brody flirted.

Ravin sent Jenna to teach them the new moves. Dealing with Jack was next. He wasn't going to make this easy for her, but she knew she had the rest of the crew behind her. They liked her ideas and gave her their full support. He turned out to be as stubborn as she expected, and to top it off, he changed from being very sweet and helpful the previous day to very demeaning and full of himself, something she picked up on the minute she walked onto the set. She called Mason and told him what she felt and how the morning was going. He promised to stop in for lunch and talk to Jack if necessary.

"Looks good." She walked up as they finished practicing the new steps.

"Ravin!" Nico called out. "What the hell! I can't believe this!" He was so excited.

"Nico, relax, darling." She laughed, hugging him back. "Sit."

They all pulled up chairs and sat waiting to hear what she had to say. "First off is there anyone here who doesn't want me to try to shoot this video?" *Besides Jack*, she thought.

"Give us a break, Ravin." Cole smiled.

"Good. Now, I came up with these changes. Let me know what you think. We only have two days to finish this before it starts costing more money. The sound stage isn't available anymore, so we can't re-do what was done yesterday, but I was thinking about moving it into the airplane hanger," she said smiling.

"Did you see the footage from yesterday?" Nico asked.

"No, Mason said he'd show me later."

"Okay, tell us what to do. We trust you; you know our music and you know us," Nico assured her.

"Yeah, we trust you, Ravin. Whatever you think will work." Vinny added.

She silently felt a strong sense of fear run through her. This was the big time, and she didn't want to screw up and allow Jack the privilege of saying "I told you so."

The day went quickly; Ravin sat and watched the screen carefully as they filmed. Mason stopped in for lunch and reminded Jack about his ticket back to Iowa if he heard anymore about his attitude with Ravin. He was as helpful as he could be the rest of the day.

Forty-Seven

"Here." Marco set down a cup of coffee.

"Thanks." She smiled as she straddled the chaise lounge overlooking the pool with the next day's papers spread out in front of her. Marco slid behind her and slipped his fingers through her belt loops.

"Want me to do anything?" he asked quietly.

"You can rub my back." She smiled back at him.

He ran his hands up her back slowly, massaging every muscle. She closed her eyes and let his touch take her away.

"You know what?" he quietly whispered in her ear.

"What?"

"I think you're pretty spectacular."

"Oh, really?"

"Really." He nuzzled his face into her neck. He gently pulled her against his chest as he leaned back on the lounge chair.

"I'm trying to work." She sighed.

"I know, but I need a little of you right now."

"You do, huh? What's wrong?"

"Nothing," he replied stately.

"Nothing? I find that hard to believe."

"I miss you, okay?"

"I miss you too."

"Good. Now get back to work. I'm just gonna sit here and hold you."

"Sounds pretty good to me." She smiled and went back to her paperwork. She never realized how much was involved in directing a video. She would have to seriously consider what answer she would give if Mason asked her to do it again. As it was, she had postponed three shoots for private paying people. She wasn't sure how much longer she would have to be in L.A. Hopefully, one more full day and she could get back to her photography.

"What time do we have to be on the set?" he whispered in her ear.

She pulled his arm around her and looked at his watch. "We have to leave in a half-hour."

"Okay, I'm gonna jump in the shower. Need anything?"

"Nope."

"Oh . . . I talked to my mom. She's gonna try to fly in sometime this week."

"I'll finally get to meet her?" A small shudder ran up Ravin's spine as she thought about meeting his mom for the first time.

"Yes, and she can't wait." He sensed her silence. "She's gonna love you. Don't worry."

"Great! Cut!" She still had a hard time yelling that.

The boys walked over and sat down, breathing heavily. Ravin sat and watched the screen re-run what they had just taped. Happy with it, she told them to print it.

The video went along smoothly, once Jack had given in to the pressures around him. Dealing with Ravin had been easier than he had suspected, and his anger toward her subsided.

"What's next?" Jack asked, walking up behind her.

"One more shot of them dancing next to the pillars and I think we'll be done."

"I'll have someone order an early dinner. What do you want?"

"I don't care." She looked back at the storyboard. She set off to set up more lights and Jack followed her.

"You know, Ravin; you don't have to set this stuff up. That's what the crew's for."

"I know, Jack, but I need them where I need them."

"So, tell them."

"I've tried; they can't see what I see in my head. Only I can figure out exactly where these go."

"I don't get you, Ravin." He sighed.

"Not many people do, Jack, not many people do." She shook her head and laughed.

"So what? How does one understand you?" He leaned in closer.

"I'm not sure what you mean," Ravin stated, wishing for an interruption.

"How does someone understand you? Get to know you?"

"I don't know, Jack. I guess you either do understand me or you don't." Her nerves tingled on edge.

"So I'll never uncover what makes you tick, huh?" He set his hand on her shoulder.

"Guess not." Her comfort level dropped and she quickly looked around for an escape.

"I never thought I'd see this day!" A familiar man's voice broke the uneasy silence.

Ravin looked back quickly. "Pauly!" she screamed and ran over to him. "What the hell are you doing here?" she threw her arms around his neck and hugged him tightly.

"I can't spend another minute on vacation, as you would call it."

"Why not?"

"Just can't sit around, not my style. And you! Look at you! Directing a freaking video! I did not believe it when Marco told me."

"You talked to Marco? When? He didn't tell me you called." She slapped his arm. "Why haven't you called?"

"Yesterday, I told him not to say anything. I wanted to surprise you."

"This is so cool, Pauly. I'm sorry, where are my manners. This is Jack Gallivan. Jack, this is Pauly."

The two men shook hands; Jack wondered who this guy was and why he was there. Pauly checked him out from top to bottom. He thought about the conversation he'd had with Marco about the trouble this guy was giving Ravin. Pauly knew that Marco was uncomfortable. Otherwise, he wouldn't have called him in. Ravin would kill them both if she ever found out that Marco had called him.

"So, have you seen the guys yet?"

"No, not yet. They just pointed you out first."

"How did you get on the set anyway?" She stared at him suspiciously.

"I talked to Marco yesterday. He said he'd put my name on the list so I could surprise you."

"Oh yeah. Ask a stupid question . . ." They both laughed.

She took him around the set and told him everything that was going on, thanking him for breaking in when he did. She explained what Jack had said and how she felt. Pauly promised that she wouldn't be alone with him again. When they reached the dressing room, they all greeted Pauly and she told them they had five more minutes. Before she dragged Pauly off to show him the footage, he looked back and exchanged glances with Marco. Marco let out a sigh, knowing Ravin would be safe and relaxed. Now he felt he could concentrate on the rest of his schedule.

After a few more hours, they wrapped it up and headed back to the hotel, exhausted but exhilarated. Mason had left a message for Ravin to meet him at the studio first thing in the morning. She fell asleep relaxed and worn out.

"So? What do you think, Ravin?" Mason asked as they finished watching the new video.

"I think it's great! But more importantly, what do you think?"

"Little lady, I *am* impressed. This video turned out better than I had imagined. I am quite pleased with the work you've done. The changes you made were right on. Good job, Ravin, good job," he said with a huge smile. Ravin sat back, secretly pleased with herself.

"When do the guys get to see it?" she asked.

"Here." He handed her a copy of the video. "Take it home and you can all watch it together."

"Are you sure?"

"Yes, this is your copy. You can keep it, but don't tell anyone. I don't usually let the directors keep a copy, but this is a special occasion. You pulled it off."

"Thanks, I don't know what to say."

"I should be thanking you. You pulled me out of a jam and I am in your debt. I'd like to work with you again. Just name your price."

"Oh, I think I'm done directing."

"Don't say that. You did a sensational job."

"Thanks, but it's a lot of work. I'm busy enough for now."

"Yeah well, maybe you'll do a few here and there for me. At least Jaded's videos. Full artistic control."

"You are serious, aren't you?"

"Very," he said with a straight face.

"I'll think about it." She smiled.

"Well, let me know." He handed her an envelope and a large bound paper book.

"What's this?"

"Payment for services rendered and a book I had made up for you. It explains everything you need to know about directing."

"Thank you. This is great."

"Good, so next time you won't be so nervous."

"If there is a next time, Mason."

"There will be. Now go. I understand you still have two photo shoots today."

Ravin walked out of Mason's office feeling alive. There was something about directing, the power, and the prestige. Something about it all made her feel more alive than ever. She held the book Mason had given her close to her chest as she met up with Pauly.

Forty-Eight

"I can't believe you have to go back to New York," Marco said sadly.

"I know, I'll miss you, but you said you'd try to get the rehearsals moved to New York." She ran her fingers in circles around his stomach.

"I'm trying. It's hard to relocate so many people."

"I know," she said, quietly looking out at the ocean.

They held each other tightly as they watched the sun sink into the water. She was going to miss California, and more importantly, she was going to miss Marco, but they both had their jobs to do, and she had to go back to New York to do hers. She also had the wedding hanging on her mind, somewhere in between all her work she had to start planning it. All these thoughts ran through her mind as she leaned her head back against his chest. She loved the way he held her, the way she felt when he touched her. She closed her eyes and let her feelings rise as he gently stroked her hair.

Rolling over, she pushed him onto his back and kissed him tenderly. His hands ran up her back, pulling out her shirt. Her skin was on fire as he removed her shirt and caressed her exposed breasts. He rolled her onto her back, pulling off her shorts with expert hands. His lips followed down her neck across her collarbone gently brushing her skin. Ravin's head spun in anticipation, it happened every time he touched her. He made love to her seductively, matching their rhythms with the waves crashing on the beach.

Ravin tucked her head into his shoulder. "I can't believe I just did that." She felt embarrassed.

"Why?"

"What if someone saw us?"

"You and your what ifs." He laughed, holding her head close to him. "So what? I love you. I've always wanted to make love to you on the beach."

"You have? You've thought about this before?"

"Yes. From the moment I touched your soft skin, I thought about making love to you." He gently kissed her face.

"On the beach?"

"Anywhere."

She rested her head back down and closed her eyes. Marco ran his fingers through her hair, thinking about how hard it was going to be to let her go back to New York. He thought how difficult it was going to be when they went on tour; months without her would be torture. He eventually pulled her up off the blanket and they walked back to their room hand in hand. They spent their last night together in each other's arms, a night filled with ecstasy and promise.

"Marco, I've gotta go." Ravin pushed him away. "They're gonna fly without me." She smiled.

"Fine, let 'em." He pulled her back against him.

"I'll see you in a week or so."

"Not good enough." He pouted.

She sighed. "You're making this harder for me, ya know."

"Good, don't leave."

"I have to and you know it."

"I know." He walked her to the gate. "Call me when you get in."

"I will, I promise."

"Okay, I love you."

"I love you." She kissed him one last time.

She looked over her shoulder as she walked down hall to the plane. She found her seat in first class and stared out the window, smiling at him and wiping away the tear that rolled down her cheek.

Marco watched the plane take off and sighed. Slowly, he walked back to the car that the guys were waiting in.

"You'll see her soon. I think we'll be able to do a lot of work in New York." Nico smiled.

"Yeah, and you'll be able to hook up with Mia again, huh?" Cole joked.

Nico's face turned red and he quickly turned to look out the window.

"So, you and Mia, huh?" Marco teased.

"Possibly," he answered embarrassed.

"I think it's cool," Cole broke in.

Forty-Nine

"Hey, Rave." Pauly grabbed her bag as she stepped off the plane.

"Hey, Pauly. What time is it?"

"It's uh, eight forty-five." He looked at his watch.

"I hate time zones, Pauly." She shook her head.

"Home?" he asked, walking out to her Durango.

"Yeah, home." She never thought those words would sound so good.

She slid in smiling at her best friend. He had flown in a few days before her to meet with her brother and make sure everything was ready for her when she got home.

"So any idea of what's waiting for me at home?" she asked cautiously.

"Just know that there are a ton of messages waiting."

"Great." She sighed and pulled out her black book, flipping through the day's schedule. The only thing written was a meeting with Roxi at ten-thirty. She took a deep breath, closed her eyes, and laid her head back against the seat.

Pauly looked over at her. "You okay?" he asked.

"Fine, just tired," she answered without opening her eyes.

"You? Tired? I find that hard to believe."

"Why? Can't I be tired?"

"Just never seen it happen before. So, what's the day like?"

"Meeting with Roxi, but that's all so far."

"Wanna a nap?" he teased.

"No! I'll be fine. I just want to take a shower in my own bathroom and eat some real New York food."

"Real food? Well, you don't have anything at home. Your mom cleaned it out last week."

"She did? Why would she do that?"

"Because it smelled, Rave. You've been gone for almost two months."

"Wow, it doesn't seem that long." She watched the buildings fly by.

"It did from this side of town. So, how did the video turn out?"

"Good, Mason gave me a copy. I want to watch it with you, get your opinion."

"Mine? Why mine?"

"Because I value your opinion."

"You do, huh? What did the guys think?"

"I haven't showed them yet."

"Why not?"

"I don't know. I guess I'm nervous."

"Well, I'm not. I know it's gonna be great."

"We'll see."

"We'll watch it tonight. Marco called already and told me to stay with you tonight."

"Why the hell would he do that?"

"He wouldn't tell me."

"Lovely. So, now you're taking orders from him?"

"More like a courtesy. He's worried about you."

"Why?"

"That hit in the desert shook him up good, and then you took off. He knows there could be someone waiting for you here."

"Yeah well . . ." She didn't finish. In fact, she was worried about the same thing. She closed her eyes and fell asleep.

Pauly shook her awake when they pulled into the garage. Slowly she got out, grabbed her cameras, and wandered into her warehouse. The smell was inviting. She knew her mother had been there. She could smell the Pine Sol she used on the floors, and the fresh laundry smell still hung in the air.

"What'd she do? Wash the couch too?" she asked laughing.

"Rave, she cleaned everything. I thought she was losing it."

"Why the hell was she over cleaning anyway? I have someone to do that."

"I know. She sent her on vacation until you got home. I think your mom missed you. You've never been gone so long before."

"God forbid I should ever move out of state!" She laughed. She walked over to her desk and looked at her answering machine, forty-three messages. "Has anyone bothered to take down the messages?" she yelled from her office.

"Yes, everyday. That's all from today."

"You're kidding!"

"You're quite popular these days."

She looked at him confused. Could everything have possibly changed this much in such a short amount of time? She ignored the machine and went into her bedroom. Throwing her bags on her bed, she padded off to the bathroom. Her waterfall shower was the first order of business. When she finished, she walked into her closet and grabbed her low-rise jeans and a T-shirt. She touched the few clothes Marco had left in her closet and thought about him. She missed him terribly. She could smell his cologne drifting from one of his shirts and pulled it to her face. Why did she have to fall in love with him? She was still scared, but she couldn't imagine her life without him.

"Pauly! Am I supposed to bring you with me everywhere or can I just fly off to my meeting?"

"You can go without me."

"Good, I'm leaving."

"Did you call Marco? I'm supposed to remind you to call him."

"No, I'll call him in the truck."

"Okay, see ya." He sat back on the couch and opened a book.

She ran down to her Durango, dialing Marco's number. His voicemail picked up so she figured he must still be in rehearsal. She left him a sexy message, telling him she was home.

"Ravin!" Roxi yelled as she walked in. She ran over and hugged her.

"Hi, Roxi! Wow! You look good!"

"Oh well, thank you. I dropped ten pounds and cut off my hair! Can you believe it?"

"You look five years younger too!" She laughed, knowing Roxi hated being reminded of her age.

"Very funny! So, let's see this ring that Brett's been bragging about." She grabbed Ravin's hand and stared at the three-carat ring perched on her finger. "Wow! Look at that thing sparkle! Very impressive, very. Come, sit, we have so much to talk about."

They walked into her office. To Ravin's surprise, Brett and all the other models were waiting to welcome her home.

After a few moments of ring envy, Ravin saddled over to Brett. "Hey, Brett." She smiled. "Vinny wanted me to tell you that he misses you."

"How was your flight?" She smiled.

"You know, shitty as always."

"Yeah well, flying back with Pauly wasn't much fun either. He's so boring; I don't know how you deal with it." She laughed.

"That's what I like most about him. I don't have to talk, which you know is good."

"True."

"Okay girls, time to go. Ravin and I have much to discuss." Roxi waved everyone out.

"We'll see you later, Rave! Maybe we can meet out for drinks later!" Lainey called out as she left.

Ravin smiled and waved back, knowing that tonight belonged to her couch, Pauly, and her new video.

"Okay Miss Ravin, tell me everything." Roxi sat across from her.

Ravin explained the whole story, leaving out, of course, what had happened in the desert. Half an hour later, Michelle brought in Chinese, per Ravin's request, and they ate and talked more.

Roxi pulled out a large stuffed envelope. "Here are your paychecks."

Ravin set them aside, hoping she would get time to go to the bank. "Thanks."

"There's more." She smiled. "Here is the check from Benny and Jerry."

"Benny? Why is he paying me? He already covered their album."

"This is from the jeans ad."

"Jeans ad? Why is he paying me for that?"

"Because, my dear, that one picture you did is hot! Jerry called and told me that his sales went up almost six hundred percent. He was so amazed that one picture could do so much, so he gave you a bonus and Benny thought it would be nice to pitch in. Not only did that picture help out Jerry, it also boosted record sales for Jaded."

"But they haven't even released the album yet. It won't be out for a couple more weeks." Ravin was shocked.

"The sales are from their previous releases. Plus, Benny released a promo CD with two of their new songs on it. This place has been going nuts this past month!"

"Wow, I had no idea." She sat there stunned, more about the fact that she had no clue about any of this.

"Of course not, you were out in California. Not much news gets out that far." Roxi laughed.

"Funny, very funny."

"No seriously, it was a huge money-maker. When they release this new album, things are gonna get even crazier. News is out about a possible engagement too."

"You're kidding? He was hoping to keep it quiet, at least for a while yet." She looked down at her hands, "I was too."

"Well, the rumor didn't say who it was—at least not yet."

"I better tell him. He'll need to do something, I'm sure."

"Good idea."

"Okay Rox, hit me with it." Ravin set down her paychecks and picked up her black book.

"Hit you with what?"

"My schedule. I know you've been building to it, so let's hear it."

"Are you sure you're ready?"

"Yeah, I think I can take it." They both laughed.

Roxi got up, went over to her intercom, and pressed the button. "Michelle, could you please send her in?" She walked back to the couch and sat back down. "I hired you an assistant."

"I already have one. Randy's my assistant. I don't want anyone else, especially now. I'll need him almost more than my camera," she said concerned.

"He'll still be with you, don't worry, but for the next month or so, you will need a personal assistant."

"Why?"

"Oh, you'll see, you'll see . . ." She drifted of laughing.

A young, attractive girl stepped into the office and stood at the end of the couch, clutching her appointment book.

"Ravin, this is Stacey. She's going to be your assistant for a while. Her job is strictly to get you to where you need to be."

"How busy am I, Roxi?"

"Very."

"Well then, nice to meet you, Stacey." She shook her hand. Something jumped inside her, but she wasn't sure why.

"Hi, Miss Capello," she answered quietly.

"No, if you're working with me, you can't call me that. You have to call me Ravin. Otherwise, I'll be looking around for my mom." She laughed at the formality.

"Sorry. Hi, Ravin."

"So . . . what's my schedule look like?"

"It's all right here." Stacey set down a piece of paper with the day printed out.

Ravin picked it up and looked over it briefly. She noticed that she was to have dinner at Capello's at seven and felt a tinge of excitement. The rest of the day was filled with two photo shoots and three meetings. Ravin took a deep breath and set down the paper. "So . . . what's the rest of the week like?"

Stacey handed her the schedule book.

Ravin flipped through the book, everyday packed with photo shoots. "Roxi . . ." She paused. "Would it be easy enough to schedule these at my studio?"

"I suppose, why?"

"Well, this way I wouldn't have to travel around with all the film and stuff. Better chance of not losing stuff."

"Great idea. You wouldn't mind people trampling in and out of the warehouse?"

"Well . . . I guess I could deal with it, at least until I'm caught up."

"That'll be fine, although I don't know if I can get this week changed. I'll rearrange the rest."

"Fine, and here." She pointed out to Stacey. "When you schedule my location shoots, could you do them every other day?" She looked up at this young, scared person and felt bad for her.

"Yes, I'll go and re-schedule them now. Anything else?"

"Just that, and the shoots will be at my warehouse instead."

"I think I can take care of that."

"Thanks." Ravin smiled as she left the room. She turned to Roxi and asked. "Where do you find these girls?" She laughed.

"She came looking for the job. She's older than she looks."

"And how old is she? Seventeen?"

"Believe it or not she's twenty years old, and she's a fabulous organizer."

"So, is this why you hired her for me? Are you telling me that I'm not organized enough?" She laughed.

"No, you will just be so busy that you will need her. Depend on her."

"I don't depend on anyone, you know that."

"I know, but I can't afford *any* screw ups. I've put this magazine on the line for you, and now I need some return, so I'm going to work your ass off!" She chuckled.

"Understood. So, this Stacey girl, is she going to be following me around everywhere?"

"You bet. I only told her a little about how you work. I figure you can tell her the rest."

"Sounds good, I guess. I don't think I need her . . ."

"But you'll humor me. She's at your beck and call; she has no boyfriend and nothing to hold her back."

"Good. Randy's bad enough leaving for his romantic weekends."

"When is he getting married anyway?"

"Three months, I think. It keeps changing. I don't know anymore." She smiled, thinking of her own wedding coming up.

"Good. Time to get to work." Roxi stood up and handed her a list of what she wanted done that day.

Ravin walked out of her office. Stacey was quick at her heels. She made a mental note to tell her not to do that.

She spent the entire day shooting and getting reacquainted with her models and her friends. It didn't take her long to feel at home. During the breaks, she explained to Stacey what she expected her to do. The most important rule was not to follow her around. Stacey asked how she wanted to receive her next day's schedules and was happy when Ravin said she wanted them the night before.

"Ravin," Stacey interrupted as she was loading her film into her black duffel bag.

"Yeah?"

"You have dinner plans in twenty minutes at Capello's. I don't know where that is, but I can find out for you."

"It's my mom's restaurant."

"Oh, sorry."

"Why? How would you know? Listen, you need to relax. Every time I look at you, you look like you're about to jump out of your skin. I don't care if you act mellow. It's better than that strict businesswoman thing. I don't work well with authority, so please relax a little. Don't try to please me so much. Okay?"

"Yes, sorry. This job just means a lot to me."

"Well, don't worry; you aren't going to lose it on account of me."

"Okay." She smiled slightly.

"I've gotta run. I haven't seen my mom in two months and I still have to stop home. I'll see you tomorrow?"

"Yes, we start at six."

"See ya then."

Ravin rushed out and jumped into her Durango. She called Pauly and told him she would be there in a minute to get him.

Fifty

After a week of shooting at Roxi's studio, Stacey had re-scheduled everyone to go to Ravin's studio. That Sunday, Ravin moved Stacey into her warehouse. Stacey insisted it wasn't necessary, that she could easily make it to work on time everyday, but Ravin insisted after finding out that she took two subways and a bus to get to work everyday.

"Listen, Stacey, it'll be so much easier for all of us."

"Okay, okay. I've given up arguing with you."

"Well, that only took a week. How much stuff do you have?"

"Just some clothes, no furniture."

"Good. I'll send Pauly with you and you can pack up your things and move in."

"Are you sure, Ravin? I mean, you're so busy and all."

"Stacey, this place is so huge; you won't be in the way if that's what you're thinking."

"No, just . . ." She paused. "Well yeah, I just don't want to be in your way," she said shyly.

"You won't be."

"Who's Pauly? Is he your brother?"

"No, more like an assistant, a very personal assistant."

"Oh, I see." She was a little confused. She wasn't sure what she meant by that, but she would figure it out soon enough.

Pauly drove Stacey back to her apartment and helped her pack up her things. He felt a little put back at the lack of belongings she had and tried to get into her head.

"Where are you from?"

"Kentucky," she whispered.

"Long way from home, aren't you?"

"Yes."

"Following a dream?" he pried.

"More like a nightmare."

"I see. Not a talker, are ya?"

"Not really." She was determined not to let him in. She knew what he was doing, and he wouldn't succeed before she did what she came to do.

Pauly searched for anything on her. Coming up short bothered him. He drove her back to the warehouse, feeling very apprehensive about letting her so close to Ravin.

Stacey kept quiet the whole ride. She didn't know this Pauly person. She had only seen him a few times in the warehouse, and sometimes he drove Ravin around. She knew Ravin was seeing Marco Deangelo from her *favorite* band Jaded, and she wondered if she was being unfaithful. She couldn't let anyone hurt her Marco, not even Ravin. She would do anything to protect the man she planned to spend the rest of her life with. He just didn't know it yet.

Ravin sat on her couch, waiting for Marco to call her back. She closed her eyes and wished she were on the beach with his arms wrapped around her. The ringing phone pulled her out of her daydream.

"Hello?" she answered quietly.

"Hi, babe."

"Marco! God, I miss you."

"I miss you too. What'cha doing?"

"Sitting on the couch, waiting for you to call."

"Sounds very unlike you."

"Why?"

"Because you don't sit. You're usually working while you talk to me."

"Sorry, I've been so freaking busy this week it's unreal. Roxi even hired me a personal assistant."

"She did? Who is he?" Marco's voice laced with jealousy.

"She, Marco. Her name is Stacey."

"Good. I'd hate to have another guy following around that sexy ass of yours!" He laughed.

"Oh, shut up!" she giggled.

"What? Aren't I allowed to be possessive?"

"Yeah, yeah. So, what are you guys up to?"

"Just finishing up some more rehearsals. We should be done in a few days."

"Cool, are you coming out here?"

"That's the plan. Benny moved our press conference out there, just not sure when."

"Another press conference? Why so many?"

"That's what I need to talk to you about. Seems the rumors are getting out of hand."

"What rumors?"

"About the engagement. Now they are saying that Tammy and I are getting married. After the baby and all, they've photographed her a few times, and seeing as none of us have commented about the engagement, they're assuming that the baby's mine and we're getting married."

"Have you talked to Tammy about this?"

"Yes, I talked to her yesterday. She assured me that nobody has asked her anything about it and she was pretty upset."

"Oh yeah, I'm sure she is."

"Now who's sounding jealous!"

"Not jealous, just protective. Big difference, Marco."

"Sorry. Anyway, she's doing okay. She got back together with the father; he apparently has a decent job."

"Is she able to take care of the baby?"

"Yes. I was about to give her some money, even though I know you'd be pissed, but . . ."

"But it would have been the right thing to do."

"I was hoping you would think that. But anyway . . . I'm going to have to tell the press about us. I can't let my fans think that I knocked her up before I married her."

"I know." She paused, feeling the panic rise.

"Listen, I know the last thing you want is to be in the spotlight, but we need to talk about this, and soon."

"We will, when you get here."

"Okay. So, how much do you know about this girl? Is she any good? What exactly is she suppose to do for you?"

"That's a lot of questions."

"I haven't talked to you in four days! I've got even more saved up."

"Oh? Like what?"

"Like . . . what are you wearing?" he asked in a sexy voice.

"Wouldn't you like to know!" she taunted.

"More than you know."

"Doctor scrubs and a tank top. What else?"

"Exactly! What else?" He laughed mischievously.

"Oh, Marco, you are bad!"

She waved and whispered hi to Pauly and Stacey.

"Who's there?"

"Pauly, he just brought Stacey over with her stuff."

"Her stuff? Why?"

"Because I told her to move in for a while."

"Why did you do that? Is that safe?"

"Why wouldn't it be? God, Marco, you're starting to sound like Pauly, ya know." She felt a little angry.

"Sorry, I would just hate myself if anything ever happened to you."

"Nothing's gonna happen to me. She's like twenty pounds soaking wet! What'dya think she's gonna do sneak in while I'm sleeping and take me out?" She laughed.

"Hey, ya never know."

Ravin laughed and rolled her eyes. "When do you think you'll be able to make it out here?"

"Soon, honey, soon. Why don't you go settle this Stacey person in. I can't wait to meet her."

"Okay, hopefully you will *very* soon."

"Can I call you later?"

"Of course. I can't promise I won't be in the darkroom . . . but if you want to take your chances!" She laughed.

"Roxi's got you that busy, huh?"

"Yeah, at least four shoots a day, and I have three locations this week alone."

"Poor baby, you need a vacation."

"Only if it's with you."

"Wouldn't have it any other way."

"Good, oh! How's your mom?"

"Good. She got in fine. I've been spending all my time telling her about you. She can't wait to meet you. She's so excited."

"Excited? What exactly did you tell her?" She felt a tinge of nervousness.

"Just that you are the most beautiful, most talented photographer in the world, that you directed our video, and that you're smart and sexy."

"Marco! You're terrible." She laughed.

"Sorry, but it's the truth."

"No, it's not."

"Sure it is, but I'm not gonna sit here and argue with you. Go get her settled in. I'll call later and we can talk privately."

Ravin chuckled. "I love you, Marco," she said tenderly.

"I love you too," he whispered quietly.

Ravin set down the phone and sighed. She hated being away from Marco. Somewhere along the way, she had fallen head over heels in love with him. She wasn't sure when, but she knew deep inside that she had. The only thing that stood between her and total happiness was the nagging past that, for some reason had decided to suddenly re-emerge. She knew she had to deal with it, somewhere, somehow. Pauly may have thought it was over, but she knew better. She could see it in Johnny's face in L.A. He knew more about this than Pauly did. Johnny had been in this type of business his whole life. Pauly wasn't involved the same way. She briefly thought about calling someone from the old neighborhood and asking for advice, but that would come at a cost. She wasn't going to risk exposing anyone, especially with Marco having to go public with their engagement. Slowly, she got up off the couch and wandered over to help Stacey settle in.

"So, do you need anything?" Ravin asked, leaning in the doorway.

"No, thank you." Stacey swung around.

"Everything good in here then?"

"Yes, it's like staying at the Plaza compared to my apartment."

"Yeah, Pauly said it was pretty severe."

"I know, but the price was right."

"That's fine, but it was a pretty dangerous area. Weren't you scared?"

"Not really. Nobody ever bothered me."

"Still, it had to be pretty bad over there. I mean, that's like total gang territory over there."

"I didn't notice anything like that."

"How could you not? Gangs, hookers, drugs, and drive-by's. That's an everyday occurrence out there."

"Is that what those girls were?" she tried to sound as innocent as she could.

"Yeah." Ravin wondered if she should even let her out alone. She was so naïve.

"They don't have that stuff where I came from. The worst I ever saw was drunken hillbillies tipping over cows."

"Tipping over cows?" Ravin laughed. "What the hell is that?"

"Cow tipping? Well, they sleep on their feet, and at night, some people think it's funny to go and push them over. I, of course, never thought it was . . . but some people." She drifted off.

"Interesting. I grew up here in the city and sometimes out in Italy, but the most nature I've come across was Central Park, the Zoo and the grapevines at my Aunts. We never had any farm animals or anything."

"You grew up in Italy? Wow! That must have been neat."

"It was great, mostly playing in the grapevines. I guess it's equivalent to cornfields, just shorter." She chuckled.

"You have such a great life. I'm amazed."

"I'm sure yours was just as good."

"Nothing like this." She motioned in the air. "I've never seen anyone with this much money. Or talent! How do you do it all?"

"All what?"

"Being an incredible photographer and shooting all those beautiful models, and . . ." She looked at her carefully. "Having Marco Deangelo as a boyfriend. Oh my! He's such a wonderful singer! So is the rest of the band. I just love them."

"Well . . ." She wasn't sure what to say. "You have your talents too. It's just a matter of finding them. I got lucky with my photography, and I guess with Marco too." She drifted briefly into a memory of their first meeting.

"How did you meet him?"

"I shot their album cover as a favor to their manager. I don't usually shoot musicians, but they were in a jam, so I helped them out."

"Wow, so it was like fate?" she asked innocently.

"Yeah, I guess you could say that. Anyway, let me know if you need anything. This place is big, easy to get lost in. I don't usually cook, so I hope you don't mind take-out."

"No, I don't. Are there any rules?"

"Just stay out of Pauly's room. That's off limits. Oh and . . ." She looked at her seriously. "Jaded stays here a lot. You can't tell anyone though. It's safer here than at the hotel, and I don't want millions of girls trying to break in here. Okay?"

"They stay here?" She was shocked and satisfied. This would be easier than she thought.

"Yes. I'm not sure when they're getting here, but it shouldn't be too long. Anything else?"

"No, I'm good."

"Ok, I'll see you in the morning."

"Goodnight."

Ravin shook her head and wandered back to the darkroom. She felt sorry for her. This girl was so lost. Ravin remembered how it felt to be lost and she wanted to help this girl out. But something tugged at her insides, a tiny nagging feeling that wouldn't go away. She didn't know why and she didn't know for whom.

Fifty-One

Ravin's morning began at three a.m. as usual. She pulled on her shorts and headed down to her gym. The one thing she missed most in California was her kickboxing. Pauly watched from the dark corner sipping his coffee. After Stacey moved in, he didn't feel settled. Leonardo was taking too long with the background information on her; it was never good when it took so long. Until he knew everything about her, he didn't plan to let Ravin out of his sight.

After a quick shower, Ravin stood in the doorway of her office, sipping her coffee and looking at the pile of proofs that lay on her desk. She heard a quiet knock on the door and knew it was Stacey.

"Either knock louder or walk in Stacey," Ravin called out.

"Oh no, I couldn't just walk in."

"Well, then knock louder. If I wasn't standing here I wouldn't have heard you."

"Sorry."

"What's up?"

"Well, there are a lot of people arriving downstairs. When should I tell them you'll be down?"

"Let's go." She grabbed her boots and shifted her coffee to the other hand. They headed down for another long day.

After three hours of shooting and dealing with hairdressers, make-up artists, and models, Ravin briefly thought about retirement. Briefly, until it hit her. Her passion for film came back strong and she was inspired. She looked over at Randy standing with her next camera ready.

"Stacey?" she called over her shoulder.

"Yes." She bounced up out of breath.

"Go into my darkroom. On the shelf to the left are a few boxes of ziplock bags. Grab them and the black marker on the table, please."

"Right away." She shuffled off, wondering what the bags were for.

"Oh shit," Randy muttered.

"You got it." Ravin smiled. "I need all three cameras and my music."

Randy set off, knowing what they were in for today.

"Oh! And film! I need lots of film!" she yelled after him.

"What exactly are we doing?" Lainey asked, perched up on the table, ready to pose for the next shot.

"You'll see." Ravin smiled devilishly.

"Oh shit." Lainey jumped off the table.

The other models looked at Lainey for an explanation. It was their first time working with Ravin, and so far they weren't impressed. Lainey walked them over to the couch and told them to hang on to their shorts. Ravin was back in full swing.

She brought them into her piano room and cleared off the top. From the closet, she pulled out some zebra striped rugs and black throws. She changed the girls into black slinky dresses and posed them seductively.

Stacey walked up and tapped Randy on the shoulder.

"This had better be good," he said, not taking his eyes off Ravin. If he missed his cue, she would be pissed.

"Marco's on the phone for her," she whispered.

"Take a message or give it to Pauly."

She stepped back and asked Marco if she could call him back. He assured her that he needed to talk to her. She looked over at Pauly, who waved over the phone.

"Marco, it's Pauly. What's up?"

"What's she doing?"

"Shooting something. She's gone mad."

"Oh no, not again." He laughed.

"Yeah, Ravin's Lair prevails."

"Well, I need to talk to her, today."

"What's up?"

"We had planned on having our wedding in October, but

Benny's got us flying across the country promoting the new album. Plus, we have an awards show in Germany or something."

"That sucks. I'll let her know if you want, but not now. She's in a groove and you know I can't break that."

"I know."

"When are you guys coming in? She mentioned you would be soon."

"Why, Pauly? Do you miss us?" he taunted.

"Yeah, something like that. Too many girls around here all the time. The only normal person is Randy, and even he's getting weird."

"Sorry to hear that. I haven't told her yet, but we're coming in tomorrow."

"You are? What time?"

"We should be in around five."

"I'll set it up. Don't tell her. I'll get you from the airport too. She needs a little pick-me-up, so leave it to me."

"That would be cool."

"Sure, I've been pretty hard on her this week. Maybe she'll forgive me if I deliver you."

"Why, Pauly? What'dya do to her?"

"Nothing. I just don't like this girl she's got moved in and shit. It's not like Ravin to pull in a stray. She doesn't know a damn thing about her and she moved her in like she's been around forever."

"You don't like her? Why? Has she done something to Rave?"

"No, that's what bothers me. Something about her doesn't sit well with me. I can't figure it out."

"This is beyond strange, Pauly. I get this uneasy feeling when I think about it too, and I haven't even met her yet!"

"Then I taught you well. I'm on it, don't worry. We'll talk more about it later though. Too public here."

"Got it. Hey, Pauly?"

"Yeah?"

"Watch her. She gets too comfortable there."

"Don't I know it!"

Pauly hung up the phone and leaned against the wall watching Stacey. She was too interested in Ravin to be an assistant. Something didn't sit right.

* * *

Ravin spent the entire day shooting. By five-thirty she was exhausted and starving. She asked Randy to order in some food and headed off to her darkroom.

"Hey, Pauly?" She stopped him.

"Yeah?" He turned around mid step.

"Did Marco call?"

"Yeah, earlier today."

"And nobody told me because?" She glared at him.

"Because you were busy." He glared back.

"You know you can interrupt me for his phone calls."

"It wasn't important, Rave. You'll talk to him later, I'm sure."

"Did he say where he was going to be?"

"No. I didn't ask."

"Pauly!" She put her hands on her hips.

"Hey! I'm not your *damn* social secretary. You want to talk to him, you call him," he shouted and pounded off. He didn't mean to scream at her, but Leonardo hadn't called him back yet and he knew it wouldn't be good.

Ravin leaned on the table shocked. Pauly had never spoken to her that way. She instantly knew something was wrong, and she had a good idea what it was. She looked over at Randy, who shrugged. Stacey kept her nose in her book, jotting notes and trying not to appear to have heard anything. Ravin closed her eyes and tried to let her instincts tell her what to do. Nothing, she felt nothing. What she needed was some time alone in her darkroom with her music. She grabbed the food off the table and flashed Pauly an angry look. He was watching Stacey though, intently watching her. She wondered if there was a reason, a reason maybe that she should be watching her too. She surprised herself when she asked her to move in. It wasn't something Ravin did. It just wasn't a smart thing to do.

"Randy, you can leave after you eat if you want."

"You sure? You don't want any help in there?"

"No, I need some quiet."

"If you're sure." He got up and threw out his garbage. He grabbed his bag and said goodnight.

Ravin stood in the doorway of her darkroom and wondered if Pauly was going to tell her why he was so pissed. She sighed, turned on her phone, and went in.

Stacey cleaned up and went off to her room. She lay down on her bed and put on her headphones. Plugging in her favorite band, she closed her eyes and listened to the sensual tones of Jaded.

"Rave." Pauly quietly walked into her darkroom.

"What?" she replied coldly.

"Sorry I snapped at you."

"You're allowed to have bad days, I guess."

"This isn't a bad day, Rave."

"Then would you mind telling me what the hell is wrong with you?"

"A couple things on my mind."

"Like what?"

"Marco told me about the rumors."

"Did he?"

"He did. You have to step up to the plate."

"Not sure if I'm ready to do that."

"You have to."

"Why?"

"Well, first of all, you don't want to jeopardize his reputation."

"And how would I do that."

"By allowing his fans to think he knocked up his old girlfriend before he married her."

"True."

"Scared?"

"More than you can imagine."

"You know it's over, don't you?"

"Pauly, it's never gonna be over."

"Why?"

"Because, my father knew too many people and I don't know who's who."

"No reason."

"Good enough for me." Her eyes studied his critically.

"Not me."

"Well, it's not your life, is it?"

"No, but I know you too well to let you run anymore. Ravin, you—"

"Don't finish that sentence."

"Fine, then tell me what you think about Stacey."

"Why?"

"Gut feeling."

"Did you check her out?"

"Do you think I would let her stay here if I hadn't?"

"And what did you find out?"

"Nothing yet."

"So, what's the problem?"

"That's it, nothing yet. My gut tells me more."

"Yeah, me too."

"So, you are still with me?"

"And what's that suppose to mean?"

"Since you hooked up with Marco, you've seemed to have lost a little bit of your edge."

"No, I haven't." She rung her hands together.

"Yes, you have."

She sighed and leaned against the counter. "Yeah, I know. I don't know where it went."

"You allowed yourself to let your guard down around him. And everyone else too. Do you really need her?"

"Roxi seems to think so."

"Do *you*?"

"No, I think I can handle it myself."

"Good. I'll get rid of her."

"No, let me do it."

"Why?"

"I feel bad for her."

"Since when do you take pity on people."

"Since I made Marco abandon Tammy at the hospital."

Pauly sat silently, thinking about what she said. "Yeah okay, I'll be outside the door. I'm not leaving your side until she goes."

"Honestly, you think I can't take her or something?"

"Marco's orders."

"Marco's! Since when do you take orders from him?"

"He's got the same gut feeling."

"He hasn't even met her yet. And when did you discuss this with him?"

"This afternoon."

"Fine. I'll be here all night," she responded sourly.

He walked out without another word. Grabbing the book from his back pocket, he sat down on the black couch and put up his feet.

Stacey stood in the hallway, watching and wishing she could hear them. She snuffed and twisted on her foot, and then quietly stalked back into her room.

Ravin spent the rest of the night developing the day's pictures. It was easier for her to think in the darkroom. Maybe it was the smell of the chemicals, or maybe the darkness. But one thing was for sure: She *had* lost her edge, not only with her ability to keep herself alive from her haunting past, but also from her photography. She noticed something was missing in it all week. She lost something when she let Marco into her world. She wasn't sure what to do. She only knew that she would somehow have to adapt. She had to get back her edge, put back up her wall, but still keep Marco in her life. It was a hard thing to balance and she needed to learn how quickly before something else happened, something as terrifying as the incident in the desert. And then there was Marco giving orders out to Pauly. This bothered her the most. Pauly was hers. She'd never had to share him with anyone before. Still, the fact that Marco had a bad feeling about this girl and told Pauly scared her the most. He hadn't even met her; he never took security seriously before. She was the one who had told him how important it was and she was the one who helped teach his security guard Tony how to watch and protect him.

She finished up around two-thirty a.m., waking up Pauly on her way out.

"Some bodyguard, sleeping on the job." She laughed.

"I was sleeping with one eye open."

"Yeah right. Are you staying?"

"Mind?"

"No."

They walked up in silence, Pauly thinking about the impending phone call from Leonardo and Ravin too tired to think at all.

Fifty-Two

"What's on the schedule today?" Ravin asked as Stacey walked into the kitchen.

"Only two shoots today."

"Only two? Why?"

"You have dinner at seven."

"With who?" she asked, rubbing her eyes.

"Capello's. It doesn't say with who."

"Well, who set it up?" She stifled a yawn.

"I don't recognize the writing." She shrugged.

Ravin took the book from her and looked at the writing. She knew immediately it was Pauly and didn't question it anymore.

"When's the first shoot?"

"An hour. Who's writing is this?"

"Why?"

"So, I don't have to ask if I see it again." She replied, trying to smother her hostility.

"Pauly's."

"Why would Pauly schedule you in a dinner? I thought he didn't have anything to do with your work."

"Probably wants me to take a break." She looked at her curiously.

"Oh, okay. I'll be downstairs waiting. Is there anything you want me to set up?"

"No."

Ravin went back to her bedroom and slipped on her jeans and a cami. Even though summer was slowly ending, it was still warm during the day. She thought about how quickly October was coming and made a mental note to start planning her wedding. She sat on the edge of her bed and wondered if she was getting married too quick-ly. She picked up Marco's picture off her end table and looked into his eyes. A comfortable feeling came over her and she decided it wasn't too quick. She loved him more than she ever thought possi-ble.

Reluctantly, she went downstairs to start her day. She was glad that Roxi was able to get everyone to come to her studio instead of running back and forth. Pauly hated it, of course. He couldn't stand the amount of people coming in and out of the warehouse. She prom-ised him this was the last time she would do this. She told him that she hoped things would be back to normal soon. Pauly knew that the normal he was use to would never be the same.

"Rave, I've got an errand to run. Think you can get yourself to your mom's? I'll meet you there."

"No problem, Pauly. What time is it?" She looked at him con-fused.

"Five."

"Okay, I'll see you there." Pauly hesitated briefly; something strange flickered in Ravin's eyes. Something wasn't right with her.

"Stacey?" Ravin called out.

"Yes." She drifted up behind her. It was one thing that drove Ravin crazy.

"Let me know when it's six please?" She ducked into her dark-room.

"Okay." Stacey made herself comfortable on the couch and began going over the next day's notes. She saw Pauly's writing again. He had re-scheduled half of the day. She would have to say some-thing this time. It was one thing to schedule in dinner, but to erase half a day? He wasn't going to get away with that, whoever he was.

Pauly stood at the gate, waiting. He watched as they filed off the private plane one at a time.

"Hey."

"Hey, Pauly. How's it going?" Brody asked, patting his back.

"Good."

"So, what's the plan?" Brody questioned, looking over at the well-dressed thug.

"This is Leonardo. He's gonna take Marco to the restaurant and I'm taking you guys back to the warehouse."

Marco shook Leonardo's hand and gave Pauly his bags. "See you all later!" he said with a smile.

"Hey, Pauly, can I ask Brett over?" Vinny jumped into the truck.

"I don't care."

"So, why are *you* staying with us?" Nico asked concerned.

"Marco don't need me to hold his hand."

"Yeah, but why did you send that other guy with him?"

"Leonardo was going there anyway."

"Not good enough." Nico looked at him.

"Okay, fine. I don't trust Stacey."

"Why not?"

"Just don't."

"Did she do something?" Cole broke in.

"Nothing specific. I just don't trust her."

"Marco said the same thing the other day. I thought it was weird to say that about someone he had never met before." Nico jumped back into the conversation.

"I taught him well."

"Taught him what?" Cole broke back in.

"Instinct."

"Aren't you born with that?"

"Yes, but sometimes you forget how to tap into it." Pauly shrugged.

"Ravin, it's almost six," Stacey called through the door.

"Thanks." She put everything away and started up to her apartment.

After a quick shower, she slipped on her black leather pants and a black silk shirt. She threw on her silver hoop earrings and headed down to her garage.

Ravin strolled into her Moms' restaurant, kissing every hello on her way to the back where her mom and brother sat at the table.

"Hi, Momma." She kissed her. "Dinner tonight? You never ask me to dinner."

"I always ask you to dinner. You're just too busy to join me."

"Sorry, momma."

"Come with me." Her mom took her hand and led her into the

private banquet room. Ravin walked in and looked around. It was dark except for the dozen or so candles that stood around the center table. Her heart skipped when she saw a silhouette of someone at the table. When she turned to ask her mom what was going on, she saw that she was gone.

"I ordered your favorite," the voice whispered from behind her.

She recognized Marco's voice immediately.

"What the hell are you doing here?" Smiling, she sauntered over, easing herself onto his lap.

"Surprise!" he whispered in her ear. He leaned in and caressed her neck with his warm soft lips.

Ravin closed her eyes and let him set her free. "What are you doing here?" she gasped.

"We had to come in and get some work done. I thought I'd surprise you."

"I hate surprises, but this is a good one." She wrapped her arms around his neck and kissed him.

"Do that later." Her mom laughed, carrying in plates of pasta. Her brothers followed in with bread and wine.

"Hi, Nicky, Joey."

"Hey, Ravin. Marco, good to see ya." Nick handed him a glass of wine.

After a while, they left them to eat.

"So, I suppose Pauly set all this up?" she asked, sipping her wine.

"He just brought me here. I called your mom and set up the dinner."

"All this spare time you had and you didn't call me!" she teased.

"Well . . . I got lucky that she was up so late."

"Well, I'm glad you're here, however it happened."

"So am I."

"How long do I get you?"

"Forever," he whispered, "forever." He looked deep into her eyes and smiled.

"That part I know, Marco! I was thinking short term."

"I'm not sure, at least a few days." He laughed.

"And the rest of the guys?"

"Pauly took them home."

"Good. And your mom?"

"She's at the Plaza." He smiled.

"Great. Now I can relax," she said with a soft smile.

"We've gotta talk." He looked down at his plate pushing his food around.

"About what?" she asked cautiously.

"Well, first of all, I've gotta go public with our engagement before the media go nuts."

"I know, Pauly told me. And?" She knew there was more and she dreaded any other bad news.

"And, well, I didn't want this to happen, but I think we're going to have to push back our wedding."

"Push it back? Why?"

"Benny has us flying around the world promoting the new album."

"You're kidding?"

"No. Didn't Pauly tell you this?"

"No, he didn't. What else was he suppose to tell me?" Her anger began to rise.

"What do you mean?"

"I mean, you're telling him about our wedding plans, you're telling him to protect me. Is there anything else you two have discussed about me that I should know?"

"Don't get mad, Rave." He was shocked at her comments.

"I am. I'm sorry, but I am."

"Why?"

"I don't know. Pauly's mine. I've never had to share him before, and now you two are all chummy talking about my life."

"It's not like that, Ravin, and you know it."

She took a deep breath. "I'm sorry. I've just had a long, crappy week. Forgive me?"

"Always. But hey, we're up for Best Group at the awards show in Germany. That's the other reason we have to go."

"Oh, that's great!"

"It is, even if we don't win."

"You will." She slid her hand on his leg.

"Wanna get out of here?"

"And go where?" She smiled.

"Anywhere you want."

"Home."

"I was hoping you would say that." He smirked.

They said goodbye to Ravin's family and walked out to her Durango, fingers entwined.

As she started the engine, she turned to him. "I know you have to tell people about me, about us. If there were a way to keep this quiet, I know you would find a way. I'm just scared."

"About what?"

"Marco, since I met you, my life has changed dramatically. Not in a bad way, but it has changed. I'm not use to attention nor do I want it. It makes everyone mad, the way I am. I've been told that if I would open up more and let more people in, I would be a better photographer or even a model. But what they don't understand is that I'm good because I won't let anyone in. I know it doesn't make much sense but—"

"But I know that's who you are and I know there are other reasons too. I don't want a wife or girlfriend that would promote our lives publicly. I'm in the spotlight enough."

"I'm just scared."

"Of your past? Is that it? Do you think that they're gonna see you and decide to come after you again?"

"Yes."

"But you're not hiding."

"I am, sort of."

"You're name is on every cover and picture out there."

"Not really. If you look closely, you'll see that it only says R.I. Capello."

"Still, they could have figured it out if they wanted to."

"Yeah, but that's not the point."

"So, what is?"

"I'm scared. That's the point."

"Don't be. I'll protect you as much as I can. I would never do anything to risk your life or reputation."

"I know—"

"Can we finish this later? We can't both fall apart at the same time."

"Why? Are you? I'm the only basket case here."

"Trust me. I'm more upset about this than you think."

"I'm sorry."

"Don't be. I love you." He reached over and pulled her chin to him. Gently touching his lips to hers, he felt alive again.

As she opened the door to her apartment, she felt the exhilaration of having her friends back and mostly the love of her life. She walked over to Pauly and hugged him.

"What's that for?" he asked, confused.

"Helping me with everything, and bringing Marco here when I needed him."

"Good talk?"

"Yes."

"Good." He smiled and walked away.

"Good morning," Marco whispered as she rolled over.

Ravin looked up into his eyes and smiled. "Ya know what?" she murmured quietly.

"What?"

"There's nothing better than waking up to see your face."

"Is that so?" He smiled.

"Yes." She stretched her arms above her head. Marco reached over and ran his finger across her chest and up her arms. Ravin closed her eyes smiling.

"There's nothing better than just being able to hold you. To touch your soft skin . . ." He paused. "I just can't seem to get enough. I'm going to be so miserable on tour without you."

"You'll do fine."

"Not without you." He ran his finger lightly across her cheek.

"I know. I've struggled here without you. It's gonna be torture."

Marco sighed; he hated loving her so much and not being with her every minute.

"Coffee?" she asked, pushing herself up.

"Are you buying?"

"Sure." She smiled pulling on her scrubs. Ravin looked over at Marco stretched out in her bed, the sheets exposing his stomach and chest. The temptation was too much as she walked over and ran her hand over his stomach. "Are you coming?"

"Not yet." He smirked.

"Funny."

"I'll be right out." He laughed.

She walked out into the kitchen. Nico, Cole, and Brody sat at the table laughing.

"Morning, boys." She smiled, walking over and kissing each one on the cheek.

"Hey, Rave! Sorry we're here so early. No coffee downstairs," Cole replied.

"No problem. I'll try to remember to get some more."

"No problem. We like it up here better anyway." Cole laughed. "So, how are you?"

"Good, busy, but good."

"Surprised?"

"Yes, very."

"Good, so what are your plans today?"

"Honestly, I have no idea. Stacey keeps my schedule pretty guarded."

"She does, huh? You should put a stop to that."

"Yeah, I will. I should find out what I've got today. I'll be right back."

She grabbed her coffee cup and headed out the door. Just as she was turning down the stairs, Stacey came bouncing up.

"I was just coming to find my schedule," Ravin said.

"Here," she said, feeling happy. She spent the night watching the group wander around the warehouse. She couldn't get up the nerve to speak to any of them, so she kept hidden in the corner.

"Thanks, but I want these the night before." Ravin held out the schedule.

"I know, but you were gone all night. I didn't see you come in. All you have is one shoot later this afternoon."

"Thanks." She turned and walked back up the stairs.

"Let me know if you need anything!" Stacey called out to her.

Ravin smiled and waved as she slipped back into her apartment without another word. Stacey sulked back to her room.

Ravin looked down at her schedule as she walked back through her apartment, happy to see her morning open until later in the afternoon.

"Here it is . . ." She paused, looking over the day as a smile spread across her face.

"What?" Cole asked curiously.

"Easy shoot today."

"Oh yeah? Who?"

"Just Brett." She smiled as Marco wandered in looking for coffee.

"That'll go quickly." Cole handed Marco the sugar.

"Yeah, if you can get Vinny away from her long enough," Brody broke in.

"This is great. I'm ready for a day off." She smiled at Marco.

"So, what to do till then?" Marco teased.

"You need to go shopping." She nodded her head. "I wasn't expecting you guys, so I have no food."

"I can go. What do you need?" Marco sipped his coffee.

"Food. I'll cook whatever you guys want."

"You'll cook? Oh, Ravin, please!" Brody begged as Cole laughed and slapped his arm.

"Sure, dinner here tonight, whatever you guys want. Take Pauly shopping with you and he'll know what ingredients I need for whatever you decide. I think I'm gonna see if I can get Brett out of bed and do her shoot early. Then we can just sit back and enjoy the rest of the day."

"Sounds like a plan to me." Cole smirked.

"Don't you want Pauly here with you though?" Marco looked at her with intense eyes.

"No, I'll be fine."

"I think he should stay. I'll call Tony back."

"I'll be fine. Don't worry."

Stacey sat in her room looking at a magazine she'd purchased a week ago. It had a huge five-page spread on the group Jaded. *My luck just may be changing for the better*, she thought. She got a huge break when she had asked to be Ravin's assistant and now . . . now . . . she was staying in her warehouse with her. She was able to study her so much more, and now Jaded was here too. She couldn't have been happier. She watched them all night, although she didn't see Vinny much and she knew Marco was upstairs with Ravin. She had hoped they would come down so she could see how she would need to act. She knew that once she got rid of Ravin, Marco would fall in love with her. How could he not? She would just become Ravin, and he wouldn't notice the difference.

She pulled out the new low-rise jeans she had bought the other day, just like Ravin's, and a cut off T-shirt. She also bought a bottle of black hair color and brown contacts. This was going to be quite a transformation. She was born with light auburn hair and green eyes, but when she was done, no one would be able to tell. She stowed away her things and went to see if anyone was downstairs yet. She hoped during the shoot she would be able to meet them, see Ravin in action, and learn how she acted around them. That was the important part, learning the comfort parts.

Stacey Wilson stood against the wall watching Missy being crowned Queen of the Fall Dance. On her arm was Stacey's true love, Rick, the one and only guy she had ever let touch her. He spent three weeks courting her and ended up taking her virginity at the drive-in. Two days later, he treated her like a complete stranger. Watching him laugh and flirt with Missy and their friends, Stacey found out that he had dated her on a bet. She vowed to get revenge. Missy was her first target, Rick was next. She would make him suffer just as she had, if not worse.

Leaving her small town was the only way out. She had read several articles about Ravin Capello, including tabloid trash about how tight she was with the band Jaded. She read about the photo shoots and how she stepped in to finish directing their last video. She watched two old videos of the band and knew Marco was the man she wanted to marry. No matter what the cost.

Ravin wandered over to Vinny's room and quietly knocked on the door.

"Yeah?" he called out.

"Its Ravin, hon. Is Brett still with you?" she asked hoping not to disturb them.

"And if she is?"

"I was wondering if I could ask her something."

"Come on in, Rave." He chuckled as he pulled on his jeans.

"Are you two decent?"

"Decent people we are not!" Brett burst out laughing.

Ravin opened the door and gave Vinny a hug.

"Hey, Rave, how ya doing?"

"Good, hon, and you?"

"Much better now." He smiled.

"I'll bet. Brett, you are my only shoot today. You're scheduled later, but I was thinking about getting it done now. Are you game?"

"Sure, why?"

"Gonna cook these boys some dinner." She shook her head.

Vinny rubbed his hands together and smiled.

"I'm game. Let me shower up." She smiled.

"I'll call Roxi and get things rolling."

"And if not?"

"Then we'll do hair and make-up. I think we can handle it, don't you?"

"Sure, what's it for?"

"End of summer party outfits."

"Oh man, that's a piece of cake!"

"Exactly. And with you as my model, it'll take us all of ten minutes."

"Is that all I'm worth to you?" Brett put her hands on her hips.

"Try the other way around. Because it's *you*, I won't have to spend all day getting a good shot. You do it right the first time." She winked.

The girls laughed and Brett headed for the shower. Ravin went back downstairs and called Roxi. She was fine with the time change and told her she would send Marley over for hair and make-up. Ravin went to the set and started pulling everything together. She called Randy and told him to take the day off. She was doing the shoot solo. He was appreciative and thanked her profusely.

"Need any help?" Nico walked in looking around.

"Sure."

"What'cha want me to do?"

Ravin sent him to the other side and he helped her set up the props. They finished fifteen minutes later, just as Brett came downstairs and Marley arrived at the door.

"Hey, Marley, perfect timing."

"Hey, Rave. I'm so glad you moved this up. I've got so much to do today. Is Brett ready?"

"Yeah, she's in the dressing room, waiting for you."

Stacey heard all the commotion downstairs and poked her head out the door. She saw Ravin pulling out her camera and wondered what was going on. She wasn't supposed to be doing the shoot until much later.

"Ravin?"

"Yeah?" She turned to Cole.

"Someone here to see you," he said pointing at the door.

Ravin turned around and saw Leonardo standing there with three other men. She set down her camera and walked over. "Hey Leonardo, what's up?"

"Not sure. Where's Pauly?"

"Went to the store with Marco, why?"

"Gotta talk to him."

"He should be back soon. Wanna tell me?"

"Not yet. Let me finger through it with Pauly first. We'll stick around and wait, if you don't mind."

"Don't mind at all. Is this about Stacey?" She looked at his face and knew it was.

"Is that her?"

Ravin turned. "Yeah that's her."

"Ravin, what's going on here?" Stacey asked, walking up.

"Doing the shoot early."

"Why? It's not scheduled until two."

"And?" Ravin looked at her accusingly.

"And well, it's not scheduled until two." She couldn't think of a good excuse.

"So, I changed it. What's the big deal?"

"I would have liked to be informed."

"Why? What difference does it make?" She shot her a look and walked away.

Stacey sat there, feeling embarrassed and angry.

"What's up?" Brett asked, walking onto the set and seeing Leonardo and his friends.

"Talk later."

Brett nodded and went to the set. Ravin picked up her camera and began shooting. Nico and Cole tried to help as much as they could. She spent half an hour on it and felt she had all she needed.

"That's good." She put down her camera.

"Think you've got enough?"

"Yeah. If not, we can always re-shoot later."

Fifty-Three

Pauly and Marco walked into the warehouse with their arms full of bags. Pauly looked around and saw Leonardo and some friends sitting with Ravin in the lounge.

"Go, man, I've got this," Marco said, looking at Pauly.

"Thanks." He handed him the other bags.

Ravin and Cole got up and helped Marco with the bags. Pauly took Leonardo to the piano room.

"What's up?" Pauly closed the door.

"Got some news."

"On Stacey?"

"Yeah, man, and it ain't good either. She was accused of murder a few years ago."

"She's gone!" Pauly yelled furiously.

"But she got off."

"Spill it."

"Well, apparently she was suspected of tampering with the brakes of some girl's car. They only thought so after they found this girl's boyfriend lying in his house with sixty-seven stab wounds, but they couldn't find any evidence proving it was Stacey so they dropped the case."

"So, she got off because she covered her tracks well? Did the guy die?"

"Yes."

Pauly sat silent for a long time.

"What are you gonna do?" Leonardo finally asked.

"Get rid of her." Pauly paced the room.

"You can't just ask her to leave. If she's screwed up in the head she could crack."

"True."

"Tell Roxi to get rid of her."

"Think she will?"

"Yeah, I think so. If you tell Roxi that Ravin doesn't need her and she's screwing up her momentum, I think she'll get rid of her."

"Good idea." Pauly chewed his thumb in thought.

"Listen, man, with Marco and the guys here, do you think you guys could stay?"

"Sure, need anyone else?"

"No, I think you guys will be fine."

"Consider it done. And, Pauly," he said as he grabbed his shoulder before he left, "If you want her gone sooner, I'm not shy." Leonardo smiled, knowing Pauly knew what he meant.

"If it comes to that, you'll get the honors."

"Pauly, I don't know what to say," Ravin said as she paced her bedroom. She was startled by the information. "What am I suppose to tell her?"

"Nothing. Let Roxi can her. That way she can't target you."

"Yeah sure, just Roxi then."

"She'll be protected. Don't worry."

Ravin left Pauly to talk to Roxi and went back into the kitchen.

"So, what's going on?" Marco asked, putting his hands on the small of her back.

"Nothing." She forced a smile.

"Bull, I can see it in your eyes."

"Fine." She let out a sigh, "apparently Stacey was involved in a murder rap or something."

"What?" he said franticly.

"I'm not sure. Pauly's holding back."

"Well, I'm just glad I'm here."

"Me too."

She nuzzled into his chest. He wrapped his arms around her and held her close. Ravin listened to her heartbeat against his chest. It was the one place where she felt safe.

"So what now?" he pulled her off and looked into her hardened eyes.

"Don't know. Have you guys seen the video yet?"

"To be honest, we haven't. We've been so busy."

"Shall we then? Mason gave me a copy."

"Yeah, sounds good."

They called everyone into the living room and Ravin was ready to hit the play button.

"Wait!" Brett stopped her. "I want to make a toast." She smiled.

"Why?" Ravin looked at her as if she had lost her mind.

"Because you are my very best friend, and because of you, I met Vinny. And you would have never met Marco either. And . . . if we had never met you guys before, Ravin would never have had the opportunity to direct a video." She smiled. "Which is something I know she's *always* wanted to do. So, here's to Ravin and here's to you guys."

She raised her coffee, as did everyone else. Ravin sat on the couch, embarrassed as everyone laughed and toasted her. Pauly stood in the doorway smiling. For the first time he saw Ravin happy and he vowed never let that get away from her.

"Okay, can we watch it already?" Ravin scoffed.

"Roll film." Marco smiled proudly.

They sat and watched the three-minute video over and over. The only part that didn't look right was the part she didn't direct.

"Ravin, that was awesome!" Nico gasped.

"Totally," Cole and Brody chimed in.

"Perfect," Vinny added.

Marco just sat back wearing a smile from ear to ear, so proud to be with her and so afraid she'd run.

"What are your plans for the next one?" Cole joked.

"Next one? Oh, I think I'm busy enough don't you?" she laughed.

"Mason made us promise to bug you until you gave in, so we're bugging you." Nico snickered. "Guys, think we can convince her?" he shouted.

They all started yelling and stomping their feet. Pauly stood laughing. There was something about this group of guys, something he had never counted on. A strong bond of friendship had formed, a bond he knew from the old neighborhood.

"I think it was perfection. I loved the way you had the camera zooming in like that," Nico said.

"Yeah, I've never been prouder to be with anyone before. You are so talented, it's scary," Marco whispered.

"Yeah, yeah. You're just trying to score points with me. It wasn't *that* great."

"I disagree." He kissed her and pulled her into a hug. "Go for a walk with me?"

"Where?"

"Well, just out to the backyard."

"Sure, why?"

"Talk."

"Okay. Pauly, we'll be in the yard."

She stood up and followed Marco outside. Together they lay on the hammock rocking slowly watching the clouds.

"The press conference is coming up."

"I know."

"Yeah." He didn't know what to say to ease her mind.

"I guess you have to tell everyone?"

"Yes, I would have liked to have kept it quiet a little longer."

"I know it was inevitable."

"Yeah."

"So, what are you gonna say?"

"I'm gonna tell them that I'm not engaged to Tammy and that I'm not the father of her baby. I'm gonna proudly tell them that you are my fiancé."

"Proudly, huh?"

"Yes, I'm very proud to be with you."

"I know. I'm pulling your chain."

"Nervous?"

"Terrified."

"Tell me why."

"I told you."

"I know, but I keep getting this feeling that's there's more to it." Ravin shrugged.

"You still think something's gonna happen to me, don't you?"

"Every second of every day."

"I thought Pauly said it was over."

"What?"

"Those guys in the desert."

"Oh yeah. I forgot about that." She looked up at the rushing clouds. Part of her wanted to scream out yes! Yes, she was terrified because she *knew* it wasn't over. She knew it would never be over unless the chain was somehow broken.

"So . . . I feel bad now."

"Why, Marco?"

"Putting you in the spotlight like this."

"I'll have to adjust then, won't I?"

"But they're gonna be following you around everywhere."

"Well, maybe they'll get bored with me, I don't do anything."

"Who knows? The media is relentless."

"I know. So when am I gonna meet your mom?" she said, changing the subject.

"Oh yeah, I should call her."

"Ya think?" She laughed.

Marco pulled out his cell phone and dialed his mom. He made plans for lunch in an hour and they went up to get ready.

Fifty-Four

"So Mom enjoyed herself last night," Marco said, lounging in Ravin's bed.

"I'm glad. I like her."

"She said the same about you."

"Good. I hear it helps when you get along with your in-laws."

"Yeah, at least you don't have to put up with my father." He looked down at his hands.

"Do you ever miss him?"

"No . . . not really. I just wish he could see what I've accomplished despite him. Do you miss your dad?"

"Every second." She stood up and started to walk away.

"Hey!" he called to her, "our fathers were different. Yours was taken from you. Our wish came true for us."

"Your wish?" She spun around and stared into his deep brown eyes. She watched his soft loving eyes turn cold and uncaring. "You wished him to die, Marco?" she asked, shocked.

"It's not as bad as it sounds," he said, wishing he hadn't brought it up.

"What do you mean as bad as it sounds?"

"Ravin, he abused us. He hit us. He hurt us everyday," he said quietly.

"I'm sorry," she whispered.

As quickly as his eyes went cold, they warmed up. He reached up and touched her face, softly, gently. Looking deeply into her black opal eyes, he whispered, "I'll *never* be like him. I will and do cherish everything in my life, especially you. Nothing could ever turn me into the monster he was . . . nothing."

"I love you, Marco." She leaned in and kissed him softly.

"I love you too, and you're gonna be late."

"Can we finish this later?"

"If you must."

"I must. I want to know everything."

"On one condition." He looked at her seriously.

"What?"

"You tell me *everything*. And I mean everything."

"Let's start with you, and if there's enough time you can work on me." She laughed. She moved quickly knowing he would chase her. He did, and they ran into the living room, laughing. They both stopped abruptly when they saw Stacey standing by the door.

"Hi," Ravin said out of breath. "I didn't hear you come in."

"I just walked in like you told me." She looked directly at Marco.

"Oh, um. This is Marco. Marco, this is Stacey." She looked at him cautiously.

"Hi," Stacey said shyly.

"Hi, Stacey, nice to meet you. Rave, I'll meet you downstairs." He said, returning to the bedroom.

"Okay." She smiled. "So, Stacey, what's first?" she asked, steering her out the door and down the steps.

"First is a make-up ad," Stacey said marking something in her book.

"Shit, I forgot my coffee." She looked around downstairs.

"I'll get it." Stacey said, not thinking twice that Marco was up there in the shower.

"No, that's okay."

Ravin began her shoot without it and without Randy. She felt a little lost that morning, same as the day before. The last two days she had felt like this, confused and restless. She shrugged it off and tried to concentrate.

Stacey stood in the corner and watched. Her plans were starting to come together. All she needed was to get a hold of Marco. Just as she was thinking about him, she saw him walk down the stairs.

"Hi, Stacey," he said walking by.

"Hi, Marco."

She watched him walk over to Ravin and kiss her cheek. He said good morning to the models in his charming way and complimented them all on how beautiful they were. He smiled and handed Ravin her lost cup of coffee.

"Thanks, I needed this. I can't seem to get my head in the game today." She chuckled.

"I noticed. You've been kinda out there when you're shooting."

"I have?"

"Yeah, last two days. Maybe Stacey's trying to drug ya." He laughed. "I'm gonna get the rest of the guys. We'll meet Stacey and then we are off to JAM."

"Sounds good."

He left without a backward glance to Stacey, causing her to become more irritated. She slipped her hand into her pocket and fingered the little pouch of poison she had been slipping in Ravin's coffee. She laughed quietly to herself at how easy it was.

Marco ran into Pauly on his was to the apartments. "Hey, Pauly." He stopped him.

"What's up, Marco?"

"Ravin, doesn't look right. I noticed it last night, and today she's kinda out there. It's not like her to be so restless. Is she okay?"

"I don't know. I saw it too the other day. She couldn't figure out what she was shooting."

"Maybe Stacey's slipping something in her drinks."

"Possible. She is with her alone a lot. Consider it done."

"What are you gonna do?"

"Go through her room."

"What if she comes upstairs?"

"You get the guys and keep her busy. She's been dying to meet all of you, so maybe you can talk to her and give me about fifteen minutes?"

"Done." He started toward the other rooms. "Oh and, Pauly?"

"Yeah." He turned around in the doorway.

"I want her out tonight."

"She will be."

Pauly grabbed Leonardo and they both walked back into Stacey's room.

"What are we looking for?" Leonardo asked, glancing around.

"Anything. Ravin's been off lately and I want to know why."

"What do you mean off?"

"She hasn't been acting normal. She's been confused sometimes, and well, I just don't know. I thought maybe it was just stress, but Marco thinks it's something else."

"Who's got Stacey's attention?"

"Marco and the guys. They should be able to keep her busy for fifteen minutes or so."

"Let's get to work."

Pauly and Leonardo carefully searched Stacey's room, putting everything back where it belonged. Under the bed, Pauly found a black suitcase. Out of curiosity he pulled it out and flipped open the top. "Holy shit," he whispered.

"What'dya find?"

"I don't know yet."

"Think she's connected?"

"No, more like obsessed. Look at this stuff, pictures of Marco and articles on both of them. She's got all kind of stuff in here."

"Take it with you. Let's go back to your room and analyze this crap."

"Think she'll miss it?"

"No, I'm going downstairs to do everything in my power to keep her busy. You go through it and get to the bottom of this."

"Thanks, Leonardo."

"No thanks needed, man. I'd do anything for you and Ravin. You know that."

Pauly picked up the suitcase and checked the room to make sure everything was back in place. Leonardo went downstairs and formed a plan to keep Stacey busy long enough for Pauly to get his work done. He went downstairs and joined Marco and the guys talking to Stacey.

"What's up?" Marco whispered.

Leonardo just gave him a look. Marco's heart sank into his chest. He knew something was going on and that it involved Stacey. He turned his attention to Ravin and watched her fumble around with her cameras.

Pauly slipped into his room and quietly locked the door. He set the suitcase on the table, took a deep breath, and sat down. Slowly, he opened the clasp and began digging through, making mental notes where everything went.

The first layer was articles about Marco and some about Ravin.

It was obvious that Ravin was the target, and as he dug deeper, he was sure. There were clothes that Ravin wore, hair color, and brown contacts. Even a pair of silver hoop earrings. She was turning herself into Ravin. Pauly felt his stomach drop. At the bottom, he found three bottles of pills. They were all labeled Nardil and prescribed to Stacey. Next to them was a package containing some kind of rodent poison. He quickly picked up his cell and dialed another friend.

"Rocco, it's Pauly," he said as fast as he could.

"Hey, Paul, what's up?"

"Check on something for me?"

"Yeah sure, what is it?"

Pauly rattled off the name of the package he had found. He also gave him the name of Stacey's prescription medication.

"Okay, pal, call you back in ten. What's it for?"

"Something's going on here with Ravin. She's got this assistant living with her and I'm checking up on some things."

"Got it. Talk to you in ten."

Pauly hung up the phone and dug further, finding articles pertaining to the deaths back in her hometown. The more he dug, the worse he felt that Ravin was in more danger than he would have thought.

Pauly stared at the phone as it rang once, then twice. On the third ring, he reluctantly answered it.

"Yeah?" he asked cautiously.

"Pauly, it's Marco. What's going on?"

"Where are you?"

"Piano room."

"Who's with Stacey?"

"Leonardo, he's got her thinking he's gonna take her out on the town."

"Good. Marco . . . we gotta get Ravin out of here."

"Why? What the hell did you find?"

"A lot. Just . . . I don't know. Call Roxi and have her re-schedule everything today. Give her some excuse; tell her Ravin's sick or something."

"Is it that bad, Pauly?"

"Yes. I'm expecting a call, so try to get a hold of Roxi."

"Consider it done." He hung up the phone and paced the room.

Not knowing Roxi's number, he called Benny first.

Pauly waited patiently for Rocco to call back. When he did, he got the whole scoop on the drug he had found in Stacey's suitcases. He also found out that what he was seeing in Ravin were the effects on a slow poisoning that Stacey was conducting. He quickly closed the suitcase and locked it in his footlocker. He grabbed his phone and called Ravin's brother Nick. He explained everything as quickly as he could and got Nick and Joey to come over. They also brought over a small army of friends.

Pauly ran downstairs and pulled Marco aside, explaining everything. Marco talked to Roxi and explained what he could to her, and she canceled everything for the rest of the day. They ran over to put the rest of the guys on alert and made eye contact with Leonardo. Leonardo slipped his arm around Stacey and led her into the back with empty promises.

By the time Pauly got everyone out of the warehouse, Nick and Joey had arrived. Ravin sat on the couch unable to comprehend everything Pauly was telling her. She greeted Nick and Joey the best that she could and held onto Marco's hand as she closed her eyes.

"Ravin! Wake up!" Marco shouted at her.

Her eyes fluttered open and he saw fear, a fear he couldn't explain.

"Pauly, we've gotta get her to a hospital," Marco said, terrified. "Ravin honey, I love you. Please wake up," he cried.

Ravin's eyes fluttered open briefly. She tried to smile and whispered "I love you" to Marco. Her eyes closed and Marco felt her body go limp against his. Tears streamed down his face as he looked over at his friends.

Fifty-Five

Marco sat at the side of Ravin's bed, waiting for her to wake up. He looked up and watched her mom talking to the doctors. Nick and Joey stood beside her, trying to understand what they were being told. Marco took Ravin's hand, stroking it gently. The entire time, he whispered in her ear how much he loved her.

"What did he say?" he asked Mrs. Capello as she walked in and sat at the edge of her bed.

"I'm not sure what he meant, but he said that the poison was now out of her system and that only she can make herself wake up. He thinks that maybe her body is taking this time to heal itself. I told him how long it's been since she's had a good night's sleep and the trauma that caused her to stop. He figured that this was her way of catching up on five years of trauma, emotional and physical."

"Well, I'm not leaving until she does."

"We don't know how long it'll take," she said sadly.

"I'm not leaving her," he said quietly, shaking his head and stroking Ravin's hand.

"Dr. Green said that the best we can do for her is to talk to her and let her know how much we love her and need her."

"That's what I intend to do," he said.

"Marco." She paused not sure of what to say. "Ravin loves you. This is something I know. She loves you deeply, and you are the only thing that matters to her outside her family." She looked down at her daughter's limp body lying in the hospital bed.

"She cares about her work too. Her photography is very important to her."

"Not as important as you are. I can see it in her eyes, Marco. You mean the world to her. If we can convince her to hold on to that, I know she'll be out of this soon."

"She's my world. I would give up everything for her. I'd even leave the group if it comes to that."

"She wouldn't let you."

"I know, but I would without hesitating."

"I know, Marco, I know."

They sat in silence, watching Ravin sleep. The blinking and beeping of the monitors reminded them that she still had life left in her. They only needed to pray that Ravin wanted to come back and live it with Marco.

Pauly and Nick went down to the cafeteria and bought a cup of coffee. Nick turned to Pauly, who was sitting quietly in the corner.

"So, who was this crazy bitch that did this to my sister, Pauly? And why didn't you know what was going on?"

"Stacey Wilson. Roxi hired her when Ravin came back from California to help her out with her schedules. She was her personal assistant."

"For what?"

"Mainly to get her to appointments on time, keep her schedules straight. Ravin has a way of losing track of time when she's shooting, especially in the darkroom. Stacey was supposed to get on her ass and tell her to be somewhere, or whatever." He trailed off.

"I want to understand how she managed to get away with slipping her poison for two weeks without anyone noticing."

"I can't figure that out either. I've never seen her doing anything suspicious or even strange."

"Were you watching her?"

"Yes, I was, Nick. The first day she was there, I got a bad vibe. Even Marco called me from L.A. and told me that he had a bad feeling about her."

"Marco called? Did he meet her before?"

"Not until yesterday."

"So, he felt it too?"

"Yeah." Pauly's guilt was hitting an all time high.

"And Ravin? Did she have any feelings about her?"

"A few, but I think she felt bad for her."

"Why?"

"I don't know."

"Where is this girl?"

"Jail."

"Think she should stay there, or should we . . ." He didn't finish the sentence. Pauly knew.

"Up to you." He looked directly at Nick.

"Prepared?"

"Think I'd let anyone hurt Rave?"

Nick just looked at him. He wasn't sure if he wanted to answer the question. He waited to see how serious Pauly was and if his loyalties had wavered.

"Nick?"

"Finish it, Pauly."

"Done." He stood up. "Personally," Pauly added.

"Marco honey, do you want to go out and stretch? Maybe get yourself some coffee?" Mrs. Capello asked.

"I'm afraid to leave her."

"I know, honey, but you've been sitting in that chair for seven hours now. Go stretch your legs, get something to eat. Maybe call your friends and let them know what's going on."

"You sure?"

"Of course. I'll be here, I'll let you know if there's any change."

"Okay, I'll be back in a few minutes."

Mrs. Capello smiled at her soon-to-be son-in-law. She saw everything that Ravin loved about him and that made her happy. She looked down at her daughter and watched her eyes moving rapidly beneath her eyelids. She wondered what she was thinking.

From the beginning, Ravin Capello was the center of her father's world. After fathering two strong, healthy boys, he was blessed with his dark-eyed princess. He spoiled her rotten, as would any doting father, but her bond with her father was special. He loved his sons and taught them everything, but Ravin was taught that and more. She recalled every memory of her father as if it had happened yesterday. On her fifth birthday, her father threw her the biggest birthday party she had ever seen, complete with tiny tables covered with white linens and teacups that served her favorite beverage. He filled their backyard with white roses and pink and white balloons. It was the biggest tea party she had ever seen.

Her mind quickly jumped to Dominic, her first love and first lover. Promising her marriage, he took her virginity at the tender age of seventeen. He was three years older than she was, and she never thought his promises were empty and filled with lies. After a year of dating, she ended up pregnant. Unable to tell her father, she turned to Pauly. Crying on his shoulder most of the night, he promised to take care of everything — and he did. It took a month for Ravin to convince her father that she loved Dominic and wanted nothing more than to become his wife. Pauly hid the fact that she was pregnant, and her father broke down and offered his blessing for a proper Italian wedding. She watched Pauly slip into the background, although he never left her side. He was behind her through everything. He was there when Dominic was shot to death, protecting her the best he could. He stood by her side through the funeral and was the one that took her to the hospital when she miscarried the baby. She could never be sure, but she always wondered why Pauly met her and Brett on the way to the jewelry store. She had always wondered if he knew Dominic was going to be hit. Pauly never spoke of it, and he reassured her that there was a reason for it and that had nothing to do with her. Even so, he never answered the question directly.

"Hey, Marco, any change?" Pauly asked as Marco was coming out of her room.

"Not yet."

"Mind if I stay?"

"No, I don't. Pauly man, you look like shit." He looked up at his pale face.

"Thanks."

"You okay?"

"Yeah."

"Need an ear?"

"No."

"I'm getting some coffee. Mind sitting with her while I go?"

"No, anyone else in there?"

"Yeah, Mom."

Pauly slowly walked into her room. He looked at Ravin lying in the bed, hooked up to machines. He walked over and kissed Mrs. Capello before sitting in Marco's chair.

"How are you holding up, Pauly?"

"Fine. You?"

"Seen better days."

He shook his head and took Ravin's hand in his. "You look tired."

"I am."

"You should go home, get some rest."

"I should stay with my baby."

"You should go home and get some rest. Marco and I will stay the night. We'll call you if there's any change."

"I know, but . . ."

"But go home. Get some sleep. She's gonna need you when she gets up."

"You're right, Pauly."

Nick and Joey walked in, looking over at Ravin, feeling helpless.

"Nick, take Momma home." Pauly said, looking over at him.

"Sure?"

"Yes, Nicky. Pauly and Marco are staying the night," she stated.

"Pauly, this is my daughter, Ravin." Mr. Capello introduced them. He then proceeded to explain to Pauly that his main job was to keep his nine-year-old daughter safe from the surrounding neighborhood. It took Pauly a while to get used to watching over her, and it took just as long for Ravin to get used to Pauly tailing her everywhere. But after a few months, they formed a strong friendship. Within a year, she began to rely on Pauly to take her places and keep her safe from the boys that readily began to notice her. Her appearance was changing from girl to woman, and her mixture of Greek and Italian heritages were giving her the best of everything. Nick and Joey noticed the gawking eyes from the neighborhood boys and alerted Pauly to watch her even more carefully. They didn't need to tell him. He'd noticed too. When Ravin met Dominic, Pauly tried his best to dissuade her from seeing him. He knew him and his type. He knew

that her father would not want his little girl to date someone like Dominic and what would happen if she did.

After a while, Ravin confided to Pauly that Dominic was her true love and she had given him her virginity. It was Pauly's worst fear. And it had happened. He decided to tail Dominic and find out what he did when Ravin wasn't around. He wasn't shocked to find out that he was a runner for the neighborhood mob boss and that he had a stash of girls around town waiting for his call. This upset Pauly quite a bit, but he didn't want to step in until one quiet night when Ravin told him that Dominic had gotten her pregnant. Pauly listened and spoke only the words that promised her that everything would be okay. He confronted Dominic the next day and told him that he had to marry Ravin before anyone knew she was pregnant. For the first time, Dominic acted like a true gentleman and stepped up to the plate, asking Ravin to marry him.

After a month of convincing her father, he agreed and the wedding plans began. Pauly shadowed Dominic even closer and found out that he not only had several girls around town, but also a wife and twin boys hidden in an upstairs apartment across town. He also found out that he was skimming money off his pick-ups. Nothing could protect him now, and if Ravin got involved as his wife, she would be hit too. Pauly had to act fast, so he turned to a very trustworthy friend, Leonardo. He told him everything he knew, and Leonardo promised to take over from there. He knew Pauly wouldn't do the hit; Pauly would need to be with Ravin. Dominic was fingered to be murdered at the end of the week.

Pauly tried to get to her as fast as he could, but he was too late. Ravin watched it happen, and he did everything he could to get her out of there. After the funeral, Pauly held her in the garden. That same night, he took her to the hospital when she miscarried the baby. Nobody except Pauly knew about the baby. Ravin was glad that he was the only person she had to share that with. She also knew that he was the only person she could trust and be comfortable with.

Marco stood in the doorway watching Pauly. He could see how much he cared about her.

"Mom go home?" Marco set down his coffee.

"Yeah, Nick and Joey took her home." Pauly got up and motioned Marco to sit. "You staying the night?"

"Yeah, you?"

"If you don't mind."

"Why would I?"

"I don't know." He felt strange.

"Listen, man, I don't feel threatened by you at all. I know how much you love her and how much she loves you. Honestly . . ." He shifted his hand into hers. "I feel better knowing she has you around when I'm not."

Pauly shook his head. He liked Marco and was glad he wasn't the jealous type.

The nurse came in, interrupting their conversation.

"I've got to check her vitals," she said making Marco get up. "Are both of you staying the night?"

"If it's okay."

"Yes, under the circumstances. I'll bring in another chair."

"Thank you."

She finished taking Ravin's vitals and jotted them down in her chart. After leaving, Marco settled back into his chair. Pauly helped the nurse bring in another chair and settled in on Ravin's other side. They both held her hand and prayed she would come back to them as they drifted off into a fitful sleep.

Stacey sat in her jail cell. After Leonardo and Rocco dug a little more, they were able to connect her to the two deaths in her hometown. Scheduled to be arraigned in two days, she only wished she would stay alive that long. She had figured out who these two guys were and she feared for her life.

Fifty-Six

Ravin's eyes fluttered open briefly. She gazed up at the dimmed lights that shone above her. After a few seconds, she realized where she was. She turned her head and saw the I.V. stand that verified she was in the hospital. Slowly, she lifted her head off the pillow and saw Marco asleep on one side and Pauly asleep on the other. A calm peace came over her and she drifted back to sleep. Her mind tried to connect the time between the warehouse and now. She couldn't remember what happened. All she remembered was hearing sirens.

Ravin felt someone standing over her and she blinked her eyes open.

"Hi, nice to see you up," the nurse whispered.

Ravin nodded, feeling slightly confused.

"Can I get you anything?"

"Water," Ravin spoke in a hoarse whisper.

"I'll get it right away." She smiled and walked out of the room, looking back briefly at Ravin and the two men sleeping at either side of her. She wondered momentarily who they were, and if that *really* was Marco Deangelo.

Marco opened his eyes and sat up in the chair. He yawned as he stretched his arms above his head. He looked down, expecting to see Ravin's beautiful eyes still closed.

"Ravin!" he cried loudly. "You're up!"

Pauly woke up from the sound of Marco yelling and looked down at her. She smiled at Marco; her eyes still lacked the sparkle she had every time she looked at him.

"How do you feel?" he asked.

"Okay," she whispered.

"Can I get you anything?" His nervousness showed.

"Nurse is getting me some water." She looked over at Pauly. Her eyes may have lacked the sparkle that Marco was use to, but Pauly could read them no matter how cloudy they appeared.

"I'll go and call your mom. Marco, do you want some coffee?" Pauly stood.

"Yes, thank you, Pauly."

He shook his head and walked out of the room pulling out his cell phone.

"Ravin honey, I was so worried," he said as the nurse walked in.

"Here, sweetheart. Take slow sips." She handed her the glass.

"Is she going to be all right?" Marco turned.

"Well, I'm not a doctor, but I think she's going to be fine." She smiled, "my name is Molly. I just got on, so I'll be here for the next twelve hours. If you need anything just call. I'll send the doctor in to check on you."

"Thanks, Molly. I'm Marco." He smiled. "Thank you for everything."

"Anytime, and thank you, Marco. But I have three daughters, so I know who you are." She smiled again and slipped out the door.

Marco turned to Ravin and took her hands in his. He looked down and ran his finger over the tops of them. He thought about how he felt when he almost lost her . . . again. Ravin stared at his face. She had been able to read his thoughts easily, but something was different this time. She had seen his fear, and his love, but now she also saw his anger.

"What's wrong?" she asked quietly as her voice came back.

"Nothing." He gazed up at her. "Just glad you're back."

"There's something else. You look . . ." She couldn't quite put her finger on it. "You look almost pissed off."

"I am. I'm pissed that Stacey did this to you."

"Ya know, it's something I've always wanted to go through." She gave a sarcastic grin to match her tone.

"No, I wasn't there."

"Marco . . ." She wrapped her fingers through his. "You couldn't have expected this to happen. I didn't even see it coming."

"Pauly did, and so did I. I called him the other day to check on you. I just kept getting this weird feeling about her. I couldn't put my finger on it, so I called Pauly."

"You did? Why didn't you tell me about this?"

"I didn't want to upset you. You've been so busy that—"

"Marco, I need you to tell me things even if you think it's gonna bother me," she broke in. "I just can't believe I didn't see this coming." She dropped her face into her hands shamefully.

"You've been preoccupied."

"That's no excuse."

"Let's talk about this later. You need to get better so you can come home."

"I'm ready now. Where are my clothes?"

"Let's see the doctor first, okay?" He smiled for the first time since she had fallen unconscious in his arms.

Shortly after, her mother and two brothers arrived, and spoke with the doctors. He told them he needed to run one more test, and as long as she felt up to it and didn't do anything but rest, she could go home. Dr. Green ran the test immediately and it came back clear. The doctor discharged Ravin that afternoon.

Marco made her comfortable on the couch. Relieved to be home she didn't argue.

"Honey? Are all these dirty?" her mom asked, grabbing a pile of clothes.

"Mom, you don't have to do my laundry. I can do it later."

"Don't be silly. I'll start a load. If I don't get back to it, you can finish it up later," she said, knowing that wouldn't happen.

"How ya feeling, babe?" Marco slid in behind her on the couch.

"Eh, a little tired."

"Are you hungry at all?"

"Not really."

"You should eat something," he said, hiding his concern the best he could.

"I'm not hungry."

"But—"

"But I still don't feel good, so drop it."

"Okay, can I get you anything?"

"You can get my proofs from my desk."

"You probably shouldn't be working yet. You should be resting."

Ravin glared at him. He had never seen that look before.

"I'm smothering you, aren't I?"

"Yeah."

"Get use to it," he stated matter of factly.

"I'll never get use to it, but . . ." She looked around at her new friends. "But I'm just glad to have so many people care about me." She smiled.

"We do, all of us," Nico added.

Ravin tried to hold back the tear as she looked up at Marco. He went to wipe it away, but she did first.

"I'll get you those proofs."

He smirked as he walked into her office. He sat down at her desk, noticing a newly framed picture. Carefully, he picked it and looked closer. It was a picture of him sitting on the beach. She had captured his silhouette in the sunset. He wasn't sure when she took it, but it was a spectacular picture. He wondered briefly how many more she had taken without him knowing.

"Here ya go." He handed her the folder. "When did you take that shot of me on the beach?"

"Oh yeah." She laughed. "After we got back from Italy. I think I went in for a sweatshirt or something. It was priceless. I couldn't help myself."

"Hey, mom!" Nico walked into the room.

"Hi, Nico. Am I the official mom for the day?" Mrs. Capello asked with a smile.

"Only if you don't mind."

"With you boys, never." She smiled.

"Hey, Marco! We gotta get going, man, press conference today."

"Oh shit! I forgot." He looked down at Ravin, asleep in his lap. He carefully pried the proofs out of her hands and slid out from underneath her.

"Rave, hon, wake up." he whispered.

"What? What's wrong?" She jolted up in a panic.

"Nothing, honey, everything's fine. I've got to go and do the press conference."

"Oh yeah." She looked around her apartment.

"Your mom is still here." He read her mind.

"Okay."

"I know they're going to ask. I've got to tell them today."

"I know."

"You sure you're okay with this?"

"What are my choices? Accept it or break up with you. Gee, Marco, tough call."

"I know, if I could—" he began to say.

"But you can't. I can't change who you are and you can't change it either. I may hate being in the public eye, but I'm very proud to be with you."

"You are?"

"You sound surprised."

"Well . . . a little, more about how easy you're accepting this."

"Well I've had a lot of time to think in the hospital, and if that's the only thing I have to give up to be with you, then it's a small price to pay."

"I'm glad you think that way because I would give up everything to be with you."

"I know you almost did."

"I'll wink at you." He smirked.

"Okay, oh and Marco?" He turned to her. "Bring Pauly with you."

"Why?"

"He can help you with any questions about my family or my past. I'm sure you'll get a lot thrown at you that you aren't ready for. He can help you, ya know, keep things quiet and controlled."

"Does this mean you haven't told me everything?"

"I don't even know everything."

"I love you. Try to get some rest." He gently brushed his lips across hers.

"Love you too." She winked.

He kissed her again and ran his finger through her hair. Somehow that always seemed to relax him.

"Hey!" she called out.

"What?"

"Where's my ring?" She felt for it on her finger.

"Why? Did you lose it already?" He chuckled.

She looked hard at him.

He went over to his other jacket and pulled it out from the

pocket. Walking over with a smile, he gently placed it back on her finger. "They made me take it off you at the E.R."

"I know. I was there. Well . . . sort of. Thanks, now I feel better." She smiled at the feeling of it twisting on her finger.

Marco walked out with Nico and met the rest of the boys downstairs. Pauly escorted them out to the limo and they drove off. Marco rode in silence, thinking how he was going to tell the rest of the guys that he had decided to leave the group, or even when he would tell them. He couldn't handle being away from Ravin, and now this happened to her. He was just grateful that he was there. He couldn't help feeling terrified about the upcoming tour. He also knew that after tonight's announcement, things would only get worse. Ravin hated being in the spotlight. Although she had told him she accepted the fact she would never be alone, she didn't realize how much her life was going to change—and he didn't know how to tell her. He didn't want to tell her. He wanted to slip away with her and start a normal life. The only way he could do that was to leave the group.

Pauly sat in the back seat with the rest of the boys going over the conversation he'd had with Nick in his head. He suggested that they wait to deal with Stacey later. He told him that he and Leonardo were prepared to deal with her, but once the announcement was made that night, she would be public knowledge and he didn't want any links. Nick agreed and felt confident that Pauly hadn't changed his loyalty toward the family.

Ravin sat with her mom, Brett, and Mia, waiting for the press conference to begin. She watched anxiously as the boys walked out

"Marco, we hear you're engaged to be married," a reported asked. It was the first question of the night.

"Yes," he replied quietly.

"Who's the lucky lady to tie up the first of Jaded?"

Marco looked over at Pauly. Pauly took a deep breath and nodded, giving him the go-ahead.

"Ravin. Ravin Capello," he answered.

"*The* Ravin Capello? The photographer?"

"Yes." He held up his head proudly.

Ravin closed her eyes. That was that. It would now begin.

"May we ask how the two of you met?"

"During a photo shoot."

"How exciting. Tell us more."

Marco looked over at Pauly as all the journalists stood excited and ready. Pauly closed his eyes, wishing this wouldn't happen.

"We want to know about this new album," a seasoned reporter broke in. "Rumor has it it's better than ever. The singles your label released are flying off the shelves." He smiled at Marco knowing how much celebrities wanted to keep some things to themselves.

The rest of the press conference went smoothly. A few questions snuck in about Marco and Ravin, but the boys were able to avoid answering them. It was over, Ravin sighed, it was over. Or so she thought. Within hours, her phone began ringing off the hook. Call after call came from distant friends congratulating her and bigwig record companies bugging her to work for them. Eventually, she let the machine pick it up and went to bed.

Marco quietly slipped into the bedroom and sat at the edge of the bed. Ravin lay on her back, asleep, her hair fanned out across the pillow. He slipped his fingers through her hair and gently touched her soft face. Slowly, she blinked her eyes opened and a smile delicately spread across her face.

"Hi."

"Hi." He smiled back.

"How'd it go?"

"Good. Did you watch?"

"Of course."

"What'dya think?"

"I think it went well."

"Me too." He propped up on his elbow and twisted her hair between his fingers. She wrapped her hands behind his neck and pulled him down to her, kissing him passionately until he pushed her away.

"You sure?" he asked breathless.

"Come here." She sighed, a soft throaty groan.

* * *

Propped up on his elbow, he carefully traced her bare spine. He watched the muscles twitch beneath his touch.

"What exactly am I gonna do on tour without you?"

"You'll survive," she whispered, wondering how she would.

"Not likely."

"Hold me."

"Anytime, anywhere."

"Here and now Marco," she playfully demanded.

"What's wrong?" he asked as he slid her onto his chest.

"Nothing," she lied.

"Nothing? Then why are you so quiet?"

"Just tired." She closed her eyes. She *was* still tired, but she was more afraid of him leaving than anything. He sensed her pain and held her closer. They fell asleep in each other's arms, both thinking about the upcoming tour.

Noooo! Noooo! Marco!

Ravin woke up covered in sweat. She glanced over at the clock. It was three o'clock in the morning. The nightmare had startled her; it had been awhile since she'd last had one. She prayed they weren't coming back as she tried to go back to sleep. Unable to after a half-hour, she gave up. She slipped out of bed, threw on her sweats, and headed down to her gym.

As she walked over to her gym, she looked around. The warehouse felt different. Somehow, Stacey's living there and poisoning her made her warehouse feel unsafe, almost dirty. She regretted letting that happen. Her warehouse had been her security, her escape from the rest of the world. Now she didn't even feel comfortable in it. She thought about the warehouse that she saw when the boys did their video. It was good enough to turn into another home, and this time, she could make it better. She could make bigger rooms attached to hers for the guys. She almost felt excited, but she had so much to do before that. She had to find out the layout, the square footage, and then see if it was possible. At least she had something to do while Marco was on tour.

By six o'clock, she had finished her workout and started upstairs. She saw a light on in the piano room and tip-toed over to the door. Her heart raced as she stood by the open crack in the door. She slowly peeked through the crack and sighed when she saw Nico sitting at the piano.

"Hey, what are you doing up so early?" she whispered, hoping not to scare him.

"Hey!" he spun around startled.

"I hope I didn't scare you." She laughed, as she opened the door and walked in.

"Well, I sure wasn't expecting anyone to be up yet. What's up?"

"Just working out."

"Yeah? Why so early?"

"Couldn't sleep."

"Why not?"

"Nightmare."

"They're back?"

"Does Marco tell you everything?" She laughed but was surprised at the same time that he knew.

"Well . . . he didn't tell us about the cute little birthmark." He chuckled.

"He told you about my birthmark?" she asked, surprised.

"No!" He laughed, "Brett did."

"Brett?"

"Yeah, big conversation one day . . ." He drifted off, waving his hand in the air.

She smiled at him, looking around feeling uncomfortable.

"What's up? Wanna talk?" He sensed her uneasiness.

"Why do ask?" She glanced around the room again shifting from one foot to the other.

Nico put down his pen and paper and patted the seat next to him. "You just look like you need someone to talk to. Spill it."

"It's nothing, really." She sat next to him and let out a sigh.

"Spill it, Ravin. If you can't talk to me, then you can't talk to anyone. I'm the easiest person in the world to talk to."

"I know. I just feel weird."

"About what?"

"About everything! My relationship, my house, your tour, my job . . ." She drifted off.

"Let's go sit on the couch. I have a feeling you need something more comfortable."

He steered her over to the couches and sat her down. Within minutes, Ravin was pouring everything out, telling Nico how scared she felt about them going on tour, how strange it felt to be in such an incredible relationship with Marco.

"Marco loves you Ravin. I've never seen him act like this before, but I know he would give the world to you if he could."

"I don't want the world. I just want him."

"So, you don't like the fact that he's going on tour?"

"Partly. I guess I sound pretty selfish, don't I?" She shook her head, feeling even more confused.

"Listen, before we met you, Marco had started plans for his solo tour while we were on our down time. He's since dropped that whole idea. Performing is in his blood, and to watch him give up his chance at a solo career really threw me. But I'd much rather see him with you. You bring out something in him that wasn't there before, some kind of new energy. It's hard to explain, but I know what I see."

"I didn't know he wanted to go solo?"

"Yeah, and part of his proceeds were going to the battered women and children charity."

"Thanks, now I feel better," she said sarcastically.

"Well, don't. I think at some point, we're all gonna feel that way. I'm sure Vinny feels like that with Brett. And for the rest of us . . . well, hopefully we'll be able to find someone as special too."

"You will. Mia looks good." She winked.

"Mia, huh? I suppose she told you about us?"

"No, but you just did!" She smiled. "Think she's a contender?"

"To early to tell, but I wouldn't be disappointed if she was."

They talked for a while. She told him about how she didn't feel comfortable in her own home and she was thinking about moving. He told her a story about when he was little, and how a burglar had broken into their house. His mom moved them for the same reason. They talked about the tour and even lightening her work load so that maybe should could do a little of the tour with them. They always had photographers with them and they would much rather it be her.

Marco woke up to an empty bed and looked around. He figured she had gone down to the gym and got up to make coffee. Wandering down the stairs, he saw her curled up on the couch next to Nico talk-ing.

"So, now you're trying to steal my girl?" he joked.

"Yeah, only if we could clone her, right?"

"Morning, hon." She smiled.

Marco handed her a cup of coffee and slid in behind her. "If I'd known, I'd brought you a cup too, Nico. Sorry."

"Don't worry about it." He smirked.

"So, what'cha guys talking about? Anything good?"

"Ravin's thinking about moving," Nico chimed in, knowing it would be easier for him to say it.

"Moving? Where?"

"I don't know." She twisted her cup in her hand.

"When did this come up?"

"Last night, this morning. Ever since I got home."

"Why?" He looked concerned.

"I just don't feel comfortable here anymore."

"Was that what the nightmare was about?"

"No." She looked down at her hands.

"Wanna tell me?"

"No," she said playfully as she looked up.

"Fine. Then I'm going back upstairs without you." He laughed.

The three of them walked upstairs, Nico poured a cup of coffee and sat with them at the kitchen table.

"Are you really considering moving?"

"I haven't thought it through yet, but it wouldn't be so bad would it?"

"Moving all this shit? Yeah!" He chuckled.

"Seriously, Marco."

"Seriously? I wouldn't be against it. If you don't feel comfort-able here anymore, then pack up and let's go. Maybe we can find a nice castle for you to live in," he joked.

"A castle, huh? And I'm sure you would want to be the king of that castle?" she played.

"Yeah, sure!"

"No, I bought that warehouse across town; it's in a better neigh-borhood too. And it's closer to my mom."

"What warehouse?"

"The one you guys shot your video in."

"You bought that!" Nico broke in.

"Yeah, I did," she answered, feeling a little embarrassed.

"Why?"

"I liked the ceiling." She felt foolish.

"You liked the ceiling?" Nico shook his head. "That's the first time I've ever heard that reason to buy anything."

"Well, maybe we should go and check it out. See if it's got any potential." Marco looked at her seriously.

"I'm sure it will."

They talked the morning away, and little by little, the rest of the crew ended up in her apartment. Looking around, she knew it was time for a bigger place.

Fifty-Seven

"Ravin, Roxi's on the phone!" Marco called into the bedroom.

"Thanks, I'll get it in here." She picked up the phone.

Marco walked into the bedroom and watched her pacing the room with the phone to her ear.

"What's up?" he asked as she slammed the phone down.

"Nothing, just anxious to get back to work."

"And what? Roxi wants to put you on leave?" he asked, reading her mind.

"Yeah." She looked at him surprised. "How did you know?"

"Just by the look on your face." He walked over and put his arms around her waist. "You could use some time off. Get yourself back into your groove."

"Well, that's not possible," she replied, wishing she didn't just say that.

"Why? Because of me?"

"Kinda, but not in a bad way." She looked at him apologetic.

"Maybe we should go back to the ocean." He cocked his eyebrow.

"Yeah, maybe." She sat at the edge of the bed and put her face in her hands. The fear that Roxi could or even *would* replace her came full force. She had never thought about being replaced. She never thought there could be someone out there with her talent. Suddenly, feeling the ego she hated so much, she looked up at Marco.

"You okay?" he asked, leaning on the dresser.

"Yeah, I'll be fine. I just need some time alone to think about what I'm gonna do next."

"Want me to take you somewhere?"

"Would you?"

"Just as long as it's local. I can't fly out to Italy or wherever today." He smiled.

"Very funny, Marco."

She got up and went into her closet to change. Pulling on a white muscle shirt and black sweatpants, she pulled her hair into a ponytail and donned a black Yankee's hat.

"Where to?" he asked.

"You drive, Central Park."

"Roxi, I can't believe you would do this," Brett said, shaking her head. She sat in Roxi's office listening to Roxi tell her that she may be replacing Ravin.

"Brett, I can't keep covering for her. I know she's been through a lot. I know this last time wasn't her fault. But it just seems that since she's found Marco, it's like she lost her drive. Something's missing and I can't put my finger on it."

"Yeah, she's changed a little. I'll admit that too. But, Roxi! She's in love, she's engaged, and she's got so much running through her head."

"Planning a wedding is very stressful. I know, I did it twice. This is why I'm giving her time off."

"You aren't giving her time off! You're getting rid of her!" Brett stood in anger.

"I know. I feel bad. I'll—"

"You do not! You don't seem to care that you are the one that hired Stacey. You don't seem to care that this person tried to murder my best friend!" Brett shouted.

"Listen, Brett, I do care and I do feel bad for her, but I can't and *won't* put my models and my magazine on the line. I knew this was coming. I knew that I couldn't rely on her forever. She'll stay on the books and she can work when she wants. She just—"

"Just can't do the major shoots! I know, I know." Brett shook her head and wondered if she should quit on protest, but she wasn't as smart as Ravin. She had nothing else to fall back on.

"Brett, like I said, she's always welcome to work here. Her pay won't change and your job is still here. I just need to find someone else to count on. If Ravin walked out on me, I would be screwed and you know it. I've relied on her for years. So far, I've been lucky. One of these days, my luck's gonna run out and I don't want to be stuck without a photographer."

Brett sat on the couch and pulled her legs up to her chest. Part of her felt glad that she was still working full speed. The other part felt like she was backstabbing her best friend. She knew that this decision was hard for Roxi and that Brett had nothing to do with it, but it still affected her personally. She loved working with Ravin and she wouldn't take well to a new photographer.

"Do you want me to stay with you?" Marco asked, pulling up the park entrance.

"Don't matter."

"Are you gonna fill me in on anything?"

"Like what?" She looked over him.

"Like, what did Roxi say that set you off?"

"I'm being replaced."

"You're kidding!" he shouted. "I can't believe she's doing that!"

"I know, but . . ." She looked over at him. "But I think its okay."

They stepped out of the truck and he walked her over to the bench.

"I'm gonna run over and get some coffee." He pointed across the street. "Will you be okay alone?"

"Yeah, I'll be fine."

"Do you want some?"

"Sure." She smiled.

She watched him walk away. Sliding her black glasses up, she did what she came to do. Watching people was very satisfying to her. She could never figure out why.

"Roxi let her go?" Cole asked, waving to Brett as she stormed through the apartment.

"Yeah, who the hell was that?" Marco asked.

"Brett, apparently she just found out too."

"Put her on. I wanna know exactly what's going on."

"Sure, hold on."

Marco waited while Cole found Brett and put her on the phone.

"Can you do me a favor, Marco?" Brett asked, still fuming.

"What?"

"Push the wedding. I don't care how you have to convince her, but push the wedding."

"Why?"

"Because she's terrified to get married. Not being married, but the actual wedding part. Maybe if she got it over with she could turn back into the Ravin I know."

"That's pretty selfish, don't you think Brett? Push the wedding so she can get back to work. Isn't that supposed to be like . . . I don't know, maybe the happiest day of our lives? You make it sound like she's getting a tooth pulled. Sorry that we've inconvenienced you, Brett. Pardon us, by all means. We'll take our happiest day and rush through it just for you." He hung up on her before she could respond. Marco shoved his phone into his pocket and grabbed the two cups of coffee as he proceeded to Ravin.

"Here. It's still hot, so be careful." He sat next to her, trying to curb his anger.

"Thanks. What's wrong?"

"Nothing," he lied.

"What's wrong?"

"I just talked to Brett."

"And she pissed you off that much? Wow, she's getting better at it, isn't she?" she laughed quietly.

"Yeah well . . . how did you know I was pissed?" He looked at her feeling his mood lighten.

"Your cheeks get red when you're mad. I saw it at the hospital too."

"Sorry."

"For what? Being pissed at Brett?"

"Yeah."

"I couldn't care less. I'm probably pissed at her too and just don't know it yet. What'd she say?"

"Mostly that she understood why Roxi was doing this to you."

"Yeah, and I do too. Let's just forget about it and move on. Okay?"

"I guess." He looked down at the concrete below his feet and felt a little helpless.

"So, when does this tour start?"

"Two weeks. Why? Did you change your mind?"

"Possibly."

"But Roxi said you can still work, just not on the major shoots."

"Yeah, in other words, I get the leftover shit. And the fact that she hasn't called to check on me after that crazy bitch *she* hired for me tried to kill me . . . well, you figure it out."

"Yeah, that bothers me too."

"Anyway, I've got other plans." She held up her chin as if to convince herself.

"You do? Like what?" He smiled seeing her spirits rise.

"I have no friggin' idea." She turned to him with a rise of panic in her voice. "What the hell am I suppose to do?"

"Vacation, definately." He shook his head. "A long one."

"And what does one do on vacation?"

"Well, you could go to a spa, fly around the world with me . . ." He smirked.

"Yeah."

"You won't be able to sit on tour, will you?"

"Probably not."

There was a long silence as each thought how the other felt. Ravin was scared about losing her job. She had never thought about not working before. Sure, she had tons of people begging her to shoot for them, but they weren't like Roxi. On the other hand, she could tour with Marco, but she knew that wouldn't last long.

"Let's shop." Marco stood, reaching for her hand.

"Shop?" She looked up at him confused.

"Yes, when I'm depressed I shop."

"You're too much." She laughed and let him lead the way.

Fifty-Eight

"So, you're going on tour with him?"

"Yes, Pauly, and unfortunately, I'm asking you to come with me."

"Why? You don't need me."

"Yes, I do!"

"Why?"

"So I can feel comfortable."

"You don't need me, Ravin. You'll have the guys."

"I know, but you're my best friend, Pauly. I can't imagine doing this without you."

"You'll be fine."

"What am I suppose to do with all my time?"

"Plan your wedding." He shook his head. "I think you should plan your wedding, I want you to have the biggest, craziest, most outrageous wedding in history, the way your father would have wanted it."

"Pauly!" She slapped his arm.

"What?"

"You're crazy, you know that?"

"I certainly would have to be to put up with you every day."

"You're a jerk!" She smiled at him. "So, what are you gonna do while I'm gone."

"Hang out. Maybe I'll get a real job or something."

"You're staying here at the warehouse, right?"

"Yeah, why wouldn't I?"

"Just making sure. I want someone here."

"I'll be here. When do you guys leave?"

"Three days. I've got so much to do!" she said, getting up from the couch.

"When are they coming back from TRL?"

"Not sure. Why?"

"I want to take everyone out to Capello's for dinner tonight."

"Everyone?"

"Everyone, the whole crew, including Mia, and if I must, Brett."

"Hey, don't be mad at her. She's got her own job to keep track of."

"Yeah, but she didn't even go to bat for you, Rave."

"Yes, Pauly, she did, more than anyone else thinks. She put herself on the line with Roxi. Anyway, I'm not mad at Roxi anymore. She did what she had to do. I've been slacking off the last few months."

"I guess. Let me know when they get here."

"I will," she called out as he left her to pack.

Ravin stood in her room looking around at all her clothes. She wasn't sure what to pack or how much to bring. She wasn't even sure how long she was going to be away.

Fifty-Nine

"Ravin honey, wake up. We're here." Marco gently shook her.

"Where are we?" She rubbed her eyes.

"North Carolina."

"North Carolina?" She closed her eyes and lay her head back on his shoulder.

"Ravin, get up. We're at the hotel." He laughed, poking her side.

Dear Pauly,

We've been on the road for three months now. I'm not sure how much longer I can take this. Its fun being with Marco and the guys, but the traveling . . . I'm telling ya, Pauly, it's killing me. The long hours on the bus, living out of suitcases, half the time I don't even know what state I'm in. We're on our way to North Carolina and we'll spend two days there. After that, I guess we're off to Australia and then Japan. It's exciting to see different parts of the world, but at the same time, I'm tired of constantly moving around. You know me. I don't take to change too well. Brett said that I'm holding up pretty well though. She spent three days with us in Virginia. She looks great, I'm glad she's still modeling, and mostly I'm glad to see it wasn't me keeping her on the covers. Ha ha! I think that's helped our friendship out too.

Anyway, I guess I'm rambling. I'm just waiting on the bus for them to get out of some press conference. I'll call you soon. I miss you terribly.

Love ya,

Ravin.

Pauly read the letter and smiled. He knew she would be going crazy on the road and it was only a matter of time before she got bored and came back. Hopefully though, Pauly thought she would get some kind of wedding plans made, and maybe even get re-inspired to get back to what she did best.

"You sure you don't want to come to the concert tonight?"

"No, does that bother you?"

"Well, I won't have anyone to sing to, but if you don't want to . . ." He paused.

"I'm getting a headache and I want to finish this invitation list. I just can't do it on the bus anymore. It's too bumpy."

"If you change your mind, just tell Carm and he'll bring you in."

"If this headache goes away and I get tired of writing, maybe I will." She smiled.

He kissed her and left to perform. She smiled as he left and flipped through some pages of her planner. She set down the list after half an hour and stared blankly out the window. What was she doing? Why was she following him around the country putting herself through the torture of making herself invisible? She noticed herself turning into Ravin Capello, Marco's soon to be wife instead of . . . photographer. She knew it was time to get back to work. She just wasn't sure how to tell Marco. It wasn't her style to follow a guy around. She just couldn't sit long enough.

She looked over when her cell phone started ringing on the side table. Reluctantly, she answered it.

"Hello?"

"Ravin?" a deep voice asked.

"Yes, who is this?"

"Ravin Capello?"

"Yes, who is this?" she asked more demanding.

"Oh good. Hi, it's, Mason Reid."

"Mason, hi. How are you?" she answered, relieved it wasn't *another* fan.

"Good, good."

"Sorry about that. I just been getting so many funky calls since the announcement aired."

"Oh, I understand. So, you two are engaged now? That's wonderful! Congratulations."

"Thank you. So, what can I do for you?"

"Well, I was hoping you read through the book I gave you."

"Yes, I did. I even have it here with me."

"You do?"

"Yes, I've been on the road with the group and I thought I'd bring it, give me something to do."

"Well, I'm happy you thought of me that way. That's why I'm calling. I'd like to start meeting with you and the guys for the next video."

"Already? They just started their tour."

"Well, Ben called and said the demand for the next video was starting, so he wanted to jump on it. Thought it could keep them on top."

"Interesting concept, but we're about to leave for Australia. When would they possibly have time?"

"Next month they have a few weeks off, and I was wondering if you wanted another shot at it."

"Oh, I don't know. I'd have to think about it and talk to Marco."

"That's fine. Take down my number and get back to me, say by next week?"

"Sounds good. I'll let you know." She hung up, feeling a little more of Ravin come back into focus. Excited, she called in Carm and had him escort her to the concert.

She stood in the front row, enjoying Marco's expression when he noticed her. During intermission, she rushed into the back and told him about her phone call.

"Ravin, that's great! So . . . what did he say?"

"We can talk about it later. I want you to concentrate on your performance."

"But, Ravin—"

She put her finger up to his lips as he gently kissed them. "You've got to get back out there."

"Are you staying?"

"Of course! Don't tell them about Mason yet. I want to be there."

"Of course, I would never take your wind."

"Thanks, hon. Now go out and do your thing." She smiled, patting her camera.

Ben offered to pay her for any shots she took of them on stage or touring the sites. As much as she loved being with them and still being able to shoot, it still wasn't the same as shooting for Roxi. She missed the creativeness of shooting covers. She missed printing her own work, watching it come to life. It was one of the best parts of what she did, watching it come to life.

"I'm gonna miss you, ya know." Marco gave her a sorrowful look.

"I know. I'm gonna miss you too, but I'll see you back in L.A. next week."

"It won't be the same without you here."

"I know, but I've got to do this. I can't sit around anymore."

"I know."

"What's wrong?" she asked, watching him stare at the floor.

"Nothing."

"Marco, what's wrong?"

"I was just wondering something."

"Like what?"

"Like . . . how we're gonna keep our relationship strong, I mean with us going back and forth from L.A. to N.Y. and touring and stuff."

"We'll do fine, Marco, you know that, don't you?"

"Yes, I know."

"Do you have faith in us? Do you want to postpone the wedding or something?" A small pang of fear ran up her spine.

"Definately not! We aren't postponing anything. And I *do* have faith in us. I just don't know how I'm gonna get along without you here with me, that's all."

"You'll be fine. Trust me."

"I trust you, more than I've ever trusted anyone before in my life."

"Good. I have to go before the plane leaves without me. I will call you as soon as I get in. Leave your voicemail on."

"Why? You don't think I'm gonna miss that call do you?"

"No, but I do think you might be on stage when I get there."

"So true."

Marco watched her board the plane and instantly felt lost without her. They both knew she would have to get back to her life eventually, but he wished it didn't have to be so soon.

Ravin looked out the window and watched Marco standing in front of the windows. She wished she didn't have to go, but she knew it was time. She felt rested, energetic, and ready to get back to work.

"Welcome to L.A., Miss Capello," the chauffeur said, taking her carry on bag from her. "Mr. Reid sent me to pick you up."

"Oh, thank you."

"I will also be your driver during your stay here in California. My name is Robert."

"Well, it's nice to meet you, Robert. Where are you taking me first?"

"Back to your suite, Miss. Mr. Reid suggested you unpack and freshen up before dinner tonight."

"Dinner?"

"Yes, he wishes you to join him at the Polo Lounge tonight at seven."

"The Polo Lounge, huh? And what exactly does one wear to this Polo Lounge?"

"I'm not sure I understand the question, Miss."

"Never mind, Robert."

They rode the rest of the way in silence. Ravin knew she would never get use to this whole chauffeur idea and hoped to remember to tell Mason.

Robert escorted her up to her suite and informed her that he would be picking her up at six thirty sharp. She unpacked her bags and sat on the bed wondering. She decided to call Brett. She would know what to wear.

"Hey," Ravin said when Brett picked up.

"Hey, what's going on? Where are you?"

"L.A., at the Beverly Whilshire Hotel to be exact."

"You're kidding? Boy, Mason sure knows how to treat ya, huh?"

"You should see this place! It's enormous."

"I know, Rave. I've been there." She giggled.

"Sorry. I called because I'm supposed to be having dinner with him at the Polo Lounge and I don't know if I'm supposed to follow some kind of secret dress code or some stupid shit like that."

"You are too much, Ravin! Since when do you care about what you wear?"

"I want this job, Brett. I won't be doing photography forever, and since I don't have a job, ya know . . ." She paused.

"Listen, babe, there isn't a dress code there, but I would highly suggest that you wear something simple and nice. I'm not talking an evening gown, or even a dress, but some simple nice black pants and top."

"I think I've got it."

They talked for a while about wedding plans and what the boys were up to.

"Oh shit!" Ravin shrieked.

"What!" Brett cried.

"I forgot to call Marco. Listen, thanks. I will call you tomorrow and let you know how everything went."

"You better! And have fun."

Ravin hung up and dialed Marco's cell. She knew he would be on stage, so she left him a sexy message. Thinking about him made her smile as she jumped into the shower to get ready for dinner with Mason Reid.

"May I help you?" the hostess asked.

"I'm meeting Mason Reid for dinner," she stated calmly.

"Right this way, Miss Capello."

Ravin followed her to the back table where Mason sat talking to a small group of people. She felt every eye follow her through the restaurant. It was something she was use to but never comfortable with. She carefully selected her black low-rise pants and a fitted white silk blouse. She wore her favorite silver hoop earrings along with her black opals and twisted her hair up into a clip letting the sides fall against her face.

'Ravin." Mason stood, kissing her cheek. "I'm so glad you made it." He introduced everyone at the table and they all sat down to order.

The four investors looked at Ravin and thought that Mason had finally gone senile. He had promised them the newest director for his company, and the most talented he had seen in many years. Sitting in front of them was this young girl. She was beautiful, but they couldn't believe this was the person about whom Mason had been talking.

Making it through dinner, as difficult as it was, she was relieved when all of the investors left. Mason walked them to the door after asking Ravin to stay for a drink.

"Hello?" she answered quietly, realizing it was her phone ringing.

"Hey," he said in a deep sexy voice.

"Hi, hon."

"How did it go?"

"Still here. The investors just left, or whatever you call them. Mason asked me to stay for a drink."

"Oh, he did, did he?" He laughed.

"Yes, I would just rather go back to the suite and try to figure all this out."

"I know, babe, I know. Will you call me when you get back in?"

"Of course, are you going to be up?"

"I'll stay up for you."

"That's sweet, but if you're too tired, then don't wait up. I don't want you to be too tired to perform."

"I'll be fine. I love you."

"Love you too."

"Good call?" Mason asked, sliding back into his seat.

"I was talking to Marco." She smiled thinking about him.

"How's he doing?"

"Good." She smiled.

"Good, let's get down to it."

"Fire away."

Mason kept Ravin there for another hour, explaining the hesitation from the investors. He told her what he expected from her and then handed her a folder of the boys' ideas. Ravin was surprised when he told her he had sent all the supplies she would need for the storyboard and asked her to start right away. She felt a little overwhelmed, but exhilarated at the same time. Mason promised to check in on her sometime tomorrow and go over any questions she had.

Ravin sat back in the limo reading through the ideas the boys had sent in. Some of them hit, some didn't. She dialed Marco's number and sat back waiting.

"Hey," he answered quietly.

"Hey, babe."

"So, are you back in your suite now?"

"Well, no."

"No?"

"I'm on my way. I was going over your ideas for the video."

"Okay, what do you hate?" he laughed.

"Nothing, I like some of the ideas."

"But . . ."

"But don't you think your fans are getting tired of the same thing?"

"Meaning . . .?"

"Meaning this is almost exactly like the video you did for 'Fire'."

"Boy! Have you done your homework! That was like on our first album." He laughed.

"I know. I was thinking of doing something a little edgier."

"Go for it." He smiled proudly.

"Don't you think you should ask the guys?"

"Probably, hold on and I'll get them in here."

He left briefly as Ravin walked into the hotel and onto the elevator. When she reached her suite, she was surprised to see boxes of supplies on the table from Mason along with a bouquet of flowers, wishing her good luck. She smelled the flowers and smiled.

"Still there?" she heard over the phone.

"Yep."

"Do you want to do something edgier?" Nico broke in.

"Yes, hold on a second." She set down her phone and slipped off her shirt. She quickly pulled on her tank and slipped into her scrubs. "I was thinking of something faster."

She spent over an hour on the phone with them. As they threw ideas back and forth, things began clicking in her head and she tried to keep up with everything. After a while, she hung up, made herself some coffee, and found a cozy spot on the terrace.

She worked all night finishing the storyboard. When she glanced at the clock and saw it was five-thirty, she knew sleep would be senseless. Instead, she laid the storyboard out across the floor and went over scene by scene. She was happy with the turnout, even happier that it was finished too.

She walked out onto the terrace and looked out at the ocean. Marco was right. There was something about the ocean that stirred her creativity. It brought her back to the world to which she was accustomed, the creative world that she preferred. Her mind drifted off to Marco and she didn't hear the door open into her suite.

Pauly quietly strolled into the suite and watched her out on the terrace. He bent down and picked up part of the storyboard. He knew she had been up all night.

Sixty

"When are we leaving for L.A.?" Vinny asked as they rushed from the concert hall.

"Three days. Do you think you can handle it, Vin? Being so far away from Brett for so long!" Nico mumbled sarcastically.

"What the hell is up his ass?" Marco looked over.

Cole and Brody both shrugged.

"I think he's drinking again," Vinny whispered.

"Oh man, I hope not. He promised." Marco glared over at Nico.

Vinny shrugged as they all boarded their tour bus and headed back to the hotel. Marco gazed out the window at the stars and again wondered if he should leave the group. They had been making albums and touring for seven years straight with very little time off between. A few years ago, Nico began drinking heavily. It was affecting the entire group as well as his music and performances. After a while, Marco and the group had asked him to either check in somewhere to dry out or do it himself. Those were the only choices they had given him. Nico choose to deal with it his way and hadn't had a drink in a long time—until now. Marco knew Nico was under a lot of pressure. They all were, but they had to find outlets for their stress. When Nico stopped writing, Marco should have known he was back on the bottle. The guilt encompassed him, knowing the reason he didn't notice was sitting alone in a suite waiting for him.

"I'm going out," Nico stated once back at the hotel as he changed his clothes.

"Where ya going?" Cole asked comically.

"Out."

"Want some company?" Cole asked, concerned.

"No, I don't." Nico said roughly as he slammed the door behind him.

"Want me to follow him?" Brody stood.

"No, let him go. Let him get it out of his system. We'll confront him on the way back to L.A." Marco opened his bag and pulled out a sandwich.

"If he lasts that long," Cole said uneasily.

"So, you're from the group Jaded?" the tall blonde asked tipping her drink slightly.

"Yes, I am. Nico is the name and fun is the game," he slurred.

"Really?" the tall blonde giggled. The shorter brunette just smiled wondering what her friend saw in him. He was a fall-down drunk and showed no promise.

Nico and his new blonde friend Gina danced the night away. They spent hundreds of dollars on champagne and he made many new friends. Unfortunately for him, he also made a very unstable enemy. Gina was playing a good game while her boyfriend sat at the back table watching. She didn't notice him the whole night, but he noticed her every move. When Nico left, he didn't notice the three thugs following him out, and unfortunately neither did Gina.

"Where are we going?" she asked.

"Home."

"Where's home?"

"I don't know. Where do you live?" He turned to her.

"Me? I thought we would go to your place."

"No, my place is too crowded," he mumbled.

"Well, so is mine." She pouted. She didn't want him to see the four kids she had sleeping on the floor in her one bedroom apartment. She also didn't want him to see her drugged out boyfriend passed out on the couch.

"Well, this is a dilemma, isn't it?"

"What should we do?" she pondered.

Nico shrugged and stumbled almost running into the dumpster as they swaggered into the alley.

"Maybe we could get a room?" She flipped her hair. "A nice one."

"We could do that." He clumsily slid his arm around her.

From out of the shadows, Gina's boyfriend aimed his pistol. He took one shot and hit Nico. Nico jerked around when the bullet hit his chest and abruptly fell to the ground. Gina screamed and looked around; nobody was in sight, so she ran.

The bouncer heard the gunshot and the scream and poked his head out the door. Crime was an everyday occurrence in this neighborhood. He looked down the alley and saw Nico's arm lying on the ground behind the dumpster.

"Shit, not again," he mumbled to himself. He waved down his partner and called the police.

Nico was rushed to the hospital in serious condition, but still alive, barely.

"Hello?" Ravin answered, rubbing her eyes.

"Hi, hon."

"Hi, what's wrong?"

"How do you know something's wrong?"

"Marco, I can hear it in your voice."

"Nico's been shot," he said gravely.

"What?" She sat up in bed.

"He was shot tonight . . . in the chest and shoulder. He's alive . . . barely."

"Marco! What happened? I mean, how did this happen? Are you okay? Did anyone else get hurt?"

"No, we're all fine. He went out after the concert tonight. They aren't sure what happened yet, but the bouncer said he left with some girl, and when they were outside, he heard the gunshot and her screaming."

"Where was his security?"

"Apparently, he didn't go with him tonight."

"Do you need me to come out there?"

"No as soon as he's stable enough, they're gonna transfer him to a rehab in L.A." He sighed.

"Marco, I don't know what to say."

"Nothing to say. I just needed to hear your voice and let you know what was going on. We have to postpone the video and the tour. I'm not sure for how long."

"Let me take care of the video. I'll talk to Mason. Do you want me to call Ben?"

"No, Cole called him already. He's on his way down."

"Marco, I'm coming too. I'll leave first thing."

"You don't have to."

"Yes, I do. He's my friend too."

"First, I was wondering if you could do me a favor."

"Absolutely, name it."

"Rent us a house on the beach and call Mia. He kept saying her name, but I'm not sure why."

"They've kinda, hooked up."

"Really? Well let me know . . . whatever. I love you."

"I love you too. And Marco?"

"Yeah?"

"Try to get some rest. You sound tired."

Sixty-One

"Yes, may I help you?" the woman at the admissions desk asked.

"Yes, could you tell me which room Nico Catone is in, please?"

"Yes, room . . ." She paused and looked at the computer screen. "Yes, he's in room four-twelve."

"Thank you." Brett smiled. She picked up her bag, turned to the elevator, and saw Ravin rushing through the doors.

"Hey, I'm so glad you're here." Brett ran over to her.

"Hi, babe. You okay?"

"Yeah, you?"

"We'll see, won't we?"

"Did you talk to Pauly?"

"Yes, he stopped by before visiting Johnny in Vegas. I asked him to pick up Mia."

"Good."

The two friends walked up to the fourth floor together, nervous about what they were about to see. Once on the floor, they knew they were close. A dozen or so security guards roamed the halls and the nurses looked irritated.

"Brody must be here," Ravin joked.

"Think he can piss off that many women at once?" Brett laughed.

Ravin smiled, knowing only Brody could stir up so many women at once.

"Hey, Cole. How's he holding up?" Brett walked up and hugged him.

"Pretty good, considering." He kissed Brett and Ravin.

"Can we see him?"

"Yeah, but only one at a time."

Brett smiled at Ravin and motioned her to go in first. She slowly walked into the room and saw Marco talking to him.

"Hi," she whispered.

Marco looked up at her, a huge weight lifted off his shoulders. He needed her so badly to help him through this.

"Hi."

"How is he?"

"Okay." He forced a smile.

"I'll be fine, I'm not dead yet," Nico managed a horse whisper.

Ravin snickered and walked over to the bed.

"Hi, baby, how ya feeling?"

"What? No flowers?"

"Well gee, if I would have thought of it. I was a little busy thinking about you to worry about flowers," she said sarcastically.

"Thanks, as long as I know you care." He let out a small smile.

"You know I care about you." She sat on the edge of the bed. "You know I love you." She smiled and brushed some hair out of his face.

"I know you do."

"So, what happened here, big boy? What were you doing out there in the badlands?"

"Just trying to have some fun, I guess." He looked over at Marco.

Ravin glanced over at Marco too. Taking the hint, he excused himself.

"So tell me Nico," she pressed, "what kind of fun were you looking for out there?"

"I don't know." He felt ashamed.

"Nico, it's me. Tell me, what made you start drinking again?"

"Pressure."

"Of what?"

"Everything, I guess." He fiddled with the edge of his blanket.

"I want something a little more specific than that."

"Fine." He closed his eyes and let it all out. "Mostly, it's stress. We've been on the road for over seven years, and I know that at some point, people won't be interested in our style of music. The industry is changing. I've been watching it closely. The new music is so different. People want single performers now. They don't want to watch a bunch of over-age guys in matching outfits dancing on stage." He let out a sigh, trying to bury his worries.

Ravin wasn't going to let him stop there. "So, you're afraid of the industry changing? Nico, I know that there's more to this than just that. Tell me, maybe I can help."

"Well, there's you and Brett." He looked away, unable to see into Ravin's face. "I'm just scared that I won't find anyone, that Marco and Vinny will get tired of all of this and just want to spend more time with you two. I would. Hell, if I had a woman like you or Brett, I certainly wouldn't want to spend all my time on the road. Ravin, I know Marco loves what he does, but I also know that part of him would just rather settle down with you and maybe start a family. When we started this group, none of us was prepared for this kind of fame. We never thought that it would take up so much of our lives. Now, Marco and Vinny have a reason to stay behind. That scares me."

"You think that they'll leave the group for us? Nico, that's crazy! They would never do that, and Brett and I would never let them."

"No?" he asked, looking at her intensely.

"I can't speak for Brett, but I know that music runs through Marco's blood. I would never ask him, nor would I let him, leave just to be with me," she answered, reassuring him that she was sincere.

"Still, it's coming to an end. I can feel it."

"So, that gives you the opening to go and get yourself hurt," she said, raising her voice slightly. "Nico, you have a drinking problem. You can't do things like this. Look how it's affected your life, as well as the lives of the people you care about and who care about you. You could have been *killed!*"

Nico looked down, ashamed. "I'm sorry," he muttered.

"Forget it, for now. Promise me something though, will you?"

"What?"

"When you're stressed out like this and you feel like you need to let it all out, call me. Maybe we can find another way for you to burn off some steam. Mia's on her way," she hinted.

Nico turned his head, trying to hide the color rising in his cheeks.

"I know everything, Nico, and I know that she likes you a lot. She isn't expecting anything, just the chance to get to know you, possibly try a relationship."

"I wasn't sure how she felt." He looked at Ravin, feeling embarrassed.

"Well, now you do, so pull it together and let's get you back out to L.A."

"Thanks."

"Switching gears here, I spoke with a realtor this morning."

"Are you buying a house?" he asked.

"Yes, my very first house."

"And where may I ask is this house located?" he lead her on.

"Well, I haven't found it yet, but it will be in L.A."

"Really?" he asked, shocked. "A city girl like you is buying beach property?"

"Yes, I am. I did ask that she find one on or near the beach."

"Why?"

"What do you mean why?"

"Why are you moving to L.A.?"

"I'm not moving to L.A. full time, but if you must know . . ." She paused, looking out the window and back at him. She leaned down and looked directly into his eyes. "I'm buying a house out there for all of us to stay in. I'm sick of hotels, and you're going to be out there for a while recuperating. Just because Marco is going to be my husband doesn't mean that I don't love the rest of you as well."

"Ravin, you are the sweetest, most loving, and caring person I have ever met, which really took me off guard."

"Is that because Benny told you I was a pain in the ass?"

"You know about that?"

"I've heard him call me worse."

"No, it wasn't what Benny said. It's just my first impression of you was very quiet and guarded, but you've opened up so much since then."

"Thanks, you guys make it easy."

She leaned down and kissed his cheek. "We should probably let Brett in. She must be going nuts out there."

"Sorry I took up so much of your time. I'm sure you're eager to see Marco too."

"Honestly, I just want some coffee." She giggled. She left the room and smiled at the rest of the waiting boys.

Brett went in to say hello.

"Hi, baby." Marco kissed her on the nose.

"Hi, baby." She smiled.

"Long talk, how's he doing?"

"He'll be fine."

"So, what was—"

"We'll talk about it later," she broke in. "How are you?"

"Better now, I'm glad you came."

"Did you really expect me not to?"

"Well, no."

"But you had to say it. I know. Have you talked to the doctors? When can he get out?"

"Well, they said probably in the next few days. They need to run more tests and make sure there aren't any complications. Right now, he's in pretty bad shape, but with good therapy he'll recover fully."

"That's good."

She snuggled her head into his chest. Marco wrapped his arms around her running one hand through her hair. Ravin instantly relaxed until her phone rang.

"Already?" He laughed.

"Sorry, I have to take this one." She smiled and he pushed her away.

"Hello?"

"Hi, Ravin, it's Elaine from the realtors."

"Hi."

"I found four houses meeting your requests. I've e-mailed them to you if you want to take a look. The first one in Santa Monica already has people interested, so if that one interests you, let me know immediately so I can start the bidding."

"Thanks, Elaine. I'll take a look and get right back to ya." She hung up and picked up her bag.

"Who's that?" Marco asked.

"Secret."

"Secret? Since when do you keep secrets?"

"Since it's a surprise."

"Oh, I see . . . I don't like surprises," he kidded.

"Yes, you do!" She laughed as she pulled out her new laptop and plugged it into her phone.

"What the hell are you doing? What is that?"

"It's a computer, Marco. Get with the times!"

"I know it's a computer. I have one. I didn't think you did though."

"I got it last month, thought it would be fun to fiddle around with. Now I'm finding it almost as important as my cell phone."

"Really? What are you looking up?"

"Well, because I promised not to keep secrets from you, I guess I'll tell you."

"Gee thanks."

"I'm buying a house."

"You are?" he asked surprised.

"I are!"

"Where?"

"In L.A. somewhere."

"You? You are going to live on the West Coast?"

"Well, only part time. I'm also gonna live in New York."

"Wow! How come?"

"Well, we're gonna be out there for a while getting Nico back on his feet. And I'm going to be directing your videos. Plus some photography, I just thought it would be better to have a house rather than live in a hotel."

"Wow! I never thought you'd do this. Well, before you put any money down . . ." he began to say.

"I know. You want to check it out and see if you like it."

"No, I want to pay for it."

"Marco, that's not necessary."

"Well, what difference will it make? In a few months, we'll be husband and wife."

"True."

"Settled. So, are these the choices?" he asked, looking at the pictures Elaine had sent.

"Seems to be."

They went through the pictures of the homes Elaine had sent to her and narrowed it down to two choices. Ravin called and told Elaine which two and set up a meeting to see the houses.

"She said we shouldn't wait until next week. These go fast."

"So, set it up for tomorrow. We'll fly out for the day and then come back here."

"You sure?"

"I'm sure."

Ravin called Elaine back and set up appointments to see the houses. They spent the rest of the day at the hospital with Nico and were kicked out around eight. Exhausted, they all met up at the hotel. They talked all night after ordering in room service.

"Which one do you like?" Elaine asked over coffee.

She spent the day with them carefully going through each house. Ravin's mind was set on the first house they saw on the beachfront. It was beautiful with huge windows overlooking the ocean. It had a huge living room area and a tremendous kitchen. Each view from every room was spectacular.

Marco knew instantly it was her favorite. "I think the first one we saw." He smiled at Ravin.

"So, shall I set it up?" Elaine asked, eager for the sale.

"Let's do it," Ravin said proudly.

After hours of paperwork and phone calls to various people, they eventually boarded the plane to take them back to Arizona. The doctors said Nico could leave in two days and they were eager to tell everyone their news.

Exhausted when they reached the hospital, they were glad to see Nico sitting up in bed cracking jokes. Marco felt the most relieved, having grown up with an alcoholic father, that Nico was in control again.

After being kicked out again at eight o'clock, they all fell back into the hotel room and discussed the options for Nico's homecoming. Marco had secretly told Nico about buying the house and asked him not to say anything until the next day. Ravin and Marco told the rest of the crew later that night over a late dinner. Brett was in shock the most. The idea that Ravin could move to the West Coast was something she never thought possible.

"Hello?" Ravin picked up the phone and looked over at the clock. It was only eight in the morning and she couldn't think of anyone who would be calling.

"Hi, hon, it's Roxi."

"Hey, Rox, what's up?"

"Sorry I'm calling so early, but I was wondering if you could do a job for me?"

Marco rolled over and looked up at Ravin. She smiled and brushed her hand across his cheek.

"What'cha need, Rox?"

"A shoot?" Roxi asked hesitantly.

"Where, when, and how much?" she half joked.

"Well, I've never heard you ask that before."

"Well, I was always on the payroll."

"Sorry."

"So . . ."

"So, I was wondering if you wanted to shoot for Lainey."

"Sure, where?"

"To be honest, I need someone to shoot her out there. I wanted it done in the Grand Canyon."

"What's it for?"

"This year's fall line is very outdoors. I'm seeing a lot of flannel come back along with hiking boots."

"Interesting. When do you need this done?"

"Well anytime you're available, but I would like it by next week."

"Let me look at my schedule and I'll call you back later."

"Thanks, hon."

Ravin hung up the phone and turned to Marco, who propped himself up on his elbow.

"What?"

"So, Roxi wants you to shoot for her, huh?"

"Yes, it's probably just more convenient seeing as I'm already here."

"I don't think so. I think she wants you back."

"Yeah right." She tucked her head into his chest and closed her eyes. She fought back the excitement that was creeping back up her spine. She secretly missed shooting for Roxi. She missed Roxi period. Roxi was the big sister she'd never had, someone she could talk to about things that Brett couldn't understand.

"Did you call her back?" Brett followed Ravin out of Nico's hospital room.

"No."

"Why not? I mean, she's giving you a second chance."

"I don't want a second chance. I didn't screw up the first one! I'll get back to her when I'm good and ready."

"Ravin, don't get cocky. I thought it was a good idea."

"Oh, so *you* set her up to this? This wasn't even *her* idea?"

"No, we were just talking. I told her about Nico and how you and Marco bought a new house out here. She thinks you're giving up on New York."

"Why would she think that?" she snapped.

"Because you bought a house in Santa Monica."

"Lots of people in this business have two, one on each coast."

"You live in a warehouse in New York, Ravin."

"And exactly what's wrong with that?"

"Nothing, it's just—"

"You know, Brett, you're starting to sound like a stuck up little—" She took a deep breath, trying not to say how she really felt.

"Like what, Ravin? Like a stuck up little bitch! Well fine, at least when your career died you had something to fall back on! You can always take pictures, even if it's for Sears! What have I got left? Huh? Tell me! Ooh, I know! I can be a washed-up, over-the-hill model who no longer has a name except for Vinny's girl!"

"What the hell are you talking about, washed-up?"

"You heard me," she said quietly and forcefully before she stormed away.

Ravin stared at her in disbelief. She had no idea what was going on. She looked over at Marco and Vinny as they stepped out of Nico's room to see what the yelling was all about.

"What the hell is she talking about?" she asked Vinny.

"You heard her. Brett feels like she doesn't have much left in her. Roxi's got seven new girls, all very young and very pretty. Brett's feeling old and replaced. She thought you would be able to understand how she felt." Vinny tried to hide his anger.

"Well then, why the hell didn't she say that! Damnit!" She stomped off to look for her best friend.

Vinny and Marco exchanged glances, shrugged, and vowed they would never understand women.

"I'm sorry, I didn't know. Why didn't you tell me, Brett?"

Ravin took her hand as they sat on the bench outside the hospital.

"Me too."

"So, what do you want to do?"

"As in?"

"Your life?"

"How the hell am I supposed to know? All I've ever known was modeling."

"That's good. My daddy taught me something. He always told me to do something that you know."

"Oh yeah, that's great advice for a model, except for the fact that once you hit your twenties things slow down—a lot."

"So, don't model. Maybe you can like coach or something."

"Coach?" She giggled and smacked Ravin's arm.

"Okay, so coach wasn't the right word, but what about like teaching or even opening up your own studio."

"It isn't out of the question, is it?"

"Who would have thought that I'd ever be directing? Huh? Certainly not me."

"True, but Ravin, you're so good at it."

"And you are so good at being a model, being beautiful without all the crap that goes on behind the scenes. I know a lot of models do certain things to stay awake or go to sleep. Sometimes they do all that crap at the same time, and now with drugs so available and popular, wouldn't you want to protect the young models from falling into that trap?"

"That's what Roxi did for me."

"Exactly. Maybe the West Coast needs someone like that."

"Ravin, I don't know." She shook her head doubtfully.

"Talk to Vinny about it. Trust me."

"Okay, only if you call Roxi back and do this shoot. I don't want her as an enemy."

"I'll call her. Don't worry."

Sixty-Two

"Now what?" Ravin stood in the living room of their new house.

"Well, I guess it could use some furniture, huh?"

"That would be good." Ravin shook her head, looking around at the empty house.

"What time did Cole say Nico would be in?"

"Some time tonight. He'll go right to the hospital though. He probably won't be able to come home for a few days."

"I think we should go shopping. Cole said to take the day to get organized." She put her hands on her hips.

"Don't you want to be there for Nico? I know you mean a lot to him."

"He told me to take care of our house so he'll have somewhere cozy to stay when he gets out."

"Where do we start?"

They stood in the middle of the room looking around, neither sure what needed to be done first.

"What did Roxi say?" Vinny pulled her closer.

"She was excited. Apparently, she had thought about it before and already bought a studio. It's just been empty because she hasn't had time to come out here and start it up. I told her that I would be willing to run the agency for her."

"She was excited then, huh? That's great!"

"It is, isn't it?" Brett wasn't sure if she felt excited or terrified.

"I think you're gonna be a great agent. You're very talented."

"No, you have the talent. I just have the experience."

"Come here, you." He pulled her close to his chest. "Have I told you how much I love you lately?"

"We're here. Now what?" Ravin looked around the huge furniture store.

"May I help you?" A tall woman walked up behind them.

"Yes, we just bought a house, so grab a pen and paper and let's get to it." Marco laughed.

"Right away." She knew a big sale when she saw one. On top of that, she recognized her newest clients. She disappeared and returned with three assistants and a pad of paper.

"Let's start with the basics." The saleswoman sat them at the comfortable table. "Do you have a color scheme?"

Ravin and Marco looked at each other puzzled.

"Is this your first place?"

"No, I have a place in New York," Ravin answered.

"Okay, so you're from New York. Let's see . . . what kind of place do you live in? An apartment, a studio perhaps?"

"I live in a warehouse."

"A warehouse? Interesting. Are you leaning more toward the rustic look rather than silks?"

Ravin looked over at Marco, who was apparently enjoying the sight of Ravin squirming.

"Maybe if we just walked around a while, I'm sure something will hit us." He took Ravin's hand, saving her from further torture.

"Thank you," she whispered as they walked away. "Color schemes, what kind of shit is that? It's either black or white, right?"

"Pretty much, although there are colors out there in the world."

"I know that!" She playfully smacked his arm.

Then it happened. Something caught her eye, and Marco had it put down on the list.

They spent three hours picking out mismatched furniture. The more it clashed with the last piece, the more he enjoyed watching the woman's face. What she didn't know was Ravin's unique ability to make it work.

By the end of the day, Ravin and Marco's house filled up with people and the decorating began. Room by room, Ravin put together a very comfortable house. It was much like her warehouse with a little of Marco thrown in. Days later, Nico moved in and started his daily therapy. Even with his arm in a cast, they began the emotional healing and the group stood by his side.

Brett got started on the new studio. Roxi wired her enough money to keep her going until she got there. Brett had full control over decorating and organizing the new place, although she called Roxi a lot to help her with ideas and help her stay in the right direction.

Ravin finished every last detail of their upcoming wedding and ceremoniously closed the book . . . at least for the time being. She waited on pins and needles, not letting Marco out of her sight. After a brief conversation with Brett, he understood and accepted it.

The photo shoot for Lainey at the Grand Canyon was two days away. Roxi flew in a crew and set everything up for her. She promised Ravin that for her next shoot, she would have to answer to Brett.

Pauly sat out by the pool, watching the hustle and bustle of his best friends. After a brief vacation and time spent with Johnny in Vegas, he felt he was becoming comfortable with Ravin's new lifestyle. As crazy as it got, Pauly was still ready for anything.

Tony, now Marco's new head of security, sat across from Pauly. He was pleased with his new title and only had to answer to Marco, Ravin, and, of course Pauly. The two of them were becoming good friends, sharing techniques on how to keep track of their charges and their bizarre schedules. Tony had been granted a gun after saving Marco's life from a deranged fan with a knife.

Sixty-Three

"So, tell me Ravin, which coast do you honestly want to spend the most time on?" Brett smiled at her as they drove out to the Grand Canyon.

"I don't know. I miss New York terribly, but at the same time, I love it here. It's so much calmer."

"I know. I'm starting to get hooked too."

"How's the model search going?"

"Okay. I've only got a few prospective clients. I haven't found that *one* girl that I'm looking for."

"The *one* girl? What do you mean by that?"

"You know, the *one* girl to carry the studio, like I use to be, and like Kyla is to Roxi now."

"So, what does this girl look like?"

"I don't know. Why?"

"In case I see her." She chuckled.

They stopped laughing when they both saw smoke spewing out the front of the van.

"Ronny, what the hell is that?"

"We overheated. Don't worry. I can see a gas station up ahead."

"Shit, this is gonna delay my shoot," Ravin said under her breath.

They pulled into the gas station, running over the hose and causing the bell to ring. Ronny got out and looked around to see if anyone was there to help him.

"Get out and stretch?" Brett asked, opening the sliding door.

"Might as well." Ravin put down her black book.

The girls got out of the van and watched Ronny approach the entrance to the garage. Ravin looked around at the scenery, the desert sprawled out in front of her from all sides. She was about to go back and get her camera when Brett reached back and grabbed her arm.

"What?" Ravin said, aggravated.

"Look."

"At what?"

"Her." Brett pointed to the girl talking to Ronny. Brett stared at the girl the same way Roxi would. She was about five-foot-ten inches tall with long dark auburn hair.

"What about her?"

"She's got the look I want."

"She does? Why?"

"Just come with me, please?" She pulled Ravin's sleeve, dragging her along.

"Tessa! What ya doing out there?" Jon asked as he came in the back door. He hadn't noticed the three vans sitting out front.

"Hi, I'm Brett Santana." She walked up to the girl.

"Hi, Tessa." She looked confused. "The bathrooms are around the corner." She pointed to the side of the building.

"No, I was wondering something." Brett looked at Ravin for support.

Ravin smiled proudly.

Jon stood looking carefully at the girls that his friend Tessa was talking to. After a few moments, it sunk in who these two were. He stood in shock.

"What were you wondering?" Tessa shifted her weight to the other side.

"If you would be interested in modeling."

"Modeling!" She began laughing and walked back into the garage.

"Well, I guess not." Brett shrugged.

"Don't give up so soon." Ravin pointed to the guy still standing in the doorway staring at them. "She may not know who you are, but I'd bet money he knows."

"Should I try to give her my card?"

"Yes, I think you should. If you think she's your 'it' girl, then do it Brett. You only get one chance."

"You're right. Come with me?"

"Sure."

The two girls walked back into the garage to give Tessa Brett's card. Tessa wanted nothing to do with it, saying that it was a cruel joke to offer her a modeling job. Ravin watched Jon carefully as he argued with Tessa, insisting that it wasn't a joke and that he knew who they were. He knew them from the fashion show's he'd been to.

Tessa, still unconvinced, dismissed them as quickly as they came. Brett felt defeated and Ravin felt a strong feeling that Tessa's mind would change soon. Brett hoped Ravin's intuition was right. She wanted Tessa to be her first unknown.

"These turned out great, Ravin. I don't know how to thank you." Roxi set the pictures down on the table. She got up and walked around Brett's new conference room. "I like how she decorated in here."

"She did a good job. I'm proud of her. I'm also thankful to you for giving her this opportunity Roxi. She feels washed up as a model. She thinks she's being pushed out by the younger prettier girls."

"I know, I know. I felt the same way at her age, and she is sort of being pushed out from what she's used to doing, like the covers for teen mags and showing off what's in for the new school year. But what she's forgetting is that there are a lot of other things she can be doing covers for. I've already had calls requesting her to do ads for make-up lines and stuff that is more sophisticated. She's got to realize that she isn't seventeen anymore, and that's not a bad thing. When she started, there was no way that she could do a shoot for say . . . what to wear to the Oscars, but now . . . now she's being requested for things like that."

"She is? Have you told her this?"

"Of course! She thinks it's just a sign of age."

"Let me talk to her. I can't stand to see her sitting behind a desk wasting what career she has left."

"Ravin, she has a lot to give still. She just needs to realize that. Don't push it. She'll figure it out when she's ready to accept it."

"Thanks, Rox."

"Anytime, I'm always here for you two. So, how are you anyway? And what's this buying a house out here all about?"

"Just easier. I hate living out of the hotels."

"So, you plan on staying out here a lot?"

"I guess I'll split my time between here and New York. I'm directing Jaded's next video as soon as Nico's feeling better, and I've got some other work lined up out here, so I'll have enough to stay busy."

"So, you're still interested in working in New York?"

"Of course."

"Good, because I'd like you to do some shoots for me."

"Sure, just let me know when so I can check my schedule and pencil you in."

"I'll fax you a list of what I need when I get back."

"Hey, baby," Ravin whispered in Marco's ear.

"Damn, you scared me!" He swung around.

"Sorry," she said, laughing and sitting on his lap. "I thought you might need some company. I see you're sitting out here all alone."

"Yes, I am lonely. You keep running off on me."

"Oh, poor baby. Let me make it up to you." She wrapped her arms around his neck and ran her fingers through his hair. Marco arched his neck, craving the feeling she gave him every time she touched him.

"Ya know it's been a long time since we've been together."

"Excuse me?"

"Not that way!" He playfully tickled her. "Do you remember how we were in New York? How every second of every day was about us?"

"Yes, are you feeling neglected?"

"No, I just don't have your full attention."

"Well you know I am planning our wedding and helping Brett and helping Nico and planning your video . . ." she said sarcastically. "Anything else you want me to do?"

"I didn't mean to make you mad. I just thought with all the things you have on your plate right now that we could use a little time for us, that's all."

"I know. I was thinking the same thing. Here we bought this big house for all of us to stay in, and I'm missing the privacy of my apartment."

"You too?"

"Yeah, just to be able to lounge around in nothing with you all day in bed . . ." She wandered off thinking about it.

"Let's go somewhere for the weekend. No work, no friends, no phones. What do you say?"

"What do I say? When do we leave?"

"Give me an hour to set it up?" He got up from the table excited.

"What about Nico?"

"Cole and Brody can stay here. And Vinny and Brett are a scream away. Anyway, he's doing good now. He just needs help with his shirts."

"You're right."

"I know I'm right. Now what kind of weekend do you want?"

"Quiet."

"Warm and sunny, beach . . . or maybe the mountains? Whatever, you name it."

"Aww, I don't know. Where do you want to go?"

"Santa Cruz? I hear there's a great Bed and Breakfast that's exclusively private and secluded."

"What should I bring?"

"Absolutely nothing." He snickered.

Ravin playfully smacked his arm and went to call Brett to tell her that they would be gone for the weekend.

"All set, we can leave tomorrow morning." Marco walked up behind her, touching her neck. "Ya know I feel a little guilty running off like this, especially so close to the wedding."

"I do too, but you know we deserve this, especially before the wedding. Things are going to go nuts very soon and we have been under so much stress. This was a long time coming. I'm just glad that we have the chance to go."

"I know. Who knows when we would have been able to do this. After the wedding I've got to get back to our tour, and you apparently will have enough work to keep you on your toes."

"Meaning?"

"Meaning I saw Roxi's face when you said you would still be living in New York part time. She wants you back. I can tell."

"She did ask me to do some shoots for her."

"I figured she would eventually. She can't dismiss your talent that easily. I mean, if it weren't for you who knows how well her magazine would do? And her models!"

"Well, I wouldn't go that far, but I do miss New York."

"I thought you would. You aren't a California kind of girl."

"No? Why's that?"

"Too hyper. You can't sit still for a haircut!"

"Ha! Very funny. What time are we leaving tomorrow?"

"I'd like to get on the road by seven."

"Okay, let me pack up some stuff and get some work done."

"Work? What work, I thought you were caught up?"

"I was, but Roxi had her office fax me a list of shoots she wants me to do and I have to figure out when I can do them."

"She's already got you working, huh? Good. I'm gonna make sure that Nico's got everything he needs."

"Good idea."

Sixty-Four

"So . . . what do ya think?" Marco asked, setting down their bags.

Ravin looked around the room. Each window had a spectacular view of the mountains. She walked over, opened the French doors, and took a deep breath.

"Marco, this place is beautiful. Come here and smell this fresh air." She laughed.

He walked over and wrapped his arms around her waist. He laid his head on her shoulder and closed his eyes.

"Ya know what I think?"

"I'm afraid to ask."

"I think I want to spend the rest of my life right here with you and this amazing view, although I'm not sure which one is better." He kissed her neck lightly causing her to shiver.

"I think that's a good idea." She turned around and slid her hands up his chest. She reached for him, craving his special touch. Slowly pushing him back into the bedroom, she slid off her jacket.

"Well, I guess I should take you here more often." He laughed.

"I've missed you." She stroked his chest, feeling the passion rise from deep within her.

"I haven't gone anywhere."

"No, I've missed you. I miss your touch, the way you run your fingers through my hair. I miss the way you take your time touching my face and kissing my neck."

"Well then, I must take the extra time you desire." He reached up and touched her face gently. "Ravin, I can't imagine life without your love. Every breath I take is because of you."

She leaned into him, kissing his neck. Marco closed his eyes and held his breath. His heart quickened and his hands began to tremble.

Slowly, she pulled his shirt over his head, tossing it onto the floor. Then she ran her hands up his chest, pushed him away, and began unbuttoning her shirt. He reached out to help her and she pushed him away again. Sliding it off her shoulders, she sat him at the edge of the bed. Marco grabbed her waist pulling her to him, kissing her stomach eagerly. She closed her eyes, waiting for her soul to be set free from his touch. She pushed him onto his back and crawled on top of him, kissing her way up his body. Marco slid his hands under her black lace bra, releasing it in one quick motion. He rolled her over caressing every part of her, touching her skin and feeling the intense heat they generated together. Ravin's head spun with desire. Her heart beat faster and faster as he unbuttoned her jeans and pulled them off.

"This way," she gasped, taking his hand and leading him out onto the deck overlooking the mountains.

"Out here?"

"Yes, make love to me out here."

Without argument, Marco took her outside, flipping on the hot tub. She looked at him and smiled, slowly sliding into the hot tub beckoning him with a wiggle of her finger. He sat across from her pulling her legs around his waist, and pressing his lips against hers. Ravin closed her eyes and allowed Marco to give her the most erotic moment she had ever experienced.

"Wow!" He looked at her smiling.

"Is that all I'm worth? Wow!"

"That's all I can think of. I'm speechless. I've never seen you like this before."

"I've never felt like this before." She felt slightly embarrassed.

"Well, I sure hope it's not the last time!" He pulled her back onto his lap, kissing her neck.

"I'm hungry." She smiled seductively at him.

"Let's go see if there's anything to eat." He grabbed a towel off the lounge chair.

Ravin smirked and laid her head back. "Let me know what you find." She laughed.

"Oh sure! Make me do all the work!"

"You wore me out. What can I say?"

Marco padded off into the kitchen laughing. He turned in the doorway and looked back at her. She sat back relaxed with her eyes closed. Her long hair fanned out in the water. Memories came rushing into his head . . .

"I'm sorry, Mrs. Deangelo, but we couldn't save your husband. We used all of our capabilities and we were still unable to save him," *the doctor said in the waiting room.*

Marco stood by his mother's side unable to cry. He squeezed her hands trying to control the relief he felt after hearing those words. 'We're free' was all he could think to himself. We are finally free.

Marco had spent all of his time at school, learning as much as he could while his friends went out on dates and hung out at the malls.

"Marco honey, why aren't you out with your friends? Why aren't you dating all those pretty girls that keep calling?"

"Because, Mom," he would say to her.

"Because why, Marco? You can't hide behind those books forever."

"I'm not hiding, Mom, I'm learning. I don't ever want to be anything like my father. If I get a good education and follow my dreams of singing, then I know I can choose any kind of girl I want."

"You are already smarter than your father. You were the minute you were born. You're father wasn't a dumb man. He was just ignorant. There's a difference."

"I know, but I want to perform. I want to be famous and when I am I can have anything I want."

"Well, just remember this. You can't buy love and happiness, and the one that will win your heart will be the last girl you expect."

"The last girl I would expect, how true," he whispered to himself and went into the kitchen to look for some food.

"What's taking so long?" Ravin walked in wrapped in a towel.

"There's no food here." He turned to her with a sour expression.

"Well, that stinks, doesn't it?" She came up behind him and slid her arms around his waist.

"What should we do?" He held her hands against his body.

"Well, I guess we'll have to go out for dinner then. I'm starving."

"Me too, except I don't want to leave."

'What? You miss room service already?"

"I guess I do."

"Marco, you are so spoiled! Get dressed. Let's go eat."

"After you." He cocked an eyebrow.

"Oh right, like I'm gonna turn my back on you!"

"Well then," he said as he lifted her up into his strong arms, "I'll just have to carry you!"

"Marco! You are crazy!" she screeched.

"About you? Yes, I am and it's only gonna get worse." He tossed her on the bed laughing.

"What kind of restaurants do they have out here?" she asked as they pulled out the driveway.

"I couldn't tell you. I hope something halfway decent."

"I thought you were here before?"

"No, what made you think that?"

"You told me you knew of a great place to go. I guess I just thought you were here before."

"No, Jenna told me about it."

"So, this is an adventure for both of us."

"Ravin, everywhere with you turns into an adventure." He shook his head, chuckling.

"Oh, shut up and drive!" She slapped his arm.

For a brief second and tinge of terror ran up her spine. She shook it off and let herself enjoy being normal, if only for a moment in time.

"Ya know, as soon as we get back all this quietness will come to an end." He looked up at her.

"I know. We've got to get that video shot before our wedding and you still have three more concert dates to catch up on."

"I know. I probably won't be able to be with you the week before, unless we somehow finish early."

"I know. That's okay. Everything's done anyway. My mom's been a huge help, so has yours, and of course, Aunt Mimi."

"I can't wait to see her again." He smiled.

"Yeah?"

"Something about her reminds me of you. It's almost as if I'm looking at you in the future."

"We are a lot alike, at least my daddy use to say so."

"Is it gonna be hard—walking down the aisle without him?"

"Yes, it will be, but I think Nicky will do a fine job."

"Won't be the same though, and that's really eating at you isn't it?"

She shook her head and looked out the window. "Do you sort of wish your father was going to be there?"

Marco looked at her blankly. "I don't know. I couldn't say."

They found a quiet little diner and sat down in the corner. The night went by fast, as they talked about the new video and their upcoming wedding. Ravin looked around feeling normal, and for her, that was something she had never truly experienced before. There was something about Marco that set her free, set her mind free from constantly looking around for something to happen. Still, she never let her guard down, and sometimes she was grateful for that. Sometimes things just looked out of place.

"Excuse me." She stood up and looked around the room.

"You're leaving me?" He pouted.

"Just to the bathroom." She smiled quietly.

Once she found the bathroom, she pulled out her cell phone and dialed Pauly.

"What's up?"

"Just a bad feeling. It's probably nothing, maybe even wedding jitters, but I just can't shake it, ya know?"

"I can be there in less than two minutes."

"You're kidding? Where are you?"

"Across the street."

"Why the hell are you here?"

"For times like these." He paused long enough without an answer. "Rave?"

"Shh . . ." she whispered quietly, looking around the corner, "I thought I heard someone. Listen, I didn't tell Marco I was making this call. I snuck into the bathroom to do it."

"Understood. I'll call ya later."

She hung up and turned off her phone, staring at it. She walked back out, sat across from Marco, and smiled.

He looked carefully into her eyes. He knew the look, and he knew she went to call Pauly. "So, Pauly good? Is he on his way?"

"How?" She whipped her head around, expecting to see him in the doorway.

"Give me a break Ravin, I may not spend every waking moment with you, but I can tell you this . . ." He paused, pulling her chin up with his finger. "I know every emotion you have and I can read your eyes like an open book."

"You can huh?"

"Yes, so tell me why you feel scared enough to call in Pauly?"

"A feeling, I guess." She looked down feeling slightly ashamed, after all this time, she should have been able to shake the feelings of always being a target.

"Well, I'm glad to see that you've got your instincts back in place."

"Why's that?"

"When I called, Pauly's line was busy. I guess we're on the same page."

"You called Pauly? Do you have a feeling we're being followed too?"

"Well, I don't know about that, but I do have a bad feeling about something. I just don't know what exactly."

She smiled at him and took his hands. "Ya know, I think we were meant to be together." Her smile slipped away as she looked out the window. The blood drained from her face as she watched in horror.

"What?" He looked around.

"Outside, someone's sitting outside." Her face continued losing more color as she spoke.

"Do you know who it is?"

"Yes." She trembled.

"Who?"

"Get Pauly on the phone *now!*" She gritted her teeth, not moving her eyes.

Marco carefully picked up his phone from the table and quickly dialed Pauly's number.

"What do I tell him?"

"Tell him—"

"Tell him not to look behind you!" Pauly whispered, causing

Ravin to jump out of her skin. Even Marco jumped throwing his napkin at him.

"Wow! What a great protector! Throwing a napkin, Marco! Gee I would have never thought of that!" Pauly laughed and slid in next to Ravin. He looked over at Ravin seeing her utter fear and suddenly became serious.

"Ravin, what is it?"

"Outside, look outside."

Pauly looked over her shoulder trying not to be seen. "Is that who I think it is?"

"Uh huh."

"Isn't he supposed to be in prison?"

"Maybe he got parole or something?"

"Rave, he got seven life sentences. Parole wasn't an option."

"What do we do, Pauly?"

"Well, first of all we get the hell out of here."

"Where? If he knows we're here, he'll know where we're staying."

Immediately, Marco got on his phone, talking fast and quietly to Tony.

"We've just got to get to the Hilton. I think it's only a few blocks from here."

"What's at the Hilton, Marco?" Pauly asked with a proud smirk.

"A helicopter."

"What about our stuff?"

"Tony will stay behind. When it's all clear he'll pick it up for us."

"Pretty impressive for a musician." Pauly smiled, shaking his head.

"So, are you going to tell me who this person is or what?"

"Not if I can help it."

"In the air, let's get out of here. Where to, Pauly?"

"Out the back. I've got a car waiting."

They carefully got up from the table. Pauly didn't take his eyes off the car. They rushed outside and jumped into his car. As fast as they could, they set off to find the Hilton.

Ravin watched Pauly looking back as they drove.

"Are they following us?"

"Yep."

"What now? Want me to drive?"

"Only—"

A bullet shattered the back window before he answered.

"Do you remember?" he shouted.

"Yes, I do!" she screamed back.

Marco watched her jump into the front seat and slide underneath Pauly, taking over the wheel without any hesitation. Pauly slid over into the back and motioned Marco up front.

"Now what?" Marco yelled.

"Get down and keep a look out for her!"

"What am I looking for?"

"Odd cars flying around corners, whatever!" Pauly yelled, returning the gunfire.

The second gunshot broke through the back window, taking out the rest of the glass. Ravin slouched low in her seat and Marco tried to cover her the best he could. Pauly popped up returning fire. Marco heard the windshield shatter behind him and looked back to see them swerve.

"Turn!" Marco shouted, pointing left. He held on as she turned the corner without losing speed. He looked back as Pauly fired again and again. "Pauly I see the Hilton, it's up ahead."

"Just go, no detours today." He sat up again and opened fire.

Marco watched the car's tire blow and it swerve into the guardrail. He could see the driver fighting for control and losing. The car soared over the guardrail and exploded when it hit the side of the mountain.

Ravin quietly pulled into the Hilton parking lot and glided to a full stop. Her hands shook against the steering wheel and nobody spoke.

"Get out and get onto the helicopter," Pauly ordered. "When you get back, call Nick immediately! I'll be in touch."

"Pauly! Don't—" She watched him jump out the back of the car and race on foot to the side of the road.

"Go!" he yelled back over his shoulder.

Ravin and Marco ran from the car into the hotel. As they ran in the doors, Tony walked up behind them. Ravin swung around, grabbed his wrist, and threw him to the floor.

"Shit! What the hell was that for?" Tony shouted, sitting up.

Marco let out a chuckle. "Sorry, Tony."

"You are! Shit man! What the hell do you need me for with her around?"

"Thought you would have learned by now not to sneak up on her."

"You're telling me!" He dusted himself off. "We're ready, but what's the rush?"

"Let's go." Marco grabbed him and pushed him to lead the way to the heli-pad. Tony looked at him curiously and Marco just glared at him.

"Not again?"

"Yes, we have to get back now," Marco demanded.

Tony led them up to the heli-pad and watched them fly away. He pulled out his room key and went to make himself as comfortable as he could without allowing himself to worry too much. In the morning, he would go and collect their things from the room and bring them back.

Sixty-Five

"Plane's leaving soon, Ravin. Are you ready yet?" Brett called into her room.

"Just give me another minute. I've got to wrap this before we go. I don't want Marco seeing his wedding gift until he unwraps it." She finished taping it and placed the small box in her bag.

"Ready?" he asked, taking her bag.

"Yep, let's go." She smiled at him. In less than five days they would be husband and wife. For the first time in her life, she felt sure about something.

"Scared?" he looked at her.

"No, you?"

"No."

"Good."

"Having second thoughts?" He cocked an eyebrow.

"No, are you?" She smirked, enjoying the foreplay.

"Well, as long as I don't get shot at anymore."

"Well, hopefully I can promise you that."

Since they returned to Santa Monica, they hadn't discussed what had happened to them. Marco remembered Ravin running into the house, nearly knocking over Brett. He could hear her screaming in Italian over the phone. He started to explain to Brett what had happened, but after a few minutes of watching her listen in horror to Ravin, he assumed she understood her.

Since then he noticed her on edge more and unable to relax. He tried to prompt her to take pictures or spend some time in her dark-room. She wasn't able to concentrate on either. Brett offered him

367

some advice: let her be. Let her deal with this. She didn't name names, but he knew this wasn't going to end. Nicky flew in with a small army, and her mother begged her to come to Italy early. Marco spent a week trying to get into her head. When he decided to give up, she asked him to walk with her along the beach. Although he was used to Pauly walking behind them, he wasn't prepared to have a dozen or so more along with them. Pauly wasn't one of them, and Ravin still hadn't heard from him.

She told Marco who it was this time and how and why he was doing this. She told him that this was the man that had murdered her father. Marco asked why Nick and Joey were never targets and she explained how she had watched him kill her father. She had also watched him kill her fiancé that she was the one who had told the police everything. Including everything her father had told her about him before he died. All that information could put almost everyone in the old neighborhood in prison for life. It was the hardest conversation she'd ever had, and he was the only person she had ever talked about this with besides Pauly.

Ravin stepped off the private plane onto the tarmac and breathed deeply.

"It's good to be home." She smiled at Marco.

"It's good to see you home." He took her hand and walked with her to the waiting limo. Brett smiled, taking Vinny's hand, and Nico, Cole and Brody followed looking around.

"This isn't your first time to Italy, is it?" Ravin asked, watching the guys look around.

"No, but we've only been here on tour. We never had too much time to see the sights or anything. Not that we would have ever thought to come to this small town." Nico laughed.

"Small town, huh?"

"Well, I did a little reading; it's not a very popular place is it?"

"Not really, but it's home."

"Well, hopefully you'll have time to show us around a little." Nico smiled.

"I'd love to."

Marco looked around at his closest friends and his soon-to-be bride and smiled. He closed his eyes and enjoyed the ride back to Mimi's vineyard.

Sixty-Six

Marco looked around as they entered the grounds of the castle.

"Why does she want to get married in a castle anyway?" Cole asked.

"I have no idea, but it's beautiful." Marco shook his head.

Ravin had briefly described it to him and promised him that it would take his breath away. She was right, it did, and he was glad she had promised him the wedding of his dreams.

They were escorted upstairs to the west wing and shown the rooms they could get ready in. Marco was slightly nervous and Nico helped him get ready.

"Listen, I know you never had a real father, and I know if he was around he'd probably tell you something horrible."

"Yeah."

"So . . . I'll try and tell you what I think my father would tell me, or at least tell you what I think."

Marco looked at him appreciatively.

"You are marrying the best person in the world, Marco. I'm going to admit to you that I'm jealous, but Ravin is an incredible person and only brings out the best in you. Treat her well and take care of her. I love her and I love the person you are when she's in your heart."

"Thanks, I don't know what to say."

"Just don't trip and don't step on her dress."

Marco let out a chuckle and finished getting ready.

The groomsmen escorted the guests into the chapel that stood on the castle grounds. Ravin's family arrived smiling, knowing Ravin's love for this castle. The other guests, including Roxi and Benny and dozens of people from both their careers, arrived in awe. No one knew exactly where the wedding was; just that it was in Italy. Ravin watched from the balcony and wished her father had been there to walk her down the aisle. She wished he could've been there to know her . . . to know Marco. She closed her eyes, took a deep breath, and felt every ounce of her father flow through her.

"Ravin, it's time." Brett opened the door. The girls looked at each other and smiled. "Who would have guessed you'd have gotten married before me?" She smirked.

Ravin wiped a tear that rolled down her cheek and walked out to meet her brother Nick.

The chapel was silent as the wedding march began. Everyone stood as Ravin appeared in the doorway. Her white wedding gown hugged her body down past her waist. She stood motionless for what seemed like an eternity; Nick put out his arm and began to walk her down the aisle. Marco watched her, his love for her reached to places her never knew existed. Fighting back the tears, he tried to smile, watching her approach him at the altar. Her train flowed behind her as if she were floating. Her hair dark hair was pulled back under her veil, and he stared at her, trying to memorize every detail, the way she still let wisps of hair fall around her face and the way her eyes sparkled from underneath her veil. He held out his hand for her as his heart beat uncontrollably. She smiled her most tender smile ever as they turned to face the priest.

The service was beautiful seeming to end before they had a chance to enjoy it.

"And I now pronounce you husband and wife. You may kiss your bride."

Marco lifted her veil and took her face in his hands. "I love you," he whispered before he touched his lips to hers. The amount of emotion that rushed through him was immeasurable. Her hands trembled as they turned and walked down the aisle together.

Ravin gripped his arm tighter and looked over to see Pauly sitting in the back of the chapel. She hadn't heard from him since Santa Cruz. She didn't even know he was still alive. Aside from the cast on his wrist and the bandage across his eyebrow, he appeared to be all right and he watched them walk toward him. His smile was as proud as she imagined her father's would have been, and his eyes danced with happiness.

They waited for everyone to line up outside the chapel before they made their exit. Ravin looked around and saw every face of every person she loved. Most importantly, Mimi's proud face filled with tears. Falling rose petals greeted them as they stepped into the horse drawn carriage and drove off to the other side of the castle for the reception.

After the toasts, Marco walked Ravin over to the piano, and his best friends and band members lined up behind him.

"What's this?" she asked, trying not to cry.

"Remember those songs I wrote on the plane the first time I came to Italy?"

"Yes."

"Well, I never let you hear all of them, but I did promise to sing them to you." He kissed her gently and sat at the piano.

Marco serenaded his new bride and tears rolled down her face. Her family looked on, feeling the same emotions.

Ravin knew her life would never end as long as he was by her side. She loved Marco more than she thought a person could love. Her father's memory drifted through her as she remembered him telling her that the one person who could take her breath away would be the only person who would love her forever. She looked over at Marco singing to her. He truly took her breath away.

About The Author

Stacey Palermo was born and raised in Western New York,
where she lives with her husband and two beautiful daughters
She enjoys writing, photography and designing book covers.
Stacey is currently working on her next novel,
and loves hearing form her readers.

zravineyes@yahoo.com

Visit her website at:
http://www.geocities.com/zraveneyes/

Printed in the United States
30447LVS00005B/40-102